Island Shifters

Book One

An Oath of the Blood

Valerie Zambito

Cover Art by Nick Deligaris
www.deligaris.com

OTHER TITLES BY VALERIE ZAMBITO

ISLAND SHIFTERS - AN OATH OF THE BLOOD (BOOK 1)

ISLAND SHIFTERS - AN OATH OF THE MAGE (BOOK 2)

ISLAND SHIFTERS - AN OATH OF THE CHILDREN (BOOK 3)

ISLAND SHIFTERS - AN OATH OF THE KINGS (BOOK 4)

ANGELS OF THE KNIGHTS - FALLON (BOOK 1)

ANGELS OF THE KNIGHTS - BLANE (BOOK 2)

ANGELS OF THE KNIGHTS - NIKKI (BOOK 3)

EDEN'S CREATURES

ISLAND SHIFTERS SERIES REVIEWS

"FROM THIS BOOK'S FIRST PARAGRAPH, I WAS HOOKED UNTIL THE VERY END."

"I HAVE TO SAY IT HAS BEEN A VERY LONG TIME SINCE I READ A BOOK AND GOT GOOSE BUMPS!"

"I WAS SWEPT AWAY BY THE COLORFUL CHARACTERS AND BRISK PACING OF THE BOOK, ALMOST COMPELLED TO KEEP TURNING THE PAGES AS ZAMBITO'S ACTION-PACKED STORY CARRIED ME ALONG."

"WITHOUT A DOUBT, THIS IS, BY FAR, THE BEST BOOK I HAVE EVER READ IN MY ENTIRE LIFE. AS SOMEONE WHO HAS READ OVER 780 BOOKS IN THE LAST 20 YEARS, THAT'S SAYING SOMETHING."

DEDICATION

All things are possible with a strong and loving family by your side. Thank you, Joe, for your sacrifice and encouragement. To Jimmy, Colby and Dylan, thank you for your patience while Mom spent all of those hours crouched over a computer. You are my heart, my soul, and my everything.
Thank you, Janice, for being my best friend as well as my sister.
Dedicated most of all to my very own Highworld angels, Mom and Janine.

MAP OF MASSA

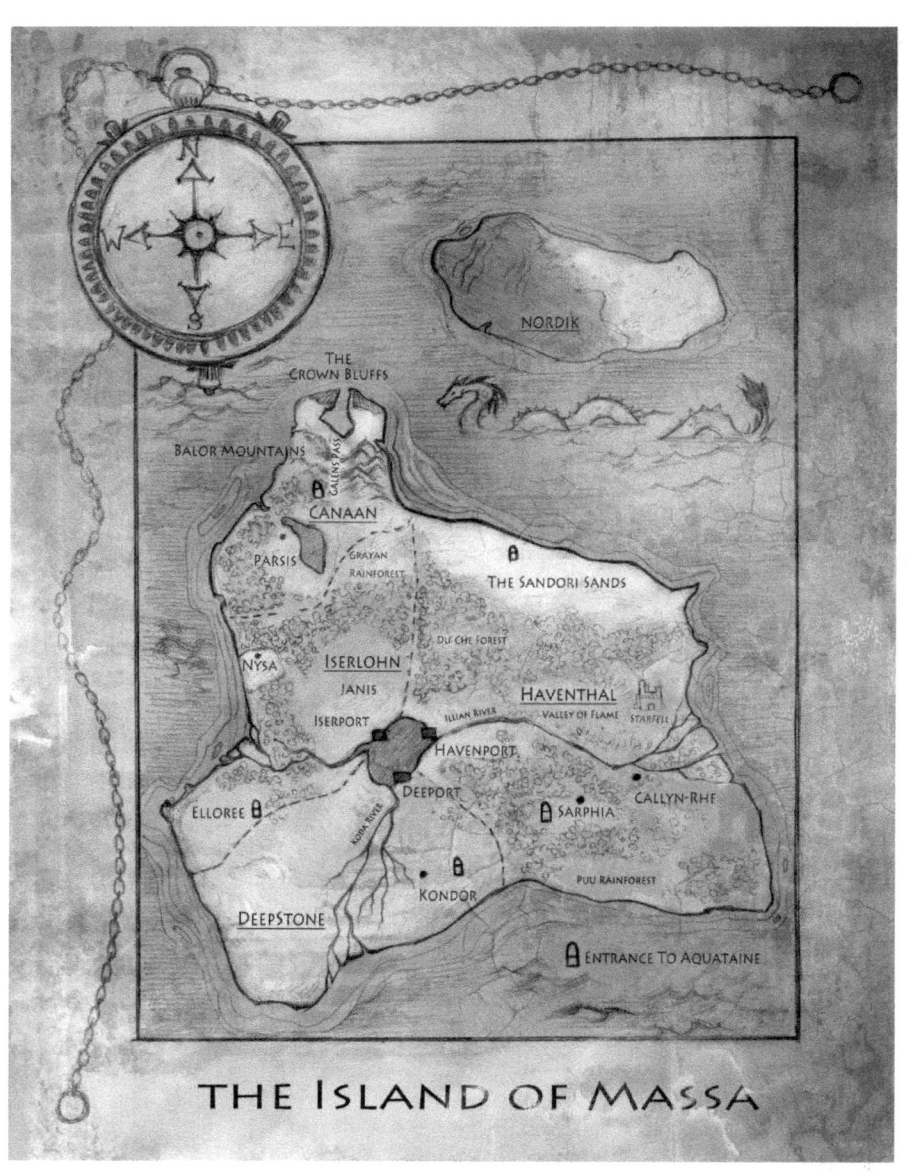

THE ISLAND OF MASSA

TABLE OF CONTENTS

CHAPTER 1

THE MAGICAL KINGDOM OF PYRAAN

"Bloody hell!" Beck Atlan pounded the ground to either side of him, his fists leaving twin, bowl-sized depressions in the dirt from the force of his strikes. With a clenched jaw, he sprang to his feet and glared at the packed benches surrounding the arena where spectators were boisterously enjoying this long-awaited jousting battle between him and his opponent. The public arguments over who would be the victor in this event were as numerous as the bets taking place in private, and Beck grimaced at the cheers pouring out of the crowd from his rival's supporters.

He picked up the fallen lance and strode to his waiting horse. Not bothering to use the stirrup, he grabbed the pommel with one hand and used his considerable strength to vault himself back into the saddle. Tucking the lance firmly into place, he trotted for the third time back to his starting position very well aware that if his opponent managed to unseat him once again, he would lose the match. Unthinkable at any time, but especially now. Especially, against this foe.

With a steady hand, he soothed his black stallion, Chasin, and stared down the length of the field at his adversary, searching once again for any weakness to stance or carry that he could exploit. The figure in black glared directly back at him through the visor of a steel helm, rigid and strong.

And, smug.

Suddenly, Beck's eyes locked in on a small movement that he would have otherwise missed had he not been so assiduously looking for it, and he permitted himself a small smile. His opponent shifted subtly and let the protracted lance stationed on the left to dip ever so slightly. An indication, he decided confidently, that the blow he delivered in the first round had found its mark after all.

I have you now, he snarled in his head. *To the left then.*

The crowd quieted as the nervous flag boy walked tentatively to the center of the field, holding the staff far out in front of him as though it were a deadly weapon.

Chasin stomped his feet and snorted, as anxious as Beck to meet the challenger in battle once again.

After what seemed an interminably long time, the boy abruptly dropped the flag in an extravagant sweep and sprinted at a dead run back toward the safety of the fence.

Chasin, needing no further signal, reared back on his powerful hind legs and bolted ahead. Beck held on smoothly, secure and certain in the saddle beneath him, adrenaline coursing through both him and his mount as they thundered down the turf. Sweat trickled down the side of his face, but he ignored it.

Beck scowled suddenly as his opponent lifted the lance into the air and repositioned the weapon on the right. The unusual move startled him, but he quickly dismissed the stunt as an obvious attempt to distract him and readied himself to even the score with this maddening competitor once and for all.

To the left, he thought again, and as the two horses converged, he drove his lance sharply at the black figure. The crowd gasped in surprise as the rider narrowly managed to avoid his thrust by plunging the lance into the dirt on the right with both hands. Using the powerful momentum generated by the speeding horse, his opponent swung upward and whirled around the shaft of the weapon. Beck could only watch helplessly as a strong kick hit him square in the chest, sending him flying from his saddle.

The rider continued through the motion of the swing and used the lance to vault forward, back arched and arms and legs clawing at the air to land back on the charging horse.

The spectators, winners and losers alike, went wild.

Beck groaned and watched with equal parts irritation and admiration as the champion rode over to him amid a plume of dust. "Gloating is beneath you," he pointed out, waving his hands to scatter the motes from around his face.

Laughing, Kiernan Everard ripped off her helmet and let her long, blonde hair tumble free. Icy green eyes stared down at him as she cocked her head. "As you should know by now, Beck Atlan, it is not all about brawn. It's about anticipating your opponent's next move, and I read yours easily in your eyes. It seems you fell for my little feint," she said, holding her left side in exaggeration.

Beck ignored her and stood, putting a finger and thumb in his mouth to whistle Chasin back to his side. The crowd suddenly exploded into roaring laughter, and Beck looked over his shoulder. "What is it?"

"You better get back on your horse, earthshifter," Kiernan said, leaning from the saddle and struggling to suppress her own laughter. "It appears the hole you just ripped in your trousers has gone straight through your small clothes."

Red-faced, Beck quickly turned from the crowd with his hands behind his back. They howled and jeered even more. Bowing in mock humor to the throng of Pyraanians, he sidled to Chasin with as much dignity as he could salvage and remounted, sneering at Kiernan the entire time.

She laughed again and dug her heels into her horse's flanks, causing the animal to leap away. Guiding the mare expertly over to the arbiter, she easily caught the winning purse he threw her way without stopping and held the bag of coins overhead as she took a victory lap around the field.

Beck grudgingly smiled and waited patiently while she graciously accepted congratulatory shouts from the crowd and then followed behind when she exited the arena to set out for Mincer's Stables at the edge of town. Wearing black leather trousers, short jacket, fitted corset and leather arm pads, Beck decided she looked exactly like the warrior princess she was meant to be. He always thought her an extraordinary blend of brute strength and subtle femininity and that belief was more in evidence today than ever. Her mastery in sword fighting, near blademaster rank, and her innate ability to anticipate the moves of much larger adversaries, made her a lethal fighter.

She was also one of his best friends.

Raising an eyebrow, he coolly appraised her slightly arched back and the soft curve of her hips as she swayed in the saddle. He could see the firmness of her thighs through the leather as they gripped the horse tightly. Silky blonde hair fell down her back in soft waves.

Still holding her helmet cradled in the nook of one arm, she suddenly glanced back and fixed him firmly in incandescent eyes that, as a mindshifter, held entirely too much knowledge about the thoughts of others.

Beck sucked in his breath guiltily and held it.

After a long moment, she smiled, amused, and gestured with her head for him to ride beside her.

He let out his breath slowly, wondering where these sudden stirring feelings were coming from. As he considered the uncertainty, he was without a doubt *very* certain about one thing. If Kiernan Everard knew, she would bash his skull in.

***

Beck caught up to Kiernan and together they followed the curve of the roadway around the square, picking their way through the celebration. Today began the weeklong biennial Homage Festival, and he smiled as the townsfolk took part in all manner of events ranging from archery competitions and arm wrestling to eating contests, and even dancing and drinking—although it was not much past the mid-day hour.

Mistress Halloran, the rotund innkeeper of the Unicorn's Tail, hurried out into the bright afternoon carrying a plate of pastries. She nodded a greeting as soon as she noticed them and shouted up to him, "Did you win, my boy?"

Heat flaring in his cheeks, he shook his head curtly.

Mistress Halloran offered him a sympathetic smile and waved as she continued on her way. Beck noted her leaving but then paused. He could have sworn that out of the corner of his eye he saw the plump little woman jump in the air with a skip of cheer! His head snapped around when he also thought he heard a snicker coming from beside him but, with the noise of the city, could not be sure.

Beck shook his head, but spared a small smile at the thought that *he* would have a place of honor at the next festival when his two-year tour of duty with the Northwatch Legion ended.

Surrounded by the Arounda Ocean and cosseted by steep cliff walls that encircled the entire island, landing at Massa by ship was impossible at any location except at a quarter-league stretch of open beach at the northern Crown Bluffs.

The law was clear. All boys who reached the age of eighteen were required to join the legion and march to the Bluffs to defend the realm against hostile forces. For the residents of Pyraan, a land of disgraced exiles, it had been this way for three hundred years and would continue to be for this protection of the land was in repayment of a debt owed to all of Massa. A debt recorded in the history tomes and owed to all of the Men, the Elves and the Dwarves by the Magical Kingdom of Pyraan.

It was only right, thought Beck glumly. After all, every Massan knew it was the magic users who destroyed the world.

***

After passing through nearly all of the merriment in companionable silence, Beck arrived at Mincer's Stables with Kiernan. Apart from the occasional bark of a dog, it was quiet at this end of the city with most residents gathered around the square and the arenas. Dismounting, Beck waited for Kiernan to do the same before leading Chasin through the wide stable doors. "I let you win, you know," he said, glancing sideways at her.

She looked at him incredulously. "You really expect me to believe that?"

"No," he said with a laugh. "Even my father confided to me that he bet a silver groat on the Princess." He held up a finger. "And, I have a strong suspicion about Mistress Halloran as well."

Kiernan smiled as she gently rubbed the nose of her mare. "You would have won if you weren't so distracted about the journey tomorrow," she conceded. "Are you excited to be leaving?"

Beck shrugged cautiously and led Chasin to one of the open stalls. "I guess so." He was actually more than excited, but had to tread very carefully. He didn't want to get Kiernan any more riled up on the subject than she already was.

She eyed him doubtfully.

"Come now," he scoffed, hoping it sounded genuine. "The entire tour will be nothing but a waste of time and you know it. It all sounds noble, but let's face it. There's no enemy out there."

"Well, at least you'll be getting out of Parsis," she replied and began to pace back and forth.

Here we go, he thought, and walked over to a row of shelves outside of the tack room to search for spare trousers. Holding up a pair and deciding they would fit, he went into an empty stall to change.

"Don't you see? I'm a prisoner here, Beck! We both are."

He laughed dryly. "That's the funny thing about exile, Kiernan, you really don't have much of a choice."

She continued her rant as if she didn't hear his response, which was probably the case. "It's worse for me on two fronts. As a shifter, I can't leave the boundaries of Pyraan, and as a female, I'm barred from joining the Northwatch Legion. It's so unfair! I should be going with you. I'm better with the sword than just about any male in this entire land." She made the declaration without even a hint of boast in her tone. She was simply stating fact.

Beck peered at her over the stable door, reluctant to say anything when she was so clearly agitated. He was in agreement with her. In his opinion, it was unfair that she not be allowed to join the legion. Small, but with an athletic build, she had proven repeatedly at the academy that she would be a very formidable legionnaire. She was also a very skilled mindshifter. She could bend people to her will simply by gazing into their eyes and transferring her own thoughts and ideas to theirs. It was a very potent and dangerous power, and she never used it recklessly. In fact, she rarely used it at all. Contrary to the name, there was very little magic performed in the Magical Kingdom of Pyraan.

For young people just coming into their shifting talents, the use of magic was permitted only during school sessions at the Parsis Academy with an experienced instructor. As for the adults, well, these were peaceful times in Massa and over the years the four metamagics of earth, fire, mind and body began to offer less and less value to their everyday lives. In fact, it began to be viewed as something unwholesome. A taint, even. A hereditary imperfection passed on from generation to generation. And, while it was important to learn to study and control the contaminant, to even use it for defensive purposes to enable shifters to uphold their oath to the people of Massa, it wasn't an integral part of their lives.

"We'll be back before you know it, Kiernan. You won't even have a chance to miss us. I promise."

"You don't understand," she murmured.

But, he did. Along with their two friends, Rogan Radek, a Dwarf and fireshifter, and Airron Falewir, an Elf and bodyshifter, they had been inseparable for the past six years. While most shifters started developing their first stirrings of power in their mid-teenage years with a mature command of the magic by their early twenties, Beck, Kiernan, Rogan and Airron began exhibiting magical tendencies as very young children and were now regarded as the most powerful shifters in Pyraan.

Beck came out of the stall and put an arm around her shoulders. "Of course I do. I wish you could join us, I really do, but you know the rules about girls joining the legion. I guess they think it would be too..." He hesitated, blushing. "...distracting or something. How would I know?"

"That's ridiculous," she snorted. "Even so, there are so few female shifters coming to Pyraan every year. What would be the harm in letting those of us who are here and more than capable come along?" As she resumed her pacing, she began mumbling something about showing *them*, whoever *they* were, that it was not over yet.

Just as she was about to launch into a new argument against the conservative rules of the Northwatch Legion, the stable doors banged open with a loud *thud* and afternoon sunlight flooded inside. They both turned to see Rogan Radek silhouetted in the doorway squinting to focus in the gloom of the stable.

"Ah, there you are," he said at sight of his two friends. Five-foot-one and tough as nails, the Dwarf barreled inside with all of the refinement of a charging bull and patted Kiernan on the back. "Well done," he said gruffly. "About time someone knocked Beck down a peg. He's too serious all of the time."

Beck pulled his white shirt down over his borrowed trousers. "Not true. What about the time I buried you to your shoulders in a sinking and left you there all night?"

Rogan smirked at the reminder. "I stand corrected. That was pretty funny... Hey!" he suddenly shouted in panic, kicking out his left leg. "What in the bloody...?"

Beck looked quizzically at Kiernan and then back at Rogan as he suddenly began hopping from one foot to the other.

"Get it out, get it out!" the Dwarf screamed, the two thick braids at his temples flailing wildly.

"What is it?" Kiernan asked, rushing to his side.

"Help!"

"Calm down, Rogan," Beck said firmly. "What is the matter?"

All of a sudden, a gray mouse appeared at the bottom of Rogan's trousers. The creature swiveled its head left and right and then leapt free of the jerking pant leg and scampered a safe distance away before turning around and rising on its hind legs to smile broadly and *unnaturally* at the terrified Dwarf.

Beck noticed Kiernan try to hide her own smile behind her hand. After all, it wasn't very often that real mice actually looked up at humans with quirky little grins of satisfaction on their faces.

"All right, Airron. You've had your fun," Beck said to the mouse.

Upon hearing the mention of his mischievous friend, Rogan narrowed his eyes at the rodent and crossed his arms over his chest, waiting. He didn't have to wait long. The air shimmered and the mouse transformed into a willowy but strapping young Elf with violet eyes and long, silver hair. Airron Falewir's perfect features were screwed up in mirth as he pointed, howling at Rogan.

"You're not supposed to be using magic," Beck said in a rote tone of voice. He used these words often with his friends and knew that it was highly unlikely that Airron, who was doubled up in the corner, was going to heed them any more today than he had any other. "Now, get dressed!"

"*Asha*, friends," Airron said, using the Elven word for greeting between bouts of laughter.

Rogan growled as his murderous eyes fixed on Airron.

Kiernan turned her back on the naked bodyshifter. "Come on, Rogan. It was just a furry little mouse. At least it wasn't a snake," she said, and shuddered visibly. "I hate snakes."

Still grinning, Airron quickly pulled on the brown tunic and leggings he must have previously stashed in one of the horse stalls and walked over to put his arm around Rogan. "Kiernan's right. Lighten up, Fireball, because you know as well as I that it won't be long before the back of my cloak mysteriously goes up in flames again."

Rogan grunted in acknowledgement.

"You have to stop grinning when you bodyshift, Airron," Beck pointed out. "It gives you away every time."

Airron barked out a laugh, and when Airron Falewir laughed, they all found it hard not to join in.

Together, the four friends headed out into the warm afternoon, blissfully unaware of the frightening events hurtling toward them. Although they did not yet know it, they would find very little to laugh about for a long time.

CHAPTER 2

AN OATH OF THE BLOOD

The full moon and star-studded sky over Parsis lent a diffuse glow to the ring of torches lining the town square creating a dreamlike quality to the evening. Activity from the festival had finally died down with just a scattering of folk remaining awake and gathered in small pockets of whispered conversation.

Beck yawned tiredly as he shifted uncomfortably on the wooden bench. Beside him, in front of the dregs of a fire, sat the thirty-five young men who would make up Troop 158 of the Northwatch Legion departing for the Crown Bluffs in the morning.

The legionnaires were quiet now, lost in their own thoughts about the journey ahead. Although usually uneventful, the trip was not entirely without danger. The most notable threats coming from Galen's Pass through the Balor Mountains where travelers had to contend with frequent stone slides, pesky dragonwasps that showed no mercy if roused, and the impish Halfies who made their home in the foothills. For these reasons and more, Pyraanians seldom traveled north of the pass.

Beck heard a collective intake of breath and looked up.

Kiernan had changed into a light blue, strapless gossamer dress that left her shoulders bare. Arm veils secured at her biceps by gold cuffs fluttered out behind her as she walked. Leather sandals laced up her legs to the knees. A magnificent sword embossed on the hilt with the royal crest of Iserlohn peeked up over her shoulder, and a small dagger rested in a sheath strapped to her thigh.

"Move over," she said to Beck as she approached, oblivious of her effect on the young men.

Beck scooted over and the scent of fresh soap and lavender spiked an unfamiliar sharp ache low in the pit of his stomach. His body shuddered, and he was grateful for the darkness that concealed the flush he knew stippled his cheeks.

Kiernan leaned in close to him. "Who is that with your father?"

Shifting again in discomfort, he looked up to see his father, the long-time mayor of Parsis, hurrying over to the fire with another man in tow.

He cleared his throat and dared not look her in the eye as he responded. "I've never seen him before."

The legionnaires around the fire and Kiernan stood as the men approached.

"Boys, I would like you to meet Commander Trent Dismore of the Northwatch Legion," his father said.

The standing legionnaires quickly saluted the commander.

"At ease," Dismore drawled.

Beck regarded the stout commander, and with his full face and ruddy complexion, he looked exactly as Beck suspected a military leader might look in these quiet times. One who had seen more dinner tables than battlefields.

"The commander will be your escort to the Crown Bluffs tomorrow. In this capacity, he is very anxious to observe your shifting skills during the testing tomorrow." When several of the boys groaned, his father quickly gestured for them to quiet. "As you have been told before, you are not expected to have mastery over your talent at the age you are."

Beck glanced to the side and saw Airron nudge Rogan and smirk arrogantly. Unfortunately, the commander also noticed and narrowed his eyes at them with an expression that promised unpleasant interactions in the days ahead.

"During your two years of service," his father continued, "you will build upon your magical knowledge and be introduced to legion battle tactics. Commander, do you have anything to add?"

Standing with feet apart and hands behind his back, Dismore glowered at them. "I have one rule and one rule only. Follow orders. It's that simple. Follow orders and we will not have any problems.

Step out of line just once and there will be repercussions that you will not enjoy."

Beck cringed. Non-hostile time or no, it was obvious the man was clinging to a very tight military tenet.

"I don't care how good you think you are," Dismore said, looking pointedly at Airron and Rogan, "but we cannot uphold our duty to the citizens of Massa unless we have strict order within the ranks. We will meet at the academy an hour before sunrise." With that, he simply walked away, the legionnaires smartly saluting his departing back.

Instinctively, Beck's father also turned to salute before he remembered himself and clapped his hands together instead. "All right, then. You heard the commander. It's time you all headed for bed. Come now, off you go."

"Er...Master Atlan, can I ask you a question?"

Beck turned to a young fireshifter by the name of Rory Greeley. Small for his age, he had little magic as of yet to command.

"Yes, Rory?"

The short youth kicked at the dirt shyly. "Well," he began, "the shifters have been guarding the Crown Bluffs for a long time now, but why, Master Atlan? I mean...I have heard about the blood oath, but how did it all happen?"

Beck's father looked puzzled. "Have your parents not discussed the debt with you, legionnaire?"

Rory blushed and shook his head. Some of the young men from the northern towns forfeited formal academic training to stay at home and work their family farms, never setting foot in Parsis until joining the legion at the age of eighteen as the law required them to do.

"Come around and I'll explain," Beck's father said, gesturing for the legionnaires and Kiernan to sit once again. He was silent for a moment as he picked up a metal rod leaning next to the fire and gently rearranged the logs to coax the blaze back to life.

"It all began long ago," Beck's father began as he sat down, his hushed voice lending a conspiratorial tone to his words. "Over three hundred years now, in fact. Back when this great island of ours was a much larger continent and home to many different races. It was a very prosperous time for Massa, and also a time," he paused reverently, "of great magic."

It would be incredible to live in a world where people didn't blame shifters for all of life's evils, Beck thought. It was something they all longed for.

"Under High Mage Galen Starr, magic's dictate was to be used for the greater good of the people. As prominent members of the Assembly of Races, Galen Starr and the seven Mages under his command were involved at the highest levels of politics to make this so. There came a time, however, when one of the Mages began to plot to undermine the government in order to usurp their power. His ultimate goal was supremacy over the lands and even suggested in private the enslavement of the other races. Little by little, his sinister plans met with success and as with most forms of power, it had an intoxicating effect. He grew drunk with it. He grew more evil."

Beck's father shook his head in silent admonition to the long-dead Mage.

"His name was Adrian Ravener, and he was a very skilled fireshifter, but his persuasive skills turned out to be even more deadly when he convinced three of the Mages to side with him. Ravener also had formidable accomplices in his sister, Avalon, and her friend, Niema Gesbina, both of whom were sorceresses. By the time Galen Starr learned of Ravener's treachery, it was too late. Dubbed *Savitars*, which means 'saviors' in the old tongue, Galen and the three uncorrupted Mages were forced into a war of sorcery against the evil Mages. Unfortunately, it cost Massa dearly."

Beck knew that his father was putting it lightly. He had heard the story many times throughout his childhood. For days, lightning rained down from the sky and burned everything it touched. The earth heaved and killed hundreds of thousands of people. Buildings, property and livestock were destroyed. Mountains fell. Entire lands disappeared when oceans converged and encircled the now smaller island of Massa.

"The war lasted for five days, and the devastation was immeasurable. Many races were wiped out completely. The *Savitars* destroyed three of the evil Mages, but Adrian, Avalon, and Niema confiscated ships and fled to the land north of here, which was once part of Massa. All of the *Savitars* perished in the war except Galen.

"Distrust was rampant after that, and the last three surviving races of people elected new Kings and made the decision to live separate from each other. As you know, the Dwarves migrated to the southern part of Massa and named their country Deepstone. The Elves moved east to the newly created Haventhal, and men carved out the land of Iserlohn in the west. Before the Kings departed with their kinsmen, however, they extracted an oath from the High Mage. An oath to make up for the loss of so many lives and for the destruction of the world as they knew it.

"Galen was brought forth before the Kings bound and naked. While he could have easily used magic to break the binds that held him, he wanted the people and the Council of Kings to know how ashamed he was of the acts of his brethren, and he held his humility out in recompense to them all. It was then that he delivered the unbreakable oath of protection on behalf of all magic shifters."

Beyond the quiet crackling of the fire, the silence was complete.

"When the Kings asked Galen by what means he would secure this debt, the Mage replied simply, 'blood.' And, they took it. With three brutal cuts to his body."

Jaimes paused again.

"The Kings also demanded that Galen gather the magic users and isolate them from the rest of the island and have them marked so that all shall know them."

Beck unconsciously raised his hand to finger the symbol of the athame, a double-edged dagger, tattooed on his neck.

The young fireshifter Rory cleared his throat and whispered innocently, "Galen Starr exiled us with his blood oath?"

"Yes, Rory. Because of Galen's oath, all shifters were exiled to Pyraan with the duty to protect the races from evil magic. We're the only ones who can."

Rogan spoke up. "So even though Galen Starr is long dead, to this day the shifters remain bound by his oath?"

"Oh, but my dear boy, Galen Starr is not dead. He is still *alive*."

A murmur ran though the legionnaires, and Beck was just as stunned.

"Still alive?" questioned one of the larger legionnaires with red hair. His bulk gave him away as an earthshifter, but Beck had never seen him prior to the festival. "Sir, you would really have to think us daft to believe such a thing."

"It is true, Heath."

"How can that be after so long?"

"That would make Galen Starr almost four hundred years old!" exclaimed Airron.

Jaimes held up his hands to calm everyone. Once he had them quieted, he explained that, yes, Galen Starr was alive and living in the Elven land of Haventhal. "He is the only known magic user living outside of Pyraan, and he is actually more like six hundred years old. After devoting many years to the creation of the Magical Kingdom of Pyraan, he petitioned the Council of Kings to live out the end of his days in seclusion in an undisclosed location. His request was granted only after weeks of immensely heated debate by the council as none of the Kings were comfortable with having any magic—no matter how benevolent—outside of Pyraan."

Again the redheaded legionnaire grunted disrespectfully.

"Do you have a problem, Red?" Rogan asked, temper rising to the surface.

"I might," replied the earthshifter with a level look.

Rogan slowly stood, along with Beck, Airron and Kiernan.

Heath laughed scornfully. "Yeah, I did hear that you freaks traveled in a pack. Come on, Jon," he said to his friend seated next to him. "I've had enough of child tales for one evening. Mages six hundred years old? Bloody hell, what a joke."

"Let them go," Beck's father warned as the two legionnaires departed.

"Someone needs to teach that one a lesson," snarled Rogan.

"For the record, it is common knowledge that the Mages of old did have access to spells that extended life. Unfortunately, all of the lore and histories of the Mage were destroyed in the war, and we have never been able to regain even a fraction of that which was lost." He stood, signaling an end to the evening's impromptu history lesson. "Off you go now. You've only a few hours before your tests and journey tomorrow. Good luck, gentlemen. Your duty is appreciated."

As the legionnaires dispersed, Beck's father pulled him aside. "I probably won't have a chance to do so in the morning so I wanted to wish you well, son. Your mother and I will miss you terribly. We are very proud of you, Beck, and all that you have accomplished at the academy. The Highworld knows, the next time I see you, you'll be taller than me!"

Beck looked down at his father and laughed. "I've been taller than you for over two years now, Father, but don't worry. The only thing I'm in danger of dying from at the Crown Bluffs is boredom."

"Just be careful. There are dangers everywhere, Beck, and you should be more mindful of that."

"I will be careful," he assured his father and smiled inwardly at the concern. An only child, Beck had always been very close to his parents. If either of them still had any family in Iserlohn, he had never met them. Beck's extended family had always been his friends and neighbors in Parsis. There was Jorge Owen, the huge blacksmith, who taught him how to ride a horse. Jakob Martyn, the hawk-faced grocer, who spent many afternoons with Beck teaching him how to hunt and fish. Of course, there was also Master Martyn's son, Ben, who taught him how to filch a pint of ale from the back of his father's store, and pretty Katrin Allendale who gave Beck his first, if awkward, kiss.

But, above all, there were his best friends, Kiernan, Rogan and Airron.

Beck bid his father good night and began the half league trek home. As he walked the well-used path with Hawthorne Lake on one side and the thick Grayan Forest bordering the other, he thought about his friends.

For some reason, he had always been the unspoken leader of the group. He guessed it was due to the inherent strength that evolved out of his dominant magic.

Like him, Airron was born in Pyraan. His parents, Jeni and Joshe Falewir, were both shifters and had lived in Parsis all their lives. Since no other Elves had come to Pyraan in over a century, it was assumed that the Falewirs were the last of the Elven magic users. The commonly held belief by the professors at the academy was that the Elves had never been very strong with magic and the spark had simply bred out of the race.

Rogan and Kiernan were both born to non-magical parents and did not arrive in Pyraan until after their abilities emerged as children.

Rogan had been abandoned in Pyraan at the very young age of six. No one knew who his parents were or why they left him behind in that way. The Dwarf chose to believe that his parents must have been alarmed by his magic developing at so early an age and did only what the laws of the land demanded they do—they brought him to Pyraan to be exiled with other shifters. Rogan often voiced his hope that his parents' actions were motivated by love and that someday they would be reunited. For his friend's sake, Beck hoped he was right.

Kiernan, on the other hand, was the cherished daughter of Maximus Everard, a leader of people and ruler of a kingdom.

He was the King of Men.

By his own law, King Maximus had no choice but to send his daughter to exile when she was twelve years old and her shifting was exposed. Over the years, the King visited Kiernan as often as he was able, but his onerous duties in Iserlohn made it very difficult for him to get away.

Hurrying down the path and lost in his ruminations, Beck was caught completely off guard when he was hit from behind with enough force to send him sprawling face first into the dirt for the fourth time that day.

Adrenaline pounded through him as he sprang to his feet and whirled around to meet his attacker in a low crouch. The ground began to rumble at his feet, churning in a rolling boil with the magic he instinctively summoned to his aid. Dust rose all about as a ball of earth erupted from the dirt and began to rotate in the air in front of him. Thinking of the black wolves that prowled the Grayan Forest, Beck peered along the roadway, ready to unleash the deadly missile at whatever delivered the blow to his back.

He tensed as a large shadow slowly peeled away from the trees on the side of the road and eyed him intently.

Even in the dark, Beck recognized those eyes.

They were Kiernan's eyes.

Sighing with relief, he reluctantly let his magic go and the ball of earth fell apart and sank to the ground.

Kiernan's snow-white Draca Cat moved silently to his side and gave him a nudge that almost sent him to the ground for a fifth time. Smiling, he reached out to pet the massive Draca whose head came up to his chest.

Extremely intelligent and fierce fighters, the cats were said to have been used in battle by the Mages of long ago. Today, the Dracas lived in solitude somewhere in the Puu Rainforest in the magically hidden land of Callyn-Rhe. Most people believed the cats to be more figments of overactive imaginations rather than made of actual flesh and blood. This belief was reinforced by the inability of people to reach the mythical land. Travelers caught up in the shield surrounding the Dracan realm were inexplicably turned around and forced onto paths designed to carry them further away no matter how many attempts were made to reach it.

Beck realized then how much he would miss him, too, when he left for the Crown Bluffs. Bajan was as much a part of the group as his other three friends. When people weren't present, Bajan often joined in on their activities, communicating to them through Kiernan. With his dignified personality, however, he did not always approve of their exploits and was eager to let them know it with a disdainful click of his tongue here or a head toss there.

"Bajan, I forgot to ask Kiernan to meet me at the lake after the tests tomorrow. Can you let her know? I want to tell her good-bye."

The cat nodded. "Thank you, my friend. Take care of her for me while I'm gone?"

Again, the cat nodded and then slipped away as silently as he appeared.

Beck turned and headed back down the road toward his house, wishing only that he make it home without falling into the dirt again this day.

CHAPTER 3

THE HOUSE OF RAVENER

Adrian Ravener gazed out of the thick paned window of the study in his Keep in Nordik, the only named city in this unnamed land north of Massa.

It was raining outside as it did most days in this dark, dreary place. His powerful conjuring over the centuries had slowly stripped the island of all life and vitality, the plants and animals destroyed to the verge of extinction. Fortunately, it had yet to touch him. Even at three hundred and twenty six years, his face remained unlined and his body hard and strong.

He sat pensively behind his desk, idly tracing a circle around the rim of his wine glass. A Cyman slave girl sat at his feet holding a wine decanter on a tray, head bent meekly and her hair falling forward, covering her face.

"It's almost over!" he hissed suddenly, slamming a fist on the desk. The slave girl flinched, almost spilling the tray.

"Patience, my brother," drawled a voice from the doorway.

Adrian turned to see his sister stroll arrogantly into his study. Avalon had the same shoulder-length black hair as he, and her physical appearance was just as untouched by the years. Although, the alabaster skin, he readily admitted, was much more complimentary on her than on him. Combined with her almond-shaped eyes and high cheekbones, she was a strikingly beautiful woman.

"Has the seer had another vision, Avalon?" he demanded impatiently.

"Yes," she replied, stopping before his desk. She held up a hand to stop him from interrupting. "Even so, it changes nothing. The plan is still intact. Your army has been created and your ships built. Now is the time to reclaim what was so unfairly stolen from us."

"I did not ask for your opinion, I asked you a question. What did the seer say?"

Instead of answering, she turned from him and walked to the window just as a flash of lightning streaked out of the dark, boiling clouds beyond the paned glass. "You know, Adrian, when you are back in power in Massa, I caution you to take much better care of it than you have this land."

Adrian slammed his fist on the desk again and stood abruptly, sending the chair toppling back. The slave girl scrambled backwards to get out of his way. "I asked you about the seer, sister, and when I ask you a question, you had better answer!"

Avalon's expression was cold as she slowly turned from the window. Without warning, she stalked over and slapped him across the face. Hard.

"Don't you *dare* think you can talk to me that way, Adrian," she snarled through clenched teeth. "I am *not* one of your slaves. Do you hear me?"

She didn't raise her voice, but the menace it contained was unmistakable.

Adrian's face mottled with rage. "You've pushed too far this time, Avalon!"

For a long dangerous moment, brother and sister glared at each other. Adrian struggled with his fury, barely able to bite back the spell that would burn her to a crisp where she stood. He could do it easily and with no more remorse than crushing an insect under his thumb, but now was not the time to take on his sister. She still figured quite heavily into his plans.

But, it was Avalon who relented. She sighed and reached up to touch his reddened cheek. "Do not expect me to apologize for something that was necessary. You must keep your composure, Adrian! All we have hoped for and dreamt about is within reach! We must keep our goal in mind at all times. Agreed?"

He nodded slightly with a tight smile that lifted only one side of his mouth. "Agreed, now tell me what the seer has prophesized." That was all she was going to get. If she wanted more, that spell was still eager to be unleashed and, well, plans could be changed.

The moment over, Avalon turned to the slave girl. "Miah, pour me some wine." As Miah hurried to comply with her request, Avalon recited the seer's words. *"In the year that the star grows weak, the ravens begin their flight; Ancient skills long since dead, resurrect in the morning light; Beware the Savitars, who are light to the dark, but fear the shadow more, who is death to the dark; Beware the star, when it shines so bright, but fear the star more, in the eternal night'."*

Adrian stroked his chin as he considered the meaning of the vision. "Childish in its simplicity, really. Obviously, *we* are the ravens and now is the time for our return to the old world."

Avalon accepted a glass of wine from Miah. "Yes, and I think we can also safely assume that Galen is the star and that he is dying."

A genuine smile lit up Adrian's face. "I believe that to be so as well, and it's about bloody time that old fool died. He has been wrecking havoc on this world for far too long."

Avalon sipped her wine and sat down. "I am curious as to why the prophecy mentions the word *Savitars*. If you will remember, the Massans named Galen and his Mages as *Savitars* in the war, but they are all long dead. Why would the prophecy mention them now?"

Adrian frowned. "Are you sure that is the word the seer used?"

"Yes, I am."

He shrugged. "In any case, we should keep the seer close to us as we travel south in the event that she has any more revelations. We need answers sooner rather than later. Dying or not, I do not intend a reunion with my former mentor without a full arsenal at my disposal."

"What about the resurrection of ancient skills? Do you know what that means?" she questioned.

Adrian blinked, surprised she had ferreted out the importance of that passage. "I have my theories," he answered cryptically, "but as yet am unwilling to discuss them until I learn more." Ignoring her raised eyebrow, he continued. "I will be meeting with Lucin later this evening and let him know of our desire to have the seer's quarters next to ours. We should be ready to sail in two days' time."

Also surprising, she simply nodded and stood. Maybe her question was only innocent curiosity?

Avalon turned to the slave. "Oh, Miah, dear, run along and tell your brother, Titus, to meet me in my chambers. I will be in need of his..." She cleared her throat in feigned modesty, "...services this evening." As Avalon started away, she unabashedly dropped her black robe revealing her nakedness beneath. The air shimmered around her as she bodyshifted into a Cyman girl and turned back to wink at Miah before closing the door behind her.

Adrian shuddered in abhorrence. The Cyman beasts repulsed him, and he didn't know how his sister could inhabit their body for even a moment.

He turned to the young slave girl, swung his arm back and slammed his fist into her face. Miah yelped and fell to one knee. "You heard her, you filthy cow, now move!"

The girl stood to leave, and Adrian glared at her in disgust as she straightened to her full seven-foot height. She wore a rough homespun tunic over her muscular frame that fell just below her knees. Keeping her head bowed, she backed her way toward the door and said in a deep voice that belied her young age, "Yes, Master."

When she finally raised her head, her hair parted revealing her Cyman heritage—one big, brown eye dead in the center of her forehead.

***

It was still dark in the small bedroom, and it felt like Beck had just closed his eyes when a hand nudged his shoulder and shook him awake.

"Beck, it's time to go."

It was Rogan.

The Dwarf stood next to his bed dressed in a dark cloak with the hood up, his face in shadows. Beneath the cloak, Beck noticed the long knife sheathed in a belt at his waist.

"You expecting a war?" Beck asked, using his palms to rub his tired eyes.

"As a matter of fact," he muttered, "I am—with Commander Dismore. Did you see the way he was looking at us? I have a feeling that the next two years are going to be harder than we thought."

Beck sat up and swung his legs to the floor in one swift motion. "So, tell me, what did you think of what my father said last night?"

Rogan slipped off his hood. "About the debt?"

Beck nodded.

"Odd, really. Of course, we already learned about the Mage War, but I'm now feeling more pride at being a shifter. My athame proclaims me a protector of the realm!" he declared commandingly, sliding his knife from its sheath and putting it through a variety of thrusts and parries with an imaginary foe.

Beck snorted a laugh. "That's funny, because Kiernan feels the exact opposite. She feels that the athame represents a chain around her neck."

Rogan just shrugged and sat down on one of the chairs in Beck's room.

"I wonder if Adrian Ravener is still alive," Beck mused aloud. It stood to reason that if Galen Starr was alive then their enemy could be as well. Maybe the legion tours were not such a waste of time after all.

Beck dressed and began stuffing the items he would need for his trip into his pack. When the room suddenly filled with light, he glanced over at Rogan who was lazily juggling three small fireballs.

"You're not supposed to be using magic," he said flatly, slinging the pack over his shoulder. He was waiting for Rogan's retort when there was a soft knock on his door and the fireballs vanished.

"Beck? Are you awake?"

It was his mother.

"Yes. Come in."

Constance Atlan stepped into the room, clutching the sides of her night cloak in one hand and a brown package in the other. Petite with short brown hair, her typical ready smile was absent this morning and her brow was furrowed. Turning her head sharply to the side, she peered into the newly created shadow left by the disappearing fireballs.

"Rogan Radek, you would not happen to be making fire in my house again, would you?" she asked sternly.

Rogan jumped clumsily to his feet, "Uh, well..."

Beck grinned as his mother attempted a forbidding look on her face and stalked over to the young fireshifter. "Do I need to put you over my knee to teach you right from wrong?"

"No, ma'am," answered Rogan lowering his head.

"Are you going to follow Commander Dismore's orders and stay out of trouble at the Crown Bluffs?"

"No, ma'am...I mean yes, ma'am!" he replied, flustered.

"Good!" His mother could no longer hold back her giggle at the look on the Dwarf's face. She rubbed the top of his head, her characteristic smile back in place. "Can I still ruffle the hair of a legionnaire?"

Rogan nodded with a smile.

"Stay safe, Rogan, I will miss you," she said softly and affectionately. Her tender words must have evoked a sense of maternal loss, because the fireshifter impulsively grabbed her in a tight hug and lifted her off her feet. She let out a startled exclamation and then hugged him back just as tightly.

After a few moments, she said, "You can put me down now, Rogan."

He did, looking up at her with a sheepish grin.

She jerked her head toward the door. "Now go so I can say good-bye to my other son."

He nodded and looked over at Beck. "I'll be waiting for you outside."

After he was gone, Beck shook his head at his mother. "He's a little old to be threatening with a strapping, isn't he?"

"Well, he deserved that!" she griped. "Last time he was here, he burned my favorite curtains."

Beck remembered well. He would bet that the neighbors still remembered, too. There was plenty of screaming going on that day.

"What do you have?"

The frown reappeared. She held it out to him. "Take it. It's yours."

Curious, he took the package and sat back down on the edge of his bed. Slowly, he untied the twine holding the edges of the wrap together and let the paper fall away, revealing a box the size of a small rock. Opening the lid, he noticed a silver pendant nestled in blue silk. He ran a finger lightly over the raised emblem pressed into the pendant and then jerked his hand back in surprise. It moved! Embossed with the image of a man's fist, the animated hand moved from side to side, the veins and tendons as detailed and alive as his own.

"What is it?" Beck breathed in amazement, picking it up out of the box by the chain attached.

His mother, who had been facing the window, turned to gaze at the ornament dangling from his fingers. "I'm not sure, but apparently it has magical properties. In any case, it belongs to you. On the day you were born, I had a visit from Galen Starr."

Beck widened his eyes in disbelief. Again, mention of this infamous Mage from the past.

"He gave me that package with instructions that it be given to you when you began your eighteenth year." She ran her hands through her hair distractedly. "With all of the preparations for the festival and your trip, I neglected to give this to you on your name day last month."

He shook his head in confusion. "Why would Galen Starr give me anything? I don't even know him."

His mother looked at him as if she wanted to say something and then thought better of it. "I had never met Mage Starr before that one day eighteen years ago nor have I seen him since. But, please wear it, Beck. I don't think Galen Starr would make this gift to you unless it had meaning." When he hesitated, she reached out to grab his free hand. "Please, Beck, I would feel better if I knew you had it on."

Beck looked into his mother's concerned eyes and wondered at the source. He said nothing, though, as he put the pendant around his neck as she had asked.

"Do you think it has something to do with my enhanced shifting powers?" he asked.

"I don't know, Beck."

"Well, I guess it will have to remain a mystery to be solved another day. Rogan is waiting for me." He stood to hug his mother. Again, she seemed preoccupied, like something was on her mind. "Are you all right?" he finally asked.

"Yes, yes. Be careful, Beck," she said softly, but intensely.

"I will." He grabbed his pack and ran out of the door with all the exuberance of a young man leaving home for the first time. He never noticed his mother watching from the window with tears making a slow track down her face as she realized with dismay that this was the first time she had ever deliberately lied to her son.

CHAPTER 4

LET THE TESTS BEGIN

The sun had yet to make an appearance, but a subtle swash of pink across the eastern horizon greeted Beck as he walked with Rogan through the enormous, twin stone pillars that marked the entrance to the walled Parsis Academy. The imposing castle had lorded over the city, serving as both a school and a dormitory for parentless shifter children, for more years than most could remember.

Beck scanned the courtyard for Airron. Regular academic classes were cancelled for the day, which allowed the legionnaires of Troop 158 to have the grounds to themselves as they milled about waiting restlessly for Commander Dismore to appear.

Beck groaned aloud when he spotted Airron standing with a defensive posture in front of the argumentative legionnaire from last night, Heath, and two of his friends. Airron had a tight-lipped smile on his face. "Uh-oh," Beck said, nudging Rogan with his elbow. "Airron has that stupid grin on his face."

Rogan looked where Beck pointed. "We better get over there," he growled.

As they started away, Rogan leaned over and grabbed a stout rod from one of the legionnaire's backpacks. "Mind if I borrow this?" he asked, without stopping.

The legionnaire watched Rogan walk away and shrugged his shoulders. "I guess not."

The trio of earthshifters belligerently watched them approach. "Looks like your reinforcements have arrived, Elf," sneered one of the boys with a mop of curly blonde hair. Jon Anders, Beck thought his name was.

"Wait a minute, Jon," said Heath, looking around. "One is missing. Oh, yes, that green-eyed witch from the campfire last night."

Without a word, Rogan stalked over to Heath, pulled out the rod and brought it down on the bridge of his nose. The earthshifter screamed out in surprise and pain. His friends growled in rage.

"How dare you!" Heath snarled, blood gushing from his nose. He waved his hands and a faint tremor ran through the ground at their feet.

Airron laughed. "Was that earthshifting or did an acorn just fall from a tree?"

Heath's face reddened. "You and your friends think you can show us all up with your mighty powers, but we're here to tell you that it's not going to happen. We might not be super freak shifters like you, but we know how to fight."

Beck ground his teeth in frustration. There were always those who were envious of their power, something they had no more control over than the color of their hair. It was ignorance, plain and simple. Intending to defuse the situation, he grabbed Airron's arm and stepped in front of him. "Look," he said to Heath and his friends, "we're not like that, all right? We're here to get a job done, just like you."

Heath flexed his fingers in a show of threat. "Really? Well, maybe we should put that to the test. You know, one earthshifter to another?"

Beck smiled lazily. "Be my guest, Heath, but trust me implicitly when I tell you that it would not work out well for you if you tried."

Heath hesitated and licked his lips uncertainly. Fortunately—for the antagonistic youth anyway—he wavered just long enough for Dismore to make an appearance.

"Legionnaires!" bellowed the commander as he exited the academy doors and entered the courtyard. "Formation!"

"Watch your back," Heath growled at Beck and turned to walk away.

Before he had taken two steps, Beck reached out and spun the earthshifter around by grasping a fistful of shirt at his shoulder and lifting him up on his toes. "One more thing, Heath," he said. "You might not be aware of this living outside of Parsis so allow me explain. It is considered a grave insult to call a gifted mindshifter like my friend, Kiernan, a witch. Next time you see her, you will owe her your heartfelt apology. Do you understand me?"

Heath glared at Beck as his friends hurried away. Beck leaned in closer, his breath hot on Heath's cheek. "Do you understand?" he questioned again.

The boy finally nodded defiantly and Beck casually released his shirt and patted it back into place. "Good. See you around."

"Line up!" Dismore shouted. "Time is short. The testing needs to be underway immediately."

With one last look at Heath to make sure he wasn't going to cause any more trouble, Beck turned back to Airron and Rogan.

"Impressive," Airron said with a grin. "Was it the challenge to your earthshifting dominance or his slur about Kiernan that got you so riled up?"

"What are you talking about, Falewir?" Beck barked. "I was defending Kiernan! You would have done the same."

"Sure, big guy. I was just about to tear his head off when you stepped in."

Beck looked on in confusion as both of his friends glanced at each other and laughed. Ignoring them, he walked away, but he had to admit that Airron had a point. It wasn't a surprise that Rogan struck out against Heath. He was known to be short-tempered and aggressive. In contrast, Airron was the laid-back prankster who was more interested in laughs and fun than in fighting. But, him? According to his friends, he was the serious one. Decisive and levelheaded. He never got riled up. So, why did he lose his temper? *Something to think about when I have more time.*

Beck ran to get in line with rest of the legionnaires.

Dismore, dressed in the light gray uniform of the Northwatch Legion, paced before them. "If there are any mindshifters here," he yelled out, "go immediately into the academy to the third floor for your test. There's an instructor waiting for you there."

Two red-faced legionnaires left the line and hurried into the school. For some reason, the majority of mindshifters were female, and the young male mindshifters who came to Parsis often found themselves the brunt of ridicule.

Dismore nodded his head once and continued walking back and forth along the line, silently consulting a parchment in his hands. Despite his admonishment that time was short, he was taking his time to look at each legionnaire closely in evaluation. *Taking his time to make sure we squirm*, Beck thought.

Dismore stopped in front of the redheaded Heath. "Demon's breath, what happened to your nose?"

"Nothing, sir," Heath replied, his voice already altered comically by the bulbous swelling.

"Nothing?"

"Just an accident," he squeaked.

"Let's make sure that the *accidents* are kept to a minimum, gentlemen. This is a legion, not a bloody playground."

"Yes, sir," most of the legionnaires answered back.

The commander shook his head. "Now, when I call your name, step out of the line and show me why you should be part of the Northwatch Legion."

"Yes, sir!" came the hearty but disorderly reply.

Dismore grudgingly nodded his head and looked down at his paper again. "Jon Anders!"

"Here, sir," said Heath's friend with the curly blonde hair.

"What is your ability, Anders?"

"Earthshifting, sir!" Anders stepped out of the line with biceps bulging in muscled power, a physical trait distinctive to all earthshifters to back up their super strength.

"Well, then, show me!"

Jon took a few hesitant steps and after glancing back nervously at the line of legionnaires behind him, he faced forward and thrust his hand out toward the soil at his feet. Like Heath's earthshifting, Beck felt a weak tremble as the young shifter attempted to manipulate the ground. Despite the line of sweat beading his forehead, a quick bubble of sprayed dirt was all he could manage.

Beck heard snickers from the line and watched as Jon hung his head in disappointment.

"You think this is amusing?" Dismore demanded, crossing the dirt to confront them faster than Beck thought possible with his bulk. "Men of the Northwatch Legion acting like silly children is amusing to you? It is disgraceful and I will not tolerate disrespect in my legion!

Get that through your thick skulls now or pack your bags and go home to your mothers!" His face was purple with anger.

Caught off guard, the legionnaires cast their eyes downward and didn't respond.

"Do you bloody idiots hear me?"

"Yes, sir!" Several of the boys banged their fists to their chests in accepted Northwatch fashion.

Dismore glowered at them for several more uncomfortable moments before turning back to Anders. "Good effort," he said to the earthshifter. "Rejoin the line."

Anders walked away, and Dismore called out the next name. "Airron Falewir!"

Airron stepped forward.

Dismore eyed him dubiously. "You are a bodyshifter, correct?"

"Yes."

"How many forms do you have?"

Beck knew that most eighteen year olds joining the legion had between six to eight solid forms that they could transform into on demand. Trained adult bodyshifters had somewhere around twenty.

Airron rubbed his chin. "At last count? I believe it was seventy-nine, sir."

Dismore's eyebrows rose to his hairline. "Bloody hell, that's impossible."

Airron tilted his head, appearing to be deep in thought. "You're right. My apologies, sir. I was mistaken. It's not seventy-nine. It's actually eighty. I got a mantath two days ago."

The legionnaires whistled in admiration. The mantath, a long-snouted mammal covered in armored plates, could grow to be as big as a small house, and Airron was the only bodyshifter on the island who could command such a large form.

Beck learned that for a form to develop within a bodyshifter, he or she used their unique magic to completely siphon off and then possess a body's exterior image. It always amazed him that it took only a simple touch for Airron to be able to shift into a whole other being.

"I would like to see it," Dismore said with eager anticipation in his voice.

Airron walked several paces away from the line and removed his clothing. His pale body then erupted upward and rows of hard-shelled, armored plates sprang up along his back. Limbs thickened into stout, muscled legs with sharp claws. A long trunk stretched to the ground.

Dismore and the legionnaires stepped back as they regarded the sight of the reclusive and massive animal. Airron elicited hearty laughter—even from their irascible commander—when the mantath rose up on wide hind legs and began to hop about, taking a playful swing at Rogan with its snout.

From there, the commander used the better part of an hour to put Airron through form after form before he finally seemed convinced that the bodyshifter wasn't lying about the extent of his abilities.

Beck clapped Airron on his back when he was finally sent back to the line. "Well done."

"*Over* done if you ask me," the fatigued Elf whispered out of the side of his mouth.

"Rory Greeley!" Dismore shouted out. "Ability?"

"Fireshifter, sir!"

Dismore produced his second smile of the day. "Ah, a fellow fireshifter. Very well then, Master Greeley, show me some fire."

Poor, unfortunate Rory was unable to produce more than a single flame, but Beck found himself quite taken by the small fireshifter and shouted encouragement to him from the sidelines. Soon, the other legionnaires joined in and the atmosphere changed from one of rivalry to camaraderie. By the time it was Rogan's turn, the entire legion was crying out for their fellow shifters in a show of unity.

Rogan amazed Dismore with his ability to create and manipulate fire. When the commander asked him to create enough light for a candle, he created flame for a torch. When asked to create a campfire, he created an inferno that shot twenty feet into the sky. He sent fire careening through the air in a multitude of shapes and sizes. His fiery arrows drew applause and then astonished gasps when they hit a small storage shed on the grounds of the academy and it burst into flames.

It was clear that the Northwatch Legion was awed by the extraordinary magic they were witnessing.

Finally, Dismore called Beck's name. "I will admit, Atlan, I've heard the stories about you and that's why I called you last. Now, do you think you can uproot that maple sapling over at the north end of the school?" he asked, pointing.

Beck looked at the sapling and immediately thrust out his hand palm down. The air vibrated with the hum of magic and instantly the earth started to churn at his feet in a violent roil. He flicked his hand, and the turbulent earth formed into a ball and shot forward like a catapult under the ground resembling an enormous worm burrowing at unbelievable speed toward the sapling. Not only did the maple sapling uproot, but every tree within twenty feet of where Beck gestured as well.

A loud cheer rose up from the legion.

Dismore nodded. "I take it you can adequately perform a shieldwall?"

"Yes, sir."

"A sinking?"

"Yes."

"Armor?"

"One of my favorites."

"Nicely done, legionnaire," Dismore sniffed, "but I think we'd better stop here to preserve the rest of the grounds of the academy."

Beck walked back to the line.

"That concludes the testing, gentlemen. Go ahead and collect your uniforms on the first floor of the academy from Mistress Button, the school administrator. Once you have changed, collect your packs and meet me at Mincer's Stables. Do not be late!"

Alarm filled Beck. "What? We're leaving right now?"

"What's the matter?" asked Rogan.

"I'm supposed to meet Kiernan at the lake before we go. I don't want to leave without seeing her."

"She'll understand, Beck. She'll have to because there is no way that you're going to have time to go to the lake."

Beck sighed, more despondent than he cared to admit even to himself.

As they started walking toward the academy doors to retrieve their uniforms, Airron, oblivious to Beck's angst, looked behind him, sniffing. "Does anybody smell smoke?"

Rogan burst out laughing.

***

The newly-uniformed Northwatch Legion sat mounted and ready to depart with packs, bedrolls and provisions secured behind their saddles. The horses stamped their feet, impatient to be moving after the confines of the stables. A light mist swirled at their feet in shadowy wisps that appeared and disappeared at random.

Commander Dismore gave the signal and they started ahead on the road that would take them north toward the Balor Mountains.

A few people, mostly the parents of the departing legionnaires, lined the streets to wave and shout out farewells to the passing company. Beck smiled affectionately at his parents when his mother called out to him and waved a handkerchief his way.

He tugged at the uncomfortable collar chafing his neck while he scanned the crowd for Kiernan. *Where is she?* He knew that she was upset about being left behind, but it was very unlike her not to be here now. He wouldn't see her again for two years. Surely, she would want to see her best friends off on such a long journey?

Shaking his head, he tried to clear the unexpected emotions surfacing again. Yes, he expected to feel sad about leaving Kiernan, but not this overwhelming sense of loss. Not this painful knot in his stomach that threatened to double him over.

If he looked closer, he knew he might discover the term for his ailment, but he refused to do so.

Not now.

He resolutely pushed aside all thoughts of Kiernan and focused his mind instead on the ride ahead and his life as a legionnaire for the next two years. Thankfully, Rogan and Airron rode up beside him and captured his attention with their usual teasing banter.

As the procession continued out of the city, Beck couldn't stop himself from glancing behind one last time, but there was still no sign of Kiernan.

Between the mist, and the shouts from the crowd, and the excitement of the morning, Beck didn't notice the extra legionnaire riding in the line that morning.

He noticed neither him nor the flashes of white keeping pace off through the trees on the left.

CHAPTER 5

A BID FOR FREEDOM

Lucin glanced up wearily from the pile of plans and maps strewn across the table in front of him when the tent flap pushed aside and his son, Titus, bent his considerable frame to enter. A wrench of grief assailed him as their eyes met. He knew where Titus had been this evening. The lecherous Avalon Ravener had finally noticed his young son, and the boy was now caught up in the midst of her voracious appetites and games. He also knew there was nothing he could do to stop it. Their gluttonous captor had moved on from the father to the son.

Lucin broke the gaze first not wishing to shame the boy further and bent back over his maps. He shook his gray head as he despaired not only over Titus, but for the plight of all of his people. As captain of the Cyman Army, he was entitled to comforts that the others lived without—a canvas roof over his head and food to eat. The soldiers were not so fortunate. They slept without benefit of cover out in the rainy, cold weather and trained for hours each day with little sleep and inadequate nourishment.

However, even they had it better than the women.

Living the lives of slaves and forced into hard labor, the females toiled in drudgery hour after hour at every trade and craft required to keep Nordik functioning. As the farmers, blacksmiths, cooks, maids, cobblers, tailors, fletchers, masons and carpenters, the women worked day and night to keep the city, soldiers and Ravener Keep outfitted and operational.

The House of Ravener had been built solely on the backs of the Cyman women of Nordik.

Even so, it wasn't the hard work that stripped the women of life—of spirit. It was the separation from their husbands and children. In Nordik, children were taken from their mothers at birth and cared for by the women who ran the orphanages. If the Cyman women performed their duties adequately, Ravener permitted them time once per month to visit with their offspring. But, it wasn't nearly enough for a mother who longed for her child.

Lucin thought of his wife, Maree, and the look of utter torment on her face the last time he had seen her. He didn't think she could last much longer. Her dress hung on her shrinking frame from lack of food, and the dark circles under her eye told him she wasn't sleeping. He clung to her tightly that day and couldn't help himself from whispering in her ear that he was close to finding a way that would one day soon free her and their people from the malevolent grasp of the Raveners. He knew it was wrong, that he shouldn't have raised her hopes so, but he would have said just about anything in that moment just to see a spark of light back in her troubled eye.

To his shame, it worked.

She smiled the first real smile he had seen in months and embraced him fiercely murmuring that she had always believed in him. Always believed he would be their savior. She told him how brave and smart he was and how much she loved him. Then, she hurried away to give the news to their daughter, Miah, who was one of the more fortunate females and worked inside the Keep.

Without a word, Titus walked over to his cot in the corner of the tent and lay down with his back turned. The boy felt humiliated by the acts forced upon him, Lucin knew. He had struggled with the same emotions when it started for him so many years ago.

Lucin closed his eye and clasped his hands to his forehead, silently beseeching the Highworld to deliver his people from evil. It had been a very long time since he had turned to prayer. The spirits had unquestionably forsaken the Cyman people to their own devices long, long ago.

Yet now, there was a minute ray of hope. Deathbed ramblings of an old woman that Lucin was now counting on to turn into a lifeline for the Cyman people.

Abruptly, he pushed away from the table and stood. Now was as good a time as any to find out if his plan would work. With a last look at Titus, he ducked out of the tent and into the mire that surrounded the camp.

It must be early spring, he thought, although it was hard to tell the seasons apart in Nordik. Every day was greeted with the same gray, overcast skies, and today was no different as the clouds overhead bulged with unreleased rainwater.

The mud was everywhere. Continual rain and lack of green growth on the ground to soak the excess water made the land a virtual mud hole. The heavy boots of the army moving through the camp churned the soil until every step sank ankle-deep in sludge. Everything and everyone lived with a perpetual covering of mud. It covered bodies, clothes, blankets and equipment. Many of the soldiers walked for a league or more in the evenings in search of a dry piece of hard ground to sleep on.

Lucin sighed in disgust and strolled purposefully through the camp. Soldiers stopped what they were doing, whether mending tools or cleaning weapons, to quickly stand and offer him a salute. He did not return them. His mind was on his destination and his meeting with Adrian Ravener. If all worked as well as he hoped, he would at last have Ravener's promise to release the Cyman people from their bonds.

Despite the foolishness of the act, he had made a promise to his wife and he intended to keep it. His children, Titus and Miah, were too young to know the joy of life that he and Maree had experienced in their early years when Ravener allowed families to live in relative peace. The Cymans were content back then with the minor comforts they were permitted. Food, blankets and shelter. More importantly, they had their families together under one tented roof, which fulfilled their basic human need for love, touch and companionship.

It was only in the last forty years or so, as the Mage became more and more obsessed with training and developing the army, that the living conditions deteriorated to nothing short of torture.

By isolating the men, women and children into three unconnected groups, Ravener stripped the Cymans of life as surely as he had already stripped the land. It was just taking longer for them to wither and die.

Lucin closed his cloak tighter around his throat as he walked toward the first checkpoint at the outer wall of the Keep. It was harder to ignore the miserable cold than his own soldiers.

His hatred of cold, he knew, came from his Desert Troll ancestry. When the Mage War rent the land of Massa in half over three hundred years ago, the entire race of Desert Trolls, who made their home in the Sandori Sands, were swept away with the cleaving.

As a reclusive, tribal race, this separation was not initially viewed as disastrous. The Trolls still had their beloved sands, and they felt fortunate to be free of the subterfuge and infighting of the Assembly of Races. It wasn't long, however, before Ravener made his presence known and enslaved the Desert Trolls and the humans unfortunate enough to be on the wrong piece of land when Massa was divided.

Ravener's many experiments over the centuries with humans and Trolls resulted in the Cyman race of today. Their imposing physical stature, strength and quickness inherited from the Trolls and their intelligence, determination and empathy from the human side. Ravener had invested years trying to breed empathy out of his Cyman warriors to no avail. Without question, the Cymans would be fierce fighters in the protection of their people, but they would never be evil.

The single eye was a manifestation of the dark magic that maligned the physical traits of Ravener's subjects.

Lucin shook his morose thoughts away as he arrived at the Keep. He returned the salute this time to the soldiers on guard and crossed the courtyard to the black iron door that led to the lower level kitchens.

The Cyman women cooks glanced up as he entered and smiled. "'Ello, Captain," said the scullery boss, Ame.

"Ame," he greeted with a nod of his head. "'Ave you seen Miah?"

"Aye, Captain, she should be just returning from the Master's chambers with 'is dinner tray."

"Good. I'm on my way there now, so our paths should cross." He started to leave and then turned back to settle a large hand on Ame's shoulder. "'Ow is your back, Ame? I know you 'ave been 'aving problems."

"O' tis all right, Captain," she replied. "En old bird like me should expect some aches and pains now and agin."

Lucin laughed for the first time in a long time. "You and me both, Ame," he said, clapping her back affectionately. "You and me both."

He left then and took the stairs to the private chambers of Adrian Ravener on the third floor. He was surprised not to have run into Miah along the way, but was unconcerned. She could have been anywhere in the Keep, despite what Ame told him.

Lucin stepped out of the stairwell and strode to the wooden doors of Ravener's rooms. He knocked loudly and after a moment, the door was opened by his daughter holding a dinner tray in her hands.

"'Ello, darling," he said, reaching out to hug her.

Miah shied away from his embrace.

He narrowed his eye enquiringly at her. "What is it?"

Miah tried to hide her face. "'Tis nothing, Da," she answered and then broke down and started to cry quietly. Lucin pulled her out of the room and set the tray on the floor. When he lifted her chin and parted her hair, he saw a bruise on her cheek.

"I will kill 'im!" he hissed in rage.

Miah grabbed his shirt and turned him around. "Please, Da, don't! It was my fault. I wasn't listening to the Master as I should 'ave. You will only get a whipping if you confront 'im!"

He shrugged away from her grasp. She was right. It was pointless. His shoulders sagged and all of the fight visibly drained from him. How was he supposed to save an entire race of people when he couldn't even protect his own daughter?

Turning back to Miah, he pressed her face into his shoulder. "Believe me, Miah," he said, his voice soft yet filled with resolve, "the dark Mage will get what is coming to 'im."

"What are you talking about, Da?" she asked anxiously, looking both ways along the hall to be sure they were alone. "Ma said something to me yesterday. She said you 'ave a plan."

"I do, darling, and after this whole affair to the south of us is over, we will be back in the desert sands where we belong, living our lives in peace." He grabbed her face tightly. "I promise you that!"

Miah looked at him with unconditional love and confidence. "I believe you, Da."

"Go now," he ordered.

After she retrieved her tray and walked away, Lucin yanked open the door to Ravener's rooms. The antechamber was empty so he continued into the living area where he spotted the source of his fury sitting in one of two armchairs facing a large stone fireplace tall enough for a man to stand upright inside.

He wasn't alone. In the other chair sat a seer by the name of Saige. The poor creature looked as if she hadn't slept or eaten in days. Her eye was glazed over and terror and pain etched her face. It was only when Lucin made his way around the furniture that he could see why. Ravener was holding a sharp knife and one of Saige's fingers in his hands. The seer held a bloodied bandage to her wound as she sat in her chair trembling.

"What is the meaning of this?" Lucin demanded, forgetting his place in his revulsion of the spectacle in front of him.

The Mage casually inspected his grisly trophy. "You know, Lucin, I do not remember inviting you into my chambers, and I certainly do not remember allowing you to question my activities. Now, get out. I have business to conduct."

The panic-stricken seer shrank back into her chair.

"You can't torture visions from this seer, Master! 'Er predictions come when she least expects it, and you can't expect to draw it out of 'er at your will!"

Ravener looked up at him. "And how would you know about such things?"

Lucin swallowed, wondering if he had gone too far. "I knew 'er grandmother who was also a seer. She 'as since passed to the spirits, but she once told me that she 'ad no control over the visions. What she saw always came true, without fail, but she couldn't control when they came."

"Is that so?"

"In any event, I think she's been through enough for one evening and 'er stress may prevent 'er from telling prophecies in the future."

The Mage looked over at Saige with a frown as though seeing her anguish for the first time. He sniffed and said, "I guess you are right, Lucin. This useless lump hasn't been able to tell me anything new for days." He waved the woman out of the room, and she jumped out of her chair as if it were on fire and ran to the door, giving Lucin a quick look of gratitude as she exited.

Ravener unceremoniously dropped the bloody finger into a bowl on the table between the two chairs. "Sit," he commanded.

Lucin did so trying his best not to look at the macabre display.

"Everything is ready for our departure in the morning," he began. "The ships have been fortified with the equipment and food supplies that will be needed. As you know, we'll be going ashore at the only possible entrance to the old world which is located at the northern end of the island with the twin bluffs." It was all Lucin could do to continue looking at Ravener when all he wanted to do was put his hands around his scrawny neck and squeeze until he breathed his last breath, but he forced himself to continue. "As you requested, all Cyman males over the age of fourteen will accompany us to war. All women and children will remain behind."

"And?"

The question startled him. "Master?"

"Oh, come now, Lucin. You took great risk interrupting me the way you did, and you've been wringing your sweaty hands ever since you arrived. If this is about your slave daughter—"

"No!" he said, cutting Ravener off, not wanting his daughter's name coming out of his filthy mouth. "I just want you to be aware of everything I 'ave done for you so you will see to repaying me in kind."

"Meaning?"

Lucin took a deep breath. There was no turning back now. "Meaning that I will go to war for you, my people will go to war for you, but we would like our freedom in return. After the war is won— and mark my words we *will* win—the Cyman people would like to come back 'ere to Nordik to live. I believe there are still good sands east of 'ere." When Ravener remained silent with his hands steepled under his chin, Lucin hurried to continue. "If the witch Niema was right and all of the magic users are exiled in the north, they can easily be defeated and you will 'ave no further opposition to your rule. You will no longer need us."

"Ah, yes, poor Niema. She served her purpose well." He paused. "Until one of your men killed her, that is."

Lucin flinched.

The witch Niema often used her divination skills to gather information about the old world for Ravener and the two were close for many, many years. She was very ruthless, however, to the Cyman people, and one of his soldiers finally had all he could take when she was being particularly cruel one morning to a group of children. That soldier snuck up behind the unsuspecting Niema and snapped her neck with his bare hands. Her death had been quick and merciful.

His death had been slow and agonizing.

"That man paid for 'is crime. I—"

"*I*? *I* tell you what to do, Lucin, and *I* am not interested in any of your pathetic attempts at deal making."

Lucin stood slowly until he towered over the Mage. "You should be interested," he said softly.

Ravener stood as well in barely-controlled fury. "It has been a long time since I have had to break you, Lucin. Maybe too long?"

Despite the horrific memories evoked by Ravener's threat, Lucin did not flinch again. He couldn't afford to when so much was at stake. "You will give the Cyman people their freedom, Master, or you will die."

The Mage stared unbelievingly at him as they faced each other. "So, let me get this straight, Lucin. Unless I give the Cyman people their freedom, I will die. Are you threatening me, Captain?"

Lucin held up his hands. "No. Let me explain. Can we sit?" he asked, hoping to get Ravener into a less confrontational arrangement.

Surprisingly, the Mage sat down. "You have thirty seconds and if your answer does not satisfy me, my whip will slice open your back."

In spite of his efforts to prevent it, Lucin gulped visibly as he also sat. But, seated or standing, he had to tread very carefully with his volatile master. "It actually 'as to do with what you were just now attempting to get from the seer. On a night not too long ago, I was called to the bedside of 'er grandma, Sashan, when she was dying. She told me then that visions 'ad come to 'er and she needed me to 'ear them."

Ravener did not move a muscle, but the hunger for knowledge burning fiercely in his eyes was unmistakable.

Lucin went on, "Sashan said it was the last 'ope of our people. Would you like to 'ear?" he asked, knowing full well that the Mage would give his right arm to do so.

"Continue."

"'*In the year that the star grows weak, the ravens begin their flight; Ancient skills long since dead, resurrect in the morning light; Beware the four Savitars, who are light to the dark, but fear the shadow more, who is death to the dark; Beware the star, when it shines so bright, but fear the star more, in the eternal night'."*

Adrian raised his eyebrows, and Lucin could tell that the words of the prophecy rang true with intelligence previously held by him.

"That hardly constitutes a death sentence for me, Lucin. I trust you have more to bargain with?"

Lucin didn't hesitate. *"For the dark to conquer the land of old, the spirits will need to sing; Until that time the only hope, is the army of the raven king; As all livings things, it is freedom they crave; and grant it he must, it is that or the grave'."*

"I was right!" Ravener hissed and sprang from his chair, startling Lucin. He slammed his fist into the open palm of his hand. "Ancient skills? Spirits will need to sing? What else could it mean?"

"Master?"

"What?" he asked, turning back distractedly. "Oh, Lucin. Yes, yes, you have your deal. You would not want me to go to my *grave* now, would you?" He laughed sardonically.

Lucin trembled, afraid to believe it. Even with the prophecy in his possession, he had little hope that Ravener would really let them go, regardless of what he told Maree. "You...you are going to free the Cyman people after you 'ave established your rule?"

"Yes, Lucin, I told you, you have your deal. The information you have provided me has been well worth the exchange." Ravener uncharacteristically reached out to pat him on the shoulder. "Oh, yes, you have no idea what you have just given me, my friend." It was all Lucin could do to stop himself from cringing at the contact. With considerable effort, he forced himself to reach out his hand to the Mage.

Ravener looked at him and cackled. "Do you really think I would abide by a gentleman's handshake, Lucin? Your naiveté truly surprises me."

When Lucin did not pull back, Ravener said, "Very well, if it makes you feel better." The Mage's hand felt limp and soft in his and again he fought the urge to recoil from the touch.

Cautiously, Lucin nodded and walked to the door, but felt Ravener's presence at his back. He had his hand on the knob when Adrian called to him. "Captain!"

He turned around slowly, warily. "Yes, Master?"

"Satisfy my curiosity if you would. Why are you so quick to take my word that I will let the Cyman people go when our mission is complete? You are much smarter than that, so it puzzles me."

Lucin blinked his huge eye. "Oh, did I not mention? You see, dear old Sashan, 'ad not two, but *three* visions to share with me that night."

With that, he slipped through the door and closed it softly behind him, grateful that he couldn't see the look on his nefarious master's face.

CHAPTER 6

SMALL SURPRISES

It was late in the afternoon and uncomfortably humid when the legion crested the hill of a deep river valley. The volatile island temperature, so cool in the mornings that frost on the ground was not uncommon, provided searing temperatures in the afternoons.

In search of relief from the heat and the press of bodies, Beck rode a distance from the others and gazed out at a countryside alive with verdant grasses, fragrant blossoms and the rushing water of a blue winding river. Serving as backdrop for it all, as fresh and crisp as a new painting—the majestic Balor Mountains.

Beck inhaled the hot mountain air, pleased to discover it tinged with the smell of two of his favorite scents—jasmine and impending rain. The bouquet of the valley was invigorating to his tired muscles, the tranquility balm to his weary mind. In contrast to the coarse racket of the legion with its creaking leather, snorting animals and jangle of bridles, Mother Nature spoke to him in a lullaby and cradled him to her breast.

Earth.

The elemental power to which he was invariably linked held power beyond measure and for the first time, he felt free to probe her secrets.

With a thrill of excitement, he causally reached out with his magic toward the terrain before him. As soon as he did, an unexpected jolt surged through his mind and he was mentally wrenched from his body. Panicking, he tried to pull back, but was as helpless as an ensnared fish on a line as the spirit of the earth seized control of the link and directed him with express purpose.

Forcing down his unease, Beck relaxed his mind and found himself soaring at breakneck speed on a cerebral journey through the earth. Weightless, he burrowed down into the rich soil of the valley and glimpsed seedlings ready to burst forth with new buds. Delving deeper along the warren of roots from a black pine that twisted through the ground in complex designs, he paused to listen to three tender heartbeats from a mother fox and her two cubs as they slept snug and unaware in their underground den. Suddenly playful, Beck plunged out of the ground to scale the bark of a hickory tree. He smiled in amusement as a normally sure-footed squirrel almost fell from its perch as it attempted to gnaw into the husk of a hickory nut.

Curious for more exploration, Beck raced back down into the ground. The life he found there! Beyond the simple plants and trees, a massive number of seething life forms teemed in the millions.

And, not only that.

He sensed the spirit of the earth itself.

Sentient. Watching. Emitting a power so vast that the hum of conscious energy radiating throughout the land thudded through his body with frightening force.

How have I never felt this before?

The truth teased and taunted until he finally understood. As an earthshifter, he had always believed it was he who was master over the earth and had only to summon the oldest of the elemental powers to his trifling needs. How embarrassingly mistaken that notion was. He might have the power to summon, but the will to act was clearly the earth's alone.

Thank you, Mother, for this humbling lesson.

After what seemed like hours, but in reality must have been mere seconds, Beck pulled out of his magical excursion and back to his corporal surroundings. He looked around hesitantly, but it was apparent that his journey had gone unnoticed by his fellow soldiers who were already making their way down into the valley.

Halfhearted after such a remarkable foray, Beck rejoined the legion and followed the procession into a small copse of trees on the western side of the valley beside the river. Saddle sore, he swung down and rubbed his backside, unused to riding for so many hours at one stretch.

Dismore ordered Rogan to make a campfire, and his friend nodded eagerly, unaccustomed, Beck knew, to being requested to perform magic outside of an academic setting. After soliciting a few of the legionnaires to help gather wood, Rogan had a large fire blazing in moments. Tasks were assigned to all of the boys, and it wasn't long before the food was cooked and consumed, the horses curried and picketed and the exhausted legionnaires settled quietly into their bedrolls.

Listening to the peaceful night sounds of the insects and the crackle of the fire, Beck put his hands behind his head and gazed up at the sky. His jumbled thoughts raced between Galen Starr and his pendant to Kiernan and her lack of farewell. Unlike Kiernan, he never felt their exile a prison term, but just accepted it as his fate in life never to leave Pyraan. He had always been very happy and content with two loving parents, great friendships and his magic. But, what did Kiernan have? She lost her mother when she was young, her father due to her shifting ability and now her closest friends. He wished he had been more sympathetic to her feelings and made an attempt to get her accepted into the Northwatch Legion. *How could I have been so callous?*

Abruptly, the ground beneath him began to churn with his roused emotions, and the surrounding dirt shot up into the air and rained down on both Airron to the left of him and Rory to the right.

"What's going on?" Airron whispered, sitting up and brushing his blanket clean. Rory also sat up and looked worriedly at Beck. The small fireshifter had become his shadow since the trip began, always finding a way to be near him as much as possible.

"Sorry," he mumbled. "It was an accident."

Rory, satisfied with the answer, rolled back into his blanket to go back to sleep.

Rogan sidled over next to Airron and Beck. "Let's have it. What's bothering you?"

"I'm fine," he answered coarsely, embarrassed that his anxiety had escaped his usual tight control. "I was just thinking again about Galen Starr and the story my father told us last night," he said, which was the truth if not exactly all encompassing. Reaching into his uniform at the neck, he pulled out the pendant with the moving fist and held it out for his friends to see. "Just before we left today, my mother gave me this pendant and said it was a gift from Galen Starr."

"Bloody hell." Airron's hand shot out and he grabbed the pendant for a closer look. After a quick scrutiny, he put his hand to his own neck and pulled forth a silver pendant that looked exactly like Beck's except for the fact that Airron's depicted a man alternately changing between human and animal instead of a fist. "My parents gave this pendant to me last week on my eighteenth name day. They said nothing to me of Galen Starr, but you can't deny that the two pendants are identical except for the images."

As puzzling as it was, Beck had to agree with his Elven friend.

"Speaking of Galen," Rogan said, "I'm curious as to why the magic users of old are called Mages instead of shifters?"

"Good question."

Beck started at the figure of Commander Dismore standing above them.

"It is?"

"Yes," Dismore replied, lowering his considerable mass into a squat. "The simple answer is that a Mage is a practitioner of sorcery. As shifters, we are able to perform elemental magic, but we don't have any spell casting abilities."

"What about the elements of air and water?" Beck asked.

"Nonexistent."

"Is it something that we can learn?"

Dismore shook his head. "With only one Mage left in the land, and in seclusion no less, it is highly doubtful that we ever will." The commander put his hands on his thighs to leverage himself off the ground, and then removed a handkerchief from his pocket to wipe his brow. Even at the late hour, the air was still thick with humidity. "Get some sleep, men. We leave at sunrise." Dismore started to walk away and then abruptly turned around. "By the way, Radek and Falewir, you get first watch. Good evening, gentlemen."

Beck laughed to himself as Rogan and Airron groaned and got to their feet to slip soundlessly into the darkness. He thought it would be impossible to fall asleep with his thoughts churning so, but in what felt like no time at all, he was roused out of his blankets at dawn.

Breath misting in front of his face, he hurried to pack his gear and had to periodically tuck his hands under his armpits to keep them warm. Thankfully, the bitter cold would be very short lived. In a few short hours, it would be blistering heat to deal with again.

Once mounted and in formation, Beck pulled up the hood of his shoulder mantle to keep off the light rain he had known since yesterday would come.

The legion made very good time traveling along the well-established roads and arrived at the base of the mountains just before sunset. The soldiers fell into an easy routine for setting up camp and each man knew his part and went about it quietly with little conversation.

The evening meal now finished, the legionnaires were swaying tiredly before the mesmerizing dance of the fire, and it was precisely this silent tranquility that made the sudden, deafening scream that rent the air so terrifying.

Beck leapt to his feet in a crouch, the earth stirring in response to his call. Somehow, his friends materialized at his side, the air around Airron shimmering and fire already called to Rogan's palms.

"Be alert!" Beck shouted, and the legionnaires stood ready with whatever modest magic they had available to them.

Dismore emerged from the trees tugging up his trousers. "What in the bloody hell was that?" he cursed. "Is everyone accounted for?"

There was a hushed swirl of activity before Jon Anders whispered urgently, "No, Commander, Heath is missing."

Beck bent down to place his palm on the ground. "Hold on! Someone approaches. Actually, several someones."

A moment later, the visitors appeared out of the shadows.

Beck swallowed. He had heard all of the childhood stories of the notorious usurpers of Galen's Pass, but the sight of the horde of tiny terrors prodding a bound and gagged Heath into the camp with spears was alarming nonetheless. The Halfies stood three to four feet tall with very muscular bodies like that of an adult human male. The strong bodies were at odds, though, with the cherub faces and curly, golden hair. From what Beck had been told, those angelic faces could turn wicked in an instant with their mean-spirited and spiteful antics. These little creatures were the reason that this beautiful region was off limits to most Pyraanians.

"What is the meaning of this?" demanded Dismore, and the tallest Halfie came forward, dressed in a loincloth, his chest and feet bare.

In a high-pitched voice, the Halfie said, "You shall not pass." He gestured to his companions, and they pushed Heath forward until the legionnaire fell to the ground on his face. Rory Greeley and the earthshifter, Jon Anders, hurried over to untie Heath and help him to his feet.

"Now you wait just a bloody minute here!" bellowed Dismore. "As you damn well know, we are the Northwatch Legion of Pyraan and we pass through here twice every two years." Dismore looked around, "Where is Verdie Vee?"

The Halfie recoiled slightly at the name. "Verdie is dead. I am Tribe Leader now and as such, I tell you that you shall not pass."

"We have always had passage before," Dismore pointed out in frustration.

The Tribe Leader nodded. "Yes, that is so, but the clouds portend great peril. When the clouds portend peril, humans are usually the cause. More specifically, magic users are normally the cause which, as I can see by the marks on your necks, includes all of you."

Dismore threw up his hands. "Oh, for Highworld's sake. Listen...uh, what is your name?"

"I am Vinni Vee, Tribe Leader, Cloud Reader, son of Verdie," he replied. "Until the clouds are clear, my fighters will ensure that no human shall pass." The Halfie tribe raised their spears and thumped them to the ground in unison.

Not all of the yells came from the Halfies in the camp, and Beck swung his head up to the mountain shelves, some of which were a hundred feet or more off the ground. Howling Halfies, including women and children, crowded each side of the pass. Most of the children also wore loincloths—others were quite naked—and the women wore one-shouldered, short tunics above the knee.

All held a rock in their hands.

"Hey, stop that!" screamed one of the legionnaires. Beck turned to see Halfie fighters sneaking up behind the soldiers and poking them from behind with their sharp spears and then darting off again before the larger humans could grab for them. One of the legionnaires shredded his clothes to rags as he shifted into a black bear and lunged at the pint-sized imps.

Rogan had had enough. Not much taller than the Halfie leader, he stalked up to Vinni and the Halfies in the pass abruptly quieted as he did so. "Tell your people to stop this nonsense now, Halfie," he threatened, "or I will make them stop. Have you ever seen what an irate fireshifter can do?"

Vinni held his ground and said in a solemn, but squeaky voice, "It is our way to be wicked, Master Dwarf, sir. It is part of our nature and we could not change it even if we wished to." He looked at Rogan and then pointed with his chin. "It would be like asking you to grow taller, sir. You cannot change your height any more than we can change our ways. It is how the Highworld made us."

Rogan actually laughed. "How do you argue with that logic?"

Dismore surprised Beck when he turned his back to the legion and whispered to him, "What do you suggest, Atlan?"

He's leaving the decision to me? Thinking quickly, he said in a low voice, "I can easily distract and pen in those closest to us with a shieldwall, but that would only serve to send a rainstorm of rocks down on our heads from those in the pass." It also wouldn't help Troop 157 at the Crown Bluffs and soon to be returning through here. He ran his hands through his hair. "Give me a minute to try and reason with Vinni."

Dismore nodded.

As Beck turned to speak to the waiting Tribe Leader, a single desperate shriek erupted from the foothills. Beck looked up and saw a young Halfie child tumble from his mother's grasp toward the rocky terrain below.

"Airron! Go!" Beck screamed.

Airron's lithe form took two long running steps and shifted gracefully into a large eagle, his clothes falling away from him. With an eight-foot wingspan, the eagle shot into the air like a missile toward the falling child and gently grasped the tiny boy by his loincloth in both talons seconds before the young Halfie would have hit the ground.

With powerful effort, the eagle climbed back into the air with its struggling cargo and wheeled around to hold the child out to his mother, wings beating furiously to hold its position.

There was no gratitude from the Halfie woman as she snatched her child back and stuck out her tongue. Free of the extra weight, the eagle dropped into a low dive parallel to the ground, and Airron bodyshifted back into his human form on the run.

"You did not let the child die. Why would you do that?" the Tribe Leader asked, seemingly genuinely puzzled over their behavior.

Beck squatted down to Vinni Vee's height. "We did it, because we would never stand by and watch an innocent child be hurt. Humans are not as bad as you think, Vinni."

"Interesting," was all the Tribe Leader said as he stared at Beck. "Strange, but interesting."

Beck extended his hand. "My name is Beck, Vinni, and it's nice to meet you."

Just as Vinni was just about to spit on Beck's hand, his eyes widened as big as saucers and he stumbled back. "Oh, dear."

Beck traced Vinni's gaze to the pendant around his neck that had come free of his uniform.

"Oh, spirits of the Highworld, you are *Savitar!*" As soon as the other Halfies closest to the camp heard Vinni's words, they turned on their heels and ran, shouting, "The *Savitars* are in motion!" and "The time has come!" It was complete chaos after that as the Halfies along the shelves scampered down out of the foothills, pushing and shoving each other out of the way as they ran.

Beck looked to Dismore for guidance, but the commander just shook his head in helplessness.

"Stop them!" Beck yelled to Vinni. "Someone is going to get hurt!"

Vinni bowed to Beck as he started to retreat. "They will be fine, *Savitar*. You may pass, but you should do so quickly. The clouds were right and darkness descends!"

Beck could only look on in bewilderment as Vinni, his fighters, and the rest of Halfies disappeared into the countryside.

***

Kiernan watched the events unfold with interest while attempting to stay out of the line of sight of Beck, Rogan and Airron. At least the problem of the superstitious Halfies seemed to have resolved itself. She couldn't afford to be delayed by their half-mad mutterings. If she was discovered by Dismore now, before going through Galen's Pass, he would surely send her back to Parsis on her own. Once through to the Crown Bluffs and Troop 157 of the legion had departed, Dismore would be forced to let her stay and train with her friends.

She smiled at the thought of their faces when she made herself known.

Especially, Beck.

That young man is going to admit his feelings for me once and for all, she vowed silently.

CHAPTER 7

A SNAKE IN THE WATER

Adrian Ravener made the long trek to the docks and watched the frenzied activity as the Cyman soldiers carried last minute supplies onto the one hundred war ships that would take him home to the old world. He adjusted his hood to keep the omnipresent rain off his face. The storm rolling off the waters kicked up heavy winds and the soldiers were having a time of it on the rocking ships. Avalon stood by his side with her arm draped through his. He heard her mumble a few words and abruptly the rain around the two of them stopped and fell down outside of the protective shield she created.

He glanced at her, nodded, and put his hood down.

"How many soldiers will we have with us, Adrian?"

"Fifty thousand. Each ship will hold close to five hundred men."

"Will that be enough?"

He looked down at her and smiled. "Plenty." Lucin's prophecy quite conveniently assured him of that fact.

He wondered if Galen Starr was in Pyraan with the shifters. Was he aware that the Raveners were returning? In Pyraan or elsewhere in Massa, a confrontation with his old advisor was inevitable, and he was looking forward to the moment when Galen realized that he had lost and Adrian Ravener had won. Galen stole everything from him, and the wizened fool would pay dearly for that theft. He just hoped the Mage stayed alive long enough so that he could be the one to deliver the deathblow. His mouth twitched upward with bloodlust at the thought. *One way or another, I will find you. And a Netherworld curse to any shifter who dares to stand in my way.*

Avalon noticed his smile and tightened her grip on his arm. "You seem in a good mood, brother. Does it have anything to do with your meeting with Saige last night?"

"Hardly," Adrian scoffed. "That boob wouldn't know a vision if it reared up and bit her nose off."

Avalon looked at him in confusion. "How can you say that, Adrian, when Saige was the one who gave us the very prophecy that set our return in motion?"

"I say that because our army captain has given me more information about the prophecies than our seer. Apparently, Lucin knew Saige's grandmother and told me of another vision that succeeds the one we have already uncovered."

Avalon whirled around to stare at him. "Come now. What would Lucin know of such things, Adrian?"

Adrian readily understood his sister's disbelief. "As I said, he gave me another vision, which I will share with you later. The more pressing nuisance is that Lucin is in possession of a *third* prophecy that he is holding over my head in order to gain freedom for the Cyman people." What Lucin did not know was that Adrian had absolutely no intention of giving the mutants their freedom once he was back in power. For now, however, he would let Lucin presume he was in control. He needed Lucin to keep the army focused on the task ahead, but the captain would be expendable after that—prophecy or no prophecy.

Adrian gazed at the ships in expectation. He had yearned for this return for over three centuries, and there was much he missed dearly about Massa. Topmost among them, blue skies, a decent glass of spiced wine and the small frame of a human woman under him. The Cyman cows did nothing for him and he only took one when absolutely necessary. Oh yes, he decided, the pleasure of a woman would be of the highest priority.

"I hope you told him he was mad!" Avalon said scornfully, startling him out of his reverie.

"Who?"

"Lucin! I hope you set him straight about gaining his freedom."

Adrian shook his head at her transparent motives. "Why? Not ready to give up your little Cyman toy?"

His red-faced sister glared at him. "I care little for Lucin or his son or any Cyman for that matter," she spat, letting go of his arm and pushing away from him. "I am three hundred and nineteen years old, Adrian, and all that I want, all that drives me, is seeing the old world again."

"Aye, me, as well, sister."

"Then you must get the third prophecy from Lucin so we can understand what we'll face upon our arrival. As a Mage, Adrian, surely you have ways of getting the information without too much trouble," she challenged.

Adrian was saved from replying when a shout came from behind them on the road. "Master! Master!"

Adrian spun around to a young Cyman army messenger. "What is it?" he responded harshly to the boy.

"I 'ave a message, Master," he said hastily and thrust a parchment into Adrian's hands, no doubt eager to be away as quickly as possible.

Adrian unfurled the note and read its contents.

"What is it?" asked Avalon.

Adrian took his time reading and then said, "It seems we will have a vacancy in the cabin next to ours on this journey."

When she looked at him in question, he said, "By her own hand, our seer has decided that she would rather visit the Highworld than the old world."

Adrian gestured toward the ship with an outstretched arm. "After you, my dear."

***

After the confrontation with the Halfies, the uneasy legion spent the evening at the mouth of the pass. At sunrise, they proceeded cautiously into the narrow split in the mountain and despite a vigilant scrutiny of the passage walls and road ahead, they did not catch sight of a single Halfie along the way.

Luck had been with Kiernan up to this point, but she knew she couldn't afford to let her guard down only to be discovered before the time was right. She'd already had one unnerving incident when Airron caught her with her face turned directly toward him and he shouted to Beck, "Hey, I can't believe it! There's—"

She slammed him hard with her mindshifting and once she had him in her magical grasp, he was hers. Airron might as well have had a metal vise holding him and his thoughts in place as Kiernan deftly inserted one of her own. Had Beck been paying more attention, he would have recognized the blank look that suddenly stole over his friend's face.

"What?" asked Beck distractedly as he was talking to the little fireshifter, Rory, who had not left Beck's side since leaving Parsis.

"Hey, I can't believe it!" he repeated. "There's...an apple tree over there!"

"Yes, that *is* an apple tree, Airron. Thank you for pointing it out." Beck looked sideways at the Elf. "Are you okay?"

"Sure," Airron said, rubbing his head and looking anything but.

Kiernan couldn't stop the giggle that escaped and hurried away from her friends before they heard.

Dismore called a halt soon after, and as soon as the legion was settled into their routine and eating their mid-day meal, Kiernan slipped silently away. She wanted to wash some of the grime off her body in a small lake she spotted through the trees. It had hardly been easy for her to bathe on this trip surrounded by thirty-six men.

Discovering a path that she was certain would lead her to the lake, she took it, but paused just inside the tree line.

She closed her eyes knowing that when she opened them again, they would be black, the telltale sign that she was connected with her precious companion.

Bajan!

She waited.

I am alone, Bajan, you may come!

Greetings, Princess.

She looked up and beamed at sight of the Draca Cat bounding onto the leaf-strewn path ahead of her.

Oh, Bajan, you can't possibly know how good it is to see you. She rushed to him and threw her arms around his neck.

Bajan made a susurrant noise of satisfaction in response to her touch. Another Draca would never let a human stroke their head in this way. As a primordial race, they were very proud creatures and considered themselves quite superior to others. Physically large and imposing, a Draca Cat had the body of a cat, sleek and muscular, but with the long, sharp talons and spiked tail of a dragon. Both were extremely deadly weapons to an adversary.

He nudged her affectionately. *Now, now. I have been in contact with you every day of this journey.*

It's not the same and you know it.

The Draca Cat pulled away and began to pace.

What's wrong, Bajan?

His tail swished restlessly in the darkened light of the forest. *Although I'm not entirely sure of the reason, there is unrest at home. The pride leader of the Draca Cats, Sovereign Moombai, has asked me to be more diligent than usual in my protection of you.*

Protection of me? But, I am no longer involved as Princess of Iserlohn. Why would I need protection? And you have not heard from Moombai in years! Is he here in Pyraan?

Bajan gave Kiernan his form of an exasperated smile. *One question at a time, Princess.*

She crossed her arms and tapped her foot, her form of exasperation.

The Sovereign sent a messenger by the name of Felice.

A female? Kiernan interrupted.

Yes.

Was she pretty?

Yes. Now, keep quiet or I will not continue. Frustratingly, he waited a full moment before doing so. *Moombai sent Felice to warn me that there may be trouble. Since I have never lived with the Draca Cats, at least within memory, I do not share their superstitious nature. I do not hold sway with their legends and prophecy. I only know that I was allowed to remain with you at the blessings of my race. My duty is to you and your protection. I will guard you no matter what the Draca Cats have to say about it.* Bajan's eyes met hers. *Although, I must admit, it can be a very trying duty at times.*

Oh, Bajan. Do you ever wish that you weren't placed in my care? Do you long for the normal life of a Draca Cat in your homeland of Callyn-Rhe?

Bajan made a distressed mewing sound and nudged her. *You know very well that the answer to both questions is no. In addition to being an irksome and stubborn girl, you are also my beloved friend. Our bond is something I would never give up.*

She leaned her head into his shoulder gratefully. It had been very difficult traveling in secret. There were many times when she just wanted to shout out to Beck or Rogan or Airron about one of the sights she had seen along the way or to talk about the upcoming training. Her only succor had been her bond with Bajan—a constant, comforting presence in the back of her mind.

Bajan had been just a cub and Kiernan six years old when her father, out on a hunting expedition, found the baby cat snuggled up to his dead mother in the woods, barely clinging to life. Having just lost her own mother the year before, Kiernan was overjoyed when her father presented the baby Draca to her to care for, and a strong attachment developed as she nursed him back to health.

She had already discovered her magical abilities by that time and, because she dared not tell her father or any of the royal staff, she was feeling extremely lonely and in need of companionship. The orphaned Draca filled the void perfectly.

Finding out that she could communicate with Bajan had been quite unexpected. Experimenting with her mindshifting, she decided to extend a single wave of thought to the cat to see if it would hold. As soon as the connection had been made, both of their eyes turned black and the force of the link pitched her and Bajan hurtling backwards through the air. The results of that experiment were a few bruises, identical-colored eyes and a bond that would last a lifetime.

Theoretically, though, the linkage she shared with Bajan could not be referred to as the traditional form of mindshifting that occurred when thoughts were conveyed by a shifter along a one-way, magically-induced pathway. With Bajan, there was a dual connection and Kiernan could actually read his thoughts and Bajan hers.

To this day, she still didn't know what had happened that fateful night twelve years ago to cause this unique bond to form between them, but she was eternally grateful for the union.

Needless to say, Bajan continued, *it does not hurt to be on guard. I am going to scout ahead to the Crown Bluffs to ensure that the way is clear. Will you be able to stay out of trouble while I am gone?*

Of course. I will be fine. Don't worry about me.

Then, I must hurry. I can travel very swiftly, but have a long way to go

Kiernan embraced him once again and bid him farewell. She closed her eyes to sever the link and when she opened them again, her eyes were green and her friend was gone.

She sighed and continued her excursion to the little blue lake vowing not to worry about Bajan. Whatever the problem with the Draca Cats, he could handle it. It was useless to dwell on the situation.

Instead, she turned her thoughts to Beck. She desperately missed talking to him and resuming their easy companionship. The exact moment when that companionship had turned into something more, she couldn't be sure, but it had.

She loved Beck Atlan.

There, I've said it.

She loved his smile, his dimples and the way he ran his fingers through his hair when he was nervous. She loved his strength. Not just his physical strength as an earthshifter, but his strength as a person. As a leader. He was kind and compassionate, yet firm and decisive. And, she knew that he felt the same way about her, although it was taking him much longer to figure it out.

At least she was out of the city of Parsis for the first time in years. That in itself was worth all of the secrecy and loneliness.

When the lake came into view, she happily ran to the water's edge and stripped off her legion-issue sword belt. The Sword of Iserlohn she kept safely hidden away in her bedroll.

Keeping her cloak in place over her head in case any of the legionnaires should unexpectedly wander near, she kicked off her boots and sat down to roll up the legs of her uniform trousers. Just as she was about to dip her toes into the water to test the temperature, she froze.

Out in the middle of the lake and slithering toward her at an alarming rate was a snake with a head the size of a boar. Two large fangs dripping with venom poked down from the open maw.

Then, Kiernan, who *hated* snakes more than anything else in the world, did something very out of character for a warrior princess.

She screamed.

***

The snake peered at the figure paralyzed in fright on the shore of the lake, its eyes moving furiously where the body—it seemed—could not. Sliding up the bank, the snake probed the air around its prey with a serpent tongue. Above all else, it tasted fear, unbridled fear.

Moving slowly over the inert body, the snake coiled around the small waist and squeezed lightly. Gliding its face close to the prey, it opened its jaws wide in intimidation hoping to get the confirmation it had come to this lake to obtain.

As soon as the high-pitched scream pierced the air, the snake had it.

I knew it.

As soon as the snake released the girl, she regained her mobility and scrambled backwards. Rolling quickly once to get momentum, she brought her foot around and landed a bone crunching kick to the snake's head. Saliva and blood flew from its mouth in a long string as its head whipped violently to the side.

The snake hissed loudly in pain.

The girl gasped in shock as the serpent's open mouth transformed into Airron Falewir's grimace as he bodyshifted back into his Elven form.

"Bloody hell, Kiernan, that hurt!"

Kiernan's whole body collapsed in relief at the sight of him. "I hate you," she managed to spew before falling back to lie on the ground.

"What?" he questioned through a mouth stained red with blood. "You're the only one who can wander around here in disguise?"

He held his hand out to her.

She grabbed it forcefully and stood. "You know I *hate* snakes, Airron."

"Well known fact, Kiernan, that's why I used it. Now, tell me, why are you here? Is something wrong at home?"

"What? No, nothing like that," she responded and walked over to her sword belt, picked it up and cinched it around her waist. "I'm actually surprised you have to ask, Airron. Did you really think I would stay in Parsis and miss all the excitement?"

Airron sighed. "Kiernan, as we've told you many times, it's not going to be exciting! We're going to be training, sleeping, and eating with the same thirty-six people day in and day out for two years. I promise you that not one of them has the requisite body parts necessary to make this anywhere near exciting for me."

Her face blushed adorably.

"At least we'll be together," she retorted and turned away. "I'll let the commander know I'm here as soon as Troop 157 departs and not a minute before! Now, get dressed so you can return before someone discovers you're gone and comes to investigate."

"Don't look!" he said with a chuckle and walked into the woods to retrieve his uniform hanging from a tree branch.

She laughed. "I've already seen you naked more times than is healthy."

When he emerged fully dressed, they started back down the path toward camp. After a moment of silence, Kiernan glanced sideways at him and asked, "So, are you the only one who knows I'm here?"

Airron shrugged. "If Beck or Rogan suspect, they have said nothing to me."

"Idiot."

"Who?" Airron asked, amused.

"No one," she muttered dismissively. "But, don't tell anyone I'm here, Airron, all right? I'll just get sent home if I'm found out too soon."

"Your secret is safe with me," he promised.

"Thank you," she said and unexpectedly reached up to kiss him on the cheek.

"Uh, requisite body parts touching my arm."

"Oh, hush."

He laughed and grabbed her shoulders to pull her close as they walked. They found the legion packing up from their short respite when they returned, anxious now to complete the last leg of the journey to the Crown Bluffs.

Airron turned to warn Kiernan to be careful, but his friend had already melted unseen into the crowd of legionnaires. He shrugged and walked over to Beck and Rogan. Rory was with them, trying to help Beck pack up his gear.

"I've got it, Rory," Beck said, not unkindly. "Why don't you see to your own things?"

"All done, sir!" the fireshifter said proudly. Much to Beck's dismay, Rory had taken to using the honorific after the Halfie encounter.

"Just Beck, Rory, just call me Beck."

Beck rolled his eyes when Rory was looking elsewhere and happened to notice Airron. "Where have you been?" he asked urgently. "Dismore has been looking for you. He was just about to send out a search party."

Rogan snorted. "He was probably out looking for another form while we're all here waiting on him."

"Don't worry, Firefly, I'm back safe and sound," Airron said, hugging the Dwarf close.

"Get off me!" Rogan yelled, shrugging out of his embrace.

"Did you hear a scream?" Beck suddenly asked. "I thought I heard someone or something scream while you were gone."

Airron didn't hesitate. "Nope, didn't hear a thing." Oh, bloody, no. He wouldn't miss the look on Beck's face when he saw Kiernan for all of the forms in the world.

Beck ran his hand through his hair and hissed, "Here comes Dismore."

"FALEWIR!"

CHAPTER 8

WHEN THE LAUGHTER STOPS

Standing concealed in the shadows of the crate-laden deck with the grunts of hundreds of men permeating the background, Titus leaned over the rail of the Cyman-built ship and tilted his head up to the sun. He couldn't help himself from moaning in delight as the wind whipped through his shoulder-length hair, and for the first time in his nineteen years of life, the air did not carry the smell of rancid decay to his nose. After a lifetime of darkness, this new encounter with light and warmth was almost more than he could comprehend.

He wondered if his father had been right and the skies east of Nordik were like this, untouched by the Mage's foul arts.

"Three days at sea has done nothing to improve my brother's temperament," came a woman's voice from behind him. "He has already thrown close to thirty soldiers overboard."

Titus stiffened but did not comment. He knew better.

Her pungent musky scent obliterated the clean ocean breeze as she walked over and stood next to him. They remained silent for long moments gazing out at the calm, open sea before she asked, "Were you aware that your father has been bargaining with my brother for the release of your people when the war is over?"

"Yes, 'e 'as told me, Mistress."

She turned to face him and put a hand on his arm. "Titus, what will you do if Adrian holds true to his word? Is your desire really to go back to Nordik?"

Surprisingly, the question caused him to hesitate. Beholding blue skies for the first time, he was suddenly unsure. Breathing in fresh air and feeling the sun's warm rays on his face revived his spirit in a way he never thought possible. But, what was Avalon Ravener really asking him? Because no matter how beautiful the woman standing next to him, she was the embodiment of darkness.

"Despite my Da's 'ope, I find it doubtful that the Master will set us free," he replied carefully.

Her big brown eyes lowered and she sighed dramatically. "I am afraid you are probably right, Titus. Although, I cannot say that I would be disappointed. Curiously, I find I am not yet ready to give you up."

Titus swallowed. "You will find a man in Massa, Mistress."

"I do not want a *man*, Titus, I want you," she said, reaching down between his legs to rub her hand possessively over him. "And, I will have you."

To his shame, he felt his body respond. The witch was skilled at exploiting his carnal urges to humiliate him.

"Look, Titus!" she shouted suddenly, pointing.

He jerked his head up and peered over the rail at the barely visible, yet unmistakable, outline of land. Hope and optimism flooded through his body, and he began to tremble. What if the Mage kept his word and the Cyman people really were standing at freedom's doorstep at this very moment? All they had to do was win the war by convincing the Massans to lay down their arms against Adrian Ravener.

Can it be that simple?

Avalon gasped, digging her nails into his arm, "Oh, Titus, we're almost home! I have dreamt of this for more years than I care to remember!"

"I must tell the others," he said, pushing off the rail and out of her grip.

"Titus, wait!" she said, her eyes suddenly hard. "Do not forget what I said. You are mine and you always will be."

And, just like that, the cold and dark slammed back into his world.

***

At dusk, sight of the twin Crown Bluffs came into sight. Two magnificent waterfalls fell in a torrent down each side of the cliffs, their roar tremendous as they thundered down and pooled into a small lake fed by the Arounda Ocean through the narrow chasm that separated the bluffs.

The spray from the falls was heavy in the air and Rogan felt the pleasant pinpricks of mist on his face as he sat his horse, overlooking the scene.

This is it, he thought. The outpost that has housed generation after generation of Northwatch Legions.

There was so much history and emotion tied to the Crown Bluffs that Rogan couldn't help but be overwhelmed in the shadow of their presence. While it truly was a stunning view, he could see more importantly that the location would be easily defendable. The narrow channel that flowed inland would prevent a large number of ships from infiltrating the island at one time, and defenders could easily position themselves on top of the wide cliffs to harry invaders from the seaside.

Rough stairs hewn into the side of the bluffs ran all the way to the top with roped-off landings at spaced intervals. A simple pulley system transported supplies in a bucket to the men patrolling there. The encampment, spread out resourcefully around the lake, consisted of two barracks for the soldiers, a dining hall, bathing stalls, and a small private dwelling for Commander Dismore.

Out in front of it all, the legionnaires of Troop 157 standing rigidly at attention to greet them.

"Look ahead, Airron!" Rogan shouted, pointing at an outhouse. "That is where you'll be spending most of your time."

Everyone within earshot laughed, including Airron whose punishment for his disappearing act cost him two weeks of latrine duty.

"Glad to be of service, my friends," the Elf said, bowing dramatically with a sidelong glance at his hooded riding companion.

Rogan noticed the glance. He also knew as surely as he knew his own name that the figure riding next to Airron was Kiernan Everard. Knowing Kiernan as long as he had, he wasn't surprised. He just wondered how long it would take until she was finally noticed and acknowledged by the others.

A legionnaire with the stripes of a lieutenant on his uniform, stepped out in front. "Welcome Commander! Welcome Troop 158!"

In response, each legionnaire of Troop 157 slammed fist to chest in perfect unison.

"We have a lot of work to do to be that precise," Beck whispered out of the side of his mouth.

Rogan nodded in agreement. To think that this motley group of eighteen year olds could look like the regimented unit standing before him seemed farfetched, but he knew they would be. Dismore would make certain of it.

The commander rode forward and dismounted. "Thank you, Lieutenant Wilem."

Dismore traded grips with the legionnaire and then looked back at the mounted recruits. "As first order of business, I must elect a lieutenant for Troop 158. As always, the journey north tells me much about my new company, and I am honored to tell you that your new lieutenant is..." Dismore paused. "Beck Atlan."

In contrast to Troop 157, who extended a professional salute to Beck, Troop 158 dismounted in a disorderly fashion and pulled Beck from his horse, mussing his hair and offering him their raucous congratulations. Heath and Jon Anders simply stood back and watched. They were coming around, but not quite there yet.

Rogan grinned when Rory Greeley started hopping up and down excitedly. "I told you!" he shouted to no one in particular. "I just knew it would be him!"

Airron didn't waste any time trying to exploit his friend's position. "Hey, Lieutenant! Any chance you can help with the latrine duty?" he asked, grinning from ear to ear.

Beck smiled just as wide. "Sorry, Airron, but I think that the commander was totally justified in his punishment."

"Huh?" Airron questioned with raised eyebrows.

Rogan listened in as Beck beckoned Airron closer and whispered "Maybe this will serve as a reminder not to be *snakey*...I mean...sneaky in the future."

Rogan didn't know what Beck was talking about, but assumed by his comment and the look on Airron's face that he also knew that Kiernan was here. How could he not? They were family, after all. The only family Rogan had known since he was six years old and his own parents abandoned him. Like Kiernan, he felt restless, but he was also angry. Angry with Galen Starr for committing generations of shifters to exile, and angry with his parents for not loving him enough to stay by his side.

He often thought that there was more to the story and the truth of it lay hidden in some dark chamber of his mind. But whenever he felt close to remembering, the images would slip away into wisps of smoke. It was maddening that he could never latch on to any specific detail. If he could remember just one, it might help to recover the rest.

Some day, he promised himself, he would find those answers. Of course, it would be easier if they weren't located hundreds of leagues away in his homeland of Deepstone.

"You coming, Rogan?" It was Beck.

He nodded and led his mount after the others.

It was late by the time both legion companies had eaten and were settled into the barracks for the evening. It was a tight fit, but necessary since Troop 157 wouldn't be departing until first light the following morning.

Rogan watched as Kiernan's slight form slipped into the building behind Airron. With a shake of his head, he stretched out on the cot assigned to him, closed his eyes and was asleep in seconds.

He was so tired that his mind refused to respond when he heard frantic shouts from outside that sent legionnaires rushing out of the doors of the barracks. Rogan sighed and sat up, surprised that light was spilling in through the windows.

Is it morning already?

He stood and took off running along with the rest of the legionnaires thinking as he did that for a journey that was supposed to be boring and uneventful, there was a plenty of screaming going on.

***

Beck was the first one out of the barracks, and he scanned the area for the source of trouble. A movement on top of the bluffs caught his eye, and he looked up just as one of the patrolling legionnaires came into view and issued a loud warning signal on his bugle with one long and two short bursts.

Enemy advancing.

What? What enemy?

Three legionnaires of Troop 157 pushed roughly past him and started up the steps in the cliff at a sprint. Dismore rushed out of his private quarters thrusting his arms into the sleeves of his uniformed shirt and left it unbuttoned as he made his way to the top of the bluff. Beck followed behind, vigorously resisting the desire to give him a helpful shove along the way.

"Demon's breath," whispered the winded commander, emerging onto the wide platform built on the cliff top.

Beck stepped around Dismore and put a hand above his eyes to shade his view. His breath caught in his throat. An armada of ships surrounded the Crown Bluffs. Large, black, three-masted vessels.

He had an instant to wonder if the ships could be friendly when shifted fire careened toward the bluff.

A waist-high stone wall built into the other side of the walkway— most likely designed for safety purposes rather than defense— provided the only barrier between him and the fire, and he dove behind it.

"Topside!" Dismore bellowed. "All legionnaires to the bluff!"

Rogan hurried over to Dismore in a crouch, snapping both arms out away from his sides as fire roared to life in each hand. "Commander! With your permission, sir!"

Dismore looked at Rogan with a bewildered expression. Despite all of the years of tours and training, the commander seemed wholly unprepared for an actual attack. Beck doubted that the man thought that this day would ever come. He doubted that there was a shifter in the last six generations that believed this day would ever come.

"Yes, yes. Go ahead, Radek. Hurry!"

"Stand back," Rogan barked as he stood upright and shifted a large, sizzling lightning bolt into existence. He ran a few steps, spun in the air, and used the momentum of the spin to heave the fire toward the nearest ship. The bolt sliced through the air with a loud *whoosh* and on its downward arc made direct contact with one of the ship's enormous sails. The material caught fire immediately and spread to the wooden decking below. Men closest to the flames screamed and jumped from the burning ship into the ocean and began swimming toward the beach. Several of the black vessels were already lowering smaller skiffs over their sides, sending them after the men in the water and others yet directly for Massan shores.

The atmosphere turned chaotic and charged with the experienced Troop 157 running along the platform and shouting orders and the inexperienced Troop 158 floundering about in confusion.

Fortunately, Dismore seemed to have finally recovered somewhat. "Fireshifters to me!"

Soldiers quickly formed at the wall and once the order was given, volleyed fire down on the enemy.

"Archers!"

Legionnaires were still scrambling up the stairs, but several archers appeared and wasted no time in taking up their bows and firing at Dismore's signal.

Beck peered down at the invaders. As the first of them made their way to shore, he shrank back in horror. They weren't men at all, but enormous, thick-skinned creatures with one eye! He never could have imagined that such monsters existed in the world, and watched dejectedly as the archers' arrows bounced harmlessly off their hides. He shuddered and then ducked as a ball of friendly fire flew close by over his head.

Taking a chance, he popped up from behind his cover and leaned far over the stone wall to look at the cliff face. He quickly found what he was looking for and thrust his hand out toward several large granite boulders embedded in the wall below him. The earth obediently responded to his summons and the dirt beneath the rocks shifted away in a controlled maelstrom of dust. Beck's legs and arms ached from his position hanging head down from the wall, but he couldn't proceed any faster for fear that he would disturb the foundation too much and cause a collapse.

His face a hardened mask of grime and sweat, he ignored the shouts and explosions above and continued shifting until three of the boulders finally came loose and tumbled down the cliff face.

Swinging back up to the safety of the bluff, he saw the first creature emerge from the ocean without noticing the danger. One of the boulders crashed into him with deadly accuracy, pounding him into the sand.

The second boulder went wide, spinning harmlessly into the ocean.

Another invader stopped to help pull one of his comrades from the water when the third granite missile hurtled into them, killing both instantly.

A blinding flare of fire suddenly erupted further out to sea, and Beck had to throw an arm up to shield his eyes. When he could, he peered back and focused on a man in black standing on the prow of one of the ships, cloak billowing out behind him.

He was human, Beck noticed, unlike the creatures that had come to shore, and also a magic user. That much was obvious as his hands were held out in front of him shifting a considerable amount of fire.

Beck turned and saw Rogan's narrowed and confident gaze on the man as he, too, shifted fire. With a loud *hiss*, he shaped a fiery club that he held in one hand and twirled in anticipation of slamming any fire balls back to the magic user.

The man stared back just as sure. He separated his fire into balls and began juggling them in the air—one of Rogan's favorite tricks. The balls spun in an orange blur above the shifter's head, creating a vortex that ultimately coalesced into one huge bright orb of fire.

The Northwatch Legion stopped to stare in shock as the fiery sphere twisted and morphed into the face of the creatures with one eye now swarming ashore. Only this image was even more grotesquely deformed with two rows of jagged teeth through which a serpent tongue darted in and out. Unexpectedly, the head turned toward the legionnaires lining the bluff and sped toward them, fiery jaws snapping.

"Bloody amazing," Rogan said in awe at the man's skill in fireshifting.

Catching sight of the danger hurtling toward their position on the bluffs, several legionnaires screamed in fright and ran toward the stone stairs on the other side of the cliff. Beck watched as the big earthshifter, Heath, pushed his fellow soldiers out of the way to get to the front of the line. One pushed back and Heath slipped from the edge, plummeting to the ground below.

Beck shook his head remorsefully. There was no way that the earthshifter could have survived that fall.

Realizing that the fight was going to take place on the southern side of the bluffs anyway, he screamed out to start more of the soldiers moving toward the stairs and away from the dangerous fireshifting. "Legionnaires! Move! Down to the camp! Everyone move!"

Where is Dismore?

Beck turned back to Rogan just in time to see him take a swing with his club at the head of the fire monster. Regrettably, it managed to evade the strike and turned its jaws instead on one of the legionnaires heading for the stairs and swallowed him whole. The screams as the young man burned were unbearable for Beck to hear, and he was grateful when Rogan honed his club into a sword and ended the legionnaire's agony.

The grisly scene caused more legionnaires to panic and two of them slipped down the seaside cliff face and onto the sand below. Beck ran to the stone wall to look down. Neither legionnaire survived, but that didn't stop one of the creatures from ripping apart their corpses.

Furious, Beck reached out his hand and the sand beneath the invader began to liquefy and pull at his boots. The creature's one eye widened in terror as he tried to escape, but the shifted sand held him fast and he sank lower and lower into the earth. The doomed invader's comrades stood by helplessly as the sand buried him up to his neck. Beck turned away only when the beast fully disappeared, silencing his screams forever.

Beck ran for the stairs. Several of the intruders had made it through the channel on their skiffs and were engaging the legionnaires in battle.

Time and motion suddenly slowed for Beck, and his feet rooted in place as he looked from scene to terrifying scene. Earthshifters with little magic to call forth were on the ground taking on the larger invaders in a physical fight to the death. Bodyshifters were summoning their fiercest forms to tear at the trespassers with sharp teeth and claws.

In time that felt mired in thick syrup, Beck struggled to turn his head to the left and saw that Rogan was still battling the fire monster, muscles straining and arms and face blistered by the alien flames. Farther down the platform, Beck finally found Commander Dismore.

He was lying face up with his eyes open and a hole in his chest where a ball of fire had slammed into him.

For the first time in three hundred years, the defenses at the Crown Bluffs had been breached. Legionnaires were dying. Young men Beck's age, most of whom had grown up in Parsis and attended the academy with him.

Dead.

His friends.

Through the haze, Beck faintly heard Rory crying out to him from the stairs several feet below. "Lieutenant! We need help!"

Beck fought to turn his head to look over once again at his best friend. Rogan continued his solitary fight, breaking down the monster with every mighty swing he took. He was the last one standing on the cliff now, and if Beck left him, he would be utterly alone.

Rogan must have sensed his hesitation, because he turned to him and screamed, "Go, Beck, I've got this!"

Rogan's words brought time slamming back into place and Beck's body jerked in response. That was when he remembered that Kiernan was down there somewhere. He nodded to Rogan and raced down the steps, passing Rory in his headlong flight into the fight.

The first person he saw as he leapt from the stairs was Airron. The Elf was sprinting to reach Jon Anders locked in mortal combat with one of the giants. By the look of the creature's open wounds, Jon had put up a good fight but the earthshifter now had his back up against the cliff wall. He was leaning into it in exhaustion, sword point dropping to the ground.

The invader grinned and made an aggressive maneuver toward Jon.

Behind him, Airron sprang and shifted midair into one of the great black wolves of the Grayan Forest, sailing onto the creature's back and digging his claws into its body. The giant bellowed in pain and twisted around to grab at the wolf clinging to its broad shoulders. The distraction provided Jon the opportunity he needed, and he took it, shoving his sword into the single eye of his combatant. The creature fell over dead, and the wolf jumped free of the falling enemy and grinned.

Beck hurried over.

"We have to get out of here...Lieutenant," Jon said tiredly. "We're no match for these invaders, and we have to save those still alive."

Beck nodded. "How many have we lost?"

"Over half," said Jon.

He was right. Retreat was the only viable option at this point. Beck approached the wolf. "Where's Kiernan? Have you seen her?" The black wolf shook his head and then loped away, hopefully to find her.

"Anders, I have to go back for Rogan. Gather up the legionnaires and meet me at the top of the valley where we first arrived."

The blonde earthshifter nodded. "Retreat!" he yelled, running through the melee. "Retreat!"

Beck studied the battlefield and at the same time held out his arms and shifted the earth. The dirt and stones ran up and over his body in a wave creating an earthen suit of armor. When he had finished, a two-inch layer of stone covered every part of his body except his eyes. "Kiernan!" he shouted over the screams of battle. "Kiernan!"

He spotted a small, hooded legionnaire near the barracks fighting one of the monsters. By the expert lunges and slices, Beck knew it to be Kiernan even before the hood slipped off revealing her blonde hair.

Howling with rage, he charged toward her, but was lifted off his feet when one of the invaders struck him from behind. He fell into the dirt, but rolled away just in time to avoid a powerful kick. He put his hands underneath him and summoned the earth to lift him upright. With his feet now planted squarely underneath him, he swung a mighty fist of stone at his foe and knocked him several feet into the air and up against the cliff wall, dead.

Another challenger rushed him and Beck ducked under his grasp and took him down at the knees. He then seized the giant by one arm and one leg and swung with all of his super strength before letting go. The body crashed into what was once Dismore's quarters, caving in one wall.

Searching for Kiernan again, Beck was relieved to see Bajan at her side and the creature she had been fighting unmoving on the ground.

Starting toward her once again, he was knocked to the ground a second time by a large explosion that rocked the morning air. He looked up at a sky littered with tiny sparks of fire and watched the lethal embers fall down onto the rooftops of the buildings in the camp and start to take hold.

Rogan ran down the stone steps yelling, "I got it! Let's get out of here!"

Distracted, Beck didn't notice one of the creatures standing over him until it was holding a legion sword to his eye—the only visible breach in his earthen armor. Beck flinched in shock when the thing spoke to him.

"Do not move," the giant commanded.

Beck looked up at the huge form and was calculating how to shift the earth just enough so that the sword point didn't penetrate his brain, when he saw something in the creature's eye that surprised him.

It was indecision.

Unexpectedly, the invader swung its head up, paused, and then threw down the weapon. Beck rolled away and followed the monster's gaze.

There was Kiernan, barely able to stand, leaning on her sword. Like the rest of them, she had been fighting for her life.

"Kiernan!" he shouted in relief, getting to his feet and allowing the armor of stone and dirt to slide off him. She stumbled over to him and into his arms.

Nothing ever felt so good to him in his life.

"We have to get out of here," she said, green eyes worried.

"I know." He reached out to wipe a smudge of dirt from under her eye. "You go. I have to make sure everyone gets out safely. I'll catch up with you."

"No need, Beck," Airron said, appearing at their side. "There is no one else. It's just us."

Beck stared at him uncomprehendingly. "What do you mean?" he asked looking around and realizing how eerily quiet it suddenly seemed. Dead bodies, human and creature alike, were strewn across the encampment. "Hell," he whispered under his breath. "Where is Anders? I sent Anders to round everyone up!"

"Over there." Airron pointed to Jon's corpse. The young earthshifter, his blonde curls matted with blood, lay face down with his own sword through his back.

Beck felt sick. All of the legionnaires and the first wave of attackers were dead.

Kiernan squeezed his arm.

"The entire legion gone?" he muttered, running a hand through his hair as he continued to survey the area in disbelief. The buildings, engulfed in flames, crackled ominously in the silence.

"Just the four of us left standing, and we don't have time for discussion," replied Airron, pointing toward the channel. "That fireshifter in black will be sending more troops in any minute."

Rogan looked at the mindshifted invader and thrust his thumb out. "What about him?"

"We take him with us," Beck growled. "I want to learn more about why they are here and what their plans are. Can you keep him under your control, Kiernan?"

She nodded and locked eyes with the creature. His head tilted to the side as he processed the thought she inserted. The invader then turned and walked away from them.

"What did you do?"

"He's off to saddle five horses for us."

"I'll need a saddle, but not a horse," Beck said and put a finger and thumb in his mouth to whistle. Within seconds, a shiny black head appeared at the top of the valley and Chasin raced down the hill toward Beck's call.

When the prisoner returned with the gear, Beck saddled him and swung up onto his back. As he waited for the others to finish, he lifted his head suddenly at a faint noise. It sounded like a cry for help.

Hauling on Chasin's reins, he kicked the horse into a trot and guided him toward the burning barracks where he thought he had heard the wail. "Dear, Highworld." He dismounted when he saw a small hand waving from under a much larger body. Beck shoved the dead man aside and found Rory Greeley beneath, bleeding from a gash on his head, but otherwise unhurt.

Beck held out his hand and Rory took it with a grim smile. "Thank you, sir. I knew you wouldn't leave me."

Beck grunted and helped Rory up into the saddle. "No, I wouldn't leave you, Rory. Not if I could help it."

Beck and Rory joined the others and all were overjoyed to discover that another of the legion had survived.

"Now we *do* need another horse," Rogan pointed out.

"He can have mine," Airron said, disrobing and stuffing his clothes into his pack. He threw it to Rogan when he had finished and shifted into a white Haventi, arrogantly rearing up on his hind legs to paw at the air.

The five riders and six horses sped away up the hill and then turned back for one last look at the valley and the generations-old Northwatch Legion encampment.

This time, they saw not the beauty of the Crown Bluffs, the waterfalls and the blue lake that they admired less than a day ago, but the smoldering fires of ruin and an unknown enemy swarming mercilessly over the land held by their forefathers for three hundred years.

Hundreds of companies of the legion, thousands of men.

Troop 158 would be the last.

Chapter 9

Friend or Foe?

The sun had already dipped below the western horizon when Beck finally slowed their hurried flight south toward Galen's Pass. Although still more than a day from the foothills of the Balor Mountains, Beck could see their mist-enshrouded tips in the distance.

Somehow, Kiernan had managed to maintain a steady stream of shifting to their prisoner, but she was now swaying dangerously in her saddle. Beck made his way over to a thinning coppice just off the road. "We'll stop here for the night."

"About time," Rogan grumbled.

Beck swung a leg over Chasin and dismounted before the big horse had a chance to come to a full stop. Rushing to Kiernan, he reached up to wrap his hands around her waist and help her down. "Are you all right?" he asked, searching her tired eyes.

"I'm fine," she said with a small smile.

Rogan offered to care for the worn out horses.

"No, Rory can do it," Beck said. "You need to take care of those burns on your arms before they get infected. There's salve and bandages in my pack."

He turned back to Kiernan. "How long can you keep this up?" he asked, nodding toward their captive.

She sighed. "Hours, if I have the ability to concentrate because the link requires periodic mental reinforcement."

Beck was impressed. He knew that for most mindshifters, a thought shifted to another person lasted for just a few seconds. "And the shifted person can't discard the thoughts you give them and act on their own, correct?"

She shook her head and a strand of blonde hair tumbled over one eye. Beck used a finger to tuck the unruly tress back behind her ear. "No. Once I've established a connection, the receiver of the magic is blocked from having any independent thoughts during that time and is powerless to counter the directive of the simulated thought."

"Does the receiver know what's happening?" he asked. Although the academy offered a cursory review of other forms of shifting, the majority of the time was spent on areas of expertise. There was never a need for more since the magic users of Pyraan never exhibited aptitude in more than one ability.

"Normally, no, because the shifting takes place so fast that the receiver just treats the foreign thought as one of their own. Again, with me, because I can cause such a large span of time to be under my control, a person familiar with magic would know a mindshifter had been involved." She glanced at the captive. "Especially, when they end up miles from where they last were."

As if on cue, the captive moaned and placed his head in his bound hands.

"Should I shift again?" she asked wearily.

"No, I want to get answers first if I can. Why don't you try to rest?"

She nodded gratefully and walked over to sit on a fallen log by the roadside.

"Get him down," he ordered Airron who, Beck was glad to note, had already shifted from his horse form and was dressed. The Elf walked over and dragged the large hostage off the horse to the ground.

Free now from the pseudo thoughts that were responsible for his every action since abandoning the Crown Bluffs, the prisoner growled and kicked out with his legs, narrowly missing Airron.

"Easy, big boy," Airron warned. "In case you haven't noticed, we're not the enemy here, you are."

The one-eyed invader glared at Airron but said nothing as he assessed his surroundings and captors with obvious mistrust.

Beck paced back and forth in front of the prone figure, large pieces of dirt flying off his boots with every determined step. "What is your name?"

Silence.

"I know you speak our language. What is your name?" he asked again, stopping.

Silence.

Rogan appeared at Beck's side, twin fireballs flaring to life in his newly-bandaged palms. "Why bother with a monster like this? I say kill it now before it brings more harm to the people of Massa."

"I'm not a monster and I'm not an *it!*" the captive roared, sitting upright and struggling against his bindings.

Rogan stalked over and under different circumstances, Beck might have laughed at the diminutive Dwarf glowering down at the gigantic trespasser. Even sitting on the ground, the considerable difference in size was unmistakable. The captive had to have been over seven feet, for sure.

Rogan leaned over him. "Not a monster, eh? Then what do you call people who invade other lands and slaughter the people they find there? Where you come from, what do you call people who butcher innocent men?"

"Adrian Ravener."

Beck heard Kiernan suck in her breath behind him. Beck's suspicions were now confirmed. The man in black on the ship at the Crown Bluffs was the centuries old Mage whose actions killed hundreds of thousands of people in the Mage War. Just like Galen Starr, the evil wizard still lived.

"My name is Titus and I am a Cyman. This is not our war, but we 'ave no choice but to fight in it. It would be best if you surrendered to the Mage so that more of your people do not die needlessly."

Beck eyed the prisoner, realizing in that moment that he was far more man than beast.

Rogan let his fireballs dissipate. "What do you mean this is not your war?"

The Cyman turned his head and refused to answer.

"We should kill him," Rogan said softly without taking his eyes from the Cyman.

Beck looked questioningly at his friend. "Since when do you talk about killing people so casually?"

"You know, it's a funny thing, Beck," he snapped, "but when people try to kill me and my friends, I tend to want to do it to them first before they succeed."

Rogan was right. These Cyman people had declared war on Massa. Their brutal actions at the Crown Bluffs by spilling the blood of innocent Massans were unredeemable. Beck thought of Jon Anders' body sprawled in the dirt.

"What do you want?" Beck hissed through clenched teeth. He reached down, grabbed the shirt of the Cyman with both fists and lifted him off the ground. The earth began to tremble along with his fury. Kiernan jumped to her feet when the log she was sitting on rolled with the wave of disturbed soil. "Tell me!"

Even had the Cyman wished to reply, it would have been impossible with the steel grip Beck had under his throat.

Surprisingly, it was Rogan who diffused the situation by putting a hand on his shoulder. "That's enough."

Beck reluctantly dropped the Cyman to the ground. "Kiernan, please shift him again. I'll be right back," he mumbled in frustration and set off into the woods. Although he felt it highly unlikely that the Cymans could have caught up to them, he didn't want to underestimate an enemy he knew very little about.

It did make him wonder. Could the shifters of Pyraan win a battle against the number of invaders he saw out on the Arounda Ocean? Would they be forced to call in reinforcements from the Iserlohn Army of Men? Maybe even the Dwarven and Elven armies? Beck readily admitted that he wasn't a good judge of the number of troops needed to win a war.

Eying a modest caprock, he climbed on top to get a view of their back trail. Although, he didn't see anything, what he heard was terrifying enough. Something hurtled through the woods in his direction at tremendous speed.

He dropped back to the ground and crouched. Whatever it was tearing his way either didn't know he was there or didn't care. He gave himself room to fight as the attacker came skidding around the caprock.

Bajan!

The Draca Cat ignored him completely as his hind legs scrabbled for purchase and he bolted in the direction of the others. Beck's alarm at seeing the panic in the usually unflappable Draca Cat sent him sprinting behind.

The shifters tensed up in surprise when they noticed Bajan, but Beck's eyes were on the Cyman warriors rushing down the road toward them. *Demon's breath, they're fast!*

"Look out!" he yelled and summoned a ball of earth, the quickest and easiest way to stop the threat. He flung the missile at the first soldier in line and it knocked him backwards into the others. His unexpected attack halted their advance for a moment, but the Cymans regrouped quickly and rushed forward once again.

There were ten of them.

Bajan leapt onto the road and issued a spine-tingling roar. His lethal, spiked tail rose threatening in the air with a promise of great harm to anyone who dared to approach.

The Cyman in the lead recognized the danger that the Draca Cat posed and held his arms out to both sides to stop his cohorts. "Give us the boy!" he shouted.

Beck glanced back at Kiernan, now rapidly shifting thoughts into Titus's mind. Face slack, the young Cyman walked over to the picketed horses and stood with his back to both groups.

"What 'ave you done to 'im?" yelled the leader. "Come 'ere, Titus!" The Cyman inched forward.

Beck stepped into the middle of the road blocking his way. Rogan, Airron and Kiernan silently joined him. The ground began to roil, flame ignited, air shimmered and the distinctive rasp of the Sword of Iserlohn echoed in the night.

Beck didn't want this to come to violence, but knew that they would win if it did. These were not magical creatures standing before him and the shifters could easily destroy them, even without Bajan's help. The Cymans fought with brute strength, not magic.

Even so, Beck suspected there was more to these Cymans and their reason for being here in Massa. Adrian Ravener had forced them into this war, and Beck was determined to find out how.

"He stays with us," Beck said. Then, he gambled. "Turn back now. This is not your war and you know it."

The soldiers looked at each other uneasily. The leader spoke up again. "Titus should learn to keep 'is mouth shut."

Beck didn't reply.

"Give 'im to us and we will leave. For now."

Ignoring the demand, Beck questioned him instead. "Why are you here?"

The Cyman hesitated for a moment and then declared, "We fight for the survival of the Cyman race. We fight for the lives of our women and children and for our very existence. Even without magic, that makes us a very formidable opponent to the isle of Massa. Do as the Mage instructs and your people will not be 'armed."

"What is your name?"

Again, the Cyman hesitated, blinking his one eye. "Teag."

"Just Teag?"

"We are not allowed surnames."

"You fight for a man who doesn't even consider you enough of one to have a proper identity?" he asked incredulously. "I don't know how the Mage has managed to coerce you into this affair, but together we can rise up against him and keep all of our people safe."

Teag snorted. "You do not know Adrian Ravener or you would not make that statement. There is no one on the isle of Massa who can challenge 'is powers. That is why 'e is 'ere. The Mage is capable of immense destruction single-handedly."

Beck smiled forbiddingly. "So am I."

Teag narrowed his eye.

"The boy stays with us, Teag, so that leaves you with two choices. Leave now and stay alive or fight and die." At his words, he felt Rogan, Airron and Kiernan brace themselves in readiness for an attack. Bajan snarled at the soldiers, saliva dripping from his jaws.

Teag glanced at his fellow companions. "We cannot win against your magic this time, but Adrian Ravener can and will. You must 'eed my words, magic user, and tell your people to surrender to the Mage."

Teag turned to go, but stopped to look at Beck. "When next we meet, one of us will not survive the encounter."

With that, the giant spun on his heel and ran with remarkable speed back up the road, the rest of the Cymans following closely behind.

Rogan let the fire in his hands disappear. "I wasn't sure how that was going to go."

"Me either," admitted Beck. "Can you and Rory get Titus mounted and ready to leave? Make sure his binds are tight."

Rogan nodded and hurried off.

The air shimmered as Airron began to undress. "I don't know why I even bother wearing clothes," he mumbled. "I'll take a look from above for another secluded spot for us to stop for the night."

At Beck's nod, Airron took a few running steps, shifted into a hawk and wheeled away into the night.

Beck turned to Kiernan. "Send Bajan to track the Cymans to be sure they are headed north and not trying to deceive us by circling around."

***

Before Kiernan had a chance to deliver Beck's order, Bajan reached out to her.

I will do as Beck asks, Princess.

Thank you, Bajan. For this and for saving my life at the Crown Bluffs.

You were in trouble again. It was my honor and duty.

I never would have imagined that trouble would take this form, Bajan. The island of Massa invaded? Our friends killed in battle? She shook her head and buried it deep within the thick fur at his neck.

You cannot imagine how worried I was when I saw enemy soldiers on the march behind you. You are safe now, little one. That is all that matters. Bajan pulled back to look at her. *Stay near Beck. For some reason, his scent has changed and he smells just as concerned as I over your welfare.*

***

As soon as Bajan sprinted away, Beck approached Kiernan from behind and rested his hands lightly on her shoulders. She didn't turn around, but leaned her cheek into the back of one of his hands.

"I'm sorry, Kiernan, but we have to keep going," he said softly in her ear. "Even if the Cyman soldiers truly are headed north, they now know where we are, and they are extremely fast. They could be back with reinforcements while we slept in our bedrolls."

"I know."

Beck turned her to face him and tilted her chin up with his finger. In her pale eyes, he found an unexpected vulnerability there that he had never before seen in his ice princess friend. How unbelievably beautiful she looked standing before him with her dirty face and her hair tumbling in a mess around her shoulders. She was so small, yet so strong. So fearless, yet so scared.

The emotions of the day washed over him in a rush. From the fight at the Crown Bluffs to the escape south to the tension of the sudden arrival of the enemy when they thought they were safe for the moment. It was all so overwhelming that he swayed on his feet thinking of how close they had all come to death. His heart started to beat rapidly at the extent of his feelings for the girl standing in front of him.

My best friend.

Staring down at the only life raft in a sea of turmoil, he grabbed for it. Without caring about the consequences, and not able to change them if he did, he cradled her head and dragged her mouth to his.

A soft moan escaped her lips in surprise. What should have been a tentative first kiss between two young people turned into a passionate hunger. Kiernan wrapped her arms around his neck, jumped up into his arms and straddled his waist, her lips never leaving his.

To Beck, it felt like the most natural thing in the world to be kissing and holding Kiernan. He would always remember this day, a day of chaos and uncertainty, as the day he fell irrevocably in love.

With Kiernan still stuck to his middle, Beck reluctantly broke from the kiss when he felt an airstream pass overhead and then footsteps running on the dirt.

Kiernan dropped to the ground as Airron approached, and Beck felt his cheeks heat.

"At least Beck has the decency to blush, Kiernan."

She smiled contently. "I have no reason to."

Airron laughed. "About time. By the way, we have company."

Beck tensed. "Who?"

"Relax, it's just the little Halfies. A few thousand of them. It looks like they're traveling with everything they own, including goats and chickens."

Beck gave Kiernan a quick intimate smile and grabbed her hand. "Let's go see what the little terrors are doing here."

"Are you sure you want to do that?" Airron asked, looking between them. "From the view up above, it sure seems like the two of you have more important things on your mind."

Beck ignored him and jogged down the road with Kiernan in tow. He skidded to a stop when he saw the Halfies. Dear Highworld, Airron had not been exaggerating. The entire tribe of men, women and children were on the road ahead pulling carts and wagons full of their belongings, including clothes, food, animals and even furniture teetering precariously atop the piles of items. Their dirty, mean little faces peered at him with distrust as he approached.

"Vinni Vee!" Beck called to the Tribe Leader. "It's not safe here! The island is under attack and the invaders are marching this way as we speak. You must hurry and find safety for your people in any way you can."

Vinni didn't seem at all shocked by what he had heard and bowed to Beck with great ceremony. "*Savitar*, you are still alive."

Beck raised an eyebrow. "Yes, Vinni, I am still alive. Did you think you might find me dead?"

"I was hoping you would not be, because you are *Savitar*, and if you die, we all die."

Beck looked around quizzically at his friends and shrugged his shoulders.

"We came to warn you, *Savitar*." Vinni's eyes moved from Beck's face to his neck. "I knew you to be *Savitar* because our legend says that they will come wearing pendants that are alive. Your pendant is alive."

Beck looked down and lifted the silver chain around his neck. The pendant certainly did look alive, and Beck marveled again at the animation within the metal. Whoever made this pendant had magical powers beyond that of the shifters of Pyraan.

"As Halfie Tribe Leader, Cloud Reader, and son of Verdie, it is my duty to come here and warn you of what has been written in the clouds. You saved the lives of the Halfie people, and it is now upon me to repay the debt so that we will not be beholden to any human. I will tell you what I know and then we must leave. That is all I can do for you, *Savitar*."

Rogan appeared next to Beck and nudged him. "Come on, Beck," he whispered harshly. "We don't have time for this nonsense. We all know that the Halfies are notorious tricksters, so we can't trust anything they say. It's a waste of precious time."

"I know," Beck whispered, "but they traveled far to come to us, so I will hear them out." He turned back to Vinni. "I'm not sure how I saved the Halfie people, but go on."

"You saved us by making your presence known and allowing us time to escape. We are traveling posthaste to Haventhal. As you are not a Cloud Reader, you would not understand. Indeed, the messages I receive are very difficult to decipher, and only a master reader such as myself should even attempt it."

Rogan sighed heavily with impatience and turned away.

Vinni stuck his tongue out at the Dwarf's departing back. "How rude! Only the foolish disregard the portents of what is to come."

"*What* is to come, Vinni?" Kiernan prompted, showing her own impatience.

The Tribe Leader took a deep breath. "When the *Savitars* are revealed, ravens will overtake the world, the sea will unleash her deadly fury and demons will walk among us."

Beck looked at Kiernan in disbelief and then at Vinni. "Is that it?"

"Yes," Vinni replied.

"Thank you, Vinni," Beck said, turning the Halfie around by his shoulders to get him moving. "Your warning has been delivered, the Halfies owe me no debt, and I thank you. Now, hurry along. I don't want any of you to be hurt."

Vinni gave the signal to his people and quite the commotion ensued as thousands of Halfies, animals and wagons filled to capacity began to turn southeast toward Haventhal.

"*Savitar!*" Vinni yelled over the noise, cupping his hands to his mouth. "One more thing! The clouds also tell me that when the *Savitars* are revealed, Pyraan will cease to exist!"

The Halfie leader stuck out his tongue one last time before eagerly following after his people.

CHAPTER 10

DUTY CALLS

The seven bone weary survivors of the invasion at the Crown Bluffs reached the outskirts of Parsis three days after they had left the Halfie tribe behind. Kiernan licked her cracked lips and reached for the water bag on her saddle. Mercifully, the captive Titus was exhausted enough that she no longer had to mindshift him. The Cyman didn't have the strength to even think about an escape let alone attempt one.

After taking a long pull from the bag, she kneaded the small of her back with her fingertips to try and relieve the pain. It didn't work, but she knew they were getting close to the outlying farming communities and thanked the Highworld when they crested a rise and a young boy in the fields gave a yelp, dropped the pail he was carrying, and ran off to announce the sight of unexpected travelers to his parents. Within moments, an older boy on a horse galloped out of the stable yard toward the city. It wouldn't be long now for word to spread that members of Troop 158 of the Northwatch Legion were returning home.

Bajan announced his departure with another admonition for her to be careful and slipped away into the Grayan Forest.

When they finally arrived in Parsis, Kiernan was not at all surprised to find City Boulevard lined with worried parents and council members. She looked over at Beck and gave him a tired smile. It seemed impossible to her that just the sight of him could make her feel so at ease when the world all around them was falling apart.

Their budding love gave her hope and strength and a determination to fight for a future with him.

He didn't return her smile. He rode straight backed and with his jaw clenched. As lieutenant, it was his responsibility to relay the events of the massacre at the Crown Bluffs and ensure that the town council members appreciated the dire circumstances facing the island. The defenders of Massa, the shifters of Pyraan, would have very little time to develop a strategy for defeating the threat bearing down on them from the north.

Beck's parents, Jaimes and Constance Atlan, and Airron's parents, Joshe and Jeni Falewir, were among the crowd waiting to hear what could have brought their children back to Parsis. They eyed curiously the large, hooded figure riding alongside them.

Jaimes Atlan stepped out to greet them with worry on his face. "Beck! What's happened? Why have you returned to the city?"

Beck slid from his horse. "Father, call a meeting of the council at once. Massa is under attack."

The crowd gasped. Several of the women let out frightened screams.

Kiernan dismounted and stood next to Beck as Jaimes grabbed his son's arm. "Beck, what are you saying?"

"I will explain everything at the council meeting, Father. We'll only have a week at most before the invaders arrive here in Parsis."

Titus snorted through the gap in his hood. "The Cyman Army will be 'ere by dawn, shifter."

Rogan whipped his head toward the Cyman. "Impossible! There were thousands of soldiers swarming our shores. You can't move an army of that size that quickly."

"It is possible," Titus said calmly. "You saw firsthand 'ow fast we can move. Unlike your legion, we 'ave 'ad years of disciplined training in extremely 'arsh conditions. We do not use 'orses or wagons or carry weaponry. We do not sleep in tents or cook meals. We do not 'unt or sit around a campfire. We are trained to survive on very little food and sleep. Mostly, the army will live on agave plants, pine bark and nuts as they travel." He paused. "I tell you this so that you understand the truth of your chances 'ere. It does not 'ave to turn into a blood bath unless you choose it to be so."

His words sent a chill up Kiernan's spine and she reached out to Beck to lace her fingers through his.

Constance Atlan moved closer, her eyes wide in alarm. "Who is that?" she whispered, rolling her eyes in the direction of Titus.

Titus reached his bound hands up to remove his hood, and there was another gasp from the crowd.

Although disconcerting to look into that one large eye, Kiernan's voice was hard as she said, "He is one of Adrian Ravener's minions, Mistress Atlan, and he is here to destroy us."

***

Kiernan walked into the overflowing town hall with Beck, Rogan, Airron and Rory, comforted to see all of the familiar faces she had come to know and love over the years. Mistress Halloran, the innkeeper, rushed over to hug her, and the woman's usual cheery features were reddened and lined with concern. Blacksmith and earthshifter, Jorge Owen, sat in the front row with Master and Mistress Falewir, looking as if he was ready—and able—to take on the Cyman Army single-handedly. Jakob Martyn, the grocer, shifted uncomfortably on the seat next to his son, Ben.

Despite the large number of people present, it was eerily quiet, and the anxiety in the room palpable.

The gathered citizens made way for Kiernan and the four legionnaires, and they took their seats at the front of the room where Master Atlan stood with the council members.

Heads twisted around when the back doors banged open and Katrin Allendale hurried over to the mayor. "The prisoner is secured, Master Atlan. I mindshifted him myself," she whispered proudly.

Jaimes patted her shoulder. "Thank you, Katrin. It would appear that your devotion to your studies has paid off."

The girl twirled giddily and went to sit in the second row next to Ben Martyn.

When she was seated, Master Atlan rose to address the crowd. "We all know why we're here. If what the self-proclaimed Cyman says is true, we have very little time to prepare our defenses."

Jakob Martyn stood. "How can we hope to win a battle against thousands of well-trained soldiers? I say we retreat to Iserlohn at once!"

Jorge Owen leapt to his feet and gestured to the athame on his neck. "Retreat? It is the responsibility of the shifters of Pyraan to protect and defend the people of Massa! We can't run from our duty and hide behind Iserlohn's skirts!"

"We're not running!" the grocer retorted with a distinct tremble coloring his voice. "We're saving ourselves to give the people of Massa a better chance to win this battle!" He looked about wildly for support as he wrung his hands. The impending hostilities were beginning to unravel the man.

Jaimes shook his head. "I agree with Jorge. We will not desert our duty in the hour of crisis when the people of this island need us more than ever. It's what we've trained to do since we joined the Northwatch Legion as young men. It's why we're here." He slammed his hand on the table in front of him. "We will not run!"

Kiernan felt more than saw the acquiescence of the shifters as they agreed with Jaimes Atlan. Her own body reacted to the words he spoke and it came from a deep-rooted pledge housed in the core of her being.

Suddenly, the air in the hall changed. Subtle at first, but then it grew into a thick, visible energy that misted throughout the room. Kiernan instinctively tensed in fright, but relaxed when she sensed that the power wasn't malevolent. Strong and determined, yes, but not harmful.

It seemed to be seeking something.

The magical vapor forcefully entered her body, and she gasped at a strange swelling in her chest that left her breathless. The mist physically lifted her off her chair and swirled all around and through her body and the bodies of her fellow shifters.

Kiernan knew instinctively that it was the centuries-old blood oath demanding fulfillment. Adrenaline coursed through her veins and resolve flowed through her mind. Every shifter in Pyraan would feel the call, whether present in the town hall at that moment or elsewhere.

There would be no retreat.

Whatever the chances, the shifters of Pyraan would stay and fight for the people they were sworn to protect.

The blood oath would have it no other way.

***

The full moon seemed an eager participant in the tireless activities taking place in the city of Parsis. Beck shared neither the moon's nor the citizens' fervor as he strode past. Having seen the size of the Cyman Army firsthand, he was more than a little concerned that the three thousand or so shifters in Parsis were not enough. Envoys had been sent to the remote settlements as a call to arms and once the newcomers arrived it would add another few thousand to their numbers, but it would take time. And, whether or not all would be able to reach the city before the Cyman Army was anyone's guess.

Everywhere Beck looked, the people of Pyraan were preparing for battle, despite his fears.

With new purpose in their hearts, the shifters had disregarded all misgivings and bolstered their preparations for war. Even Jakob Martyn was now readily devising battle tactics with his fellow bodyshifters.

Needing no prodding prior to the blood oath's not so subtle reminder, Jorge Owen vigorously directed the shirtless earthshifters at creating defensive barriers, gleans of sweat layering their abnormally muscular chests. With casual waves of their hands, great holes in the ground opened up and the excavated dirt used to construct the enormous walls from which the shifters would make their stand against the invading army. Other earthshifters carried large boulders with ease to reinforce the bulwarks from behind.

Under Rogan's direction, the fireshifters were busily inventing elaborate strategies to throw at the enemy, and the ideas for destruction were becoming more lethal as the night wore on.

Earlier that evening, Beck's father had asked Airron to take their only bargaining chip, Titus, south and out of the fight to await further word. He had originally asked Kiernan to do so, but she adamantly refused to leave. Airron hadn't wanted to abandon the conflict either, but the mayor convinced him that a strong shifter was needed to guard the Cyman, and ultimately he relented.

His father had also wisely instructed that as many horses as possible be corralled to the south in the event an emergency retreat was required, and Beck made sure that Chasin was among them.

Kiernan was busy doing her part teaching some of the younger shifters how to use a sword. She had changed out of her drab gray legion uniform and into a dress and sandals. Beck smiled as he took a moment to watch her. Even with a deadly weapon in her hand and a grim look on her face, she looked beautiful to him.

Finally, he turned away and jogged along the boulevard searching for his mother. He had been told that she was helping to sequester the older women and children into the underground storage cellar of the town hall, but with all of the people in the streets, he was having difficulty locating her.

He hoped that the troublesome Halfies had made it safely to Haventhal. To his surprise, he had come to appreciate the spirit of the little imps. Against Vinni Vee's very nature to be mean, he traveled out of his way to warn Beck that danger was coming. Even though Beck didn't believe that the Halfie could actually read such a warning in the clouds, he had to admit that Vinni had been right. Danger did find him. Not only did it find him, it threatened to devour him.

His thoughts of Vinni quickened his footsteps. He had to find his mother to get the answers he was sure she had. He thought back to the night he left for the Crown Bluffs when she seemed distracted and evasive. Yes, his mother had been holding back information from him, of that he was now certain.

He finally found her expertly guiding a group of older women to the shelter of the hall. Her face looked drawn, and Beck felt his heart tug for her. No matter what happened, he promised himself, he would see to it that she stayed safe.

"Mother!"

She looked up at his call and used the back of her hand to move a loose strand of hair from her eyes. She smiled at him.

"Can I talk to you for a moment?" he asked when he reached her.

"Of course. Katrin, can you please take over for me?"

The mindshifter nodded and took the lead. She peeked up from under her long eyelashes to give Beck a demure smile.

He smiled politely to her and led his mother to one of the small benches that lined the square.

"I'm worried, Beck," she admitted as she sat down.

"We all are, Mother," he said putting his arm around her shoulders and hugging her close to his body. "But, I will protect you. I won't let anything happen to you or Father."

She stared up at him as if seeing him for the first time. Again, she looked like she wanted to say something to him, but wasn't sure how to put it into words. He remained silent while her internal struggle took place.

At last, she reached out and cupped her hand under his chin. "Where did my little boy go?" she whispered. "The mother in me just wants to pick you up and run with you as far from this place as possible." Beck grinned inwardly at the mental picture in his mind. "But, the shifter in me knows that not only can I not keep you from harm, but I fear you are our only hope."

"As *Savitar*?"

He felt her stiffen. "Where did you hear that?"

"You wouldn't believe me if I told you," he confessed. "What does it mean? Why have I been called *Savitar*?"

Her gaze roamed his face as though measuring him up in some way. "Do you remember when I told you Mage Galen Starr visited me when you were a baby and he left you that pendant?"

"Yes."

She stood from the bench and turned her back to him. "He also told me at that time that you had been born with enhanced shifting abilities that would be needed in the future to ensure the safety of the island. He told me..." She paused and choked back a sob. "Dear Highworld, he told me that you had inherited a future filled with danger and combat."

Beck quickly went to her. "Mother..."

She spun around to face him, tears coursing down her cheeks. "Do you know what it felt like to be a new mother and be told that about your baby son?" she cried. "After that visit, I vowed to give you the best childhood possible to make up for the life you were destined to lead. I had no other children so I could devote all my time to making you happy."

Beck felt taken aback by her sacrifice. "I do have a great life, Mother, and that's why I treasure it so much." He gave her a small smile. "If, as you say, I will play a role in this battle, I have you to thank. You have given me more tools for this day than either the academy or the legion. You taught me to appreciate life and to fight for life."

She grabbed the front of his shirt. "Don't you see, Beck! Without your knowledge or consent, an unbelievable burden has been thrust upon you." She laughed resentfully. "I guess I always hoped that it wouldn't come to anything, but it has, and I've put you on the front line of a war. I should have taken you and ran, Beck. Hidden you from harm! Oh, why didn't I?" she moaned. "I had years to do something and now it's too late! What kind of mother am I? What kind of mother deliberately puts her son in harm's way?"

Beck dropped to his knees in front of her and hugged her around the waist. "A mother who cares for the people of Massa. A mother who did not have any other choice because she is bound by a blood oath to protect and defend." He looked up at her tenderly. "A mother I am proud to call mine."

She made a pitiful sound low in her throat and wrapped her arms around his head. "Oh, Beck. I am so sorry."

"I'm sorry, Mother, that you didn't have any more children because of me."

Through her tears and pain she said, "I didn't have any more children because of me, not you. My heart was so full of love for you, that there wasn't room for another child. It was my choice."

Beck held her for a long moment before finally letting her go. "Where can I learn more about why I have been named *Savitar*?"

She shook her head, sniffling. "You could seek out Galen Starr in Haventhal, but no one knows where he is or if he is even still alive."

"Airron also has the same pendant. Is he *Savitar* as well? What about Rogan and Kiernan?"

"I honestly don't know, Beck. All I know is what I did to you."

"You did nothing to me, Mother," he said firmly. "And, I'm going to prove that to you by keeping us all safe. I promise."

CHAPTER 11

ENEMY INVASION

Kiernan heard them coming with her heart in her throat as she lay between Beck and Rogan in a furrow atop one of the fortifications created by the earthshifters. As the strongest magic users in Pyraan, the council ordered that they position themselves at the top of the barricade for the higher vantage point that would allow them an unobstructed view of the battlefield.

The ominous sound of thousands of feet rushing toward her in the pre-dawn darkness was as frightening as it was meant to be. Jaimes Atlan warned them that Adrian Ravener would try to intimidate them. He would want them to make mistakes out of sheer terror.

I am with you, Princess, said Bajan, crouched behind her. *Do not be afraid. Any creature that gets close will have me to deal with.*

Bajan, just in case—

Do not make it sound like the end, because it is not. You will have time to torment me for many years to come.

I don't mean to torment you.

I would not have it any other way.

Despite her fright, she smiled at the Draca's words.

Her gaze slid over the shifters down below organized into a U-shaped tactical formation. The earthshifters were stationed on the ground in front of the center bulwark and the fireshifters lined the top. Bodyshifters concealed themselves on the western flank in the Grayan Forest, and the mindshifters were scattered along the eastern edge of the U in hastily created earthen domes that would offer a bit of protection as they produced their unique form of mayhem. The advantage of the formation was in its solid defensibility against a larger opponent. The Grayan Forest and Lake Hawthorne created two natural barriers that would make it impossible for Ravener to send his entire army at one time. He would be forced to funnel in smaller units on the road west of the lake where the shifters would be waiting to dispatch them.

Regardless, thought Kiernan, every person there knew that the greatest threat came from Adrian Ravener and not the Cyman Army.

The long, sinister blare of an enemy battle horn wrenched Kiernan back to the present in a rush. Every fiber of her being urged her to run, to get away from there. Death was coming, and she was right in its path.

Closing her eyes, she took a deep breath and drew on the power of her magic to calm her mind. She was a warrior, she chided herself. A protector. If death was coming for her, it would have a fight on its hands.

More composed, she opened her eyes and glimpsed the Cyman Army as it appeared on the northern horizon like a black stain against the brightening sky. She was again staggered by the speed with which they moved. The huge, thick-skinned bodies charged into view with ear-splitting howls and did not slow their breakneck pace until they reached the shores of Hawthorne Lake.

Kiernan held a range finder to her eye.

She spotted Adrian Ravener immediately as he was the only one mounted. He rode through the center of the Cyman Army and stopped at the edge of the lake. She idly wondered which farm he had stolen the animal from along the way.

All was still as the Mage sat silently appraising Parsis and her defenders.

Kiernan's eyes widened in shock as his body abruptly lifted off the horse and rose into the air. The Mage flew over the lake toward the shifters, black cape billowing out behind him.

The sun picked that very moment to peek up in the east, but the light could not compete with the inky blackness emanating from Adrian Ravener. He wore death and darkness like a mantle wrapped tightly around his shoulders.

How does he fly?

Once past the lake, the Mage flitted down effortlessly to land on the south shore. Dressed in all black with his dark hair secured at the nape of his pale neck, he paced the water's edge with the dangerous grace of a predator. His youthful visage was a bit of shock as Kiernan expected a three-hundred-year-old wizard to look ancient and withered.

"So," drawled Ravener, magically magnifying his voice and spreading his arms wide, "this is the Magical Kingdom of Pyraan." He looked around at their quickly constructed defenses and laughed scornfully. "I can sense where every shifter in this city is hiding, and I can tell you that it is not enough."

Kiernan tensed as Beck pushed angrily to his feet. "What do you want, Ravener?"

Adrian shot forward in a blur of black and hovered directly in front of Beck.

Kiernan had to give Beck credit. He didn't flinch.

Neither did the fireshifters next to her as they collectively rose from their positions, the sound of their simultaneous shifting of fire a chilling warning that hung in the air.

Adrian completely ignored them.

"What do I want?" the Mage repeated. "I want the island of Massa, what do you think I want? You people have had hundreds of years to rule this land and what do you do? You accept banishment as a way of life. You sit hiding away in a corner of the island like naughty children who have misbehaved."

"This land should be of no concern to you," Beck declared.

Adrian laughed with contempt. "This was my land long before yours, young shifter, and it appears that I am the only one strong enough to rule it. You people are weak! You allow yourselves to be treated like servile bodyguards by peasants. It's absurd. You are magic users!" he roared, the clouds in the air above him roiling in response to his dark emotions. Lightning lit the sky and a sudden peal of thunder boomed causing the shifters to duck involuntarily.

"Where is the Cyman that you kidnapped from me?" the Mage asked.

Jaimes Atlan spoke for the first time from his position on the ground with the earthshifters. "He is far from here, but unharmed. He will be returned as soon as you agree to depart."

Adrian rolled his eyes. "This is really pitiable. You are even bigger fools than I imagined if you thought I would turn around and scurry back to Nordik simply because you hold the son of the captain of my army."

Kiernan glanced at Beck at that piece of information.

"I am not the sniveling coward that the shifters have proven themselves to be." Ravener swooped down to Master Atlan. "Who are the *Savitars*?"

Master Atlan shook his head in confusion.

"Think hard, sir! This is a very important question. Your answer will dictate succeeding events!"

"I honestly don't know what you're talking about."

"Very well." Ravener darted back up to Beck. "You have proven yourself to be an outspoken young man, so you must have half a brain at least. I have a task for you. As my emissary, you are to travel to the lands of Men, Dwarves and Elves and demand their surrender. In order to avoid a war, the three Kings must appear before me at Starfell Keep in Haventhal and declare their unconditional relinquishment of power."

Beck snarled. "Why would I do your bidding, Mage?"

"Because if you do not do as I ask, shifter," sneered Adrian, "you will be personally condemning the people you have sworn to protect to death." He shrugged. "Your choice, of course."

Kiernan put her hand on Beck's arm to restrain him from being goaded into action.

Ravener glided close to her, but addressed Beck. "If the Kings do not surrender to me by Earthshine, I will kill every single man in this land and keep the women and children for my slaves. I have found that the women are much more enjoyable to have around anyway." He reached out to touch her hair.

In the space of a heartbeat, she unsheathed the dagger secured to her thigh and screamed with effort as she swung the weapon in a deadly upward arc toward the Mage's throat. Bracing herself for the biting impact of the dagger on his flesh, her body spun off balance as the weapon sliced nothing but air.

"Kiernan!" Beck screamed as she slid down the embankment.

On instinct, she rotated her body around and dug her sandaled feet into the wall to try to slow her descent. The fall would probably not kill her, she had time to think, but it would hurt her. Hurt her bad. The earthshifters wouldn't be able to disturb the earth to soften her fall or they would risk toppling hundreds of shifters.

She still had her dagger in her hand and she used all of her strength to stab it into the hardened earth below her. As she slid by, she reached out with her other hand and grabbed the dagger, stopping her fall. Legs swinging beneath her, she struggled to find a crevice with her feet to relieve the strain on her arm muscles, but could find nothing. She groaned with the exertion of trying to hold her entire body weight with the tenuous grasp she had on the small dagger. Sweat poured into her eyes and her slick palms began to loosen their grip. Mentally, she braced herself for the inevitable plummet to the ground below.

And then, he was there. Her white savior.

Grab my neck. Bajan, poised above her on the wall, lowered his head within reach. She let go of the dagger first with one hand and then the other to wrap them around the cat's thick neck. She clung to him as he turned and scaled the wall, sharp dragon talons piercing deep into the earthwork with each step.

As they neared the top, Beck reached down and hauled her to safety as if she weighed no more than an infant. Breathing heavily, she flung herself onto her back on the barricade.

Beck knelt down next to her. "Are you all right?"

She nodded, trying to catch her breath.

The shifters, incited by the Mage's dire threats and Kiernan's fall, exploded into action now that she was safe.

The bodyshifters emerged from the Grayan Forest running at top speed, arms and legs shortening, muscles bulging outward, mouths elongating into snouts, teeth lengthening into deadly fangs as the majority of them shifted into wolf form.

The ground roiled dangerously, creating tremors and fissures from the fury of the earthshifters.

The night sky lit up as the fireshifters released their deadly arrows at the Mage and then sprinted for the crude stairs at the back of the bulwark to rush to the aid of their friends.

Kiernan staggered to her feet and Beck held on to her arm for support.

All the while, a maniacal laugh spewed from the figure that hovered over the middle of the lake. Ravener's voice boomed over the shouts and snarls of the angry shifters. "I did not want it to come to this, but you have proven that you are of no value to me. The Magical Kingdom of Pyraan must be destroyed!"

Ravener glared at Beck still standing on the rampart. "Go!"

With that, he spiraled straight up into the air, arms waving as he prepared a dark conjuring. The air and earth responded in tandem to his sorcery making it difficult to stay upright. The clefts opened by the earthshifters widened and people screamed as they teetered on the edges and then tumbled into the deep voids. A ferocious cyclone of blowing wind touched down in the square and sucked people, trees and property into its deadly funnel, spinning them violently and spitting out the broken pieces.

Kiernan cried out, but stood unmoving, uncertain what she could do to stop what was happening.

Over all the screams and furious winds, another terrifying sound of destruction hammered unstoppable toward the city of Parsis.

Kiernan blinked in horrific realization.

Death had finally arrived and there was no way out.

A tidal wave of water close to a hundred feet high appeared on the northern horizon, rushing over the land and destroying everything in its path.

"My parents!" Beck screamed, launching himself off the rampart in an impulsive attempt to get down to the ground to save them. As he jumped, he slammed into an unseen obstacle and the collision threw him back down onto the rampart.

She reached out her hand. There was an invisible barrier in front of them!

All she could do was watch helplessly from behind the shield as the water poured in over the city of Parsis and all of its inhabitants. The shifters tried to flee, but there was nowhere to go. By constructing a semi-circular shield in front of Beck on top of the bulwark and another for his Cyman Army, Ravener transformed Parsis into a virtual water bowl from which there was no escape for the shifters of Pyraan.

People were swept from their feet as the water crashed over their heads. Arms and legs flailed frantically in an attempt to reach the surface, but a swirling eddy dragged them down, preventing them for getting to the air they so desperately needed.

The basin filled quickly.

People were dying.

"Help me break this thing!" Beck shouted, slamming his fists against the shield with all of his super strength. His skin broke under the repeated contact, leaving blood stains streaked across the barrier. Rogan shifted and struck at the shield with a club of fire, and Kiernan battered it with her sword. They worked together obsessively, and all three were covered in sweat, blood and tears as they tried to save the shifters.

The water was up over the top of the bulwark now and rising, the city totally submerged.

Then, the bodies came.

Kiernan covered her mouth with her hand as they floated by with eyes and mouths open in silent screams. Jorge Owen's body bumped up against the barrier, and she flinched in revulsion.

Beck rushed down the back stairs of the rampart and uprooted a tree. In anguish, he ran back up to the shield and swung the trunk with all of his might, struggling to find a way to create a rupture. He growled and screamed, endlessly battering at the barrier.

Suddenly, the tree dropped from his hands and he stood still.

Kiernan gasped as Constance and Jaimes Atlan appeared before them. Both were still alive and holding hands.

Beck pressed his face to the shield and wailed. "I promised her! I promised!"

The elder Atlans reached out to him and Beck tenderly touched their hands through the barrier, tears leaving dirty runnels down his face. His mother had just enough time to mouth that she loved him before the eddy spun her away, arms outstretched to her son as she sank down into her watery grave alongside Beck's father.

Beck threw his head back and howled, the barricade listing dangerously.

"Beck!" Rogan warned.

Somehow, he understood and released his magic and sank to the ground. His sobs were heartbreaking to hear and Kiernan dropped down next to him to cradle him in her arms.

Thankfully, he never looked up to see the rest of the grisly scene parading before her eyes. Some of the bodyshifters had tried to shift into a fish form that would have saved their lives, but were stopped grotesquely halfway through the transformation. Ravener's conjuring must have stripped their abilities.

She saw the body of wolves. She saw pretty Katrin Allendale who looked as if she was asleep as she passed by with her pale, ghostly face frozen in death. Mistress Halloran, Jakob Martyn, Joshe and Jeni Falewir, professors from the Parsis Academy, friends—all drifted slowly past her. When the children and babies came into view, the despair became too much to bear, and she leaned over to the side and retched. On hands and knees, she trembled as her stomach muscles contracted painfully. The sickness refused to stop.

After what felt like an eternity, she felt Rogan touch her arm, and she brushed her hair away from her sweating brow and got to her feet.

She looked out over the top of the swirling bowl of death in time to watch Ravener and his Cyman Army heading east toward Haventhal. As they moved on, the Arounda Ocean filled in behind them. For as far as Kiernan could see, it was nothing but blue water outside of their shield. Pyraan was completely flooded and every living thing that once called this land home was gone. Everything and everyone. Gone.

They were all that was left of the Magical Kingdom of Pyraan.

CHAPTER 12

NO MUD

Beck felt numb as he rode silently behind Kiernan and Rogan. For hours, he debated whether his grief was going to render him insane or just kill him on the spot.

Everything happened so suddenly that he found it difficult to wrap his mind around the reality. In a vicious act of violence, he had lost everything in his world. His family, his friends, his home. All gone. And now, the prospect of venturing into the unknown and vast land of Massa after a lifelong confinement in exile only served to exacerbate his feeling of aloneness and smallness.

He noticed Kiernan look back at him worriedly as had been her habit on the painful ride. Her green eyes, filled with such compassion, soothed his broken heart. His watery eyes burned with gratitude and a ghost of a smile lifted the corners of his lips as he realized that he really was not alone. He still had Kiernan, Airron, Rogan and Bajan.

"There he is," Rogan said, pointing ahead to where Airron stood on a boulder off the road waving his arms to get their attention

As soon as they approached, Airron smiled and jumped down. "I didn't expect to see all of you here. What happened? Is it safe to go back?"

Beck shook his head, suddenly finding it difficult to swallow. "No, Airron, we're not going back."

Airron tilted his head, waiting for him to say more and, when he didn't, turned to Rogan. "Tell me what's going on."

Rogan cleared his throat uncomfortably. "I...I'm sorry, Airron, but the land of Pyraan is no more. Adrian Ravener razed the land and killed everyone."

Airron's perpetual grin slowly vanished as Rogan's words registered in his mind. It would take time for him to process the news, Beck knew. He had lived through it and still couldn't believe it had happened.

"What?" he asked softly. "But, we had thousands of shifters there."

"We are all that is left, Airron."

Bajan walked over and nudged Airron consolingly, but the Elf didn't seem to notice the big cat leaning against him. "My parents?" he asked, looking at Beck. "Your parents? They are all dead?"

"Yes."

"I should have been there!" he yelled, backing away from them. "Why did I let your father talk me into leaving?"

Before Beck could reply, Airron's body shimmered and contorted downward, and he disappeared in a covering of feathers and wings and shot into the air.

"Let 'im go, 'e will be back," said a deep voice.

Beck whipped his head around to the Cyman prisoner, Titus, who stood in the middle of the road with no bindings and his arms crossed at his chest.

Beck crouched instinctively, but Titus held his hands out and said, "Do not worry. I am not going to 'arm you."

"It's not my safety that I'm worried about," Beck growled.

"I told the Elf I would not try to escape and 'e took off the rope. I 'ate Adrian Ravener as much as you and want to see 'im destroyed. If there is a way we can do it without 'arming the Cyman people, I would like to try."

"Why do you hate your leader so much?" Beck asked, suspicious of the Cyman's motives.

"I will tell you, shifter, but let us first settle at camp and wait for the Elf. Then, I will tell you why there is nothing I desire more in this world than to be the one to drive a sword through Adrian Ravener's black 'eart."

***

Beck was stirring Airron's pot of stewed rabbit and leeks over a fire when the Elf reappeared. It was painful to see such grief etched on a face usually crinkled in laughter. Beck was just grateful that his friend hadn't been there to witness the horror of their parents' final moments. The image of his mother reaching out to him would be the source of his nightmares for many years to come.

"Do you want something to eat?" Kiernan asked Airron gently as he sat down on the log beside her.

He shook his head. "No. I'm not hungry."

Kiernan reached over and squeezed his hand. "I hope you realize that we're here for you, Airron. We are your family and always will be. You do know that, don't you?"

Airron nodded. "You know what it feels like to lose a parent."

"I do. I was only five when my mother died, but I remember her well and the pain of losing her."

Beck dished out a plate of the rabbit stew and handed it to Titus. The big Cyman shifted on the log and took the food hesitantly. Beck didn't know if it was his extreme grief or that he just didn't care anymore, but he decided not to bind Titus. There was something genuine about the young Cyman, and Beck believed him when he said he would not try to escape.

"There is no mud 'ere," Titus suddenly blurted out.

Beck reached behind him for a few twigs and threw them in the fire to keep the blaze hot. "Mud?"

"That is all we 'ave in Nordik. Mud."

Beck looked up in surprise. "Well...we do get mud after a rainy spell, but the sun dries it out quickly," he said, not sure if he was understanding Titus correctly.

"We 'ave no sun."

"Of course, you do," Beck scoffed.

"We 'ave no sun. The Mage's dark arts 'ave blocked the sun for many years. There is only cold and rain...and mud."

Beck shuddered. *How can something so intrinsic to life be absent?*

"I feel for your loss," Titus said to Airron. "I sometimes wished death for my own Ma rather than she keep living a life of pain and suffering as one of Ravener's slaves."

"Why do the Cyman people allow this?" Rogan asked. "Is there no way to defeat the Mage?"

"You were there, Dwarf! You saw what 'appened with your own eyes. The Mage destroyed thousands of your magic people with little effort. There's no fighting that." He put down his plate and stood. "That is why I tried to tell you to surrender. It did not 'ave to end this way. Your parents did not 'ave to die."

That riled Rogan. "The shifters did their duty, Cyman! If they had bowed down to the Mage, they still would have died. It just would have been a much slower, painful death, like the one your people are living!"

"I 'ear you, Dwarf. 'Tis just that the shifters were the only chance your island 'ad. The only chance my people 'ad. It will take powerful magic to destroy Adrian Ravener."

"Don't count us out just yet. We travel to the land of Iserlohn now with the hope that the King of Men can aid us in uniting the lands against Ravener."

"Unification is your only 'ope against the Cyman Army. You," he said, pointing to each of them, "are the only 'ope against the Mage. You must figure out a way." He sat back down and speared a hand through his shoulder-length hair, clearly agitated. "Would you like to 'ear what you are fighting to avoid? What 'tis like to be one of Ravener's slaves?"

They all nodded.

"Even though the Cymans are good people, they will stop at nothing to advance Ravener's plans. They 'ave come to believe that fighting for the Mage is what is going to save their loved ones. For years, Ravener 'as brainwashed and dominated the Cyman male. One of 'is cruel games is to parade the women slaves naked and chained together by their necks in front of the men as they train. If a soldier so much as looks up at the women or slacks for one second in the training, Ravener 'as that soldier's Ma, sister or daughter whipped raw. The female is left lashed to a pole for the entire night in the cold temperatures, and all the soldiers 'ave to listen to 'er cries for 'ours."

He took a deep breath. "The males are whipped and starved and tortured on a daily basis. We do not get much time with our families. Only enough so that we do not get too 'ardened and forget why we fight. The Mage also did something even more tortuous on the voyage 'ere. 'E gave us false 'ope. 'E vowed that as soon as we defeat the people of Massa, 'e will give us our freedom. It is a lie, but the Cymans 'ang on to that shred of 'ope with everything they 'ave."

He paused. "And, all of what I just told you about the men, it is ten times worse for the women."

Kiernan let out a distressed breath.

"Why is it that you know the truth and can see through Ravener's lies?" Airron asked.

Beck answered before Titus. "Because his father is captain of the Cyman Army."

Titus looked at Beck. "Yes, 'e is and 'e is not fooled. 'E has seen great evil at Ravener Keep. If there is a way to leverage this war with Massa to the Cyman's benefit and spare 'uman life in the process, 'e will find it. 'E is a good man."

"Are there other Mages where you come from?" Kiernan questioned.

"No. There is just Adrian and 'is sorceress sister, Avalon Ravener."

"Is she here with him? In Massa?"

Titus nodded.

"What can you tell us of her? Is she as evil as her brother?"

Titus's eye glazed over. "In my opinion, the witch is worse. Ravener listens to 'er and she whispers evil in 'is ear. She is sick and likes to play 'er own kind of games with the Cyman male." Red spots colored his cheeks, but he went on, explaining how the Cyman people came to be through Ravener's experiments with humans and Desert Trolls.

Beck's face hardened into rock. "I have sympathy for the plight of your people, Titus, but I will fight them to the death as long as they stand with Ravener. I can't let what happened in Nordik be repeated here in Massa."

Titus nodded. "And, the Cyman people will fight Massans to the death until they get their freedom."

Beck held out his hand to Titus. "Friends until enemies?

Titus took it. "Friends until enemies," he confirmed.

Beck waved his hand and dirt rose up off the ground to cover the fire. "We should get some sleep. We have two days of travel before we get to the border of Iserlohn."

Abruptly, Bajan rose up off the ground beside Kiernan and started to growl. Next, came the soft scuffling of boots on the road. Beck quickly stood and peered between the trees surrounding the clearing of their campsite. His jaw fell open. "Rory?"

The young fireshifter flinched. "Yes, it's me."

Beck ran out to greet him, the rest of the group following close behind. He grabbed the smaller boy in a bear hug that lifted him off his feet. "How did you escape the flooding?"

"I was looking for you and made it around the shield just in time."

"This boy has the blessings of the Highworld, that's for sure," Airron declared, mussing his hair. "Twice now thought dead and then resurrected from the ashes!"

Kiernan gave him a hug and Rogan patted his back. When Titus came into view, Rory turned to face him with a glare.

"Don't worry," Beck told him. "He won't hurt you."

"Rory, do you think it's possible that anyone else survived?" Airron asked hopefully.

"No. There is no one else. Pyraan is gone."

***

Kiernan rode with the hood of her cloak up in the light drizzle of the early afternoon. This visit back to her homeland had her more on edge than she realized it would. She trailed behind her companions as they approached the northern border of Nysa, and her anxiety intensified with each passing moment.

Despite the nerves, however, her heart and mind longed for home, and old memories flooded through her. She recalled the big kitchen on the first floor of the palace and snatching freshly baked cookies with her best friend, Larkin Malley. She thought of her caretaker, dear Miss Belle, who became a surrogate mother to her after her mother died. Kiernan smiled fondly thinking about the Royal Guard and how they would all take turns teaching her to fight with wooden swords in the courtyard near the stables. She remembered spending countless hours helping the groundskeepers in the beautiful gardens or simply reading a book beneath one of the large willow trees. It had been a very idyllic and indulgent upbringing for a little Princess, and she had always felt treasured by the people of Iserlohn.

But, that was then. She wondered how they would feel about her now. After her father discovered her shifting ability, she was swept away to Pyraan so quickly and discreetly that she never had the chance for a proper good-bye to those she loved.

Up ahead, Beck stopped his horse and waited for her to catch up so he could ride next to her. It would be tricky on the narrow path of the heavily wooded forestland in which they now rode.

"How are you feeling?" he asked as she squeezed in beside him.

"Better when you're near," she answered and leaned over to kiss him, the horses dancing between them. He kissed her back, placing his hand on the back of her head.

"Mmm...this is something that I can get used to." With his lips still pressed to hers, he murmured, "Keep your eyes up front, Falewir."

Kiernan heard Airron chuckle, and it was a nice bit of levity that they all needed.

Beck broke away, but held on to her hand. "Kiernan, as soon as we deliver Ravener's demand to your father, I plan to continue on to Deepstone and then Haventhal."

"I know. I'll be ready to go with you."

Beck squared his shoulders. "That's not a good idea. You'll be safer in Nysa with your father and his armies."

"I go where you go," she said, fixing him in her green eyes to make sure he understood that she would tolerate no argument. Although, she looked forward to returning to Nysa, Beck was her home now.

"Kiernan..."

Suddenly, she alerted on the unmistakable whisper of several bowstrings being drawn taut.

"Hold!" she hissed to the others, and they all stopped immediately when they sensed the caution in her voice.

The Royal Guard is here, Princess, and it is about time. To think, a person of your distinction skulking in the back woods instead of receiving the royal escort as is your due.

Kiernan smiled at the hauteur in evidence in the thoughts of Bajan. *As you well know, I have not had a royal escort in several years, my friend.*

Hmmrf. Ridiculous human rules.

"Beck," she murmured quietly, "make sure Titus keeps his face hidden." At his nod, she inched her horse past the others to the front.

An authoritative voice rang out. "You have entered the land of Iserlohn! State your purpose!"

Guardsmen wearing the scarlet and black of Iserlohn materialized from behind the trees. Their tunics marked them as Nysa's elite Royal Guard, also known as the Scarlet Sabers for the thin, single-edged curved swords they carried at their hips.

Kiernan stopped her horse and Bajan sidled up to her side.

"Does a long overdue visit home warrant passage?" she asked coyly.

The officer in charge who halted the group strode forward, naked sword in his hand. "I will ask one more time, state—" The officer froze in his tracks when he saw Bajan and then looked up at her.

"Kiernan?"

She smiled at his impetuous lack of formality. "Yes."

He realized his mistake and immediately dropped to one knee, left fist on the ground in from of him, and the Scarlet Sabers accompanying him followed suit. "Forgive me, Princess! It has been a long time since you've been home."

Kiernan looked down at the fair-haired head bent in deference.

"Colbie, is that you?" She casually lifted her right leg over her saddle and dismounted.

"Yes, Your Grace, I'm now captain of your father's Royal Guard."

Kiernan laughed. "Royal Guard now, is it? Does my father know, Colbie Nash, that the last time I saw you, you were trying to steal a kiss from me in his stables?"

The young captain blushed fiercely as snickers came from the Sabers behind him. "Quiet!" he snarled over his shoulder and immediately bowed his head in front of her again.

"Please rise. All of you."

As they did so, Colbie asked, "May I inquire as to your purpose, Your Grace?"

"I am here to see my father, Captain," she answered, reverting to protocol. She needed to reestablish her authority with these men lest they decide she was no longer within her right to give commands as the Princess of Iserlohn.

Colbie impulsively reached out to move her hair from her neck, revealing her athame. "The rumors are true," he confirmed. "You're a shifter."

"Yes."

He backed away a fraction, and that modest movement stung. Much more than she thought it would. Fortunately, she didn't have time to dwell on hurt feelings. In order to give the people of Massa a fighting chance of survival, she had to get to her father.

"The King never really explained where you went," he told her. "At first everyone thought that you were simply away on missionary duties, but as time wore on, the rumor of your exile surfaced."

"It is true. I have been living in Pyraan for the past six years, but recent tragic events require that I speak to my father immediately. Our business with him is urgent. Please lead the way, Captain."

She turned and walked back to her horse. To her surprise, she realized that the Sabers had not moved. With her hand on the pommel of her saddle, she caught Beck's eye and read the meaning in his look. He would remain silent. This was her homeland and her battle to win.

"You must return to Pyraan, Your Grace," Colbie said quietly, his blue eyes filled with remorse but firm. "It is the law. It is the King's law."

Her anger flared and she stalked back to him. "Captain, my patience is running thin. I can't return to Pyraan because there is no Pyraan! It does not exist! I am issuing a royal order for you to escort me and my traveling party to my father immediately. Either comply with that order or I will ride through you. Which will it be?"

All was silent in the woods.

"Well, Captain Nash? Are you going to refuse a command from the Princess of Iserlohn?"

So much for subtlety.

Long ingrained tradition won out and the captain immediately dropped to his knee and banged a fist to his heart. "Of course not, Your Grace. We will escort you at once."

Kiernan let out her breath slowly. "Thank you, Captain. Please rise."

Colbie stood, gave a rapid hand signal and the Sabers melted back into the woods, presumably to retrieve their mounts. The young captain broke the tension by smiling at her and taking the reins of her horse. "Allow me, Princess."

She smiled back and gestured to the rest of the party to dismount and follow their lead.

As she walked ahead on the pathway with the captain, he leaned his head close to her to whisper, "For the record, Your Grace, I *do* remember that kiss."

Kiernan gasped aloud as she looked at her old friend. "You did not kiss me, Colbie Nash! You tried, but you were unsuccessful."

He looked at her and raised an eyebrow. "Oh, believe me, I was successful, Princess. I have thought often of that kiss over the past six years."

Kiernan felt a faint tremor beneath her feet.

"Kiernan," Beck growled, appearing at her shoulder. "We need to move faster if we're to reach Nysa before dark." He snatched the reins of her horse from Colbie. "Lead on, Captain."

***

After several hours of navigating the forest, Kiernan finally glimpsed her childhood home through the leafy foliage ahead. *If a palace can be referred to as a home.*

High twin turrets thrust up from behind a black, granite curtain wall that rose fifty feet into the air. Crimson and black pennants flapped in the late afternoon wind from the spaced intervals between the crenellations of the wall.

In contrast to the stark stone of the outer wall, however, Kiernan knew that the city that lay beyond held remarkable beauty and grandeur. *The colors of nature may be Beck's world, but the colors of the city are mine.*

She hadn't realized how excited she was to show Beck her old life. In Pyraan, she never dared to dream that it would ever be possible.

Now, though, she erased all emotion from her face and mentally steeled herself for the commotion her unexpected arrival was sure to create.

Captain Nash led the way through the throng of tents that made up the public marketplace outside of the walled city. All around them, hawkers eagerly promoted their wares offering an assortment of trinkets, beads, ribbons, cloth, dyes, tools and even delicious-smelling cinnamon cakes and roasted meats. The aromas made her empty stomach grumble in protest.

They passed charlatans dressed in colorful headdresses attempting to seduce customers into their establishments with the promise of rich fortunes in their futures, and a man with a painted face walked on stilts to the delight of the children following behind him.

On any given day, the sight of the Royal Guard returning to the city escorting travelers would be cause for hushed whispers and speculation. Today, sight of the enormous snow-white Draca Cat padding regally in front of the Sabers sent the people in the market into a frenzy, and the shouts rang out.

"It's Bajan! Look! Bajan has returned!"

"No, it can't be. He is exiled with the Princess!"

"If Bajan has returned, do you think the Princess is here as well?"

Now, they were rushing forward, necks craning to get a glimpse of the travelers.

"Is that her?"

Kiernan slowly and deliberately lowered the hood of her cloak so there could be no mistake.

A cheer went up from the people of Nysa and they all dropped to one knee.

The Princess of Men was home.

CHAPTER 13

THE LAND OF MEN

Beck felt as though he had entered another world when the wide iron gates of Nysa opened in front of him. He had never seen so many buildings, and lights and people in his entire life. Numerous merchant shops and stately two-story manors lined the main cobblestone thoroughfare, and a veritable maze of streets and alleyways branched off in every direction.

The modest buildings and homes in Parsis paled in comparison to the opulence in Nysa, and Beck felt conspicuously out of place. He could see now why Kiernan had always felt so trapped in Pyraan. After having grown up with all of the bustle and luxury of a large city, the much smaller Parsis must have seemed very remote and backwards.

As was the case outside of the city, the Nysians bent a knee to Kiernan when they saw her, but Beck noticed that two people, a man and a woman, only bowed their heads to her. When he asked her why, she explained that they were a higher-ranking lord and lady of King Maximus's Court rather than common folk, so a nod was acceptable.

Common folk? Am I not common folk?

Suddenly feeling awkward at the displays of veneration to the girl he loved, he fell back in line. Bajan had no such difficulties. He strolled out in front of Kiernan, accepting the excited welcome of the people with the posture of a cat getting his ears scratched.

Rogan nudged his horse up next to Beck. "We've been extremely lucky so far, but someone very soon is going to notice old Big and Scary over here," he said, jerking a thumb at Titus.

"I know. Any ideas?"

He nodded. "As soon as we get to the palace, the groomsmen working the stables will come to get the horses. I'll just tell them we have a sick friend and ask if he can lie down in one of the lofts. Airron can help me get him inside out of sight while you and Kiernan talk to the King."

Beck raised an appreciative eyebrow. "It might work. Go tell Airron and Titus so they can play their roles, and I'll talk to Kiernan. Rory can come with us." He rode back up to the front next to Kiernan and informed her of Rogan's idea.

She nodded in agreement. "It will be better if I can explain Titus to my father before he actually lays eyes on him."

"What do you think your father is going to do about Ravener's demand for surrender?"

Kiernan barked out a laugh. "You have never met my father, Beck. He will not take kindly to this ultimatum and will fight like a cornered lion to protect his people."

Beck's stomach tightened as he thought of his parents and the rest of the shifters in Pyraan. "You saw what happened when we decided to fight."

She turned to look at him. "Are you saying you think we should just give up?"

"Of course not!" he said at once. "But you now know what a Mage of Adrian Ravener's power is capable of." He reached over to grab her hand. "We need to get to Galen Starr somehow."

Kiernan shook her head. "My father won't want to hear that, Beck, nor will any of the people of Iserlohn. They mistrust magic. They'll want to fight the only way they know how. With swords."

"And that is the fight we must avoid at all costs," he said ruefully.

***

With Rogan, Airron and Titus safely tucked away in the stables, Colbie Nash and half a dozen of the Royal Guard led Kiernan and Bajan along with Beck and Rory toward the sweeping stairs of the palace. A trumpeter from the balcony above the doors signaled the royal procession refrain, but it was unnecessary. Word had traveled fast. The double doors etched with the Golden Lion of House Everard were thrown open wide and people rushed out to line both sides of the stairs to greet her. Those gathered were in all manner of dress from soldier uniform to servant livery to formal attire.

Tears welled in Kiernan's eyes as she greeted people she had not seen in years.

"Kiernan!" The shriek came from the top of the stairs, and a pretty, dark-haired girl came running toward her with skirts lifted high in both hands exposing her leather ankle boots and a bit of leg stocking. The girl ignored the disapproving looks from the women and threw herself into Kiernan's arms. She was shorter and softer in body than Kiernan and had the most gorgeous dark blue eyes.

"It's so good to see you, Larkin," Kiernan told her, breaking the embrace to stare at her face. "I've missed you so much, and I have so much to tell you!" Just like that, she was twelve years old again, anxious to share all of her secrets.

"Well, well," came a deep, alto voice from behind Kiernan. "If it isn't my little girl come home."

Kiernan spun around.

"Miss Belle!" she yelled and ran up the stairs to bury her face in the ample bosom of the dark-skinned woman.

"Hello, child," she said, rubbing the back of Kiernan's hair. "It's been much too long. And look at you! You're as thin as a reed!"

Kiernan smiled. "I've missed you, Miss Belle, more than you know. Where is Father?"

"Oh, that ole curmudgeon should be on his way. Let's get you inside and cleaned up and fed first." She gestured for Beck, Rory and Bajan to follow. "You, too, Mistress Larkin. I know you won't want to be away from Kiernan now that she's returned home."

Kiernan ran back down to thread her arm through Larkin's and sighed with relief. Beyond her greatest hope, the people of Nysa seemed genuinely pleased at her return. She wondered if they truly accepted that she was a shifter or if they simply chose to believe that the rumor was untrue.

She stopped in her tracks when she noticed her father standing at the top of the stairs in front of the open palace doors. As soon as she saw the look in his eyes, she realized that her relief may have been premature.

***

Kiernan didn't remember later if it was her magic that warned her or if she had actually heard the *thrum* of the bowstring as it was released. Either way, a fraction of a second after noticing her father on the steps above, her head snapped to the right and she pushed Larkin to the side, drew her sword over her back and swung it in a sweeping arc high overhead to cut the hurtling arrow out of the air.

Captain Nash, on the step below Kiernan, shouted, "Assassin! Protect the King!"

The two Sabers who preceded the King out of the palace, crashed into him, pitching him backwards onto the marble floor of the foyer.

Colbie turned, flung himself down the steps and leapt onto the shooter, sending the second shot of the would-be murderer flying wide. The assassin collapsed to the ground and tried to shake the Royal Saber off his back. Without the slightest hesitation, Colbie lifted the head of the hooded man by the jaw and drew his knife across his throat.

The brutal deed complete, the Saber stepped away and let the man's head thud to the ground, blood spraying across the cobblestones.

"Who would dare such a thing?" someone spat.

In response, Colbie flipped the assassin over and stripped off his hood. Horrified gasps issued from those on the steps.

It was a Cyman soldier, his one eye fluttering closed.

More screams suddenly erupted from the eastern end of the thoroughfare and the main outer gates. Kiernan's eyes turned black.

Bajan! Hurry and find Rogan and Airron. Tell them to meet us at the entrance gate.

The Draca Cat hesitated. *I will not leave you.*

Kiernan reached up and grabbed the enormous furry face between her hands.

You must. And, afterwards, I want you to stay and guard Titus. He must remain hidden. His life will be forfeit if he is discovered now. Do this for me, Bajan.

His life means nothing to me.

All life has meaning. What kind of Princess would I be if I did not value life? It is my duty to serve and protect.

Yes, to protect the people of Massa.

To protect the innocent, Bajan. There may be a time when I will have to kill to protect the innocent, and I will do so without hesitation, but Titus has not proven himself my enemy yet. I must go. Please do as I say.

The Draca gave her a frustrated nudge and then sprinted toward the stables. Beck, who had been waiting patiently while she conversed with Bajan, grabbed her arm as soon as her eyes resumed their natural color and propelled her down the stairs.

Weaving through the pedestrians on the street, they arrived at the outer wall just as the gates to the city were opening for a second time. Frightened citizens began pouring through in a panic from the marketplace beyond.

Kiernan elbowed Beck and ran for the stairs that led to the gatehouse above.

The sentry standing guard inside looked over as the door opened and immediately stood to block their way.

"Stand down, soldier, it's me, Princess Kiernan."

His face registered shock and he nodded respectfully to her. "Your Grace."

The fact that he did not kneel, told her that the wall was now considered a battlefield. Soldiers did not observe convention during times of war.

"What's happening?" she asked him.

"We're not quite sure, Your Grace, but I suggest you take a look."

Opening the gatehouse door to the parapet, she pushed through the assembled soldiers and scanned the open plains east of Nysa. Although she expected it, she still inhaled sharply at sight of the host of Cyman soldiers.

A scuffle behind turned her around in time to see Rogan and Airron plow through the gatehouse door, followed by the irate sentry.

"It's all right, soldier," said Kiernan. "They're with me."

The soldier looked at Rogan and Airron for a long, hard moment before returning to his post in the gatehouse.

A thunderous roar sounded from beneath them and the wall trembled as Nysa's Cavalry charged out through the open gates to offer protection to the people still streaming in from the marketplace. On the finest and fastest horses on the island, the renowned regiment tore out into the open grasslands in a flagrant show of strength, reigning in their mounts in a dramatic stop as they faced the enemy in a barefaced challenge.

"Princess!" barked a gruff voice. "You shouldn't be here right now! It's too dangerous. I'll have one of the Sabers escort you back to the palace."

Kiernan recognized Bo Franck, captain of the Iserlohn army, muscling his way toward her. Whereas Captain Nash was responsible for the protection of King Maximus and the royal family, Captain Franck led the defense of the city. At age five, Captain Franck had been the one to teach Kiernan how to ride her first pony and at the age of six, how to swing her first sword.

Kiernan smiled fondly at him. "I'm not a little girl anymore, Captain Franck."

He did not smile back, but said just as fondly. "To me you are."

"As your Princess and, more importantly, as a shifter, I am asking you and your men to stand down."

The captain's eyebrows rose into his hairline. "We can handle this, Your Grace. We don't need magic to protect us. Never have and never will."

She sighed. "Can you do it with no lives lost, Captain? Because we can."

Her old instructor looked at her in assessment for a long moment before nodding reluctantly. "But, balls, girl, just be careful. Your father will hang me by mine if you get hurt."

Beck growled next to her, bringing her focus once again to the plains. A Cyman in the middle of the throng raised his arms and taunted the Calvary. Kiernan recognized him as the soldier they encountered after the destruction of Pyraan.

"It's Teag," she said. "He's the one leading this horde." She also remembered the threat Teag issued to Beck just days before that one of them would not survive their next meeting. *Beck Atlan is not going to die this day, Teag. Not if I have anything to say about it.*

"I don't get this," Airron suddenly said.

"What don't you get?" Beck asked.

"Why are they here? If my estimate is correct, there are at most five hundred troops out here. How can they possibly expect to oppose Nysa's armies?"

Kiernan shouted for a range finder to get a closer look. "Maybe they don't mean to fight," she said as a Saber handed her the tubular device and she peered through the shaft. "This could just be a scouting mission. After all, Ravener probably doesn't know much about the capabilities of Massa's militia."

Beck ran his hands through his hair. "No. They will fight."

Rogan looked surprised at his conviction. "Why do you say that?"

Captain Franck turned to face them. "What in demon's breath is a Cyman? Is it as big and ugly as the group sitting out there?" he asked, sweeping his hand out to the east.

"Yes, Captain, those are Cymans," Beck replied. "If I'm correct, Teag and his soldiers are Ravener's sacrificial lambs. He knows they won't survive this encounter, and I'd bet that the assassin wasn't even meant to succeed in killing King Maximus." When everyone looked at Beck in question, he continued. "Remember what my father said? Ravener specializes in terror. He probably feels that if he can frighten the people of Massa enough, they will do anything he asks. They'll bow down to him."

"Who is Ravener?" the captain interrupted.

"A Mage who wants to rule Massa," Beck answered offhandedly and turned back to the shifters. "Although Ravener knows that the Cymans will be destroyed, he probably figures that they will at least take out a large number of forces along the way. In his mind, this would be a fair trade for the fealty of Iserlohn's people. I also don't think it's a coincidence that Teag leads this force. He's being punished for not bringing back Titus as he was ordered to do. This is his death sentence."

"Who is Titus?" asked Captain Franck in exasperation.

"A Cyman soldier," Kiernan answered and then looked at Beck. "So, the Mage is forfeiting this battle to win the war."

"Exactly."

Kiernan jerked around at the sound of the now familiar Cyman war horn and hundreds of Cyman soldiers began sprinting at remarkable speed toward Nysa.

She leapt up into the space between two crenellations, and her friends did the same.

"What about archers?" Captain Franck asked in a panic, and the archers along the wall brought up their bows.

Kiernan shook her head. "Won't work! They have skin as thick as a mantath!"

Captain Franck paced the length of the parapet. "Stand down, soldiers! Stand down!"

Beck was the first to react by throwing out his hands and rippling the ground before the Cymans and sending the first line sprawling. Those that went down didn't stand a chance as the forces behind continued to advance, trampling them to the ground.

Even though the Cymans were immune to the archers' arrows that couldn't penetrate their hardened skin, it was not so with Rogan's arrows. The screams of soldiers and the smell of burning flesh filled the air as fire slammed into their ranks.

Kiernan cringed. *This is nothing short of a slaughter. How can Ravener send his warriors to their deaths in this manner?*

Yet, still they came.

"Call in the Cavalry!" she shouted.

Captain Franck gave the order and the signal was sounded for the mounted unit to retreat. They did so reluctantly, Kiernan noticed. These were soldiers trained to fight and a fight was exactly what they were looking for.

She noticed the frown on Beck's face as he created a sinkhole and fifty Cyman warriors perished when they were buried alive. It wasn't easy to take a life, no matter how justified the act.

Airron's black wolf slithered through the mounted troops returning through the open gates to shred warriors with his sharp claws and teeth.

By the time Beck, Rogan and Airron were finished with their deadly magic, there were only two Cymans left standing. One of them was Teag and he stumbled close to the wall, bloodied and exhausted. He laughed bitterly as he looked at the carnage around him.

"We meet again, Massan," he snarled up at Beck.

"Yes, we do," Beck acknowledged.

The Cyman fell to one knee as he laughed manically. "Come off your wall and let us negotiate your surrender!"

Kiernan turned to one of the soldiers nearby. "Throw your sword over the wall." He hesitated at the unusual request. "Do as you have been ordered, soldier."

Unsheathing his weapon, he did as she asked.

Kiernan watched the sword land and then sought out the Cyman standing next to Teag with her magic. The soldier snapped his head up to look at her and she slammed the link in place. Teag looked on suspiciously as his last remaining comrade walked to the fallen sword, picked it up and, with a mighty two-handed swing, took his head off at the shoulders.

"We do not negotiate with the enemy," she said unapologetically.

CHAPTER 14

HOMECOMING

Kiernan made her way wearily back to the palace with Beck, Rogan and Airron, and on the way met up with Rory who had been hurrying to intercept them. Kiernan had forgotten all about the young fireshifter.

"Where were you?" she asked.

"Your friend, Larkin, had me cornered," he said angrily. "The girl has the arms of an octopus."

Kiernan patted his shoulder. "I'm sure she meant no harm, Rory."

"I'm not so sure about that," he murmured. "But, that's not why I'm here. Your father wishes to see you in Grace Hall immediately."

Kiernan nodded in resignation. "Thank you, Rory."

Grace Hall, named after her mother, Queen Grace Kenley Everard, was the pride of Nysa. Accented in black marble, the entire concaved domed ceiling featured a magnificent painted replica of the city in a stunning display of color. Kiernan's mother commissioned the fresco a year before her death, but fell ill before its completion.

For the most part, her father used the hall to take commoner appeals. People traveled to Nysa from all over Iserlohn to petition the King and his vassals for everything from settling land disputes to seeking employment to requesting foodstuffs for their families.

The sudden sound of hoof beats racing toward her from behind turned her around. Charging up on a splendid Palomino, the mounted man yanked cruelly on the horse's bit to stop the animal directly in front of Kiernan.

She recognized him as Lord Davad Etin, a house member of her father's Court. He was finely dressed in a silk coat and trousers in the red and blue of House Etin, and his handsome face was pinched in disapproval as he looked down at her. "So, the rumor is true."

She sighed regretfully. As soon as she stepped off the parapet and the Iserlohn soldiers shied away from her, she knew what would be coming. "Which rumor would that be, Lord Etin?" she asked coolly.

"How about the one where you and your cohorts killed five hundred men in cold blood using magic?"

She flinched inwardly, but outwardly remained unperturbed. "Those men, if you wish to call them so, were enemy forces who have invaded Massa, Lord Etin. Our actions were wholly justifiable and saved the lives of hundreds of Iserlohn soldiers who would have perished had they met those warriors on the battlefield."

"So you say."

"I do say, and you will address me properly, Lord Etin! Your insolence is tiring and inappropriate."

He bowed from his saddle. "Forgive me, Your Grace. The use of magic shifting and the arrival of monsters out of a child's nightmare have me—and others I might add—a bit off balance."

"I can understand," she freely admitted.

He cleared his throat. "What would you have done with the bodies, Your Grace?"

"Burn them. Good day, Lord Etin."

Without another word, she turned and strode into the castle. She could sense that Beck wanted to say something to her, but she kept her eyes to the front and led a hurried pace to Grace Hall. If she stopped now, her tenuous grasp on her composure would crumble to pieces.

The servants they met along the way gasped at the sight of the stomping Princess and either dropped low to the ground in a curtsy or fled in the other direction. Apparently, news of her shifting had traveled to the castle much faster than she did. She forced down the butterflies in her stomach and stopped before the two Scarlet Sabers outside of the hall.

The soldiers immediately knelt with fists to the ground in front of them. "Please rise," she ordered.

They did so and announced her presence to her father inside.

"She may enter," came the deep reply.

Kiernan swallowed and went in. Her father, sitting stoically on his official throne, watched her come.

He was not a very tall man, but possessed an imposing physique with broad shoulders and muscular arms and legs. He had dark, shoulder-length hair with long sideburns and dark eyes that, when fixed on you, felt as though they could read every thought you ever had. At least that was what the twelve-year-old Kiernan had always thought. For some reason, the eighteen-year-old Kiernan was feeling the same way.

The long walk under the domed ceiling seemed to take a lifetime. When she reached his throne, she knelt before him, took a hold of his hand and laid her cheek upon it. It took all of her resolve not to cry. This man was home to her. He was love and safety and warmth.

Maximus stroked the back of her head. Despite the circumstances of their separation, she had always known that he loved her very much.

"It is good to see you, daughter."

She looked up into those knowing eyes and blurted, "I just killed a man."

"I heard."

"I do not regret it, Father. I did what I had to do. I only regret that the citizens of Nysa had to find out about me in this way."

"It is unfortunate. You know how they feel about magic."

Kiernan narrowed her eyes. "It is how *you* feel about magic, Father. The people follow the lead of their King."

Her father sighed loudly. "I do not wish to resurrect a six-year-old fight with you, Kiernan. The law is the law."

She decided not to pull any punches. "Magic saved your life today," she said, referring to the thwarted attack of the assassin. "But for magic, I may be Queen right now."

The King snorted. "Bah! It would take more than a skulking coward to send me to the Highworld!"

Kiernan stood, deciding to let the argument go. Her father was right. This was an old fight and one she would not soon win. She gestured behind her to the others. "Father, these are my friends Beck Atlan, Rogan Radek, Airron Falewir and Rory Greeley."

The boys gave her father awkward bows.

The King stood. "As friends of Kiernan, I welcome you to Nysa. Are you all shifters?"

"Yes, Your Grace," Beck answered for them all.

Her father gave him a pointed look. "Are you any good?"

Beck looked surprised, but answered honestly. "Yes, Your Grace. I am."

The King grinned. "Better than the young fireshifter behind you, I hope. The boy couldn't even create a flicker of a flame when I asked him to."

Beck smiled and looked at Rory who had his eyes firmly on the ground. "He must have been nervous, Your Grace."

The King waved his hand dismissively. "Whatever the reason, he did inform me of the tragedy of Pyraan." He looked at Beck and then Airron. "I am sorry for your losses. I actually had the opportunity to meet both of your parents several times over the years and found them to be very fine people."

"Thank you, Your Grace."

"Thank you, Your Grace."

Dark eyes glittered dangerously. "We will get these bastards, you have my word. All of Iserlohn's soldiers are being recalled to Nysa as we speak."

Beck cleared his throat. "Your Grace, with all due respect, I'm not sure that this is a war that Iserlohn can win alone. The combined might of all three lands may be needed to even stand a chance."

"Bah! The Scarlet Sabers and Iserlohn Army can defeat these animals. They are made of flesh and blood, are they not?"

"Yes, but it is the Mage we are concerned about."

The King waved a hand. "We will discuss further at dinner this evening."

"Dinner? Father, we really don't have time—"

"Kiernan, there is etiquette to be followed even in times of war. This dinner with my Court has been planned for weeks now, and I do not intend to cancel. I will need their support in any case. Now, tell me about these Cymans," he ordered.

Kiernan recounted what Titus told them of the Cyman's human and Desert Troll genealogy and of the horrible experiments inflicted upon them by Adrian Ravener.

The King gave her a penetrating look. "So, why then do you have one of these creatures hiding in my stables? He smells and he's scaring the horses."

Demon's breath, she cursed to herself. "He is one of the Cyman soldiers that we captured during the initial conflict with the enemy at the Crown Bluffs in Pyraan."

"Why is he still alive?" he demanded.

"Originally, we kept him alive to gather intelligence about the invaders."

"And now?"

She hesitated. "He...is a friend."

His eyes held disappointment. "I had hoped that your decision making would have improved with age. Princesses need to be wise in order to lead their people."

Kiernan stiffened her back. "I am a shifter first, Father. By your decree."

The King's lips flattened into a straight line. "I will see you at dinner," he said brusquely. "And, I expect you to wear your House colors. That dress is entirely unsuitable."

It was a dismissal.

***

When Beck offered to walk her to her room, Kiernan asked one of the servants to show the others to their chambers so they could wash before dinner.

"I guess that went as well as could be expected given the circumstances," he said just outside her door, leaning his shoulder into the stone wall of the corridor.

"Went well? My father is a condescending, arrogant pighead! But, I suppose," she conceded, "that he does genuinely care very much for the people of Iserlohn."

"As do you," Beck replied with a lazy smile.

"Yes."

He reached out to finger one of the curls framing her face. "I'm discovering many new sides to the girl who has been my best friend for six years. Sides I knew nothing about, Your Grace."

"Do not call me that! Ever!" she said forcefully and spun from him. When he laughed, she glanced back over her shoulder. "Do you like all my different sides?"

He pushed off the wall. "No."

Her shoulders stiffened.

"I *love* all of your different sides. Even those qualities of your father's that he's passed down to you."

"Oh, you brute!" She playfully raised her arm to slap him, but he caught her wrist in his large hand and an electrical current surged through her.

He stared at her hungrily. "Would it be proper for me to enter your bed chambers, Princess Kiernan?"

She found it hard to breathe. "It would be highly improper for you to do so, Master Atlan."

He moved closer. "Are you sure?"

Her heart leapt into her throat. "I...I am quite sure. However, it appears that we really have no choice in the matter."

"No, we don't," he confirmed.

Still gazing into his blue eyes, she fumbled behind her for the handle. The door opened and they stumbled inside together.

Beck kicked the door shut, grabbed her by the shoulders and swung her up against the wall. He pressed his body hard against hers. "I've never wanted anything as much as I want you right now," he growled and brought his mouth down on hers.

She responded instantly, her lips opening to his. The world shifted as they melted together, burning in their desire for each other.

His hands were not idle. Stroking the side of her face, her neck and then further down to caress the curve of her breast through the delicate fabric of her dress.

His touch produced an unexpected spasm down low in her body, a pleasure-filled throb she had never experienced before, and she moaned against his mouth. She pulled him tighter, inhaling his scent, and ran her fingers through his hair.

Beck snatched her wrists and pinned them above her head on the wall while his knee snaked between her legs to hold her in place. His head bent to her throat and nipped at her skin.

She was on fire.

He looked down at her with eyes heavy with need and slowly, very slowly, lowered one of his hands to the tie at the back of her dress.

The strap came loose in his hand, and she whimpered as the garment fell down to her waist, tumbling her breasts free. She bit her lip shyly as he looked at her.

"You are so beautiful," he said in a ragged breath.

He cupped one of her breasts in his hand and ran a thumb over her nipple. Longing raced through her, and her knees buckled. Beck caught her, picked her up and carried her to her large, canopied childhood bed.

He carefully set her down and she inhaled sharply as his fingers brushed her hips to gather her dress and slide it the rest of the way down her body. His eyes soaked her in for long seconds before he leaned down and his mouth found her breast, his breath hot on her skin as he ran his tongue over its surface. She arched up into him with a strangled cry.

Beck stood to remove his own clothing and she admired his powerfully built body through brazen, lidded eyes, impatient to have him back in her arms.

At last, he lowered himself on top of her and she had never felt so loved, so complete in her life.

CHAPTER 15

DECLARATIONS

Beck entered the transformed Grace Hall for the King's dinner with Rogan and Airron. There appeared to be close to thirty people in attendance, and he recognized several of them. He nodded politely to Bo Franck, the graying captain of the Iserlohn Army, and Captain Colbie Nash of the Scarlet Sabers. Lord Davad Etin was there as well in the same brilliant red and blue coat he had been wearing earlier. Poor Rory Greeley was backed into a corner by an assertive Larkin Malley and having what appeared to be a one-sided conversation.

There were several other men in military regalia that he didn't know, and the lords and ladies of the King's Court were all present, dressed elegantly in the colors of their Houses.

"Pardon me," said a soft feminine voice, and they turned to a lovely brown-haired woman of about thirty years. "I have never met an Elf before," she said looking at Airron. "You are really quite beautiful."

Airron lit up in his trademark grin. "*Asha*. Thank you, my lady," he said, lifting her gloved hand and bowing dramatically.

"I am the Lady Lillian Knapp of House Knapp, but please call me Lilly."

"And you may call me Airron, Lilly." Airron boldly fixed the lady in his almond-shaped, purple eyes. "If you are interested in learning more about the Elves, Lilly, meet me in the royal gardens after the dinner, and I will teach you everything I know."

"Which isn't much," Rogan murmured under his breath to Beck.

Lilly met his gaze. "I would like that, Airron."

"Until then, Lilly," he said and let go of her hand with another flourish.

As soon as she walked away, Airron said, "That woman is going to make a man of me yet."

"You are seriously not right," Rogan grumbled, shaking his head.

Beck ignored the banter and looked around at the beautiful hall and the incredible workmanship of the mural above his head. In the glow of candlelight, dinner tables were dressed impeccably with scarlet and black linens and placed strategically throughout the great room, all facing the King's much larger table on the dais where his throne had sat earlier.

A hush went over the room and a liveried servant stepped forward. "Lords and ladies, honored guests, may I present to you, the Princess of Iserlohn, Princess of Men, Kiernan Grace Everard."

Beck turned and sucked in his breath at the vision before him. He had never seen a more beautiful sight in his life. *Except perhaps the one my eyes feasted on earlier this evening*, he corrected himself with a smile.

Tonight, Kiernan wore a high-waisted, red silk gown with a low-cut square neckline. The silken material, gathered just beneath her bosom under a black velvet ribbon, hung to the floor in shimmering waves. Her long blonde hair was piled artfully on top of her head with soft ringlets loosely framing her face and neck. The crowning touch was the ruby and onyx tiara that glittered in the light of hundreds of candles. A velvet choker around her neck discretely hid her athame from view. *Her idea or her father's?*

As always, Bajan stood by her side, his green eyes narrowed and probing.

Captain Nash stepped forward to take Kiernan's hand, and he held it high between them as he escorted her to the King's table.

King Maximus entered the hall behind his daughter, and before he could be properly announced, he said loudly, "Please have a seat. As much as I abhor mixing business with pleasure, we have important matters to discuss."

***

Kiernan glanced over at Beck, now taking a seat at one of the tables with Airron and Rogan, and her stomach tightened in pleasure. She barely noticed as Captain Nash bowed over her hand and kissed it before holding out her chair and then taking the seat next to her for himself.

Her father stepped up onto the raised dais behind them and addressed the crowd. "Thank you all for coming. Regrettably, what was supposed to be an informal dinner must now be deemed a war council."

The Nysians murmured in surprise and glanced around uncomfortably at each other.

"As you know," her father continued calmly while the guests hurried to take their seats, "a host of invaders attempted to breach the outer wall to Nysa earlier today. Fortunately, the Iserlohn Army was able to repel the attack."

Kiernan looked at her father with a raised eyebrow.

"One of these invaders even managed to get into the city and make an assassination attempt upon my life. My daughter, the Princess, stopped him with her sword."

Shocked gasps were followed by nervous applause.

"With great remorse, I must now inform you that the fears of our ancestors have come to pass, and the protective measures they put in place centuries ago have failed." He paused. "The shifters of Pyraan have been defeated."

More anxious twitter broke out from the guests. Kiernan did not like the way this was going.

"The very same Mage who started the war over three hundred years ago has invaded Massa through the Crown Bluffs in the north, and all of the people and the land of Pyraan have been destroyed. With the exception of five shifters who escaped this massacre, magic is no more."

She gritted her teeth at several shouts of approval.

Suddenly, the doors to the hall banged open and two Sabers entered with a large struggling man between them, a black hood thrown over his head.

The nervous guests scraped back their chairs and turned toward the commotion at the door.

The King kept on as if nothing at all were happening in the back of the room. "This Mage must be stopped at all costs. He is ruthless and devious and intends to enslave the people of Massa. He covets our women and children."

Lord Etin's chair crashed to the floor as he stood. "Never! Iserlohn's swords will cut him to bloody pieces!"

Kiernan thought she saw a slight smile on her father's face. The cunning orator continued with deliberate fervor in his voice now. "This Mage leads a mutant army to do his killing! To kill Massans!" Her father lifted his arm and pointed to the figure in the back. "Guests, behold! I give you the face of the enemy!" All eyes turned in time to see one of the Scarlet Sabers roughly pull the black hood off the prisoner.

Titus stopped struggling and rose proudly to his full height amidst the screams of the women.

Kiernan stood. "Father, please don't do this," she pleaded quietly.

He ignored her, his voice growing harder. "We will avenge the shifters who gave their lives protecting the people of Massa!"

Applause.

"We will persevere in the defense of this great nation!"

Applause.

"We will throw these animals back into the sea from which they crawled!" the King roared and basked in the thunderous applause generated by his words. He pointed again to Titus. "Starting with this one!"

The guests leapt to their feet with shouted pronouncements of unmitigated allegiance to their King.

Kiernan knew she had to stop this. She tried to meet Beck's eyes over the heads of the crowd.

The doors swung open a second time and a tall, handsome man with long blonde hair strode into the room disregarding the protests of several servants. He appeared to be in his fortieth year with a strong, chiseled face that was mostly unlined. A black cape hung from his broad shoulders and flowed out behind him as he walked into Grace Hall. The most remarkable thing about him was his eyes, thought Kiernan. They were startling blue in color and seemingly wise and knowing beyond his years. A hint of mischief twinkled just beneath the surface.

"Apologies for my lateness, Max," he said to the King informally. "I was unexpectedly delayed."

Her father snorted. "I should have known you would show up, Starr. You always did have a nose for trouble."

Starr? Galen Starr?

The elusive Mage strode swiftly through the newly dubbed war council directly to her father's table and bowed. "And you, my dear King, always had a knack for rousing the masses," he said softly, out of earshot of the others.

Her father smirked. "It has been a long time, Starr. I just regret that our reunion is due to unfortunate circumstances."

"Why else would I be here except for unfortunate circumstances, Your Grace?" he quipped. "May I have the floor?"

When her father nodded, Galen walked to the back of the room to stand in front of Titus, still being held securely by his arms. The Mage shook his head in regret. "My apologies to you, young man. It seems my former apprentice has much to answer for. With your permission, I would like to speak to you in private after this council as there are many questions that I need to have answered."

Titus looked taken aback, but nodded his head.

Addressing the Sabers with authority, Galen said, "Return this man to his cell until I can speak to him, but do not harm him." It was an order. "On your way out, see to it that we're not interrupted by anyone, including servants. Dinner will have to wait."

The soldiers hesitated and glanced at Colbie Nash. "Do as he says," the captain commanded.

As soon as Titus and the Sabers left the hall, Galen walked forward and addressed her father. "Again, my apologies, Your Grace, but events on the island are spinning out of control and time is of very limited supply. If you will, please introduce your guests to me. I would like to know to whom I speak."

The King glared at Galen. "Very well, Mage, but you are testing my patience with your pomposity."

Galen bowed his head in acknowledgment, but Kiernan again noticed an underlying sparkle in the man's eyes.

Her father walked off the dais and Kiernan and the others followed. He introduced the two captains and several of their top officers. Next, he introduced the six lords and ladies of his Court,

Lords Etin, Winslow, Hamilton and Paxton, and Ladies Conry and Knapp. Lastly, he presented the shifters.

Once the introductions were complete, Galen approached Bajan and bowed deeply at the waist. Bajan clicked his tongue, clearly satisfied at the display of respect. "I am honored to meet you, Draca. I have had many dealings with your Sovereign, Moombai, over the years and hold the Draca Cats in the very highest of esteem."

Bajan's eyes turned black.

Princess, thank the Mage and tell him I am pleased by his words.

After Kiernan translated, Galen bowed once more and turned to face the war council with outstretched arms. "Let us all sit down. It is imperative that you understand the occurrences that have led us here and what must be done to repel this invasion of evil." He walked toward the tables and, with a casual flick of his wrist, several chairs skidded across the floor to rearrange into a half-circle.

Lord Etin's face reddened in fury. "Your Grace! I'm sure the Mage must have a purpose for all of his dramatic antics, but flaunting magic in the face of the law? In the palace of the King?"

Before her father could respond, Galen put his hands up again in concession. "You are right, Lord...Etin, is it not? Forgive me, Lord Etin, but my gift is such a natural part of *who* I am that I have forgotten *where* I am." He held his hand out to the chairs. "Please. No disrespect was intended."

The wary council members took their seats and Galen, throwing his cape back to billow out over the back of his chair, sat down with them. "Let me start by telling you why Adrian Ravener has chosen this time to start a war with the island of Massa." He paused. "It is because of me. Because I am dying."

Kiernan looked around the room at all of the stunned faces that must have mirrored her own. *This imposing, vibrant man is dying?*

"With my death, safeguards I created long ago to stop Ravener will be vulnerable. As you all should know from our histories, there were four original *Savitars* who defeated Adrian Ravener in his original quest for dominion. He has now returned three hundred years later for the very same purpose. Adrian is a magician of immense power and will give no quarter. He must be utterly destroyed. The only way to do so is to unlock an ancient magical counter that—"

Captain Franck snorted an interruption. "Bah! An arrow through his black heart will kill him the same as any man."

Galen nodded. "True, but he will be well guarded, and while he is well guarded, he will be conjuring dark arts."

"What must be done?" asked Captain Nash.

"Despite your mistrust of magic, the naming of four new *Savitars* is compulsory to success. Only they will have the power to reach and summon the counter."

The Mage stood up to walk behind the seated guests. "It will not be easy." He put his hands on Rogan's shoulders. "It will take a master fireshifter to light the way." He moved to Airron. "It will take a bodyshifter of many forms to locate the trail." He touched Beck. "It will take a mighty earthshifter with the strength to carry the day." Galen stood behind Kiernan. "And, it will take Princess Kiernan Everard, and only Princess Kiernan."

She turned to look up at him. "Why me?"

"Because of your connection with the Draca Cats. The power we seek is in Callyn-Rhe."

She tilted her head in question. "But, how do we find it? I had always been told that Callyn-Rhe is impossible for humans to find."

Galen shook his head. "Not impossible. Each of you should be in possession of a pendant. These four pendants, when joined, create a map to the shrouded Callyn-Rhe. There is where you will find the weapon to counter Ravener's plans."

The King, who had been quiet throughout Galen's dire assertions, walked over to him now with barely controlled rage. "How long have you been making these plans, Mage? How long have you known that you would be using my daughter to wage war?"

Galen's blue eyes filled with regret. "I have known for many years that this day would come, Max."

Her father's fists clenched at his sides. "You didn't find it necessary to share this information with me? With the other lands?" he asked in disbelief. "We could have had years to prepare!"

"We need her, Max."

"Maybe your way is not the only answer, Starr! If you will recall, it didn't turn out very well the last time the people of this island entrusted their welfare to you!" Galen didn't flinch, but Kiernan could see the sorrow in his face. Her father went on mercilessly. "Hundreds of thousands of people perished, Galen! Their blood still stains your hands! I don't want to see another Mage War. There has to be another way!"

Galen reached out to put his hand on her father's shoulder. "There is no other way, Max. I wish there was." He looked directly into his old friend's eyes. "She is pureblood."

The tension stretched between them as everyone in the room watched the silent battle that waged between the Mage and the King as they glared at each other for several long moments. Jaws twitched. Chins lifted. Fists open and closed.

At last, Maximus shrugged Galen's hand brusquely off his shoulder and turned toward Kiernan, taking her hands in his. "What say you, daughter?"

She didn't hesitate. "I must do as Galen requests, Father. I am the only one who can communicate with the Draca Cats." She didn't bother to remind him of her blood oath. He wouldn't understand. Still, she knew her father was hoping to hear her rail against this unconscionable task being requested of her. To denounce Galen Starr and his enigmatic claims. But, she did none of those things and thus unwittingly handed the victory of this evening to Galen Starr.

The King was silent as he contemplated and paced in front of the war council. He stopped in front of Beck, Rogan and Airron with a measuring gaze. "Will you also travel to Callyn-Rhe with my daughter?"

Her three friends stood as one and she smiled. "We will."

He turned to Bajan, sitting passively on his haunches at her side. "Will you travel to your homeland with the Princess and protect her? Lay down your life for her if you must?"

Bajan nodded.

"And so it is!" he bellowed, whirling back to the guests. "As the shifters have agreed to do their part in defeating the bastard Mage, so do I pledge to rout the Cyman Army. We march in one week for Starfell!"

Kiernan scraped back her chair. "Father, you must wait for the armies of the Dwarves and Elves. There are tens of thousands of soldiers in the Cyman Army!"

The King scoffed. "We have already discussed this. The Iserlohn Army and the Scarlet Sabers can handle these interlopers, daughter.

We may be outnumbered, but we have advantages that the Cyman Army does not such as maneuverability, knowledge of the terrain and the best battle strategists in the land."

Airron stepped forward. "But, Your Grace, with assistance from the Elven Gladewatchers—"

"Don't forget the Dwarven Iron Fists!" interrupted Rogan.

The King nodded. "Yes, yes, both units would be very formidable allies and if they arrive at Starfell, I will be grateful for their aid. But, we can't depend on them. Ravener has demanded a response by Earthshine which is six weeks away. It will take all of that to outfit the army and march to Starfell."

Lady Knapp leapt to her feet. "House Knapp supports King Maximus! The Shadow Panthers march to Starfell!"

Lord Etin nodded his head. "I care not one whit for where the shifters go, but you have my support as well, Your Grace. The Eagles of House Etin fly for Starfell!"

One by one, the Royal Court voiced their backing by committing their forces to the engagement.

"House Winslow's Couching Wolves with the King!"

"The Red Dragons of House Hamilton to Starfell!"

"The Thundering Bulls of House Paxton charge to the Valley of Flame!"

"House Conry's Savage Badgers will not be denied!"

The King unsheathed his sword from the scabbard at his hip and lifted it high into the air. "It is decided! But, if it is surrender that Ravener is expecting, he will be sorely disappointed, for he will only receive the sharp points of our swords!"

Iserlohn was at war.

CHAPTER 16

AN EXPENDABLE PAWN

While King Maximus was making his declaration of war, Rory Greeley slipped out of the doors to Grace Hall. He moved past the nervous servants milling about and went in search of the holding cells. Fortunately, most people seemed to forget he was around which left him ample opportunity for covert exploits.

He had to ask several servants for directions along the way, but finally found the correct location. Two brawny guardsmen in black and red tunics stood in front of an arched door that Rory was told led down to the underground cells. He walked purposefully toward the pair, and the guards watched him come with suspicious eyes.

These are soldiers who know their duty and take no chances. Rory was fairly certain that they wouldn't let him through simply by making the request, so he tried another tactic.

He smiled disarmingly. "Pardon. I was wondering if you could point me in the direction of the guest chambers. I have only just arrived with the Princess and must confess with some embarrassment that I can't remember the way to my room."

One of the guards pointed down a corridor that led, Rory knew, to the guest chambers.

He fixed a confused look on his face and scratched his head. "Are you sure? I have already been down that way, sir, and couldn't find them."

The guards exchanged a glance and then one nodded, probably the senior of the two. "Stay at your post, Vance. I'll show him the way."

Rory thanked them both and followed behind the guard. Before they turned the first corner, he risked a peek back over his shoulder to confirm that Vance was still in position and looking forward again.

He was.

When the burly guard leading him turned to provide further directions, Rory struck. Although small, he was skilled at combat and knew how to immobilize a larger opponent. The unsuspecting soldier didn't have a chance. A well-placed blow to the side of his temple dropped him like a stone.

Eyes darting up and down the corridor, Rory lifted the man under the arms and dragged him to the first door he saw.

Luck was with him. A quick look inside revealed a short set of stairs that led down to what appeared to be an empty wine cellar. Grunting with the effort, Rory yanked the unconscious man inside the door and let him tumble down the stairs to the bottom. He raced down after the guard and pulled him into a darkened corner.

After wiping the sweat from his forehead he undressed and placed his clothes in an empty barrel for safekeeping.

Then, he did the unthinkable. What no bodyshifter in Pyraan would ever consider. What all shifters considered a heinous, despicable act against humanity. He placed his hands upon the guardsman and absorbed his form.

The air shimmered and the body on the ground sunk in on itself as Rory's smaller stature shifted upward. Arms and legs lengthened, light-hair turned dark, the bristle of a beard popped out on his chin.

It took a few moments to orient himself to the man's height and bulk and strip off the soldier's uniform. Once dressed, he shoved the shrunken corpse further into the shadows of the room, staggered back up the stairs in his new body and headed back down the hall toward Vance and the cell doors. Smoothing his uniform, he approached the other guard.

"Open it up," he said, gesturing to the door with his head.

"What are you doing, Penske?"

"I just ran into Captain Nash. The prisoner is to be readied for interrogation immediately. King's orders."

Vance shrugged and unlocked the door. "Need help?"

"No, stay here. This won't take long."

***

Kiernan threw open the balcony doors of her bedroom chambers and stepped out onto the cold mosaic tile with bare feet. Leaning against the stone balustrade, she inhaled the night air hoping to dispel some of the unease that wormed its way inside of her. War loomed and the greatest chance of victory Massa had depended on whether she and the other shifters successfully penetrated Callyn-Rhe and uncovered her secrets. She shook her head. *The Mage is holding something back, I'm sure of it. But, what?*

Restless, she turned and walked back into the room.

Bajan was curled before the fireplace impassively grooming himself. She glared at him.

Well?

Well what?

Massa will soon be at war.

Yes, I heard. Lick, lick.

We are going to your homeland of Callyn-Rhe.

Yes. Lick

Bajan! I need your help here! I have so many questions.

I am not surprised. Lick.

The first of which is what kind of power do you think is hidden at Callyn-Rhe?

I cannot be sure. I have never been there.

Do you think we will be able to find it?

We must. Lick, lick.

I wonder what Galen meant by me being a pureblood?

There was a knock on the door.

Finally, someone I can talk to, she sneered at Bajan. He didn't so much as glance in her direction as he continued his cleaning.

She answered the door to find her childhood friend standing outside. "Larkin! Come in."

After a brief embrace, Larkin walked in and sat down on the bed with a lively bounce. "I've really missed you!" she complained, lying back with her hands behind her head. "It's been positively boring around here since you left."

Kiernan smiled and sat by her on the bed. "You? Bored? Never."

The dark-haired beauty turned on her side to look at Kiernan conspiratorially. "So, out with it! Tell me all about your handsome earthshifter. Every detail, mind you!" she demanded.

Kiernan's cheeks heated and she rose from the bed. For some reason, she no longer wanted to discuss her relationship with Beck. It was too special, too intimate now, and all hers. "We're not little girls anymore, Larkin, sharing every little secret," she chided.

Larkin sat up, her smile vanishing. "Truth be told, we didn't share all of our secrets back then either, did we?" Larkin looked in her eyes. "Why didn't you tell me?"

Kiernan didn't have to ask what she was talking about. She shrugged. "Scared, I guess. I knew that if I was found out, I would be sent to Pyraan, so I kept it to myself for many years."

Larkin grabbed her hands. "I was your best friend, Kiernan. I never would have betrayed your secret."

"I know. I am sorry."

Apparently, satisfied with the apology, Larkin changed the subject. "What is the matter with that friend of yours, Rory? He acts very strange, Kiernan, and gives me the creeps."

Kiernan laughed. "You couldn't tell that from where I've been watching! You've been cornering the boy every chance you get."

"Only to get answers," she sniffed. "He slinks around all the time, poking his nose in places where it doesn't belong."

At the sound of another knock, Kiernan got up and opened the door wide in invitation to Beck, Rogan and Airron. After they stepped in, she looked out in the hall in both directions. "Where's Rory? Isn't he with you?"

Airron lifted his shoulders. "No. He wasn't in his room."

Kiernan shut the door and Beck leaned in close to give her a small kiss on her lips that sent a jolt through her entire body. She resisted the urge to hug him close to her. There, burrowed within the strength of his arms, was comfort and safety. Out here, there was nothing but danger and anxiety.

He pulled back to look at her, his blue eyes full of the singular knowledge he now possessed. He wiggled his eyebrows at her and smiled.

"Stop it!" she hissed, her face warming.

Beck laughed aloud and the innocence of the sound helped to soothe her frazzled nerves more than anything else could have.

Suddenly playful, she turned to Airron. "I thought you were going to meet with Lady Knapp?"

Taking a seat next to Larkin, Airron bounced on the bed causing the girl to squeal. "Alas, the lady appears to have fallen out of the mood for love. Pronouncements of war tend to do that, I've heard."

Rogan shook his head. "Has everyone gone mad? I don't know what is in the air around here, but we have important matters to deal with." He looked at Larkin. "If you will excuse us?"

Larkin resignedly made her departure amid hugs and a promise to see Kiernan again before she left Nysa.

As soon as the door shut behind her, Rogan wasted no time. "Airron was right. The pendants that he and Beck have in their possession do have a connection. Now, Kiernan and I just have to locate ours so we can unlock this map. Kiernan, any idea where yours might be?"

She shook her head and sat on a chair to put her sandals on. "None, but I will ask my father this evening to see what he knows."

Rogan looked worried. "I wish I knew where to search for mine. I suppose I'll have to start with my family home in Deepstone."

Beck nodded. "Makes sense. We should also go see Titus to let him know what's happened. I want to reassure him that we'll be back for him once this is over. Let's go."

Beck and Airron walked out the door, and Kiernan laced her arm through Rogan's in comfortable companionship as they followed behind. "Don't worry, Rogan, you'll find your pendant, I know it. And, just think! You'll finally get a chance to visit the homeland you haven't seen in years."

His brown eyes brightened slightly. "I just hope I get the same warm welcome that you did here in Nysa."

She nodded. Despite her fears, it had been a warm welcome.

But, it was getting colder by the moment.

***

Unmoving, Titus kept his eye to the ceiling as a guard turned a key in the lock on the door to his cell.

He had known it wasn't a good plan to come here into the city, but he'd had very little say in the matter. He was a hostage after all. As accommodating as the shifters had been to him, he was still a prisoner of war, a war initiated by his people.

But, he had grown fond of his travel companions, and began to hold out hope that everything would work out for both of their peoples. He took sinister delight in the images of war that swirled in his head of the shifters destroying Adrian and Avalon Ravener in a hundred gruesome ways to give the Cyman people their freedom.

"Titus?"

He turned toward the door and swallowed, all hope disappearing in an instant when the guard entered his cell.

The only way he could describe the look in the man's eyes was dead. This was a dead man walking and it terrified him. He had seen the look many times before.

He bolted up out of his cot.

The air shimmered and the big guard shifted into Avalon Ravener.

"Hello, Titus." The sound of his oppressor's voice sent his heart racing in his chest and he began to tremble. He instinctively glanced around for a way to escape, but quickly realized there was nowhere to run. There never had been.

She slithered over to him and put a hand on his face. "Oh, Titus, it is such a shame that you were taken. I really was looking forward to enjoying more time with you." She reached down between his legs and squeezed, twisting cruelly until he cried out in pain.

"Please, Mistress," he grunted.

She let go and he fell to his knees with his hands pressed to his groin.

Her lips hovered close to his ear. "You do understand, Titus, that I cannot leave you alive in the hands of the enemy?"

"Please Mistress, don't kill me."

Her whisper was callous and cold. "I have no choice."

He couldn't help himself. He began to sob, and she looked down at him in disgust. She abhorred weakness.

His mind reeled furiously, rummaging for any possible chance at survival. Finally, hating himself, he said, "I could still be of value to you, Mistress. I could get information to you about the Massans' plans."

Avalon grunted. "I already have all of the information I need, Titus. I have been privy to all sorts of interesting intelligence." The air shimmered again and Avalon shifted smoothly into Rory Greeley.

Titus gasped in shock. "If you know what they are about, why 'ave you not killed them?" he asked, tears falling from his eye.

"Oh, I plan to kill them, lover. Just as soon as I get all four pendants and the map that leads to this ancient power Galen Starr was yammering about." She waved her hand dismissively in the air between them. "You weren't around for that little disclosure."

He grabbed at Avalon's hand in Rory's form. "Please, I don't want to die! I'll do anything you ask!"

For a fleeting moment, Titus thought he saw a shred of decency pass across Avalon's eyes. She exhaled noisily and moved close to him to cradle his head to her chest. "Oh, Titus."

Suddenly, the sound of voices drifted down to them from the top of the stairs.

"'Elp!" he screamed, pulling away from Avalon. "Someone 'elp me!"

Avalon stood back, shifted into the guard and plunged her sword into his throat just as Beck Atlan slammed the cell door open with a crash, his eyes wild.

"What is the meaning of this?" he screamed, grabbing Avalon's shoulders and slamming her up against the stone wall.

In the guard's form, she held her hands in the air. "King's orders."

Titus fell over to the floor from his knees.

Kiernan ran to him and gently lifted his head to her lap. "Airron! Get a healer in here. Quickly!"

Wheezing forcefully, Titus attempted to speak, but try as he might, he couldn't get the breath to do so. Avalon had severed his windpipe. He looked up and noticed tears on the Princess's cheeks.

For me?

Her voice grew faint as she urged him to hang on.

If only he could warn her that she was in danger.

If only he could ask her to tell his Da that he loved him.

If only he could tell her how sad he felt that they weren't going to have the chance to become better friends.

But, he died in her arms before he could say any of these things.

CHAPTER 17

BETRAYALS

The concussion of a loud thunderclap reverberated through the palace walls, but Kiernan barely noticed as she stormed through the corridors with Beck, Rogan and Airron keeping pace beside her.

"Open the doors!" she barked to the two Scarlet Sabers standing in front of her father's personal chambers. The guards hesitated, and Kiernan was so angry that she briefly considered mindshifting them out of her way. Fortunately, her father staved off her actions by opening the doors from the inside.

Bewilderment creased his features. "I thought that was you. What is it, Kiernan?"

Without a word, she walked past him into the room and waited. As soon as the doors closed behind her friends and father, she whirled on him, tears in her eyes. "How could you?" she demanded. "Galen Starr ordered that he was not to be harmed! He was an innocent and you gave the order for his execution! No, not execution, a heartless murder!"

"What in the world are you talking about, Kiernan?"

"You know very well, Father, that I am referring to the Cyman that you were holding prisoner. You gave the order to kill him!"

"I gave no such order," he asserted.

Kiernan faltered at her father's denial, and gratefully Beck stepped in to seek clarity.

"Well, he is dead, Your Grace, and the guardsman who committed the act said it was on your orders."

The King's expression turned grim and he stalked to the doors and threw them open. "Ryan! Summon Captains Nash and Franck immediately along with the two guards at the holding cells. Do you know who they are?"

Ryan nodded. "Vance and Pen—"

"Get all four up here now!" he bellowed and slammed the doors shut. He turned back to Kiernan. "We will get this straightened out, I promise. I can't tell you that I'm sorry the Cyman is dead, but the order did not come from me."

"But, the guard said—"

"I did not give the order, Kiernan," he interrupted, gripping her upper arms. "You have to believe me on this."

She took a deep breath to calm her emotions and turned away to stare out at the storm lashing against the windows. Bajan was out there somewhere hunting. Hopefully, he would make fast work of it so he could return safely to her side.

When she finally felt like she was back in control, she faced her father once again. "Forgive me."

He waved her off. "No apology necessary. We will get to the bottom of this." He motioned with two fingers to a servant lurking at the back of the room, and the girl rushed forward to pour wine.

Kiernan accepted the proffered glass. "While we wait, Father, I must ask you about the pendant that Galen Starr mentioned."

He shook his head and shrugged. "I have never seen such a pendant. If it exists, your mother must have had possession of it. Her jewelry is still locked in her dressing rooms, and you are welcome to go through them."

"I will. Thank you. I....Again, I am sorry for accusing you."

Her father reached out to stroke the side of her face with a sad smile. "You look so much like her, you know. You have her spirit, too, that's for bloody sure!" he chortled. "You must know that I would give anything to have our situation changed, Kiernan. Truly, I would."

"How so?" she asked, genuinely curious. "What would you wish differently?"

"For one, I wish more than anything that your mother was still alive and here with us. Every young lady needs a mother to guide her, and the Highworld knows I haven't made a very good show of it."

"Father..."

"She would be as proud of you as I am," he said, cupping her cheek in his large palm. Eyes full of regret, he stepped away and turned his back to her. "For another, I wish that you could take your rightful position by my side as Princess of Iserlohn."

"I am not sure I understand."

He looked back. "You are a shifter, Kiernan. The law calls for your exile."

His words cut her to the bone. *He still doesn't want me.*

Rogan set his wine glass down with a splash. "Your Grace, there is no longer any exile. Pyraan does not exist."

"Not only is Pyraan gone," Beck pointed out, "but the men and women who gave their lives in defense of this island. Now, you would exile five shifter survivors? One of whom is your daughter?"

Her father shifted uncomfortably. "It is inevitable that more shifters will be born each year, and they will need a place to train and be raised away from ordinary people."

Hurt turned to fury. "Father, shifters *are* ordinary people who just happen to have been born with magic. You can't seriously be considering this!"

The King threw his wine glass against the fireplace with a roar, the lightning outside of the window briefly illuminating the harsh resolve on his face. "It is the law! What good are laws if the King arbitrarily disregards them for his own personal interests? Besides, the people of Iserlohn will never accept a shifter Princess!"

At those words, her shoulders slumped. "I ask again, Father. The people or you?"

His face a blank mask, he said, "You will have all of the provisions and mounts you require for your journey ready by morning. The Iserlohn Army will meet the shifters at the Valley of Flame by Earthshine."

Kiernan struggled to keep the pain from her voice. "Fine," she said softly. "At least all of the years of pretense are now at an end. I will not burden you with my presence any longer than necessary. I shall leave in the morning and will not be back." Despite all effort, she couldn't stop the single tear that trailed down her cheek. She rubbed it away harshly, annoyed.

"Kiernan, that's not..." her father began, but she didn't give him an opportunity to continue as she brushed past him and slammed the doors on her way out.

***

Beck didn't immediately follow Kiernan, knowing she needed time to herself. She remained intractable in her belief that magic shifters be accepted for who they were, and it would take time for her to come to terms with the fact that most people, including her own father, did not share her view. He loved that about her. Her unwavering courage to stand and fight against people and causes much larger than she.

When he eventually did seek her out, he found her in her mother's dressing rooms on her hands and knees, throwing clothes and boxes all over the floor, two young handmaids hovering anxiously behind her. She looked up at him when he entered, frustration filling her green eyes. "It's not here! I've looked everywhere."

Beck knelt beside her. "I asked one of the servants to send for Miss Belle. According to them, she was closest to your mother and may know where the pendant is."

Kiernan sagged. "I should have thought of that." She leaned over to kiss him on the mouth, ignoring the giggles of the handmaids. When she finally pulled back, she glanced over his shoulder. "Lola and Leah, you may leave now."

"Yes, Your Grace." The girls curtsied low to the ground and scampered away, hands covering their grins.

After they left, Kiernan stood. "Don't do it."

"Do what?" he asked, frowning down at all of the clutter at her feet.

"Don't talk about my father or Titus or anything else for that matter. I don't want to talk and I don't want to cry anymore."

He did as she asked and remained silent.

Crossing her arms at her chest, she said, "My only concern now is recovering my pendant so we can leave."

He nodded and picked up one of the boxes on the floor.

"My father is a pig-headed, arrogant bastard. Exile? Really?"

He returned a velvet slipper to its rightful box.

She started to pace. "Oh, I *am* Princess of Iserlohn, Father, on that you can be certain!"

He continued to straighten the room.

"Well?"

He couldn't help but laugh.

"What is so funny?" she demanded, hands on hip.

He stood and gestured her closer with outstretched arms. "Whatever happens, Kiernan, all that matters is that we'll be together. Even if they exile us in the Sandori Sands, I'll be happy as long as I have you."

She walked into his embrace and reached up to lace her fingers behind his head. "I knew I fell in love with you for a reason. You always know just what to say."

"Will you love me forever?" he teased.

"And, then some."

The door to the outer sitting room opened. "Kiernan?"

"In here, Miss Belle," Kiernan responded, pulling away from him.

Her former caretaker appeared, filling up most of the doorway with her large frame. Her eyes went wide. "Whatever are you doing, girl?"

Beck noticed Kiernan's face flush before she realized that Miss Belle was talking about the disaster she had made of the dressing room. "I'm looking for a piece of jewelry, Miss Belle, a silver pendant. My mother must have had it, but I can't find it anywhere."

Miss Belle visibly blanched. "Are you talking about that two-eyed pendant?"

Kiernan ran to her. "Yes! That must be it. You have it?"

"I have it, and I will gladly give it to you. It makes my skin crawl, it does. The eyes blink!" She shuddered. "Your mother asked me to give it to you on your eighteenth name day, and I was planning to have a messenger deliver it to Pyraan."

Beck looked at Kiernan, smiling. "What did I tell you? You will learn one of these days that I am very rarely wrong."

Kiernan punched his arm. "Where is it?" she asked Miss Belle.

"I will have it brought to your room. Now, make off so I can clean up your mess." Shuffling into the room, the woman boldly looked Beck up and down.

"Miss Belle!" Kiernan admonished.

"What? I've never met an earthshifter before. And, a very handsome one at that."

Beck laughed.

The outer door opened again and hurried footsteps approached. "Princess!" It was Lola, the young handmaid. "Come quickly. I have been ordered to escort you to Mage Starr's rooms straight away."

Kiernan grabbed Beck's hand. "This can't be good."

CHAPTER 18

DEATHBED CONFESSIONS

Rogan and Airron were already present in the Mage's sitting room along with Bajan, who Kiernan was relieved to see was safely back from his hunt. Captains Nash and Franck were there as well, huddled around a table covered with maps and conversing softly. Both knelt with left fist to the floor when she entered.

The King's back was to the door as he poured himself a glass of wine. He did not turn around.

A soldier, presumably one of the guards from the holding cells when Titus was murdered, stood before someone lying on a sofa and covered with a blanket.

Kiernan gasped quietly when the guard turned to kneel to her and revealed Galen Starr. The vitality and health of just hours ago had vanished, leaving a face gaunt and ancient and that appeared to be...sliding off of his skull. *Dear Highworld, what happened to him?*

"Please rise," she told the three men.

"Come closer, Princess," croaked the Mage. "Guardsman Vance was just describing the events surrounding the death of the young Cyman. I must warn you, it is very disturbing." He waved his hand weakly toward the guard, prompting him to continue his story.

The uneasy guard stood and cleared his throat. "After it was discovered that the King had not ordered the interrogation or execution of the Cyman prisoner, we went looking for Guardsman Penske to get answers. We searched for hours until a servant ran screaming from one of the wine cellars." The guardsman gulped audibly. "We found Penske there in a corner of the cellar. He...I am not quite sure how to put it. His body was emaciated as if all of the air and fluids had been sucked out of his body."

Airron grunted in disbelief. "He was bodyshifted?"

Kiernan refused to believe it. Shifting a human form was unconditionally forbidden in Pyraan and its practice rejected outright by any moral and reasoned human being. It was just not done. Not ever.

The Mage nodded. "Yes. I viewed the body myself and can confirm it to be so."

The two captains drew closer to the conversation and were now listening intently. Bajan rubbed protectively against Kiernan.

Beck shook his head. "But, Mage, Airron is the only bodyshifter left in Massa, and I can assure you he did not kill this guard."

Airron looked sick.

Galen again waved a weak hand. "I do not think Airron was responsible, Beck, but what of the other shifter with you?"

"Rory?" Kiernan questioned. "No, he's a harmless fireshifter with not much magic to command. It couldn't be him."

"When was the last time you saw him?" asked the Mage.

"Not since dinner."

Without warning, the Mage began to hack and wheeze violently into a handkerchief in his hand. The fit went on for several uncomfortable seconds. Just as Kiernan started forward to try to help, the coughing subsided and Galen straightened himself on the sofa, breathing heavily.

"It...it appears that we have a rogue bodyshifter here in the castle who has managed to kill two people," Galen managed to get out.

Comprehension flooded through Kiernan. "Wait. Are you suggesting that it could be a shifter who never went to Pyraan?"

"It is possible," rasped the Mage.

Her father spoke up for the first time. "You may go now Vance."

The guardsman immediately bowed and headed for the door, looking relieved to be away from the focus of attention.

The King asked Colbie Nash to acquaint the shifters with the Massan maps on the table. The captain nodded and motioned them over. "How familiar are any of you with the geography of Massa?"

"Quite a bit from our studies at the academy," Rogan replied.

Colbie gave Kiernan a warm smile. "I understand that you've all decided to travel to the other lands first before going to Callyn-Rhe?"

"Yes," Kiernan confirmed.

He pointed a finger down at the table and drew their gazes to a point on the map south of Nysa. "Tomorrow at dawn, you will travel by horse to Iserport. Midway is the small town of Janis where you can get off the road to spend the night at an inn and get a decent meal. Once in Iserport, you will take the ferry to Deeport and travel the Koda River to Kondor to meet with King Rik and the Dwarves. You will be provided with traveling papers to verify your purpose." He pointed back to the map. "After delivering your message to the Dwarves, head northeast to Sarphia and King Jerund. According to Mage Starr, your pendants will lead you to Callyn-Rhe from there."

"Easy enough," said Airron.

"No, Airron, it will not be easy," Galen whispered. "Come closer. There are several things I need to caution you about." When they gathered around him once again, the Mage said, "First, your presence will not be welcome as you journey across the island. The people of Massa are very leery of shifters and even other races for that matter. Free travel between lands is very infrequent, so there is no telling how they may react. You must do whatever you have to do to protect yourselves and your mission."

The shifters nodded.

"Second, even with the map, Callyn-Rhe will be difficult to reach. That you all survived the destruction of Pyraan is the only miracle we can count on in the days ahead. Your ingenuity and strength are what will enable you to prevail."

He paused to catch his breath. Kiernan thought he was going to launch into another choking fit, but a servant rushed over to give him water and he gulped it greedily. "Third, there is quite a bit of prophecy written about this time, but one concerns me more than the others and specifically relates to the quest for Callyn-Rhe." Galen glanced surreptitiously at the King. "It reveals the fate of the seekers of the power."

"Go on," pressed Beck.

"The foretelling claims that during the journey one will be betrayed, one will be lost, one will be gravely injured and one...will die."

The room went completely silent.

Her father recovered first, stalking over to Galen, eyes blazing. "If you were not already dying, Starr, I would kill you myself!" With that, he stormed from the room.

"I truly am sorry," the Mage said, looking even more fragile after the King's avowal. He looked at each of them with watery eyes. "I did not think it was wise to hide the truth from you. Do you still accept this undertaking? Even after hearing those prophetic words?"

Kiernan felt like her knees were about to buckle, but she resisted the urge to reach out and cling to Beck. It was unthinkable to imagine a life without one of her friends in it. Without Beck in it. It could even be her life that was to be forfeit. Even so, she didn't have to consult with the others when she said, "As you know, Mage, we have no choice. Your blood oath demands that we continue if there is any hope to save the people of this island."

Galen nodded as though expecting those very words. "If you will all excuse me, I would like a few words alone with young Beck."

***

As everyone began to file out of the room, Rogan stepped over to the sofa. "Pardon, Mage, for the interruption, but I was wondering what you can tell me of my parents."

Galen coughed. "I wish I could give you what you seek, fireshifter, but the truth is I never knew them."

Beck patted Rogan lightly on the back and watched the dejected Dwarf nod his thanks to Galen and walk out.

"Why did you just lie to him?" Beck asked when the door closed behind his friend. Ever since Beck had known him, Rogan had been desperate to find out the truth about his family. And, just as long, Beck had always secretly worried that the truth would never live up to the fantasies Rogan had conjured over the years.

Animation crept into the newly wrinkled face. "Very perceptive, I am impressed."

"Can you answer the question?" Beck persisted, knowing through pure instinct that the Mage was holding information back.

Galen shrugged his thin shoulders. "He already knows the truth. The loss of his parents was a very traumatic event for him, so he has blocked it out of his mind. He will remember when he is ready."

Galen began to wheeze, and Beck knelt beside the sofa. "Can I get you more water?"

"No, I am fine." With trembling hands, he reached under the blanket and produced a book that he held out to Beck.

"What is this?"

"A very valuable item. It is called the Protetor and it protects within its bindings the only written record of Mage teachings. It is bespelled and only you can read its contents. Anyone else who opens the book will see only blank pages. Guard it well, Beck, it is a powerful magical tool and one that is essential to your quest. The Protetor contains every spell, charm, incantation, and curse known to me. It is all yours. The people of Massa need the wisdom of a Mage to guide them."

Beck hesitated, knowing that it wasn't just the book itself that he was being coerced into accepting. It was the string attached—that Beck use the knowledge contained within to become a Mage. He shuddered at the thought.

Feeling like he had no other choice, he took the book from the pale outstretched fingers and examined the exterior. It was small, black and non-descript, with no writing on the front or spine. He looked at the Mage in confusion. "Why me?"

Beck noticed a glint flare in Galen's eyes. "Because you are my great, great..." The Mage paused. "Too many greats to list...grandson."

For some reason, Beck didn't question the legitimacy of Galen's revelation. "On my mother's side or my father's side?"

"Mother. You are both direct descendants of the Starr lineage."

Beck thought back to the discussion he had with his mother before Ravener's destruction of Pyraan. Whatever her reasons for not telling him then of his ancestry, Beck did not hold it against her. She did what she did out of love for him and nothing else. "Is that why I have been named *Savitar*? Because I am your descendent?"

"Yes. Just like Kiernan, you are pureblood."

"What of the others?"

Galen's voice grew softer. "All of the new *Savitars* are descendants of the original *Savitars*. The power of the blood oath runs deeper in you four than in any other shifter. Your strength comes from your patrician blood. Kiernan is a descendant of Garret Kenley. Rogan from Regan Rojin, and Airron from his mother's side through Arias Sarphia. Garret, Regan and Arias were at my side in the defeat of Adrian Ravener. Sadly, they did not survive the encounter. Our progeny will have the unfortunate honor to rid this land of him once again."

Beck twirled the small book in his hand, contemplating all that he had heard. "I can't take this, Mage."

"You must, Beck! You must also promise that you will carry the Protetor with you until this is over." A long-fingered hand reached out to grab him with surprising strength. "Promise me!"

"But, I will never be a Mage. I am a shifter. It's who I am."

"Learn from my mistakes, Beck!" implored the dying man. "Take the knowledge from this book and start over. Create a world where magic is to be used for good again. A world where shifters can come out of hiding!"

"I...I don't know if I'm strong enough," he admitted.

"You must be," he said once again, and Beck had to lean in close to hear his next words. "You are the only one who is."

The Mage produced one last weak cough and then his head slumped to the side. After six hundred years of walking the earth, Galen Starr was dead.

A pitiful roar rose up from outside of Galen's rooms. Beck scrambled to his feet and ran out into the corridor, shoving the Protetor into his pocket as he went. Looking around wildly, he saw Kiernan kneeling on the floor with her arms around Bajan's neck. The Draca was lying still, a line of blood trailing from his nose and staining his beautiful white coat.

***

The Cyman Army was just bedding down for the evening when Lucin heard a deafening scream from Adrian Ravener's tent. He rushed in and found the Mage lying on the floor with a manic smile on his face and blood trickling from his nose.

"It is done, Lucin. The portals are now open."

CHAPTER 19

CAPTURED INNOCENCE

The laughter of the two young Elves as they frolicked through the woods was so pure and ethereal it defied description. The delicate lilt of their voices evoked sensations of sheer ecstasy.

Anyone listening to them would have known that they were of the Elven race. Anyone watching them would have known that they were in love.

The male affectionately grabbed for the girl, but she gracefully leapt out of his reach, her feet barely touching the ground as she flitted through the Du'Che Forest.

Several young deer ran alongside, keeping pace with the Elves, and rabbits and other small animals darted in and out of the brush, hopping beside them in delight. Not to be forsaken, bluebirds sang out and swooped down through the tree branches, joining in the merriment.

Face flushed with enjoyment, the girl stopped and whistled. She held a thin hand out high and one of the birds alighted on her finger. She spoke softly to it, a mischievous glint sparkling in her violet eyes. The bird rose in the air and dove at the head of the Elven boy. His laughter rang out as he ducked and took off running, this time the girl in pursuit of him.

Suddenly, the boy froze in place, his hand held up in caution. He made a quick hand signal to the girl so she would understand not to talk. The two melted into the forest background as silently as a breeze drifting through the trees. The boy stopped and pointed through a gap in the woods, and the female's eyes widened in shock. The space beyond the trees undulated strangely as though underwater. And, in that wavering landscape was a large hole that gave the impression that a circular rent had been torn into the fabric of the world, revealing a new universe beyond.

Despite a warning hiss from her companion, the girl moved closer and reached out to touch the rippling backdrop. Her hand recoiled. *It pulses with evil!* she signed to him and motioned him forward. Together, they peeked through the hole and received their first glimpse of the Cyman Army passing through the Sandori Sands in northern Haventhal.

Who are they?

A better question is what *are they?* he replied, fingers moving fast.

She nodded and shuddered. *Look at their single eye! They look like ogres. They are traveling beyond our sight, but how?*

Magic.

Do you think they mean us harm? she asked innocently.

I know they do. Let us go and tell our fathers. They will know what to do.

The youngsters turned to flee and two huge hands reached out of the trees and grabbed each Elf by the upper arm. The female let out a scream, and the tall, monstrous soldier who held her hit her across the mouth to silence her. "Quiet!"

The boy struggled against his captor with murder in his translucent eyes. Quickly realizing it was futile, he stilled and signed to his companion. *Do as they say, and let them think we are submissive. We will find a way to get free. They are big and clumsy.*

But, how did we not hear their approach, Falcon?

I told you, magic.

"Arlan. I think they're talking to each other with their 'ands," said one of the soldiers.

"'Come on, let's tie 'em up."

"Wait!" shouted the girl as she wrestled her arm away.

I love you, Falcon, she signed quickly.

And, I you, Siole.

After the exchange, the soldiers made short work of binding their slight wrists.

"Look at their ears and silver 'air, Cyrus. They must be the Elves that Lucin was telling us about."

Cyrus stared at them intently. "What should we do?"

Arlan shrugged his shoulders. "We can't let 'em go. Lucin said that 'e wanted to avoid conflict with the Elves until the timing was right, but these two will go back and tell others."

Cyrus shook his head. "You know what will 'appen if we bring 'em to the Mage."

It wasn't a question.

Arlan sighed. "We 'ave no choice. When it comes to our purpose 'ere, it is Cymans first and Massans dead last."

Cyrus nodded and dragged the young female Elf through the breach in the shield and into the sand toward the army.

***

Kiernan awoke early the next morning and silently dressed in the damp, chill air. It was always cold in the palace in the early hours, she remembered, before the sun had time to infuse its warmth into the day. Bajan lay relaxed by her bed, but his eyes watched her every move as she packed her belongings and ran a comb hastily through her hair. After securing her scabbard and sword over her back and fastening her dagger on her thigh, she said, *Let's go.*

The castle was silent as she made her way along seldom-used passageways and exited through the servant's quarters. Gray skies and a light drizzle to match her mood greeted her and she pulled her mantle up over her head. *It's just as well. I would prefer not to be recognized as I travel.* After last night, she no longer considered herself the Princess of Iserlohn. *I'm a shifter with a job to do, and it's painfully obvious that my father feels the same way.*

With a heavy heart, she also made the decision not to bid farewell to Miss Belle or Larkin or any other of the royal staff. The wound was too raw for her to expose, even to those she loved most, and lengthy partings would have only intensified the pain.

Arriving at the stables, she went through the open doors and breathed in the nostalgic aroma of hay and horses. *I spent many wonderful years in this stable, but, I will never be back here. I will never again lay eyes on the beauty of Nysa or her people.* She wiped away an unexpected tear with the back of her hand.

Bajan startled her as he bumped up against her side to rub affectionately against her.

The King does love you.

Really? If that is how he shows love, I would hate to be his enemy.

He will come around to the irrationality of his beliefs.

She snorted. *I will not be around in the unlikely event that happens, Bajan. We are never coming home.*

Home is where your heart lies.

She smiled. *True. I leave a piece of it here, but the rest will always be with you and Beck and Airron and Rogan.*

Especially Beck.

She didn't deny it.

Turning from her friend, she walked over to the exquisite blue roan mare that she would ride south to Iserport. Her name was Milan and one of her father's prized mounts from King Jerund J'El's personal stables. *A final gift from a long-suffering father to his wayward daughter*, she thought bitterly. Well, she would take her. She would have need of a quick and intelligent horse beneath her.

The stable doors opened and Rogan, Airron and Rory walked in amid loud conversation and laughter. Rogan had questioned Rory about his whereabouts the previous evening, and the fireshifter confessed to feeling overwhelmed and slipping out of Grace Hall after the war council for a walk in the gardens.

Beck entered next, giving her a small, knowing smile that sent shivers through her body. Behind him were the two Scarlet Sabers that would accompany them on their journey. Gage Gregaros, a wiry, gray-haired man and Bret Schwan, younger at around twenty years, with a muscular build and short, blonde hair. Kiernan preferred to travel without an escort, but Colbie Nash insisted she accept the two Sabers as an extra safeguard.

She nodded to the men as she rechecked her backpack for their traveling papers. Since passage between lands was restricted, they would all need to rely on the King's Decree of Purpose to avoid difficulties.

It was disconcerting to her how the countries operated independently of each other with very little trade or creative exchanges. The three Kings rarely met, thus allowing the isolation and racism to grow more pervasive every year. Regardless of the reasons, it was a state of affairs that needed to be rectified—especially now that a common enemy had emerged.

Kiernan mounted and led their party of eight out of the stables and through the deserted streets of Nysa. Kiernan heard Rory ask Beck how long it would be before they arrived in Iserport. She smiled at the little fireshifter who seemed to have matured so much in the past week. He had considerably more confidence today than the nervous boy she had met for the first time at the Homage Festival. It wasn't surprising considering the horrors they had lived through. *The Highworld knows I feel older than my years.*

"We should reach Janis in two days and Iserport in another three."

At the tall iron outer gates, running hoof beats sounded on the road behind. Kiernan turned and watched Colbie Nash race toward them, his crisp, dignified black and scarlet uniform contrasting with his tousled hair and red-cheeked, youthful features.

He looks like an angel.

Colbie reined in and gazed at her for a long moment, but then addressed Beck. "I hold you personally responsible for her safe return."

Beck nodded. "As does the King."

He glanced at her again, but cautiously this time as if not sure how she would react to his next statement. "I plan to fight you for her, you know," he said, turning back to Beck.

Beck shrugged. "Can't say as I blame you, Captain."

Colbie lifted an eyebrow. "You're not concerned?"

"No."

"Maybe you underestimate me."

Beck shook his head. "On the contrary. I think you're an honorable man and one who Kiernan holds in very high esteem. In any other circumstance, you would be a very worthy opponent."

"But in this?" he inquired.

"It has already been decided. She is mine."

The young captain looked carefully from Beck to her, and whatever he saw in their eyes must have convinced him. He danced his horse close to Beck and Chasin and held out his hand. "Take care of her."

Beck shook Colbie's hand and nodded. "My life on it."

Without a backward glance, the captain spun his mount and disappeared back along the quiet city streets of Nysa.

Beck looked at her, waiting for her silent confirmation. She had to admit to being a bit put off by the verbal contest between the two men. She was no mindless git after all who expected the men in her life to speak for her. But, in this instance, Beck was right. It was already decided.

She tilted her head in approval and guided Milan through the gate.

Once outside of the city, Gage Gregaros took the lead at the head of the group with Airron and Rogan next, Beck, Kiernan and Rory in the middle, and Bret Schwan bringing up the rear. Bajan sprinted ahead and turned west into the forest to feed. Luckily, he recovered fully from his episode the evening before. The Draca told her that he didn't remember much about the event, only a blinding pain that exploded in his head and sent a strange ripple throughout his body.

Of course, it hadn't escaped the notice of any of them that it occurred at the exact same moment that Galen Starr had died. But, what it could mean, they hadn't a clue.

CHAPTER 20

THE WRATH OF A PRINCESS

Two days later, the outline of the town of Janis came into view in the distance. Beck wiped his brow. The rain had cleared after the first day of their departure from Nysa, and the sun had beat relentlessly down on them from a cloudless sky ever since.

Riding warily toward the open gates, he hoped for nothing more than a trouble-free stay and a good night's rest on something softer than dirt.

Two guards patrolling a raised walkway above the entry eyed them as they passed through but made no attempt to stop or question them.

Inside the walled town, a number of shops, an inn, tavern and church lined the main road. Small, well-kept homes dotted the side streets where children played in the yards, running in and around lines of laundry flapping in the light breeze.

Beck stopped in front of one of the larger buildings that declared the establishment within to be The Lantern Inn.

Gage Gregaros dismounted and offered to go in and secure rooms for the evening. As the Saber stepped up onto the wooden platform that encircled the town's establishments, Beck frowned at a disturbing noise. The sound of flesh striking flesh and then a woman's cry came from the alleyway between the inn and a merchant's shop. Dismounting, he tied Chasin to a post and walked around the corner.

A heavy-set, bearded man, sweating with exertion, stood over the top of a woman on the ground, her arms held up in front of her face to ward off the man's fists. She appeared to be middle-aged, her disheveled hair falling free of the chignon she wore at the nape of her neck. The fading remnants of an older bruise yellowed her cheek.

The man didn't see Beck approach from behind and was poised to throw another punch at the woman when Beck reached out and stopped the man's fist in his own, just inches from her face.

"What the...?" The man twisted around to look at Beck in surprise.

The woman scurried away, whimpering.

"What are you doing, man?" Beck demanded.

"None of your business," he spat, trying to yank his arm free.

Beck watched Kiernan hurry over to the woman and usher her out of the alleyway holding onto her shoulders for support.

"This is between me and her, now get lost," the bearded man growled, still trying to pull his fist loose.

Beck held on tight. "It's a very small man who would beat a woman."

The abuser's face screwed up in anger, and Beck could smell ale on his breath. "Yeah, well, she oughta learn to obey a little bit better."

Beck glared at the man in disgust and walked out of the alleyway still holding the man's fist. The woman beater didn't have any choice but to stumble behind his long strides.

Beck shoved the man into the street. "Now, get out of here before I lose my temper."

People walking along stopped to stare.

The door of the tavern across the street banged open and two men stalked out, eyeing Beck as they approached. "What's going on, Sully?" one of them asked.

Sully got back to his feet. "A bunch of strangers sticking their noses where they don't belong, that's what's going on."

"Need help?" the other man asked, spitting tobacco juice onto the road through a gap in his teeth.

Sully looked from Beck to Bret and Rory, and then Airron and Rogan, who were standing idly by—Rogan with his arms crossed at his chest and Airron leaning against one of the horse posts casually chewing a piece of grass.

"Well, well, if it ain't a Dwarf and an Elf. I shoulda known there was something off about you people. We don't take to your kind around here."

"Do you take to my kind?" Beck asked and waved a hand in the air. A small tree next to the wooden platform in front of Sully responded to his summons, and its thin branches shot forth and wrapped around the man's wrists, wrenching them high above his head.

Sully shrieked in surprise and struggled as the branches pulled him upright to the top of his toes. Sully's two friends backed away, one narrowing his eyes suspiciously at Beck. "Look at his neck!" he said, pointing. "He's one of them shifters that are supposed to be banished up north!"

The bystanders in the street scattered like leaves in a strong wind.

Heavy footsteps on the planks behind Beck caused him to turn. One of the largest men he had ever seen in his life was standing on the platform, glowering. Beck assumed he was the Lantern's innkeeper by the apron tied around his generous waist. "Go on home, Sully. I'll take care of Cara, and these folks here."

Beck let his magic go and Sully rubbed at his wrists when the tree branches snapped back into place.

The innkeeper gestured with his head to Beck and the others. "Get inside."

"Come on now, Jase! You're gonna let these people stay here after how they just treated me? I've got my pride, you know!"

Jase stared down at the despicable man. "A man who has pride in himself does not beat his wife, Sully."

"It ain't the end of this, Jase," Sully yelled, backing away from the inn.

The large man simply shook his head and disappeared back into his establishment.

Beck followed behind.

Several people seated at tables in the dining area looked up as they entered, but resumed their conversations when it looked as though the trouble had passed.

Beck held out his hand. "Thank you, Jase."

The innkeeper waved an enormous hand. "Bah! It's high time someone stood up to that bloody coward. Most people around here would rather turn a blind eye than take him on."

"So, why did you?"

"Two reasons. One, I'm ashamed that it took strangers coming to my town to oblige me into doing the right thing by one of our own. Two," he said, turning to Kiernan and settling his large frame down to the floor on one knee, "if you are traveling with the Princess of Iserlohn, it is my honor to serve."

Kiernan shook her head. "But how...?"

"Your eyes, Your Grace. I haven't seen you since you were a little girl, but those are eyes that once you've seen 'em, you never forget 'em."

Chairs scraped back as the diners in the inn hastily knelt.

"Please rise," Kiernan said clearly so that all could hear.

When the big man stood, Beck said, "We appreciate your kindness. If there is anything we can do to repay you, please tell me."

Jase tilted his head. "That thing you did with the tree. Are you one of them earthshifters?"

"Yes, I am."

"Well, my water well out back has pretty much dried up and I've been digging for over a week now with no luck. My back is not what it used to be," he admitted, rubbing it tenderly. "Do you think you can remove some dirt for me and find a spring for a new well?"

Beck nodded. "Sure. I'll do it right now."

"Are you sure it's no trouble?"

"No trouble at all," Beck assured him.

Jase clapped Beck on the back. "You know, Iserlohn sure could do with more shifters around. Think about all of the good you could do for people!"

Beck smiled. "I wish everyone felt the way you do, Jase."

"If you don't mind my asking, what about your exile? Are the shifters free?"

They had decided before the trip not to mention the invasion to the citizens of Massa if they could avoid it. They didn't want to cause undue panic before the Kings could rightfully call their arms to bear and address their people as they saw fit.

"I hope so, Jase. I really hope so."

***

A muffled noise sent Kiernan springing upright in her bed at The Lantern Inn.

Something is wrong.

She quickly swung her legs to the side, slid into her sandals and began to lace them, listening intently for the sound to repeat itself so she could identify the source.

Her head whipped up. *There it is!* It sounded like a woman's cry.

Cara!

Kiernan had been up half of the night with the woman trying to instill some confidence into her. Before Cara retired to her own room, she assured Kiernan that she was feeling stronger and that Kiernan's words had emboldened her to stand up to her husband.

Kiernan raced to the window of her room and looked out. Standing in the street in front of the inn was Cara's husband, Sully, with two of his cronies, and they were lifting a struggling Cara onto one of their horses. Before Kiernan could so much as shout for help, the four were mounted and tearing down the street toward the outer gates.

With a curse, Kiernan slapped her scabbard over her shoulder, checked to see that her dagger was still in place on her thigh, and sprinted from the room. She took the stairs two at a time, leaping past the last four rungs at the bottom. Landing smoothly, she pushed outside into the night and headed for the inn's stables at a dead run.

She skidded to a stop in the hay outside of Milan's stall and hastily bridled the mare. Without taking the time to saddle her, she took a running jump onto a stool and flew at the animal's back. The unexpected maneuver startled Milan, but she allowed it, familiar now with Kiernan's scent.

"Git!" she screamed, grabbing the reins and nudging Milan roughly with her knees. The horse needed no further encouragement to run as she tore out of the stable doors and raced out onto the street. Kiernan's only concern as the buildings flashed by was reaching Cara and seeing her safely away from Sully.

The wooden doors were just banging shut behind the three kidnappers as Kiernan bore down on them.

"Open the gates!" she yelled.

A man dressed in dark clothes on top of the walkway over the entry swung a bow into her vision and loosed an arrow at her. She reached over her back for the hilt of her sword and drew it, contemptuously cutting the arrow out of the air.

With one hand, she reined in Milan, and the horse reared up before a lone night guardsman on the ground. Gritting her teeth, she peered through the wooden slats at the kicked up dust from the fleeing horses.

She brought the horse down and pointed her sword at the guardsman's throat. "Open the gates! Now!"

Kiernan could never have imagined the imposing figure she cut atop her elegant horse, eyes blazing with determination and her voice resonating with command.

A princess warrior in all her rage.

The guard cowered from her and quickly scurried to obey. She sheathed her sword and guided Milan through the widening aperture as soon as the horse was able to fit through and raced away into the night.

The kidnappers were leaving a conspicuous trail in their wake, and the capable Milan would be upon them in no time. Kiernan laid her torso flat over the horse to give the mare as much speed as possible.

A whisper of movement off to the side caught her notice. Bajan charged out of the forest to the west and was soon keeping pace beside Milan, sinew and muscle rippling powerfully with feline grace as he ran.

Up ahead, two of the kidnappers peeled away and sped off in different directions while Sully slowed his horse. He had to know that she would catch up with him eventually. Still, it unnerved her that the others were getting away.

When he came to a stop, he dismounted and dragged Cara down with him, holding a knife to her throat.

It took all of Kiernan's skill to stop the racehorse, who wanted to continue on with their spontaneous sprint.

She drew her sword and swung down. "Let her go," she ordered Sully, with Bajan backing up her command with a heart-stopping, savage growl.

Cara struggled against Sully, but he held her tight to him, using her body as a shield.

Kiernan's eyes turned black.

Leave him to me, Bajan. I don't want the woman hurt.

Just one bite.

No.

As you wish.

Kiernan strode closer to Sully and Cara in a non-aggressive stance with her sword still in her hand but held away from her body toward the ground.

"Are you all right, Cara?"

"Never mind, witch!" Sully snapped. "Now get back from me or I'll kill her right now." To prove his resolve, Sully jabbed Cara with the knifepoint, and she cried out as a bead of blood blossomed on her neck under her chin. Cara turned to look at Sully with heat in her eyes. Turning her body to the side, she surprised Kiernan and Sully both when she wrenched her arm back and rammed her elbow hard into his abdomen. He loosened his grip on her just enough that she managed to escape his grasp.

"Run!" Kiernan shouted.

With his buffer suddenly gone, Sully dropped the knife in his hand and unsheathed his sword. Kiernan growled and closed with him. The two exchanged blows, sparks flying when metal collided. Kiernan easily parried Sully's thrusts and tried to establish a link so she could mindshift him, but the crafty criminal somehow closed his mind to her. *How is that possible?* No matter how many times she tried to open a pathway, her shifting was turned away.

Tiring of the dance, she slashed out at his neck and a fountain of blood spurted from the gash. Bellowing in rage, Sully made a clumsy lunge at her and, using his own forward momentum, she grabbed his beefy wrist in her hand and spun him to the ground.

"I don't want to kill you," she said over the top of him, "but I will if you ever go near your wife again."

Sully sat up and spat at her, pressing a hand to his neck wound.

Behind her, Kiernan heard a yelp. She twisted around and saw Bajan yanked harshly backwards to the ground by a rope twisted around his neck. Sully's cohorts had looped a noose over Bajan's head and were pulling the rope tight in opposite directions. The Draca Cat hissed and clawed in pain as he tried to break free of the tightening deathtrap.

Snarling in fury, Kiernan whipped her dagger free of its sheathe and in one smooth movement, hurled it underhanded in the direction of one of Bajan's captors. The dagger embedded itself in the man's chest just as Sully hit her from behind.

She went sprawling in the dirt, and the brute jumped on her with his sweating bulk and punched her in the jaw. "Not so high and mighty now, are ya?" he sneered, sitting astride her to pin her arms to the ground with his knees.

She thrashed under him, but the man was easily more than twice her weight. She could hear Bajan struggling to breathe and she cried out in rage and frustration. *Demon's breath!* Even with one of the men dead, Bajan was too weak now to save himself. They were both going to die out here, and there was nothing she could do to help either one of them.

Sully lifted his sword, the point hovering directly over her breastbone. "Like I said before, we don't take to your kind around here. Enjoy the Netherworld, shifter!" Before he could begin his downward thrust, a primal screech rang out and Cara buried Sully's own knife in his temple.

Sully started to slump over and Kiernan helped him on his way with a violent push. She scrambled out from under him and turned toward Bajan. The Draca hacked coarsely on the ground, but Sully's accomplice had already let the rope drop from his fingers.

"What happened?" the man asked, looking around at his surroundings in a befuddled manner.

Kiernan glared at him until the realization became clear. This man had been mindshifted! And, the link had abruptly ended when Sully had been killed. That was how Sully had been able to convince the citizens of Janis to ignore his abuse of Cara. He must have been methodically planting thoughts and lies in enough people that the rest were too scared to stand up to him.

First a bodyshifter in Nysa and now a mindshifter here in Janis? What is going on?

Kiernan bent down to retrieve her sword. "Get out of here," she commanded the man. After seeing his two friends dead on the ground, he didn't have to be told twice. He took off at a sprint back toward town, not remembering he had a horse hidden somewhere in the darkness.

She went to Bajan, but he was already sitting up. *Are you all right?*

He nodded his big head. *It is I who must thank you for my life this time.*

Trouble follows us, my friend. I don't think it will be the last fight we will have in the coming days.

No.

I will see you shortly, she told him with a parting hug.

When Bajan left, she removed her dagger from the chest of the man she killed, wiping the blood away on his cloak before sheathing it. *This is the second man I've killed. First Teag and now this one. I did what was necessary to protect the lives of Cara and Bajan, but the Highworld knows, I don't have to like it.*

She would tell Jase what happened when she returned to town so the bodies could be retrieved and their actions reported to their liege lord or lady.

Cara approached and knelt in front of her. "Thank you, Your Grace, but you shouldn't have risked your life coming after me! Yours is so much more important than mine."

Kiernan sighed tiredly. "All life is equally important, Cara. Let's go."

She mounted Milan while Cara climbed on Sully's horse. Together, they rode silently back to Janis in the pre-dawn light.

After parting from Cara in front of the inn, Kiernan stabled Milan before heading to her own room on the second floor, anxious for bed. Just as she put her hand on the handle of the door, Beck came out in the hallway, stretching languidly. "It's about time, sleepyhead. I knocked earlier, but you weren't awake yet. Come on, now, you can't loll around all day. It's time to leave."

CHAPTER 21

ISERPORT

Late in the afternoon on the third day after leaving Janis behind, Beck looked down from a small hummock at the city of Iserport sprawled up against Lake Traverse.

Wavering in the heat of the sunlight like a mirage, Iserport's gray mass appeared dingy and unwelcoming, considerably disparate to the city of Nysa, and even to Janis. Noticeably more populated, the inhabitants looked worn and ragged as they moved sluggishly through the streets in the heat among buildings squat and rundown. Surprising to Beck, Iserport was not walled, but spread out haphazardly around the lake.

Each land, Beck knew from studying Gage Gregaros's maps, had their own transportation port on the lake through which the movement of goods and people would be ideal if such passage was desired. It wasn't. According to the Scarlet Saber, the port cities were little more than military outposts, restricting the small number of ferries that utilized them.

Beck thought it absurd. Unlike animals, men had the ability to shape their own world and to seek out ways to better their lot in life. The people of Massa, with their old grudges, seemed determined to allow time to slip inexorably by without progress and let the world shape them into pale and colorless replicas of what could be. The lands should be flourishing with trade instead of hunkered down in segregation. He wondered why they didn't see this. Were the blinders that tight? The resentments that deep?

He glanced at Kiernan. In contrast, she looked so beautiful and full of life with her hair glittering in the sunlight and hanging down to her waist in golden waves. And, Jase the innkeeper had been right about her eyes. They were unique not only in their color, but in the compassion and spirit that dwelled there. *Whatever it takes, I have to keep her safe.*

More so than he had in Janis, anyway.

Kiernan had told him and the others after they left about Sully and his abduction of Cara. Beck shook his head as he recalled her modest shrug after he scolded her for tearing off alone into the dark after three men. He would have done the same thing, she insisted firmly, seeing absolutely no distinction between the two.

Gage Gregaros pulled him from his thoughts.

"We've been fortunate so far, Atlan, but it's important here, more than anywhere else, that we don't give anyone a chance to detain us. It could mean the end of our journey if the soldiers on patrol discover a shifter among them."

"We have our papers from the King," Beck pointed out.

"Yes, and they will probably, and I mean probably, help us in getting things sorted out eventually, but it would cost us valuable time. Better to be cautious and avoid discovery if we can."

Beck nodded and made sure his athame was covered. He instructed the others to do the same and asked Airron and Rogan to remain hooded. Not a pleasant experience in the heat, but necessary.

They wouldn't see Bajan again until Kiernan called to him to board the ferry to Deeport. The potential to attract unwanted attention was high enough with a Princess, Dwarf and Elf in their party without the addition of an enormous mythical Draca Cat.

"I'll take the lead," Gage said. "There's a small inn near the wharf where few questions are asked. A stable borders the property where we can leave the horses, but I must confess that I'm not optimistic that the animals will still be here if and when we return. We don't have a choice, though. The horses must stay behind."

A sharp pang of disappointment cut through Beck. He would be devastated to lose Chasin. The horse was one of his last tangible ties to Pyraan and the memories of his life there. He transferred both reins to one hand and patted the silky black neck with the other.

"Don't worry, old friend," he crooned. "I'll be back to find you when I return. I promise."

The party spurred their horses forward to follow Gage onto a thoroughfare in serious need of repair. Beck wrinkled his nose at the smells in the air as they picked their way through the muck—both refuse and human—that littered the streets.

Wagon drivers rumbled through the melee cursing and shouting at pedestrians in language rough enough to color the cheeks of most men Beck knew. The people didn't seem to notice or care as they pushed and shoved their way through the throng to reach their destinations.

The buildings, in crumbled neglect, were packed as tightly together as the people on the streets with very little space between establishments. Gage told Beck that the most lucrative occupations in Iserport were those that catered to the transient soldiers. Away from home and with little to do, the young men felt more at liberty to indulge in their more wanton desires, namely drink, gambling and women. Consequently, the taverns and brothels of Iserport did very well while other more legitimate businesses closed their doors. The more upstanding citizens of Iserport left if they were able and wallowed in poverty if they were not, leaving the dregs of society to run amok.

Beck wondered if King Maximus was aware of the destitution here. Did he ever even leave his safe, walled city?

Beck felt a tug on his pant leg.

"Do you have a copper penny, sir? Just a penny for some food?"

Beck looked down at a small, dirty-faced boy of about seven years. He was naked from the waist up, his bottom half clad only in a pair of ill-fitting trousers that he had clearly outgrown long ago. Sad, round eyes wrenched at Beck and he moved to retrieve a coin from his pouch.

Bret Schwan's hand lashed out and grabbed Beck's wrist in a steel grip. "Give that boy a coin and we will never make it to the docks," he whispered out of the side of his mouth.

Beck looked around cautiously and spied several hard-faced men lining a narrow alleyway across the street eyeing the scene with debauched interest.

"Sorry, boy, but we have no coin," Bret said loudly, shooing the youngster away. "Off you go now."

The incident disturbed Beck, but he trusted the Saber's instincts, and they were accosted no further as they continued to wind their way toward the wharf.

After what seemed like hours to Beck, the travel-weary party reached their destination, The Queen's Lair. To his relief, it looked in slightly better condition than most of the others they had passed.

The two Sabers went next door to coordinate the care of the animals with the stable owner and within a few moments returned with two young boys to retrieve the horses. "Make sure they get rubbed down good and fed well," Bret ordered sternly. The two boys nodded their heads impassively and went about their work, just one more chore in a day already full of them.

When Bret excused himself to arrange for their board with the innkeeper, Beck watched Kiernan approach the young grooms. She leaned down and whispered to them, and whatever she said caused their dirty faces to light up into the first genuine smiles Beck had seen since arriving in Iserport. When she returned, he asked her what she had said to them.

She shrugged. "I just told them that if the animals were still here when we returned, I would give them a florin."

"A gold florin!" exclaimed Beck. "That's more than they would ever see in a lifetime."

"I know, but I want my horse back!" she justified to him. "I couldn't bear to see either Milan or Chasin sold off or mistreated."

Beck was impressed that she thought to bribe the grooms, but was doubtful her plan would succeed. "What if the boys or the stable owner decides to sell them?"

She gave him a smug smile. "They won't. I told the boys to give me sixty days. If I don't return for the horses within that time, they are free to do with them as they will. They would never receive anything close to gold by selling them, so they promised to sleep in the stables with daggers across their laps until I return." Her green eyes were full of confidence. "Those boys will guard those horses with their lives."

A still hooded Airron sauntered over, head swiveling as he gaped at several heavily made-up young women entering a ramshackle brothel on the other side of the street. "I think I'm going to take a little look around. See the sights."

"No, Airron," Beck said.

The Elf laughed and patted his shoulder. "Relax, Beck, I won't be found out. You have my word."

"Not a good idea."

Airron grabbed Rogan's arm. "I'll take the big fireball with me."

Rogan snorted. "No thanks."

"Fine. I will take the little fireball instead," he said and walked away dragging a reluctant Rory behind.

Beck sighed as he watched them leave.

"You can't just let them go," Kiernan said, her steel-edged words laced with reproach.

Beck raised his eyebrows. "He doesn't need my approval, Kiernan. He makes his own decisions."

"And, if he gets noticed for being either an Elf or a shifter? What then? You heard what Gage said. We can ill afford to be waylaid here."

"Don't worry, Airron will be careful. He knows what we're about."

She stared at him, hands on her hips. "This is not a carefree excursion into the Grayan Forest, Beck. People are depending on us." She tilted her head. "Perhaps you would rather join Airron in his escapade? Is that it? Forget about all of this and have a little fun?"

He stared at her, astonished and hurt that she would say such a thing. "Why would you suddenly question my commitment? I am well aware of what is at stake and, more importantly, what has already been lost. I was there in Pyraan, Kiernan. Remember?"

"Yes, and that's why I'm surprised at your recklessness."

The comment stung. "I don't deserve that, Kiernan, and you know it. But, I'll go after Airron as you have so forcefully suggested. Go get some rest inside."

He walked away then, his already heavy shoulders hunched even further with the added weight of Kiernan's rebuke.

***

Hours later, Kiernan recalled those curved shoulders as she restlessly paced her room and mulled over her comments to Beck.

She still didn't understand what had caused her to doubt him like that. Especially, after all they had endured. After all *he* had endured with the loss of his parents. In the end, she could only attribute her behavior to her exhaustion from traveling and her argument with her father. It didn't matter the reasons. She would find Beck and make it right with him. Surely, he would understand after she explained herself.

A knock sounded outside of her door.

Beck!

She stumbled in her haste to the door, righted herself and threw it open.

It wasn't Beck, it was Rory.

"Rory! What are you doing here? Where's Beck?"

Rory slid his foot inside the threshold and pressed it up against the door. "Are you going to invite me in, Princess?"

She wasn't sure why, but she hesitated. "It's late, Rory. Just tell me if you know where Beck is."

"Let me in and I'll tell you."

Grudgingly, she opened the door for the young shifter. She smelled wine on him as he passed. "And, stop calling me Princess. What is wrong with you?"

He flopped on the bed with a giggle. "Sorry, Princess."

She gritted her teeth in annoyance. "Well?"

"Our dear Beck has decided that all duty and no fun can be very dull indeed. He is outside the doors to the inn at this very moment if you would care to see for yourself."

"See what? You're acting strangely, Rory. Is it the drink?"

He laughed. "No, no. I just thought you deserved to know that Beck has decided that one woman is simply not enough for him."

This boy is not making any sense. I'll just have to find out for myself what he's rambling about. Kiernan grabbed her cloak and sword and rushed out into the corridor and down the stairs. She didn't look at any of the patrons in the dining area as she stomped out the front door.

The streets were busy even at this late hour. Reluctantly, she pressed into the mass of people who in turn bumped and pushed at her rudely as she walked among them. *Where is he?* She craned her neck to see over the heads of the crowd, scanning each side of the street. *Decided that one woman is not enough?* She snorted dismissively and resolved to have Beck speak to Rory about his drinking.

Then, she saw him.

He was leaning against the stone wall of a brothel on the opposite side of The Queen's Lair with two young ladies pressed against him, trailing kisses down the length of him. He was smiling as he stroked the hair of one of the young women.

Kiernan stood there in stunned shock. It felt like someone had clamped a vise around her lungs and she couldn't get a breath. When she saw Beck throw his head back and moan in pleasure, she turned and fled. She slipped several times as she ran and her knees began to bleed freely.

"Hey!" screamed a woman on the street as Kiernan collided into her.

"Sorry," she mumbled, her surroundings blurry and indistinct through tear filled eyes. She didn't care. She just wanted to get away. Away from Beck, away from her father and away from this bloody quest.

To demon's hell with them all!

No destination in mind, she moved blindly through the crowd until it began to thin. Brazen young men made lewd comments to her as she passed, but she barely heard them.

Distantly, she became aware of footsteps close behind her.

Too close.

She turned to look and an arm whipped around her neck, spinning her hard against a soft body. Before she could react, the murmur of whispered words in her ear caused her vision to haze and the energy to seep away from her. She knew she should be fighting, but no matter how hard she tried, she couldn't move arms that suddenly felt like lead weights.

Why am I so weak?

Unexpectedly, she felt herself lifted off the ground. Her mind screamed out one last coherent thought before darkness swallowed her.

Bajan!

CHAPTER 22

LAND OF THE DWARVES

"Do you think we should wake him?" Beck heard Rory ask.

"He still looks a little green to me," Rogan replied, reaching down to lift one of his eyelids.

Beck growled and swatted Rogan's hand away clumsily. His head ached dreadfully. "What happened?" he croaked.

Rogan dragged a chair over to Beck's bedside. "You tell me. Do you know how hard it is to tear an amorous earthshifter from his intended quarry?"

Beck opened his eyes. "What? Speak some sense, man!"

"I found you in the street last night in the arms of two, shall we say, ladies of dubious honor. Were you drunk?" the Dwarf asked, sounding perplexed.

Rory snickered.

"Of course not!" He had no interest in other women or excessive drink. *So, why can't I remember what happened last night?*

Rogan leaned back in his chair and engaged in his favorite pastime coaxing three fireballs to life in his hands. "Forget about it. It happens," he said philosophically as he juggled.

Beck shook his head emphatically despite the shooting pain to his temples. "You don't understand..."

There was a knock on the door, and Rory went to answer it.

Beck groaned and lifted his head enough to see that Airron was in bed, snoring softly. Well, that was one less thing to worry about. The only concern on his mind now was talking to Kiernan and resolving their argument. He still didn't agree with what she'd said, but her frustration with him left an achy, hollow feeling in the pit of his stomach.

"It's Gage," announced Rory.

The Saber came into the room. "Good," he said looking around. "Most of you are here. I'll be going down to the docks to arrange our passage to Deeport this morning. It shouldn't take long, so make sure everyone is ready to leave within the hour."

When Gage left, Beck got out of bed, staggered to the basin and splashed cool water on his face. Feeling only slightly more human, he said, "Wake Airron. I'll go tell Kiernan."

Throwing a shirt over his head, he lurched out into the corridor. Two doors down, he knocked loudly and waited. There was no answer. After giving it a few more minutes, he left.

"Kiernan's not answering," he blurted as soon as he returned to the room.

Rogan shrugged. "Maybe she's downstairs already."

"No, I don't think so." Beck walked over to Airron now sitting on the side of his bed and combing his fingers through his long silver hair. "I need you to get in there, Airron."

"Kiernan's room?"

"Yes. I can't explain it, but I think something is wrong. I'm worried about her."

Airron stood up at once. "Enough said. I'll do it, but I better shift in here."

The air around Airron flickered with magic. It seemed as though the Elf had disappeared into thin air as his tall frame shrank down to the floor and his mouse appeared from under the pile of clothes.

Rogan growled in his chest at sight of his nemesis.

The mouse scurried from the room and Beck sat down to wait, exhaling deeply to ease the growing apprehension inside of him. Rogan was right there beside him, laying a comforting hand on his shoulder. "We'll find her, Beck. There are any number of places she could be, so don't borrow trouble. We've already bought enough of our own."

Beck nodded appreciatively to his friend.

Airron came back a few moments later and shifted. "She's not there, but as far as I could tell from my low vantage point, all of her belongings are still in the room."

"I suggest we go down to the dining room," Rogan said. "We can ask the innkeeper or some of the guests if they've seen her."

Not sure what else to do, Beck nodded and followed, but Kiernan wasn't downstairs and no one had seen her. He argued to his friends that they needed to split up and search the city streets for her and to his great relief they agreed.

Now, pushing once more out into the streets of Iserport, the smells and noise battered at his senses. After so many years of exile, he didn't think he could ever live in the proximity of so many people. He needed more land around him. He needed earth.

More than a head taller than most of the people around him, he surveyed every face, building and alleyway he passed. He spoke to the two young grooms whose names, he'd learned, were Seth and Tobias. They had not seen the pretty lady with the green eyes, as they referred to her, but promised to help look. Motivated, no doubt, by the promised gold florin.

Beck searched for an hour. There was simply no sign of Kiernan. He returned to The Queen's Lair despondent and grew even more so when the others reported the same negative results.

"What could have happened to her?" he asked aloud to no one in particular.

Airron's features were pained as he spoke up. "I regret being the one to voice it, Beck, but in my opinion Kiernan would never leave like this. Not voluntarily." The implication hung in the air between them. If not voluntarily, then someone had taken her against her will. His thoughts were naturally running in that direction as well—his heart just refused to catch up with them.

"I won't leave without her," he told them adamantly.

The door to the inn opened, and the Sabers walked in.

"Do you have the passes?" Beck asked.

"Yes, we have them," said Bret Schwan.

"Are they good for tomorrow as well?"

Bret said that they were, so the group agreed to continue the search for the missing Kiernan. But, they didn't find her that day or the next.

Beck was sick with worry. He couldn't eat or sleep and spent every waking moment pounding the streets, looking for any sign of her passage. It wasn't until dinner on their third night in Iserport that Rogan said quietly, "We have to continue on, Beck."

"I told you. I won't leave her."

"I know, but I need to retrieve my pendant and the Dwarves and Elves need to know the island has been invaded. Earthshine is less than five weeks away."

Earthshine. The phenomenon that happened once a year on the island where the sunlight held sway for twenty-four hours straight. Most Massans rejoiced during the event and celebrated with all manner of festivity and merriment. By choosing this occurrence as a demand for surrender, Adrian Ravener had turned this joyous occasion of light into something dark. Beck doubted that the Massans would ever look forward to Earthshine with the same zeal in the future.

If there is a future.

"What do you suggest?" he asked Rogan wearily.

Rogan stroked the bearded stubble on his chin as he considered. "While you stay here and continue to search for Kiernan, I'll travel ahead to Kondor to find my pendant and speak to King Rik, and Airron can travel to Sarphia to warn King Jerund. We'll all meet up again in Sarphia."

Rory looked annoyed. "And, me?"

Beck waved a hand at him dismissively. "You should go with Airron to Sarphia."

The fireshifter glowered. "I don't want to go to Sarphia. I'll stay here."

Beck thought about Kiernan's words that he was being too casual in his duty. "No, Rory!" he said harshly, standing abruptly and knocking his chair backwards. "You are to go with Airron to Haventhal. Do I make myself clear?"

He felt all of their eyes on him as Rory reluctantly nodded.

By the next morning, his friends were all gone, continuing on in their sworn duty. Beck felt the same pull, but fought it. When he had lost everything he had cared about in this world, Kiernan had been the one to see him through the pain. He wouldn't abandon her now. If he had to tear down this decrepit city brick by brick to find her, that's exactly what he'd do.

***

Luck was with Rogan when he boarded the ferry at Iserport with Gage Gregaros. The port soldiers gave King Maximus's Decree of Purpose a hard look, but ultimately permitted them passage. As they had hoped, the soldiers also had not recognized Gage as one of the Royal Guard, but it didn't stop the Saber from mumbling something under his breath about the whole lot needing a sturdy reminder of Iserlohn's chain of command.

It took the better part of the day for the ferry, under the power of long sweeping oars by four muscled oarsmen, to reach Deeport.

Beneath a clear blue sky and gentle rolling waves, Rogan looked out over the expanse of Lake Traverse at the homeland he'd left behind twelve years ago. Nicknamed the Land of Stone, the entire city had been carved out of the sandstone cliffs of southern Massa, and the Dwarves' penchant for and skill in architecture, sculpting and ceramics could be seen even from the distance.

A slat on the ferry creaked behind him, and he turned.

"How does she look, shifter?" Gage asked.

"Gorgeous," Rogan said in awe, looking back toward land, "simply gorgeous." Everywhere he looked, from the stone docks to the surrounding streets, he saw nothing but Dwarves. So many Dwarves! *Dear Highworld, it feels like home.*

When the ferry finally bumped up against the dock at port, Rogan resisted the uncharacteristic urge to jump up and click his heels in excitement. Instead, he bid a reserved farewell to the Saber, who would be returning to Iserport to help Beck in the search for Kiernan, and disembarked.

It suddenly occurred to him that for the first time in his life, he was on his own.

He'd grown so used to the presence of his friends by his side. How could he not? They had been his surrogate family for as long as he could remember. Even so, he was anxious for this time alone to probe Deepstone for answers to questions he had kept bottled inside for many years. Answers to the identity of his real family.

He intended to begin his search further south in the capital city of Kondor, but learned on the ferry ride that he would be unable to secure passage on the Koda River until the next morning, so he set about fincing an inn to spend the night.

In good spirits, he smiled widely and hefted his pack over his shoulder. Walking down the dock to the city streets below, he fervently hoped to receive the same warm welcome in Kondor that Kiernan had received in Nysa.

Unlike Iserport, the lakeside city of Deeport was very well kept. Industrious Dwarves everywhere swept streets, picked up trash or tended to stonework. Elaborate buildings rose up out of solid rock in a complex labyrinth of tunnels and channels with nary a blade of green grass or tree to be seen.

Rogan cheerfully strolled through the stone warrens nodding politely to the people he passed. The Dwarven males were all similar in appearance, stout of build and with beards of varying lengths and often decorated with an array of braids and beads. Curiously, almost all were armed with sword, axe or mace. Rogan had studied the customs of different races in the academy and he knew that, in addition to masonry and mining, the Dwarves were renowned for their metallurgy. The finest horses on the island might come from Haventhal, but the finest weaponry was crafted in Deepstone. And, for the most part, the weapons remained in Deepstone. Only the wealthiest of Massa's citizens could afford to import the heavily taxed product.

The females were thinner and softer than the males, although just as well armed with an assortment of ornate knives with gem-encrusted hilts.

No one paid him the slightest mind as he walked the streets. *Just another Dwarf among many*, he thought with pleasure, used to being in the minority, not one of the majority.

He eventually found an inn that looked reasonable and pushed his way into the dimly lit establishment. A small number of patrons sat at tables enjoying drinks and conversation.

Taking an empty seat at the bar, the height of the stool bowled him over. He had lived for so long in a world created for human men, that he was pleasantly surprised to see that all of the furniture in the inn had been created to fit the stature of Dwarves. Such a minor detail, but one that touched him deeply. Deepstone was a world made specifically for him and, in his memory, he had never had that before.

The barkeep, a bald fellow with an earring dangling from his left ear, walked over, wiping his hands on his apron. "Whatta ya have?"

"Wine." As the barkeep went about complying with the request, Rogan asked if any rooms were available. The man said he did, for a silver groat. Rogan thought the price a bit steep but nodded and handed over one of the coins that King Maximus had given to him. The barkeep put the coin between his teeth and bit down. Apparently satisfied, he pointed to the stairs in the back of the room and told Rogan to take the third room on the right.

Rogan offered his thanks and sat back to sip his wine in silence.

All at once, a shout of alarm cut into the quiet, and Rogan heard the sound of running footsteps outside of the inn. He toppled his stool as he jumped off and went through the door. Looking in the direction of the running Dwarves, he noticed acrid smoke spilling from the second floor of one of the residences across the street. A Dwarven woman hung out of a window in an attempt to breathe in fresh air around a stream of black smoke billowing out around her head. Citizens on the ground were waving to her and encouraging her to jump.

"I can't!" she screamed, shaking her head back and forth.

"We'll break your fall! Now jump!"

Still she refused, her white knuckles grasping the edge of the window in terror. She was so paralyzed with fear that she couldn't move even though her hair was starting to singe.

Rogan ran to the building. "Move!" he shouted to the bystanders. Without thinking of anything except saving the woman, he immediately threw his hands in the air and began weaving. Through his magic, he quickly discovered the origin of the fire—a taper that had fallen to the floor and caught the woman's carpet and draperies on fire. Moving his hands in an intricate pattern, he shifted and massaged the energy of the blaze into a long, sinuous fiery tube. Once contained, he ordered the woman to duck, which, miraculously, she managed to do. As soon as her head disappeared under the window sill, he wrenched his hands over his head and jerked them skyward, sending the flames shooting out of the open window. There were surprised gasps as the stream of fire rocketed into the sky and exploded into a shower of sparks that drifted harmlessly back down to earth.

Rogan turned to address the crowd to assure them that the danger had passed and was hit hard from the side and slammed to the ground. His arms were roughly pinned behind his back and three soldiers in the blue and maroon of Deepstone hauled him to his feet.

"Is he marked?"

Another tugged Rogan's shoulder mantle down, exposing his athame.

"Yes."

"Well, isn't that something," one of the soldiers with a long black beard and a scar down the side of his face said. "You are under arrest, shifter. I don't know what you're doing here or why you thought you could use magic, but it's going to cost you."

Rogan struggled against the soldiers. "I was saving a life! A few minutes more and that woman would have burned to death!"

The scarred soldier responded by clenching his hand into a fist and slamming it into Rogan's stomach.

Rogan grunted in pain and would have dropped down to the ground had the two other soldiers not been holding him up by his arms.

Blackbeard reached out and yanked him up by his hair. "We don't use magic to solve our problems in Deepstone," he hissed. "You can now go to Kondor to spend a nice long time in a cell to think about that. Then, I suspect the King will have you carted back to Pyraan where you belong."

The soldiers dragged Rogan away, passing the bald-headed innkeeper who had already taken his silver groat and was now standing by watching his capture impassively.

When they arrived at the wharf, the dockworkers noticed the soldiers' uniforms and, where there had been no passage previously, a skiff was made available to take them directly to Kondor. The soldiers hauled him on board the small boat and unceremoniously threw him into the bottom face down. Within moments, the skiff moved away from the dock and they were headed south down the Koda River.

Welcome home, thought Rogan.

Then, he started to laugh hysterically into the floorboards of the boat and, despite all effort, could not stop.

CHAPTER 23

LAND OF THE ELVES

Airron decided that the Elves of Massa were the most decorous race he had ever met. The dockworkers went about their tasks assiduously with very little engagement in conversation.

What few he encountered, anyway.

He was surprised to find that Havenport wasn't a city at all. Just a wharf with two wooden docks and a few merchant shops that butted up hard against the Puu Rainforest. The villages of Haventhal, he had been told, lay beyond the towering trees.

Airron gazed toward them wistfully. He had family somewhere within that forest, but he didn't know their names or how to find them. Maybe someday he might get the chance to search them out, but not today.

Without the comfort of an inn, Airron, Rory and Bret Schwan, were forced to spend their first night in Haventhal in their bedrolls outside of the rainforest. They decided to purchase supplies at one of the dockside shops in the morning and then Airron and Rory would continue their journey to Sarphia while Bret returned to Iserport.

Airron spent a fitful night at their makeshift camp, and was the first to wake the following morning. He set off for the wharf without waking the others, anxious to spend time talking to Elves for the first time in his life.

He lifted his hands to pull up his hood but stopped short, realizing with satisfaction that it was unnecessary. The combination of silver hair and violet eyes so unique in other parts of Massa would be unexceptional here.

A slight wind picked up as he made his way across the open grassy knoll between the docks and the Puu. All was quiet except the gentle sound of the waves lapping against the shore. He didn't see any of the Elves as he approached the road that fronted the shops. He tried a few doors and was surprised to find them all closed for business and locked up tight.

A muffled sound flowed to him on the breeze. *Singing?* Walking further down the road, he saw them then. All of the Havenport Elves were down by the lakeshore standing in a circle with joined hands. Their lips moved in unison to the words of a chant, the cadence in their upraised voices captivating, the lyrics poignant.

The grief that Airron carried around with him like a lead weight since the destruction of Pyraan seemed to lighten with each word. Sorrow was replaced with thoughts of joy as he watched the Elves gesticulate in prayer, their beautiful faces bathed in rapture, silver silken strands floating in the wind.

Suddenly feeling like an interloper intruding on a private ritual, he reluctantly backed away and returned to the docks to wait.

The Elves returned to their duties several moments later. One of the dockworkers that Airron had met the previous day approached him. His name was Loren and he walked with an elegantly powerful grace as though one with the earth and forest around him.

"*Asha*, brother," he said, clasping forearms with Airron in the traditional Elven welcome. "If you plan to stay in Haventhal, you cannot miss the Morning Song to Elán."

Red-faced, Airron admitted his ignorance of Elven customs. Loren explained that Elán of the Earth was the Elves' woodland deity and daily devotion at sunrise was expected of each and every Elf.

Airron smiled. "When my duty is over, brother, I will be back here so you can teach me all I need to know about being a proper Elf."

"It will be my pleasure."

Airron remained to chat with Loren and a few of the others for a time, and then purchased the items he needed for the trek on foot to Sarphia. Walking back to camp, he realized with a measure of contentment that he had gained more than supplies that morning— he had gained a friend in Loren.

When he returned, Rory was awake and sitting by the fire, quietly stroking the embers, but Bret was nowhere in sight.

"Where's the Saber?" Airron asked, letting his bulging backpack fall to the ground.

"Gone."

"What do you mean *gone*?"

"Left for Iserport. You must have missed him at the wharf."

Airron shrugged. "Looks like it's just you and me then, kid." He walked to the fire and kicked dirt over the smoldering cinders. "And, there's no time like the present. Let's go."

Airron led the way onto one of the narrow paths into the Puu. Ducking his head under the trailing vines and ferns hanging over the entrance, he winced at the sudden thick humidity that enveloped him. He expected the interior to be cooler in temperature similar to the Grayan Forest, but it was hot and sticky, and beads of sweat popped out on his brow.

His head swiveled in all directions as he walked, amazed at the plethora and size of the plant life in the Puu—palms, ferns, orchids, mosses, bamboo, and the forest giants, the ficus trees, that soared one hundred and fifty feet or more into the sky. The heavy foliage that encroached on both sides of the path restricted his visibility of what lay beyond and he silently prayed that a snake or jaguar native to the forest didn't drop down on his head.

Eventually, the trees began to thin and the first of Haventhal's villages appeared before him. Airron inhaled sharply and stopped to stare.

Winding paths twisted through a landscape of lily-filled ponds, colorful gardens and trees alive with twinkling lights—the source of which Airron could not even guess. Quaint cottages were sprinkled over the area, some on the ground, others built into the branches of the trees. Silver-haired Elven children flitted swiftly through the village on toes that barely touched the ground, the lovely sound of their laughter enchanting. The adults were busy laboring over one chore or another.

Loren explained to Airron that although the Elven people toiled during the daylight hours, they loved to sing and dance and give thanks to Elán at night. He assured a skeptical Airron with a twinkle in his purple eyes, that the Elves really did know how to have fun.

As profoundly moved as he was at seeing an Elven village for the first time, he felt an odd detachment to the people. In contrast to the humans and Dwarves he grew up with in Pyraan, he was light on his feet, but compared to the indigenous Elves of Haventhal, he felt clumsy and heavy. He didn't have anywhere near their wraithlike movements and swiftness.

"Are you going to stand there with a stupid grin on your face all day, Elf?" Rory asked, startling him.

He hadn't even realized he had been smiling, but it vanished quickly when two soldiers in uniformed tunics of green and brown suddenly emerged from the trees on either side of them, hands on the hilts of their swords. "*Asha*, good folk. It is not often that we get strangers to our village. May I ask your purpose?"

Airron nodded and took his pack off his back. "Of course, I have—"

"Slowly," said one of the soldiers, lifting his sword a fraction out of its scabbard. "Whatever you have in your pack, bring it out slowly."

Airron swallowed and reached in to retrieve King Maximus's decree and handed it to the Elf.

The soldier read it very carefully, continuing to eye Airron as he did. The document only disclosed that he was a messenger with an urgent communication for King Jerund. It did not mention the invasion; that was for the King's ears only.

"I am Gardien Leif Oliver and this is Gardien Raine Aubry of the Haventhal Army. Sarphia is a five-day journey along that path," he said pointing to a road that led further east into the Puu. "It seems your business is urgent. Would you like an escort?"

Airron shook his head. "Thank you for your kind offer, brother, but we don't wish to be a burden. We will be able to find our way."

Oliver nodded. "Very well. Safe travels to you." With that, the Gardiens disappeared, melting back into the forest walls.

"Come on," Airron said to Rory and guided him through the hard-working village and into the darkened forest beyond. After walking in silence for several moments, Airron turned to Rory. "It's dark here. Why don't you give us a little light to see by?"

Rory's shoulders stiffened. "I can see clearly enough."

"I guess you're right," Airron said. "We can do without. Not to mention that it would be impossible anyway."

Rory stopped in his tracks. "Pardon me?'

Airron smiled but his violet eyes narrowed dangerously. "You are no more a fireshifter than I and you know it."

Rory glared thoughtfully at him for a moment before throwing his head back in a disturbing laugh.

Airron recoiled as the red-cheeked innocence that was Rory Greeley morphed into a dark, sinister presence with hate in his eyes.

"Well, well, one of you *Savitars* has brains after all. What gave it away?"

"Many things. Who are you?" Airron's eyes never left the imposter as the air began to shimmer in the precursor of a bodyshifting, and a beautiful woman appeared in front of him.

Airron briefly mourned the death of the little fireshifter they had all thought miraculously survived the destruction of Pyraan, but then quickly put it behind him. He would need all of his concentration on the task at hand. The woman circled him, and he shadowed her path, eyes never leaving her face.

She tapped a finger on her chin. "It will be nice to have an Elven form as I travel through Haventhal," she murmured. "Of course, it would mean I have to kill you first."

Airron tensed his muscles as he prepared to fight. "You killed Bret Schwan, I presume."

"Of course. That is one body that will never be found."

His jaw clenched. "And, Titus?"

"My, my, clever little thing."

"Kiernan?" he demanded.

She glowered in frustration. "Unfortunately, no. The fool of a girl ran off before I could get her pendant. Adrian will be quite furious with me."

Airron's suspicions were now confirmed. Avalon Ravener stood before him and the knowledge was not comforting.

She stopped and faced him. "Enough of the questions. It is *your* death I am most concerned with now. After all, it will fulfill the second of the prophecies that the bothersome Mage blabbered about." She checked her fingernails. "Yes, I heard all about it standing on the balcony outside of the Mage's chambers."

"What do you mean by the second of the prophecies?"

"I have already betrayed the earthshifter by ensuring that the Princess caught him with two whores. Of course, neither knew that I bewitched the boy with a glamour spell, but that's besides the point."

Comprehension hit at that moment and a rush of terror-induced adrenaline coursed through him.

So, it was to be him.

He was the one to die.

Better me than any of the others, he told himself shakily. Even so, he didn't want it to happen. He enjoyed life too much.

He fixed the witch in a defiant stare. If she wanted his death, it would cost her.

"I guess I will have to satisfy myself with your pendant until I meet up with the Princess again. Toss it over." Avalon held out her hand, and Airron acted.

The air flickered as he shifted into a Meeko lizard, one of the most powerful and agile creatures on the island. A single bite from the reptile's powerful jaws could sever an arm. But, he was going for the throat.

The lizard scrambled forward, sharp claws digging into the dirt and leapt at the witch.

Avalon proved just as fast, her body contorting downward into the shape of a Puuvian goliath arachnid.

The lizard flew through the sudden empty space, tumbled over the ground and slammed up hard against the trunk of a ficus tree.

The oversized spider, at least two hands in length, raced after the fallen lizard, swarmed up its leg and sank pointed fangs into the soft tissue of its underbelly, injecting a fatal dose of venom into its bloodstream.

Demon's breath!

The spider's murderous task complete, it scuttled back to the road and shifted into the form of Avalon Ravener. Not satisfied, the witch picked up Rory's sword from the ground and stalked to the Meeko. She grunted with effort and swung with a two-handed chop meant to take the lizard's head off.

The Meeko managed to twist away in time and shifted into an eagle—the same eagle that saved the little Halfie child in the Balor Mountains a little more than two weeks ago.

The venom spreading quickly now, Airron found it difficult to maintain his magic.

The eagle flapped its enormous wings and reached out toward Avalon with sharp talons, raking viciously at her face.

She cried out in pain, three long welts on her cheek pebbling with blood. She slashed her sword at the bird, but it wheeled behind her and tore a chunk of flesh from her back with its beak.

With a harsh yell, Avalon exploded in size into a primate with a thick black body and muscular arms. The ape beat its chest once and then used human-like hands to grab the eagle out of the air and smash it to the ground with sickening force.

The eagle, dazed, attempted to lift off, but was heaved into the air a second time and slammed down to the earth.

The bird did not move again as it lay broken on the path, blood pooling beneath it in a small river. The air around the eagle flickered once, and the form reverted to Airron's battered Elven body.

Avalon limped over to him. "Like I said, *Savitar*, second prophecy fulfilled." She bent down and grasped his pendant, ripping it from his neck. After tucking the pendant away in her pack, she returned to him and put her hands on his head.

No!

Airron's mind desperately urged his ruined body to respond. To get up, to roll away, to lash out at Avalon before she turned him into a shrunken corpse like the guard in Nysa. But, it was no use. His body was beyond taking orders.

But, he could still register fading sights and sounds.

Avalon's sudden scream as she batted her hands around her head at what looked like a bird clawing at her scalp.

Running footsteps.

A curse.

The witch gathering her clothing from the ground and hastily retreating into the forest.

Then, he was alone. Alone and cold. *Dear Highworld, I can't remember ever feeling this cold!* His body convulsed and his teeth chattered uncontrollably. He wished he had a warm blanket to throw over his shoulders, or a nice burning fireplace to warm his hands or even a mug of Master Martyn's ale.

Wait. Master Martyn is dead, isn't he? They're all dead.

Airron smiled when he realized that he would not be alone for long. Where he was going, the shifters were sure to be waiting for him.

CHAPTER 24

THE SEARCH

It was the fifth day of Kiernan's disappearance, and Beck still had not uncovered a single clue as to her whereabouts. Thoughts of her haunted him. He lived a waking nightmare, not knowing if she was alive or dead, hurt or scared. He agreed with Airron's assertion that she hadn't left of her own volition since all of her belongings, with the exception of her sword, were still in her room.

She had simply vanished.

Beck stalked the streets like a man possessed and entered every tavern, inn and shop in Iserport, enquiring of everyone he met if they had seen a woman of Kiernan's description. He spoke to men in rough coats and even rougher faces enjoying a game of dice or cards. Soldiers, innkeepers, barmaids, citizens on the streets. Anyone he thought might have the answers he needed.

Pulling his cloak around his shoulders in the rain, he looked up at the sign dangling above the door of one of the seedier taverns he had yet to visit. *The Rearing Horse* it read, with an image of a stallion rearing up on hind legs under the faded script.

He pushed inside, wrinkling his nose at the thick pipe smoke. All of the tables were full, the raucous crowd slapping their knees in crude delight at a young serving girl dancing timidly on one of the tables.

"Do not be shy, lass! Show the good fellows a bit more leg!" yelled one of the patrons drunkenly. Color blossomed in the girl's face, but she did as she was told and lifted the bottom of her wide skirts to show off her calf.

Beck shook his head. The girl's eyes had a now-familiar desperate cast to them. No doubt, the coin she made at the tavern supported several members of her family. He had heard similar stories many times during his hunt for information.

He threaded his way to the bar easily enough. One glance at his bulk was enough to turn most men aside with ease. He ordered a mug of ale and leaned back on the bar with his elbows to study the clientele. Riffraff, mostly. There were no soldiers in sight or women except the barmaids. That was precisely why he was here. The innkeeper at the Queen's Lair advised him that if he was thinking that foul play had been involved in the disappearance of his friend, he should go to The Rearing Horse. That lot, he was told, would be aware of the undercurrent of all criminal activity in the city, whether they had a part in it or not. And, of course, coin and drink would loosen most tongues.

"Lass, if you do not show more leg, I will get off this chair and show it for you," came a shout from the same drunken man in a disheveled brown cloak.

The girl visibly blanched and held her skirts tight to her body. She couldn't have been more than fourteen or fifteen years.

Demon's breath.

Beck pushed away from the bar and strode to the front of the room. He held his hand out to the girl. "Get down."

She looked at him warily before placing her small hand in his. He helped her down and walked her to the front door. After reaching into his pocket, he pressed two silver coins into her hand. It was more than she could make in six months dancing at The Rearing Horse. "Take this," he told her, "and find another job."

Tears welled in her eyes as she looked up at him gratefully and attempted a clumsy curtsy. "Thank you, my lord," and she was off, running into the night like a frightened deer.

Beck turned away and went back to his ale at the bar.

"You!" someone screamed.

Beck turned slowly toward the voice. It was the man in the brown coat. Beck kept his face impassive, but now recognized him. He was one of the men who had come to the defense of the wife beater, Sully, in Janis. "Grab that man! He's a bloody shifter!"

Beck stood motionless as the murmurs of the men around him grew in intensity. One rough ran to the front door of the inn and threw the lock, and Beck noticed the barkeeper duck into the kitchens.

"Do I know you?" Beck asked casually.

"You bloody do know me, shifter," the man said, pointing at him. "You killed my friend, Sully!"

Beck shook his head. Kiernan told him everything that had happened that night. "Unfortunately, I did not have the pleasure. Sully's wife killed him."

Feet shifted uneasily, but the men held firm. They probably didn't know or care who Sully was, but they still had a shifter in their midst.

All was silent for a moment as the men sized him up and then with a roar, Sully's friend charged him.

Idiot.

Beck straightened and when the man was within an arm span from him, he reached out, grabbed him behind the head and slammed his face into the edge of the bar. The man crumpled to the floor.

Outraged bellows spewed forth and the rest of The Rearing Horse patrons swarmed over him. As he was driven to the floor, he kept his knees tucked under so he could use his legs as leverage. A fist hit him in the jaw on his way down. He twisted his body onto his back and kicked out sending three men crashing into the now vacated tables around the bar.

Another large hand licked out at him, this one holding a knife. Beck yanked his head back just enough to avoid a slicing cut. Turning again to protect his face, his back and ribs were pummeled by the string of men who managed to get close enough to his prone body.

Over the grunts and curses of his assailants, he heard the front doors crash open and saw through a gap in the legs surrounding him that it was Gage Gregaros with two Iserport soldiers.

The men scattered at sight of them, and Beck staggered to his feet, his jaw and ribs aching painfully.

"You all right?" Gage asked him, glancing down at Sully's friend, still out cold on the floor.

He nodded.

One of the patrons pointed at Beck. "Arrest that man! He's a shifter!"

A soldier who looked vaguely familiar stepped forward. "King's business," he told the patron forcefully. "Go back to your drink."

Before Beck could say a word, he was whisked out of the tavern like a pile of garbage for the midden heap.

His struggles were half-hearted. "Gage! I didn't learn anything yet!"

The Saber was furious. "What do you not understand about laying low, Atlan?"

Beck attempted a few more protests but they were ignored, and he was dumped in his room in The Queen's Lair with a command to stay put.

Reluctantly, he did as instructed and that evening, he broke down, lying alone in the dark with his torturous thoughts. Whenever he considered that he may never see Kiernan again, his heart raced uncontrollably with panic and he had to take long, deep breaths to calm his mind. He wanted so badly to hold her again. They had only just discovered their feelings for each other and it seemed so unfair that they not be given the chance to build a life together.

His stomach clenched as he imagined her in the hands of vicious and evil foes, berating himself ruthlessly for not shielding her from harm as he promised King Maximus and Captain Nash he would do. Kiernan had been right in all of her accusations. He was negligent and careless, and she was paying the price.

He couldn't help himself. He wept. He wept for the loss of his parents and home. His shifter friends. Titus. Galen Starr. But, mostly for Kiernan.

The following day, a maid knocked on his door twice, once to clean his room and once to deliver food. He sent her away both times without opening the door.

He spent another pain-filled night in his room, but with the rise of the sun on his seventh day in Iserport, he slowly climbed out of his depression. The light of the morning brought new hope to him, and he clawed for it, deciding he still had the will to fight. Still had faith that Kiernan would be found.

He rose from his bed, washed at the basin and went downstairs. He found Gage Gregaros in the dining room eating alone at a table.

Beck pulled out a chair and sat next to him. The Saber's mouth tightened when he saw him, but said nothing and continued to eat.

"I'm not going to apologize, Gage. I will do whatever I have to do to find Kiernan."

The Saber grunted.

Beck tried for safer territory. "Is Bret back?"

"No, but he should have been days ago. I've sent word to Captain Nash that he's missing."

Another one of our party missing. Could they be related?

Gage finally looked up from his plate. "We'll find her," he said, but the words no longer sounded as optimistic as Beck would have liked.

Despite Beck's exhaustion, the pair started out again, steering clear of The Rearing Horse. They searched long into the night without results, and it was well past midnight when Beck returned to his room and flopped down on the bed.

Still, sleep didn't come. His mind and heart raced in turmoil. It was apparent now that Kiernan had been kidnapped, but by who? Why? *Did her captors know that she was the Princess of Iserlohn? Or could it be that Adrian Ravener was involved?*

Beck jumped off his bed, went to the window and threw open the shutters to breathe in the pungent night air. A few people were still on the move outside of the inn.

A flash of motion suddenly caught his eye. He peered into the shadowy recesses of an alleyway across the street. That's when he saw the glow of green eyes.

Bajan!

Beck waited for the stragglers to pass by, whistled softly and stepped back. In a streak of white, the Draca Cat bounded across the road and leapt into the second-story window.

"Bajan, what are you doing here?" he asked, sticking his head out of the window to see if any bystander happened to witness the Draca Cat's jump into the building.

It looked clear, so he pulled back and shut the window.

Bajan paced the room, his nose to the ground.

"She's gone, Bajan."

A distressed whine sounded low in his throat.

"She needs our help. Do you think you can you track her?"

The Draca Cat gave him a look that suggested he was an idiot. His optimism flared. "Come on then."

Together they went out into the hallway. Beck didn't see anyone, but laughter drifted up from the dining area downstairs. He tried the door to Kiernan's room. Finding it still locked, he smashed his fist straight through the wood and reached in to open the door from the inside.

When he was sure no one had heard the splinter and crack of wood, he slipped inside.

Except for Kiernan's backpack and a few personal items on the table by the bed, the room was empty. Beck repacked her belongings and turned expectantly to Bajan. "Now, what do we do?"

Beck cringed when the cat sprinted out into the hallway and raced down the stairs.

A woman in the dining room screamed as soon as she saw Bajan, and chairs scraped back as people stumbled to get out of the Draca's way.

Indifferent to the reaction of his presence, Bajan scrambled through the diners and out into the night. Beck held up his hands. "It's all right! He is very friendly. Please! Don't be afraid."

Beck ran out of the inn to catch up and located Bajan standing at the far end of the street. He sprinted toward him. "Have you found anything?"

Bajan whined and circled the same location over and over. Beck could read the cat's frustration easily. Kiernan's trail ended right here in the middle of the street.

She had disappeared into thin air after all.

***

Kiernan slowly opened her eyes and regretted it when a sharp pain exploded inside her head. She shut them tight again to stop the throbbing, but it didn't work to alleviate her pain.

That one brief glimpse revealed to her that she wasn't in her room at The Queen's Lair, but in a room filled with white. White walls, white floor and a white coverlet thrown over her body.

She turned over and cradled her head in agony.

"I can help you," said a female voice from the corner of the room.

Kiernan flinched at the unexpected presence, but didn't lift her head. "Then, help," she croaked out.

The woman approached the bed, and Kiernan felt the movement of the mattress as it sank under her weight. "My name is Helenite, and I am a healer." The woman gently prodded Kiernan to turn over and pressed soft fingertips to her temples. Kiernan felt a strange tingle and her body stiffened in response.

"What...?"

"Quiet now, and let me finish here."

Helenite mumbled a few unfamiliar words over her, but all Kiernan cared about was that the pounding in her head seemed to be subsiding. When Helenite finally released her, Kiernan opened her eyes and sat up.

The healer sitting next to her was exquisite. She had lovely almond-shaped eyes and full red lips. She wore her long brown hair pulled back into a single braid. A pale green satin gown revealed a generous amount of bosom.

Kiernan self-consciously ran her fingers through her own tangled hair, feeling extremely dull and frumpy in the woman's presence. "Where am I?"

"The questions must wait until you are fully healed." Helenite rose from the bed to leave.

"Wait!" Kiernan said, grabbing the woman's arm. "How did I get here? Where are my friends?"

Helenite gave her an indulgent smile. "Everything will be made clear in time."

Kiernan started to get out of bed. "Yes, well, time is one thing that I don't have."

"Stop that, young lady," Helenite scolded, pushing her back down by her shoulders. "You have been unconscious for days, and your body needs to recover."

"Helenite, I beg of you. Just tell me where I am!"

"You are home, Princess."

She raised an eyebrow. "Home?"

"Yes, now close your eyes and rest. I'll be back for you shortly."

The last thing Kiernan wanted to do was sleep, but after another mumbled word by Helenite, she felt her eyes grow heavy.

When she awoke sometime later, she felt much stronger. From the bed, she again studied her surroundings. The furnishings were sparse, with a small table by her bedside holding a basin and pitcher and a wardrobe in the corner. She threw off the coverlet and the cool air that greeted her body told her she was quite naked. With cold pimples rising on her skin, she padded over to the wardrobe to see if her clothes were there.

She found only a single garment inside—a beautifully-draped, silk ivory gown. Kiernan fingered the luxurious material and gasped in surprise. It was identical to one that had been owned by her mother. Seeing the gown uncapped a well of emotion and the memory of that day.

Mother stood in front of her mirror twirling to get a view from every angle of the silk ivory gown she wore. "How do I look, Keke?"

"Lovely, Maman."

"Do you really think so?" her mother asked again, nervously biting her lower lip.

"Yes, Maman. Father always thinks you look beautiful."

At the mention of her father, her mother's face grew melancholic. "He is a great man, Keke, remember that always."

"I will."

Her mother caught her eyes in the reflection in the mirror and held them. "But, you must never discuss your magic with him."

"I won't, Maman. I'll never tell anyone. I want to stay here with you."

"I want you to stay with me, too, darling," she said with a smile and walked over to grasp Kiernan's hands. "And I promise, someday soon you will be wearing a beautiful gown like this and a young Prince will ride up and sweep you away!"

Her mother picked her up into the air and whirled her around the room as she giggled in delight.

But, it would never turn out as her mother had promised. Her Prince had discarded her and her mother was dead. End of tale.

A tear slipped from her eye. She hastily swept it away and slammed the wardrobe shut just as the door to her room opened.

It was Helenite.

The healer looked at Kiernan with a raised eyebrow. "As Princess, you are probably used to a handmaid, but we dress ourselves here."

Kiernan blushed. "No....no, I don't need help. I was just looking for my dress."

"It's being laundered. You can wear the one in the wardrobe. It is your size."

Kiernan opened the wardrobe door once again and stared at the gown wistfully for a moment. Finally, she removed the dress and stepped into it under the watchful eye of the reticent healer. She had to admit that the cool silk felt nice against her skin. The comfort of fresh clothes felt like an extravagance after so many days traveling.

Helenite nodded in approval. "Come," she said and walked out of the white room.

Kiernan followed behind.

The healer swayed seductively as she walked down the corridor, the green gown flowing attractively around her hips and legs. *Who is this woman?* There was no doubt in Kiernan's mind that Helenite was able to command some form of magic, but how was that possible? She had always been led to believe that the island of Massa outside of Pyraan was chaste of magic. *Yet there was the bodyshifter in Nysa, the mindshifter in Janis and now this mystical woman in front of me.*

Kiernan bit back her questions, realizing she would have to wait. Helenite said everything would be made clear. *But when?*

The hallway they traveled led to a four-story foyer with a marble fountain in the center depicting a figure of a laughing young woman capturing in her hands the water that gushed up from the basin below. Something about the fountain seemed familiar to Kiernan, but she couldn't imagine why that would be so.

Helenite skirted the fountain and crossed the large chamber to a set of double doors located to the right of a grand staircase. The woman held open the door and pressed her hand to the small of Kiernan's back to usher her inside. A loud voice boomed from the center of the room. "Welcome, Princess Kiernan!"

Applause rang out from every direction.

Kiernan flinched in shock and glanced hesitantly around a vast circular hall. Hundreds of people—all women, it appeared—stared down at her from balconies that edged four floors. Every woman present wore her hair in the same braided style as Helenite, and each gown was more exquisite than the next.

A petite figure stood alone in the middle of the room. "Come," she encouraged with her hands outstretched toward Kiernan. "My precious gem, you are home at last."

Kiernan looked back for Helenite, but the healer had disappeared. Annoyed with the lack of answers and feeling like she had no other choice, Kiernan strode toward the woman. "What is going on here? Why are you holding me prisoner?"

The woman appeared to be twenty years older than Helenite, a thick braid of graying hair lying over one shoulder. The diminutive figure nodded in greeting. "I am Gemini and these," she said loudly, her arms sweeping the room, "are more of my precious gems. Gems, let me introduce Princess Kiernan Grace Everard, the newest candidate for our coven!"

Coven?

Again, the women clapped enthusiastically.

Kiernan leaned in close to Gemini. "Look," she said in an urgent whisper, "I don't know how I came to be here, but I really must leave at once."

Gemini peered at her closely and then reached out to touch her face. "You look so much like your mother."

Kiernan drew back from the touch. "You knew my mother?"

"Yes, and I know you as well. You have been here before." Without giving Kiernan a chance to respond, the woman stepped around her and once again addressed the audience. "As you all know, my Gems, it typically takes months of careful study to determine a woman's stone. It is an intimate and personal bonding and many factors weigh into the decision before the appropriate placement can be made. A woman's personality, physicality, magical prowess and desire all play a key role in the selection."

Excited murmurs drifted through the hall.

"However, knowing what I do of Kiernan Everard, there can only be one suitable stone. I am pleased to pronounce that our newest Gem will train with...Citrine!"

A woman with red hair let out an animated shout, and the women around her offered their congratulations.

"Kiernan's Friend of the Coven Ceremony will be held at next month's gathering."

Kiernan glared at the older woman. "Now, wait just a minute—"

Gemini lifted her hands. "Thank you all for coming out to greet Kiernan. You may now go back to your duties."

Kiernan watched as the lovely mob dispersed.

Gemini reached for Kiernan's hand. "We have much to discuss. Let us now retire to my rooms for a private conversation. Are you hungry?"

Kiernan pulled her hand away. "No! I am not hungry." She tilted her neck to expose her athame. "There's been talk here that I won't even pretend to understand, but I'm a shifter and one way or another, I'm leaving this place. Now, step aside."

"No."

"No?"

"This is your home now, Princess, and the sooner you get used to that idea, the better it will be for you."

Kiernan distantly heard the murmur of Gemini's spell a moment before she hit the ground.

CHAPTER 25

DARK ARMY

Adrian Ravener paced his tent like a caged tiger, fed up with the heat and the endless leagues of sand that ended up everywhere—in his bedding, his clothes and even in his food. *If we don't get out of these accursed Sandori Sands soon, there will be hell to pay.*

How he longed to travel through the green woods and highlands of Haventhal again. They were so close—he could see the forest edge just south of where they traveled—yet so far. Strategically, he knew that it was necessary to travel through the Sands. The Cymans with their Desert Troll heritage were at home here and moved quickly and efficiently over the land. It would have been nigh impossible to travel through the Du'Che with fifty thousand soldiers. Even so, magically veiling an army of this size was wearing on his mood as much, if not more, than the sand.

The other advantage of traveling in the relative anonymity of the Sandori was the privacy it afforded him to test out his new powers. Galen Starr's death made the attempt possible now, and he silently thanked his old mentor for his long overdue demise.

Adrian glanced over at the young female Elf crouched in the corner of his tent. *She is a feisty little thing.* Even now, glaring at him with disdain from her lowly position on the floor.

He did learn something new about the Elves of Massa since two of his soldiers captured this female and her male companion. It started when three enormous brown bears charged out of the Du'Che and tore apart twelve Cyman soldiers before they were able to be put down. Peculiarly, during the rampage the bears continued to try to advance toward the tents holding the two Elves despite the mortal injuries inflicted upon them. It took a considerable amount of interrogation to get the testimony, but it had been worth it. The male Elf finally admitted that he, and all the Elves in Massa, had an inborn nexus with nature's beasts and could command them at their behest.

Adrian found the news quite shocking. He knew that it couldn't be mindshifting at work because animals just didn't process thoughts the same way humans did. It is true that the Mages of old were able to communicate with the Draca Cats, but they were magical creatures, not wild animals. *Is it shifting at all or an unknown form of sorcery?* The boy didn't know, and Adrian believed him. With the amount of stress put upon him, he would have said if he had known. Either way, it now required him to camouflage the army not just from the Elves, but from the animals of the Du'Che as well.

He walked over to a table in his tent, poured himself a glass of spiced wine, and stared at his young captive. The army was halted for the evening and he was alone with her. Unfortunately, her male companion had not made it through the questioning. He succumbed to his injuries that very morning. *It is just as well,* Adrian thought, eyeing the girl appreciatively. *She is only one that I need now.* After centuries of looking upon Cyman women, the small, feminine body of this little Elf fascinated him with her silver hair falling in silken strands down to the small of her back. He licked his lips and set his wine glass down.

A cough at his tent door stopped him.

"What is it, Captain?" Adrian asked impatiently without removing his gaze from the girl.

Lucin ducked to enter the tent, helmet in hand. "Everything is ready for tonight."

Adrian nodded. "Any word from my sister?"

"Not yet, but we do 'ave sentries posted. You will be sent word immediately if she arrives."

"Food supplies?"

"Meager."

"Deserters?"

"Very few. The Cyman soldiers 'ave been bred for this day."

"Thank you, Captain," he said and gestured to the door. "You are dismissed. I will be along shortly."

Lucin glanced at the Elven girl in the corner, and Adrian could see the sympathy in his eye. It infuriated him. He just didn't understand this emotion that he had long considered a weakness in the Cymans. "Get out, you idiot!"

Lucin's eye turned cold as he bowed and exited the tent.

The little Elf laughed and it sounded like the tinkle of a bell. "Even your own people do not like you."

"Fortunately, it is not a prerequisite of the job."

"Where is Falcon?"

Adrian shrugged. "He is fine. As long as you do what you are told, you will both be freed unharmed."

"What else would you have of me, sir? You have already robbed me of my body and my dignity. What else would you have?"

Her words angered him. This little slip of a girl belittled him when no one in his entire life had ever dared speak to him in such a manner. Struggling to keep his feelings in check, he smiled at her. "I would like your participation in a special ceremony to be held at midnight. You will be there as a representative of the Elven race, and after this ritual you and your companion may go back to your homes."

Her slanted purple eyes stared at him with suspicion. "What kind of ritual?"

He waved his hand in dismissal. "A simple ceremony that requires the presence of an emissary. That is all."

Her eyes flickered with hope. "Can I see Falcon first?"

"Soon." He leered at her hungrily, and it excited him when she began to tremble. He bared his teeth in a wicked half-smile. "Let us begin with the first part of the rite which involves partaking in the pleasures of the flesh."

The young girl's eyes deadened in grim hopelessness as she slid down and spread open her shaking knees. Tears dripped from her eyes as he approached, tugging at the lace of his trousers.

***

Lucin prowled through the Cyman camp, barking and growling at anyone who tried to speak to him. All of the arrangements had been made according to the instructions of the Mage and within the hour, Ravener would engage in his despicable dark arts. For what purpose, Lucin could not even guess.

Sickened, he stalked away from the army and its raucous noise and foul smells and disappeared over a towering dune. Once out of sight, he ran, pumping his arms and legs until his muscles protested in pain. He ran until he could continue no further and collapsed into the white sand. Even in the moonlight, the Sandori Sands glistened in blinding splendor, the landscape ever changing into exotic shapes as the dunes crested, caved, and swirled in the strong westerly winds. Hearty scrub grasses and plants dotted the terrain, but mostly it was a sea of glorious white as far as the eye could see.

Soon, he promised himself. *Soon, this whole campaign will be over and I'll be back with Maree, Miah and Titus.* He worried so for his son, his fervent hope that the Massans wouldn't harm an innocent boy.

Innocent? Who am I kidding? The Cymans were as complicit as Adrian Ravener in this whole sordid affair! Did the shifters they encountered in the north think the Cymans were innocent when they swarmed their shores with murderous intent? Did the young male Elf named Falcon think so when he took his last torturous breath crying out for his love? What about the Elven girl? Given the chance, she'd thrust a knife in Lucin's heart without batting an eye and been justified in doing so.

He shook the disturbing thoughts away. They were halfway through the Sands now, and he just had to see as many of his people as possible safely through to Earthshine. That was all he could do.

Pushing to his feet, he returned to camp and once again strode through the army without stopping. He slipped into the forest beyond and made his way toward the ritual location.

Earlier that evening, Lucin selected the requisite number of soldiers to participate in what Ravener called his war ritual. He had ordered Lucin to send the twelve Cymans to a clearing a full league south into the Du'Che Forest. *Whatever Ravener has in mind, he does not want to be overheard.*

Lucin had been strictly forbidden from attending the ceremony, but he wanted to see for himself what the Mage planned. If his men were to be a part of these war rituals, Lucin wanted to see that they were safe.

When he finally arrived at the clearing, he noticed the soldiers already present and standing within a circle of stones. Ravener had instructed that torches be staked into the ground outside of the ring, and they flickered eerily over the twelve anxious faces.

Lucin chose an enormous old oak and hauled himself onto a sizeable limb that looked like it would provide a good view of the clearing. But, he felt foolish. *Here I am, the captain of the Cyman Army, dripping in sweat and lying across a tree branch twenty feet off the ground to spy on my master.*

A miserable hour later, his head twitched up at the sound of movement coming from the far side of the clearing. Ravener strode out of the darkened forest gripping the upper arm of the Elven girl, Siole. Her eyes were frightened and wild as she looked around at the soldiers.

"Where is he?" he heard her question the Mage suspiciously. "You said Falcon would be here."

Ravener ignored her and proceeded to the center of the circle of soldiers where he forced the girl to her knees. He looked around at the men. "There will be no speaking during this ceremony. You must thank Captain Lucin for your presence here this evening as it is he who has honored you for this service. Let us begin."

Ravener reached down to lift the Elf to her feet, and Lucin could see the small body shuddering uncontrollably in fear. The sleeves of the Mage's cloak fell to his elbows as he began to weave his arms in the air in front of the girl, his lips moving in a silent chant.

The words were indecipherable from Lucin's position, but he could see the impact they were having on Siole. Her body stopped shaking, and she snapped rigidly upright before Ravener. Her eyes spun in her head, but she seemed unable to move any other part of her body. Horrible moans issued from her mouth, sending the hair on the back of Lucin's neck standing straight up. The soldiers shuffled their feet in agitation at sight of the girl's obvious torment. White froth began to bubble at her lips.

Suddenly, Ravener let out a primal scream and fell to his knees in front of Siole. As the Mage knelt with his head down, Siole's mouth opened wide—wider than was humanly possible. Lucin put his hand to his own gaping mouth to cover his horrified gasp.

The oral cavity continued to elongate and Lucin heard the cracking of her jaw. Shadowed fingers appeared at the maw opening and widened the mouth further. Impossibly, the silhouette of a head poked through and a ghostly apparition started to crawl out of Siole.

Dear Highworld, what am I witnessing?

When the specter finally slithered free, it shot into the air and the little Elf crumbled to the ground, an empty husk devoid of life.

The creature alighted to the ground and solidified into a flesh and blood demon. It was definitely female with naked breasts exposed around a tight fitting black outfit and billowing cape tied at the neck. Horns protruded from both sides of her temples and pointed upward in sharp lethal tips. Her smile revealed two rows of tiny serrated teeth.

"Niema," the Mage breathed reverently.

The evil that emanated from the dead sorceress brought all of the soldiers falling to their knees and covering their heads in soft groans. Lucin almost tumbled to the ground as his body shook in an uncontrollable desire to flee from the abomination in his presence.

"It has been a very long time," rasped out the demon, her voice chafing away at Lucin's sanity. "I must thank you for the delicacy. That is the first time I have tasted a fledgling Elven soul." The demon slid her long forked tongue out to lick at her lips. "Delicious."

"Niema, I am honored that it is you who has answered my call."

The creature barked out a brittle laugh as she hovered over the kneeling Mage. "I have accepted your offering. What is it you wish, spiritshifter, for I see you have earned this title."

"I am in need of your assistance to secure my position as ruler of this island. The sniveling leaders here want nothing more than to abolish all magic." He looked up expectantly. "You wouldn't want that, would you, Niema?"

Her red glowing eyes narrowed at Ravener. "Galen Starr is dead at last?"

"Yes."

The demon flipped into the air backwards in satisfaction and swooped down to within inches of Ravener's face. "Magic is needed in *all* of our worlds, spiritshifter. I will help you."

"I am in your debt, Niema."

She ran a clawed fingernail under his chin. "Yes, you are. And, just as I, spiritshifter, each demon you call forth will demand a living portal through which to emerge here into this mortal world."

He nodded. "Since I haven't yet built up the power necessary to summon the number of demons I need, I ask for your help."

Niema smiled sinisterly and licked her lips again in anticipation. "Shall I start with these twelve?" she asked, sweeping her arm around the circle.

Horrified screams escaped from the men and one collapsed to the ground.

Ravener raised an eyebrow. "But, of course. That's why they are here. You may begin."

Niema cackled and began weaving the air, bidding the demons of the Netherworld to her side.

Lucin's fingers dug into the bark of the branch beneath him as the men on their knees were jerked to their feet by sorcerous strings, even the man who had fainted. Tears streamed from his eye as he watched the mutilation of his men and the horrors that crawled from their outstretched jaws.

Ravener looked on in delight as twelve male demon spirits soon swirled in the air around him. They were caped and horned like Niema, but taller and more muscular.

Beckoning them close, the Mage gave them their instructions. Four demons each were to go to the leading cities in Iserlohn, Deepstone and Haventhal in search of the *Savitars* in the unlikely event they were still alive and to terrorize the citizens of the land along the way. "Frightened people have a way of convincing their Kings to surrender," cooed Ravener to Niema.

The twelve horned shadows howled and streaked away into the night.

Lucin watched them go and then glanced back at the clearing and the thirteen bodies that lay on the ground. *Only a coward would watch the events of this night perched in a tree and do nothing!* Lucin berated himself. *But, what could I have done?* If he had tried to intervene, he would have been killed. That much he knew.

But, he did vow then and there to destroy Adrian Ravener. It didn't matter when or how, only that he be the one to do it.

Without warning, the female demon snapped her glowing red gaze his way. The temperature around him dropped and his breath clouded in front of his face. She hissed as she crouched, forked tongue darting in and out.

Adrian held up his hand. "Do not worry, Niema, there is no threat out there. It's just the captain of my Cyman Army. Although he apparently finds it hard to follow orders, he is harmless."

CHAPTER 26

PRECIOUS TROUBLE

Every muscle tensed as Kiernan waited behind the door of her white room with her dagger clenched tightly in one hand.

Soon, one of the women would be back, and she would be waiting.

It remained a mystery to her why she was being held captive. If these women were of benevolent intent, why was her door locked? From the outside? Why did they keep spelling her into unconsciousness?

Gemini said that she knew Kiernan's mother, so at some point the Queen must have brought her here. But why? What was Gemini referring to when she said that Kiernan would be trained? It was all very intriguing, but she simply didn't have time for games and innuendo. Beck and the others must be worried sick by now.

As soon as she thought of Beck, her heart sank and she looked up toward the ceiling to blink back the tears that threatened to fall. No, most likely not worried at all and still wrapped up in the arms of another woman. *How could his feelings for me change so abruptly?* His betrayal made no sense to her, and all attempts to accept that he just didn't feel the same way about her as she did him caused unbridled pain to stab through her.

Footsteps sounded outside in the corridor, wrenching her back to reality. She readied herself for a fight. *I don't want to harm anyone. I just need to scare them into letting me go.*

There was a knock.

When she didn't respond, a key was inserted into the lock and the door opened. Kiernan held her breath as a dark-haired woman dressed in a blue velvet dress entered her room.

Kiernan sprang forward, grabbed the woman around the neck, and held the dagger less than an inch from her throat. "Looks like we'll have to do this the hard way," she snarled into the woman's ear. "I'm getting out of here and *you* are going to show me the way."

"Princess, you don't want to do this," the woman said calmly.

Too calmly?

"Yes, obviously I do." She nudged the woman's back roughly toward the door. "Now go. If you make any move—"

"*Bindeno!*"

Kiernan's dagger dropped from nerveless fingers and she fell back onto the floor, stiff as a board and unable to move no matter how hard she tried. She couldn't even move her lips to scream.

The dark-haired beauty stared down at her. "Do not let our looks fool you, Princess. We're not weak and delicate. We can be ruthless if we have to be. After all, they don't call us witches without good reason."

If Kiernan's rage could have broken the spell over her inert body, it would have exploded into a million fragments. She had never felt so helpless in her life, her fate so completely in another's hands.

The woman's gorgeous blue eyes were confidently smug. She appeared to be around Kiernan's age, although it was hard to tell with these women.

"My name is Sapphire," Kiernan's tormenter announced and then stepped one leg over Kiernan to straddle her in a very humiliating fashion. "If you continue to push, Princess, you will be pushed back. Hard."

If Sapphire expected Kiernan to nod, it was a cruel joke.

The woman tossed her black braid over her shoulder and squatted. "I should probably leave you on the floor all night to teach you a lesson, but I won't. Gemini is waiting. Try it again, though, and you will be very, very sorry."

Sapphire mumbled a counter to her spell, and as soon as it lifted, Kiernan let out a frustrated scream and jumped to her feet.

"What in the hell was that?" she shouted. "How do you know magic? What are you?"

Sapphire held her head high. "I told you. I am a witch, or a sorceress if you like that name better."

"So, you're telling me that this is some kind of witches' coven?"

"Exactly what I am telling you."

"Really? And, how does Gemini know my mother?"

Sapphire grabbed Kiernan by the upper arm in a vise-like grip. "Come. I'll take you to Gemini and, Highworld bless her, she can answer all of your irritating questions herself."

"Fine," Kiernan said, and gave the sorceress a sickly sweet smile as she jerked her arm free.

The sorceress raised her eyebrows, but said nothing.

Kiernan found herself escorted down the same corridor and into the foyer with the fountain, but instead of going to the hall across the white marble floor, Sapphire led her up the wide staircase to the first level of balconies.

They passed several women, all in formal attire, who nodded politely to them. At the top of the stairs, Sapphire continued along the hallway until she came to a simple wooden door with no sign or decoration.

At her knock, she was granted admittance from a voice on the other side of the door.

The petite Gemini came from around her desk as soon as Sapphire and Kiernan entered.

"You may go now, Sapphire. Thank you."

Sapphire curtsied deeply to Gemini and left.

A provocative scent permeated the room. Kiernan's mood changed in an instant, and she felt herself growing tranquil and relaxed.

Gazing around, she decided the best way to describe the décor was a blend of disordered comfort. A beautifully carved, but cluttered, writing desk sat directly across from the door. Off to the side was a wooden sofa upholstered in blue cut velvet brocade and strewn with plump colorful pillows. A bookshelf in the corner contained a sizeable library of well-used tomes, and Kiernan walked toward it unsteadily to scan the titles on the spines. Among the collection, she found *Manipulation of Magikal Herbs, Dream Acumen* and *The Prophetic Age*. Scattered between the books was a variety of ritualistic items including mortar and pestle, crystals, pentacles, pewter chalice and even a cauldron.

A true witch's lair, she thought in amusement.

Turning back, she spied a three-legged ornate censer vibrating softly on the corner of Gemini's desk and emitting a sweet smelling vapor into the air. The source of her artificial serenity, no doubt.

Gemini spoke, interrupting her perusal. "My apologies, Kiernan, for the last time we met. But, using your own words, you left me no other choice."

Kiernan pointed to the censer. "Turn this off. I like to have my wits about me when I face my enemies."

Gemini smiled indulgently and walked over to pull the rosewood incense stick from the censer and ground it into the sand on the bottom. "Sit down, Kiernan," she said pointing to the velvet couch. "Let me explain."

"Explain first why you kidnapped me and why I am not free to leave. If your answer satisfies me, we might have something to talk about. If not, sorcery or no, get out of my way, because I'm leaving."

Gemini clapped her hands in delight, her blue eyes twinkling. "My, my, they say that Princesses are born, not made, and you certainly give truth to that adage. Although you have not been a Princess for many years, you certainly still act like one."

Kiernan scowled. "I act like a person who is being held against her will!"

"Where is your Draca Cat?" Gemini asked, startling her.

"How do you know about him?"

"The bond between your ancestors and Callyn-Rhe goes back many, many years. A Kenley should never be without the protection of her Draca Cat."

Kiernan finally sat and Gemini joined her.

"First, let me explain who we are."

"Sorceresses," Kiernan said evenly as if she had met them every day.

"Yes. I have been rescuing female shifters from the dreadful fate of exile in Pyraan for years. Without the benefit of training in the art of elemental magic as a shifter, the girls are taught instead the use of gemstones in sorcery. Just like mind, body, fire and earth, gems contain an enormous amount of energy that we use for healing, divination, spell casting and combat, just to name a few applications.

Each gem has its own unique purpose in witchcraft, and we study them all here."

Kiernan jaw dropped. "That explains why we saw so few girls coming to Pyraan."

"It explains some of it, certainly, but we only have a little over four hundred girls and women here in Elloree. There should be more."

Four hundred shifters in Iserlohn? Untrained shifters, but shifters nonetheless. Kiernan felt her heart soar. "How do you find the girls?"

"Actually, they find us. Our vocation here is not entirely clandestine. People talk. When parents are faced with a daughter's shifting abilities, the first thing they think about is how to keep their child from exile, so they bring them here and we care for them and train them."

"You mean you teach them magic?"

Gemini looked at Kiernan as if she were daft. "Of course! We are magical beings are we not? Did you not learn to use your craft at the Parsis Academy in Pyraan?"

"Well, yes, but only because we were required to use shifting to protect the lands. We didn't use it in our everyday lives."

Gemini shook her head in disgust. "Bah! What rubbish! Why not? Don't tell me you subscribe to the archaic and ridiculous notion that having magical ability means you are defective in some way?" The sorceress rose to her feet. "What a waste! All these years of exiling and subjugating people solely because of a gift they possess. A gift that can heal and create and, yes, defend if necessary."

Kiernan felt that same way and gave much of this same speech to Beck during the Homage Festival, which seemed a lifetime ago now.

"And to think," Gemini raged, "this all started because of an oath my absurd brother took!"

Kiernan snapped her head up. "Brother?"

"Yes, my dear. My full name is Gemini Starr, sister of that idiot, Galen Starr."

"Did you know that...?"

She waved a hand in the air. "Yes, I do know that my brother has passed." She shrugged. "I hadn't seen Galen since he took the oath. I concealed myself from him because I knew that if he found this coven, he would have commanded us all to exile. He wouldn't have had a choice because of the oath. Of course, I'm certain he heard of my activities, but this palace is bespelled with an invisibility veil that affected only him. Yes, I loved him, but exile was an area in which we most definitely did not see eye to eye."

Kiernan felt like she had to defend the dead Mage. "I agree with you that shifters don't deserve to be exiled, but Galen did a lot of good and it all came from his desire to protect this land and its people."

Gemini smiled. "Yes he did, and that was his biggest flaw. He wasn't objective about the situation. He felt so responsible for the Mage War that I think he would have agreed to anything back then."

"You were there?"

She laughed and the sound reverberated throughout the room. "Yes. I was several years younger than Galen and, before you ask the next question, yes, he did share one of his Mage secrets with me, the LifeFire Tonic." Gemini walked over to the chaotic bookcase and after moving several items out of her way, pulled forth a vial that swirled with a red mist. "While not immortal, I have had prolonged existence in this world through regular use of this tonic. However, I have not, and will not, share it with any other person. I gave my word."

Gemini returned the tonic to its rightful place and though her movements appeared uncomplicated, Kiernan felt confident that no one would ever be able to retrieve that vial except the sorceress herself.

Kiernan was curious about something. "As a shifter, then, do you not feel the pull of the blood oath?"

She shook her head. "No, because I haven't been marked." She pointed to the tattoo on Kiernan's neck. "The mark of the athame unleashes a very powerful energy into the body—into the soul—that binds the oath."

Fascinated now, Kiernan thirsted for more. "Tell me everything you know, Gemini. Starting with my mother and our bond with the Draca Cats."

CHAPTER 27

OLD GRUDGES

"You are one strange Dwarf," commented one of Rogan's escorts with a long red beard while dragging him to his feet from out of the bottom of the skiff.

Rogan couldn't decide whether his earlier hysteria sprang from the stress of the situation or the irony at being freed from exile at last only to be arrested and thrown face first into a boat. Whatever the case, it had taken two days to navigate the Koda River, and Rogan was stone cold sober now. But, with his disheveled clothing and matted hair, he knew he probably looked like the demented creature they thought him to be.

"I want to see the King," he said hoarsely.

Redbeard laughed. "Oh, yes, and I want to date the Princess of Men."

"She's already taken."

The soldier looked at him askance and then shook his head. "I'm afraid it's the dungeons for you, my friend."

"Nice homecoming," he snorted to himself as they walked down yet another stone dock, all the while wondering if the Dwarves harbored some deep-seated resentment against wood.

In the comfortably cool morning hour, citizens paid little mind to the soldiers, and contentedly went about their business without a hint of the danger that loomed. Rogan wasn't sure of the name of this riverside city, but knew that Kondor was located some distance away still on the eastern border of Deepstone. Somehow, he had to find a way to convince the soldiers on the journey to give him an audience with the King. *I will protect the Dwarves from Adrian Ravener whether they wish it or not!*

"Homecoming?" asked the other soldier who had not yet spoken. He had a light brown beard that just dusted his chin, which meant he was close to Rogan's age. "I thought you were a shifter born in Pyraan?"

Rogan shook his head. "I was born in Kondor and then exiled when I was six years old. At least that's what I've always been told."

The soldier stopped in his tracks. "What is your name?"

"Radek. Rogan Radek."

The young soldier sucked in a breath and glanced at his partner. "Maybe we ought to bring him to the King after all."

"Yes, you should!" Rogan said trying to shrug off his captors. "In my pack, you will see that I carry a Decree of Purpose that will authenticate my need to see King Rik."

Redbeard untied Rogan's hands just long enough to strip him of his pack. The Dwarf pulled out the decree and read through it carefully. "Wait here," he said to his companion. "I'll arrange for horses and dispatch a messenger ahead of us with this," he said, holding up the decree.

The younger Dwarf nodded and led Rogan to a stone bench at the edge of a small square, gesturing for him to sit. "I thought you were dead."

"Dead? You recognize my name?"

"Of course. You don't remember me?"

Rogan shook his head. "Sorry, no."

"I'm Dillon Hamderk. We were friends. Good friends. We lived next door to each other."

The thumping in Rogan's chest sounded loud in his ears. "Do..." *Oh, Dear Highworld.* "Do...my parents still live next to you?" he asked and held his breath as he waited for Dillon to respond.

Dillon lowered his head. "No, I'm sorry. They died many years ago."

Rogan felt like someone had just rammed a wooden club into his abdomen, and he fell back onto the hard bench. Just like that, his search had come to an abrupt end. All those years of wondering what his parents were like. All that time fantasizing about a reunion in which his parents would gather him in their arms and tell him how much they missed and loved him. With a few short words, his dream had ended and there was no family standing at the end of it.

He turned his head so Dillon wouldn't see the tears that welled in his eyes. He wondered why he didn't remember Dillon when the young Dwarf so clearly remembered him. "Did I have any siblings?" he managed to croak out, his face still averted.

"Not that I am aware of."

"Who lives in the house now?"

"No one. No one has lived there since your parents died."

Rogan knew he was taking a risk, but had little choice in the matter. Dillon was his only potential ally in this land. He lifted his head to look the soldier in the eyes. "If we were once good friends as you have just told me, then I should be able to trust you."

"You can. I swear it on my life."

Rogan breathed out a sigh of relief. "I need to see if any of my parents' belongings are still in that house. I'm looking for a pendant that I must retrieve without fail."

"I'll see what I can do, but I'm sure that once the King hears what you have to say, he will release you from detention and you can search for yourself. I'll guide you there if you like."

"I would. Thank you, Dillon." He cracked a smile. "I wish I could remember more about our friendship."

"Me, too."

***

A hard, three-day ride later over an otherworldly landscape of bare red rock, the city of Kondor appeared on the horizon. Rogan's body ached in places he never knew existed and his throat grated from constant thirst. So much so that he almost cried in relief when the dust kicked up from the horses of their escort could be seen in the distance.

"Who are they?" Rogan asked Dillon.

"The Iron Fists, the King's elite personal warriors."

They were outfitted in the same blue and maroon as Dillon and Redbeard except with the addition of black sashes tied at their waists. Without any conversation, the Fists came on fast and surrounded them, creating an impenetrable ring around their small party.

They moved toward Kondor at a clipped pace now and within a short time, the stone palace of the King of Dwarves came into view. Crossing beneath a portcullis into the courtyard of the castle, Rogan took notice of the soldiers standing on the wall above warily watching his progress.

They're afraid of me.

Servants scattered out of the way of the imposing entourage as they dismounted, and the Fists led the way promptly up the palace stairs. Rogan didn't have time to blink as he was ushered directly into a great hall where King Rik Rojin stood waiting near his throne.

Rogan skipped a step, momentarily taken aback at the naked hatred burning in the King's eyes.

Taller than any other Dwarf Rogan had ever seen, he had a long, flowing white beard that he wore gathered at the middle with a gold and ruby clasp. A simple gold circlet sat regally upon his head.

Dillon and Redbeard released their hold on Rogan's arm and went to stand with the Iron Fists who had spread out efficiently throughout the chamber.

Rogan walked forward, hands still bound, and dropped to his knee in front of the King. "Your Grace."

"What are you doing in my land, shifter?" the King growled, malice rolling off him in waves that seemed strong enough to physically sweep Rogan from the room. The King held the decree limply in his right hand.

"I have just come from Iserlohn—"

"The affairs of Iserlohn do not concern me," interrupted the King, sitting down on his throne and tossing the parchment to the ground.

"Your Grace!" Rogan cried in astonishment. "You don't understand. The island has been invaded by the Mage, Adrian Ravener, who fled to the north at the end of the Mage War. He brings with him an army of thousands! If you don't aid us in this fight, Ravener will make slaves of us all!"

Rogan heard the Fists shuffle their feet behind him. *Good!* If the King chose to act irresponsibly, he needed the Dwarves to be witness to it.

"I believe you exaggerate this Mage's capabilities for your own purpose, shifter."

"And, what purpose would that be?" Rogan asked in bewilderment.

"Your freedom."

Rogan couldn't understand why this King was directing such loathing at him. Although they had never met, it felt extremely personal. "You are right, Your Grace, my freedom is something I desire, but I desire my life more."

The King turned away and waved his arm. "Escort this shifter to a cell."

When the Fists moved toward him, Rogan struggled to his feet. "My name is Rogan Radek, Your Grace. If you're going to condemn an innocent man to imprisonment, you should know his name first!"

The King turned back to look at him, eyes burning. "I know *exactly* who you are."

"How?" he demanded, impatient for answers. "Mage Starr was unable to tell me anything of my heritage on his deathbed. What can you tell me?"

The King, for the first time, appeared disturbed. "Starr is dead?"

"Yes."

"I thought that old buzzard would outlive me for sure." The King appeared to be lost in his memories for a moment and then snapped his fingers. "Iron Fists! Take him out of here!"

Without use of his hands, Rogan could only dive and roll out of the way of the advancing soldiers. "You can't do this! Even if the Dwarves wish no part of this fight, I must continue on! I have been named *Savitar!*"

Two Fists jumped on him.

"If King Maximus wanted help from me," the King bellowed, "he should have thought better of his choice of messenger!"

"I don't understand!" Rogan screamed. "Why do you hate me so? At least tell me that!" The King silently watched as the Fists wrestled him toward the door. "You are a coward, King Rik! A coward!"

"Silence!" the King roared as he stood from his throne. "I am no coward, *nephew*. When your father, *my brother*, tried to flee with you when your vile shifting abilities were discovered, I made the most courageous decision of my life to save this land and my people. I killed him! My own brother! All because of you! Now get the bloody hell out of here before I kill you, too!"

CHAPTER 28

RUMINATIONS

Gemini Starr idly fingered the embossed hilt of the royal Sword of Iserlohn that lay on the bureau behind her desk. It had remained there untouched since Kiernan Everard surrendered it to her five days ago. The Princess had been with them almost five weeks now, and Gemini had spent the majority of that time indoctrinating Kiernan into the ways of the coven, instructing her on their core values, philosophies, hierarchy and the use of gemstones in sorcery.

Gemini's mother, also a sorceress, had taught her very early on about the extraordinary power contained in gemstones. Those early teachings were precisely why she founded the coven in Elloree after the Mage War against the express wishes of her brother, Galen. She simply refused to sit back and do nothing while every shifter girl born on the island was flung into exile instead of being given a chance to hone and develop her unique talent. Because of their innate shifting capabilities, every woman in the coven had the gift of magic and so had the ability to work with the stones. Each "Gem," as the women liked to refer to themselves, worked with one specific gemstone and directed the energy contained within to master a skill used in witchcraft.

Gemini's own daughter, Sapphire, worked with that most precious of all blue gemstones as it contained the metaphysical properties for her chosen craft of spell casting. Born Dayna Starr, her daughter was so Named when she achieved her position as Sect Leader. All the women who worked with sapphires to create spells answered to her daughter. When Sapphire died or could no longer hold her position for any reason, another woman from within the sect would then be raised up and Named Sapphire.

Gemini continued to stroke Kiernan's sword. *The Princess is one of us now. As it should be.*

After Kiernan learned that her mother brought her to Elloree as a young girl in her desire that she one day become one of the Gems, the Princess began to succumb to Gemini's persuasive reasoning. The rejection of her father and a quarrel with the young man she loved made it easy to manipulate the vulnerable Princess into shedding former ties and agreeing to join the coven. If a thread of guilt wormed its way into Gemini's conscience, she quickly stamped it out. What she was doing was necessary. It was what Kiernan's mother—Gemini's dearest friend—wanted for her daughter, and she would fulfill that wish.

She related to Kiernan how her mother paid a visit to the coven thirteen years ago with a young Kiernan in tow. As a descendant of the powerful original *Savitar*, Garret Kenley, Queen Grace knew it was inevitable that Kiernan would be a shifter, but she desperately wanted more time with her daughter. More time to instruct Kiernan in the nuances of magic and royalty and to impart the special wisdom that only a mother can provide during the journey to womanhood.

Kiernan cried openly at that point, Gemini remembered.

The Queen had been adamant that King Maximus not find out about Kiernan. Unbeknownst to anyone in Iserlohn, Grace herself was also a powerful mindshifter and when she arrived in Elloree with Kiernan, she reunited with her bonded Draca Cat, Moombai.

According to records from as far back as a millennium, Kenleys and Draca Cats stood side by side in combat and in peace through an unbreakable bond wrought through magic. As custom demanded, a baby cub due to be born in less than a year had already been promised as Kiernan's lifelong protector.

When Moombai delivered the prophetic news that dark times were advancing on the island and that the young Kiernan would be named *Savitar*, Grace grew anxious. The Queen, already aware that her daughter's skills would be needed due to a fateful visit from Galen upon Kiernan's birth, seemed more eager than ever after hearing it from Moombai to hide Kiernan away from the rest of the world. She begged Gemini to accept Kiernan into the coven.

When Gemini agreed, Grace promised to return to Elloree with Kiernan in two weeks time after further preparations could be made. Unfortunately, the Queen became sick with fever during her travel back to Nysa, developed an infection and died.

After the Queen's premature death, Gemini made several attempts to visit Kiernan and even delivered the baby Draca Cat at one point, but the King refused to admit her. He kept the young Princess under very strict guard until he discovered her abilities at the age of twelve and sent her off to Pyraan.

Kiernan listened to the entire account without speaking as she gazed out of the window of Gemini's chambers.

It took another full four weeks after that conversation for Kiernan to surrender her sword, but she finally did so. The last symbolic cast off of her former life.

Because of her warrior skills, Gemini placed Kiernan with Citrine who used the lemony gemstone she was Named for in combat. The gemstone lent incredible speed and strength to the witches who were able to invoke its power.

Coincidently, it was Citrine who now startled Gemini out of her ruminations by knocking on the door and entering with Diamond, the Divination Sect Leader.

Citrine, her fiery red braid hanging over her shoulder, spoke first. "I apologize for the interruption, High Priestess, but we have had news that fighting has broken out on the island, mostly in the more populated cities and villages. My sources tell me that we are under attack, although not by an army. They tell of shadows that paralyze with fear and kill innocents."

Gemini's features remained composed. "Is Kiernan correct in her assertion that Adrian Ravener is behind this?"

Citrine nodded. "Yes."

"Diamond, what predictions do you have to add?"

Diamond tugged on her blonde braid, uncharacteristically agitated. Usually, the pale-haired sorceress was composed ice. "It's devastating, Gemini. I saw great destruction in our future. Dead bodies littering the streets, homes afire, chaos."

"Can it be averted?" she asked, already knowing the answer.

"Only through the combined might of four new *Savitars*, but their identities remain clouded. We must find them, Gemini," Diamond implored forcefully. "Find them and set them in motion to destroy Adrian Ravener!"

Gemini rose and looked pensively out of the same window that Kiernan did weeks ago when she learned of her legacy. "Leave me. I must deliberate about our course of action."

***

Kiernan rubbed her aching neck as she soaked in a copper tub of hot water in her room. After weeks of working with Citrine and the other Gems of the sect, her body was bruised from head to toe. They used only practice swords in their combat training, but the power of the citrine gemstone around her trainer's neck infused the woman with a strength and swiftness that proved impossible to counter.

She sat back and sighed, content to be here with the Gems. After Pyraan, she didn't think it would be possible, but she had found a place where she could put her warrior and shifting skills to use for good. She owed her gratitude to Gemini for offering to take her in when she had nowhere else to go. Nysa was no longer an option for her, and Beck, the man she loved more than anything in this world, had rejected her. Yes, this was where she belonged. Among women of her own kind.

Every now and then, she felt a guilty pang for abandoning her duty, but Gemini assured her over and over again that the armies of Massa would be able to handle Adrian Ravener if battle did ensue. In all likelihood, the sorceress scoffed, Ravener would be content to retire at Starfell and live out his days without incident.

Whenever concern niggled at her that she was the only one who could lead the others to the weapon in Callyn-Rhe, Gemini laughed in her face and admitted that her brother had always been a bit of an alarmist and storyteller.

Gemini's assurances assuaged her blood oath.

She did miss Bajan very much, but doubted he would understand what she was going through. At some point, she hoped to reunite with him, but not now. He was better off with the *Savitars*. With Beck.

Oh, Beck.

Kiernan sank lower into the steaming water. Unbidden, a soft moan escaped her lips as she recalled his tender touch and the fire his caresses ignited in her that last evening in Nysa. They had promised each other that they would always be together.

Why did he lie?

She screamed in anguish at the image in her mind of his dimpled, smiling face as he stroked that young woman in his arms.

With a final kick at the copper tub, she stomped out naked, threw herself across her bed and sobbed.

Hours later, exhausted, her tears had finally dried and she resolved to put Beck Atlan out of her mind once and for all.

After all, Gemini would be very disappointed to learn she had been thinking of him.

***

Beck jogged down the deserted street, Bajan loping at his side. He ordered all of the citizens to remain inside their homes or in one of the cavernous warehouses located at the pier after sunset to keep them out of harm's way. For weeks now, he and the soldiers stationed in Iserport had been battling four demon shadows. Weeks now that he had been unable to search for Kiernan. He swallowed past the bile that tickled his throat whenever he thought of her.

Unbidden, his mind drifted to Galen Starr's dire prophecy, but he resolutely pushed the thought aside and set his mind to the task at hand. As soon as he defeated the last of these nightmarish creatures come to life, the sooner he could resume both his search for Kiernan and his journey to Callyn-Rhe.

At an intersection, Beck stopped and flattened his body tight against the side of a cutlery shop. He risked a quick look around the corner and saw Gage ushering the last of the citizens to safety. The Saber moved with a calm, deadly grace that made Beck extremely grateful to have him by his side. Together, they had managed to destroy three of the demons, but not before the creatures brutally killed over a hundred innocent people, mostly women and children. It seemed Ravener's minions were intent on targeting the weakest inhabitants of Iserlohn in order to subjugate the strongest.

Unexpectedly, Bajan let out a growl, deep in his chest. A terrifying sound that quickened Beck's breath because it meant that the last remaining demon was near. For some reason, the Draca was able to sense the demons where the humans could not.

Beck jerked his head back around. This last female demon had proven very hard to defeat and as such had roamed the city for over a week now killing indiscriminately.

Across the street, he detected a shift in the shadows and watched as the demon slowly detached herself from concealment between two buildings. The wraith, when it coalesced into mortal form, was tall, muscular and caped in black. Large, exposed breasts swung obscenely as she moved. Sharp horns protruded from her head in pointed tips.

When she opened her mouth and released a screeching, inhuman scream, Beck fought the urge to cover his ears. The scream had the opposite effect on the Draca Cat, and Bajan's answering roar was just as intimidating as he peeled away from the wall and rushed at her.

Fangs bared, Bajan used his powerful leg muscles to close the distance and leap into the air, outstretched jaws snapping for the demon's throat. The creature easily pivoted out of the way of the enraged Draca, and spun with extreme swiftness to grab Bajan around the neck. The Draca let out a choked cry as the demon lifted him off the ground and squeezed his throat. Bajan's deadly tail lashed out at the beast's head and one of his spikes embedded in the top of her skull with a stomach-turning crunch.

Beck sprinted toward the two foes locked in combat and threw out his hands as he ran, an earthen missile exploding upward from the road and spinning violently toward the demon.

Still connected to Bajan by the spike in his tail, the creature just managed to lurch out of the projectile's path.

Beck anticipated the maneuver and crashed into her at the same time that Bajan whipped his head around and sank his teeth into her neck, the three of them pitched forward to the ground in a heap of snarling muscle. Beck raised his arms, laced his fingers together and smashed his fists into the demon's face. Her head snapped to the side, a grotesque indentation caving in her cheek.

Turning back to him, her fiery eyes suddenly locked on the sliver pendant that spilled from his shirtfront.

"*Savitar!*" she hissed.

He had only a second to wonder where the archers were before she was on him, ripping and clawing at his chest in an attempt to claim his pendant. Beck kicked out with his heavily built legs, and her head ripped from Bajan's tail and she sailed through the air. She landed hard, but immediately shrieked and charged at him again. Fortunately, it was then that Beck heard the *twang* of released bowstrings and dove to the side as two Iserlohn soldiers on a rooftop let loose their arrows. Stumbling back upright, he saw that one of the arrows had hit its mark, now firmly seated in the demon's chest.

Beck knew he had to act fast before the creature reverted to wraith form. As long as the demon was in contact with an earthly object, they discovered, she couldn't alter. The demon, still intent on his pendant, didn't seem to notice the arrow and hurtled forward.

Big mistake, fiend.

He reached out to one of the trees on the side street, and branches groaned as they snapped outward toward the demon and seized her in a leafy binding around her waist, pinning her arms to her sides.

"Fire!" he screamed, and Gage ran to him with a burning torch. The demon saw the fire and began to howl. Another detail they learned over the past terror-filled weeks—as dwellers of darkness, both fire and light were fatal to the demons.

Taking off at a run, Beck grabbed the torch from Gage and sprang into the air. With all his strength, he drove the flame directly into the open screaming maw of the she-demon. The red eyes glowered in rage before bursting apart in an eruption of black ash.

Beck rolled to the ground and lay flat on his back, panting as he fought for breath. After so many weeks, he found it hard to believe it was over.

The two dozen soldiers who had been fighting side by side with him sprinted over. "Thank you, earthshifter," said one with blonde curls who looked, if possible, younger than Rory. Beck recognized him as the same soldier who helped Gage escort him to his room after the debacle at The Rearing Horse. "If not for you and the Draca Cat, we would have many more dead on our hands."

Beck nodded. "I think the city is safe for now, but continue to have people remain indoors at night. If any more wraiths appear, use fire to destroy them. They can be defeated."

The soldier held out a hand and pulled Beck to his feet. "We can't stay. Captain Franck has summoned us to Starfell. Only a small detachment will remain here in Iserport, but we will instruct them properly."

Beck reached out to shake his hand. "It has been an honor to fight with you. Good luck."

"To you and the other *Savitars* as well. Word has spread of the invasion, and it appears all of our lives depend on your success." Surprisingly, the young man knelt down in front of Beck and held out his sword in both hands parallel to the ground. "My life before yours at Starfell. This I swear as my binding oath."

"Soldier..." Beck stumbled, moved by the declaration of fealty. "It's not necessary to give—"

The young man interrupted him. "It is. As a shifter, you are bound by a blood oath to protect this island, which means you would lay down your life for me. But, as *Savitar*, it is more important that I lay down mine for you so that you survive to battle the Mage. As a man and a soldier, I can do no less."

Beck stepped back in shock when every soldier standing on the deserted street knelt to the ground and offered their swords and oath.

Finally, he bowed his head solemnly. "We serve each other, then. What is your name?"

The young man stood. "Lieutenant Kirby Nash, sir."

Beck tilted his head in question. "Any relation to Captain Colbie Nash of Nysa's Scarlet Sabers?"

"Yes, sir, he is my brother."

"He is fine man. It seems honor runs in your family."

"Thank you, sir."

Beck smiled. "Just Beck, Lieutenant."

Kirby smiled back. "Just Kirby, sir."

"Until Starfell, then."

Exhausted, Beck left the men and made his way to The Rusty Nail with Bajan by his side. They moved from the Queen's Lair a few weeks back when their grid search for Kiernan took them further west. He ran out of King Maximus's coin early last week but the innkeeper, grateful for all Beck and Bajan had done to protect the city, refused to accept any further compensation. It was just as well since he didn't have any to give.

Bajan had developed a considerable amount of admiration from the citizens of Iserport, especially the children, but the Draca tolerated all of the attention without his usual posturing. It had been more than a month now that Kiernan had vanished, and the toll showed through on both of them. Each had lost weight. Beck's face was gaunt and stubbled from lack of shaving, and Bajan's beautiful white coat had lost some of its natural luster.

"Beck! Over here!" He turned to find Gage rushing toward him. "I'm afraid I have bad news, Atlan."

Every muscle in Beck's body seized. *Please, no. Not Kiernan.*

"One of the *Savitars* is down. I found out earlier today but didn't have a chance to tell you. Airron was poisoned by a venomous spider in the Puu Rainforest on his way to Sarphia. To be truthful, I'm not sure if he is even alive."

Beck ran a hand through his hair. "Dear Highworld."

"That's not all. In addition to the spider bite, Airron was severely beaten. When he was found, his ribs were broken, he had a fractured skull, and had lost a large amount of blood. The Elven healers did all they could for him."

The news shook Beck, and he turned from the Saber for a moment to compose his emotions. "Rory?"

"Missing as well. And, I must leave at once for Starfell. The Iserlohn Army is only a few days from the Valley of Flame and will be ready to engage the enemy."

"What of the Dwarves and Elves?" he asked, finally turning.

Gage shrugged. "That's the strange part. There are no reports that either army is on the move. With the *Savitars* out of commission as well, it appears as though the Iserlohn Army stands alone in this."

Beck swallowed, despising himself for what he was about to say, but he had no other choice. The time had come. "I'll be leaving as well. First to Sarphia to meet up with Rogan and then on to Starfell." Without all four pendants, Callyn-Rhe would continue to remain undiscovered and the power they needed buried within her depths, but he would still fight. As long as there was breath in his body, he would fight.

Gage nodded and gripped Beck's upper arm in understanding.

Beck gave him a small smile of gratitude. "Thank you for all you did to try and help find Kiernan. I owe you a debt you have only to name."

"No debt owed. She was my Princess."

Beck inwardly recoiled at the Saber's use of the past tense when referring to Kiernan.

"Then again," Gage said, "there is this demented Mage I would like to have help in killing."

Bloodlust flared in Beck's chest. "My pleasure."

CHAPTER 29

DESCENT INTO DARKNESS

Preoccupied with thoughts of the upcoming battle, Beck entered his room at The Rusty Nail. Bajan went off to hunt before their voyage tomorrow as it was uncertain when he would have a chance to do so again.

At the washbasin by his bed, he leaned over to splash his face and his hands started to shake. He gripped the rim, unable to move for a moment as he contemplated his departure and all that meant.

I'm leaving Kiernan behind.

Leaving her in the hands of a fate only the Highworld knew. He tried to convince himself that he would be back, but deep down he knew it wasn't true. Not with Iserlohn standing alone in this war.

He suddenly froze at the shuffle of feet behind him and yelped in pain as an assailant stabbed him in the lower back. He spun around with a growl, magic igniting within his body.

Standing in front of him with a spear in one hand and the other covering his eyes was the Halfie Tribe Leader, Vinni Vee. He wore the ragged clothes of one of the orphaned children who haunted the streets of Iserport.

"Pardon, *Savitar!*" he squealed. "You know it is in my nature to be wicked. Please forgive me!"

Beck reached behind his back and his hand came away with blood. "Hell, Vinni, did you have to stab me? What are you doing here, anyway?"

"I am here once again to give you valuable information, *Savitar*," he said, shaking his golden locks. "Honestly, I don't know how you manage without me."

Beck retrieved a cloth from the side of the basin and reached around his back to hold it against the small wound. "Help that is a little less painful would be appreciated."

Vinni stuck his tongue out, and it mystified Beck how the imp's behavior came so instinctively. Most of the time, the little Halfie didn't seem to be aware of what he was doing until the vicious act was complete. He just did what came natural and, unfortunately, that meant being ill-behaved.

"I came to tell you that the Princess of Iserlohn is going to be kidnapped!"

Beck's jaw dropped. Maybe there was more to the Halfie's foretelling abilities than he previously gave credit. "I know, Vinni—"

"The Gems will have taken her," he declared.

Beck looked at the pint-sized terror quizzically. "The Gems?"

"Yes, the Gems! The witches who live in Elloree! Goodness, you are a little slow for a *Savitar*."

Beck's heart soared at the news. This was his first solid—even if it was written in the clouds—clue to Kiernan's whereabouts. Impulsively, he reached out and hugged the little Tribe Leader. "Thank you, Vinni! You don't know how much you've just helped me, my friend!"

Vinni cocked his head at the show of emotion from Beck and tentatively returned the hug. "You know, *Savitar*, this feels kind of pleasant. Does it always feel like this to...to show kindness?"

"Yes, Vinni, it does."

"Hmmrf. Something to think about." Vinni released him and headed for door. "Good-bye, *Savitar*."

Beck held out his hands in question. "What? No kick in the stomach or another stab in the back?"

Vinni turned around slowly, his apple-cheeked face pensive. "Not this time, *Savitar*. Not this time." The Halfie lowered his head with a shake and walked out the door.

***

Rogan lay unmoving in the corner of his cell. He lost track of how many weeks he had been confined to King Rik Rojin's cells. It really didn't matter. He was never going to be freed. His friends would never know where to find him and, even if they came searching, the King would only mislead them with untruths.

He wondered if Beck had found Kiernan. Were they in Sarphia now? With Airron? When he didn't show up with his pendant, what would they do? Without a counter to Adrian Ravener's magic, the Mage would have free rein to kill all who stood in opposition and enslave those who did not.

It was hard not to feel guilty, as the reason for his current predicament fell squarely on his shoulders. He was the one who sauntered directly into Deepstone without any consideration of how the people would feel about having a shifter in their midst. For all they knew, he was a fugitive from exile. As a group with Beck, Kiernan and Airron, and along with King Maximus's decree, they had a chance of succeeding. But, Rogan traveling alone, as it was now painfully clear, had been a huge lapse in judgment and it had been his idea to split up. With Kiernan missing, Beck was in no condition to see things reasonably. Rogan centered his argument conveniently on the need to find his pendent, but his real intent had been to find his family.

A family that no longer existed in this world.

That wasn't entirely true. He still had an uncle, albeit one who wanted to secure a heavy weight around his neck and throw him into the Koda River.

He sat up from the stone floor, leaned against the wall and let his gaze slide over the only items in the tiny cell with him—a bucket of his urine and a plate of bread and cheese that the guards had left earlier and still sat untouched near the door. He wasn't hungry. He realized he was growing weak by not eating and moving about, but he couldn't find it in himself to care.

He flinched at a squeak coming from the shadowed corner of the cell that signified the arrival of one of the many rats that shared his dwelling and nipped at him while he slept. His fingers were raw and bloodied from their nighttime attacks, and he watched as the large rodent made its way over to his food.

He can have it, he thought, lying down and turning his back to the rat and his meal.

Sometime later, he jerked awake simultaneously by a rat chomping down harshly on this thumb and the sound of a key being inserted into the door of his cell. He batted the rat across the room and it smashed into the opposite wall with a horrible *thud.*

Rogan peered at the two figures bent over the lock and squatted onto the balls of his feet. Because of the guards' wariness of his magic, it was out of character for them to get this close to his cell. Usually, they just slid his plate of food under the iron bars with a long pole, well out of sight.

The door came unlocked and two Dwarves slipped furtively inside.

"What do you want?" he asked roughly.

"It's me, Dillon."

Rogan straightened from his crouch. "Dillon? What are you doing here?"

A sarcastic feminine voice answered. "Saving your hide, obviously."

Dillon threw Rogan's pack to him. "Come on, we have to leave before someone notices that the guard upstairs with his head on the table is not taking a nap."

Rogan stared at the duo questioningly. "Did you kill him?"

"No," replied Dillon, and then he asked with curiosity, "Would it matter?"

"To me it would. The guard is not guilty of any crime, and I could never condone the harm of innocent people. Especially on my behalf."

The female snorted. "How noble. Can we discuss after we get out of here?" she asked, looking anxiously back toward the stairs. She wore her long, auburn hair down, hanging casually around her shoulders, and it seemed out of place with her austere soldier's tunic.

Dillon nodded. "Rogan, this is Janin, a soldier in the Deepstone Army and, Highworld help me, my best friend. It's the only reason she's here breaking every Dwarven law in existence."

Janin turned and shook her head at Dillon playfully. "Not the only reason. I happen to think King Rik is being a blunderhead and that we need to get this shifter out of here. Unlike the King, who appears to harbor prejudice on this subject, I can see reason. Let me see.

Either we free this Dwarf or we end up enslaved by a fanatical Mage." She went to the cell door. "I always was a fan of logic."

Janin hurried out and led the way up the stairs with Rogan and Dillon close behind. At the top of the stairs, Rogan saw the guard with his head facedown on a wooden table. He did appear to be sleeping and, hopefully, that would buy them some time.

Rogan stepped behind the desk to grab his belt and long knife hanging from a peg behind the guard, and they sprinted out of the room and down a stone passageway, moving fast. Whenever they heard voices, Janin directed them into a shadowed alcove until the way was clear. After several long moments of running, they exited through an exterior door.

Rogan breathed in the fresh night air greedily. It smelled like sheer ecstasy after having been closeted underground for so long. His legs, unused to movement, trembled from the exertion and it was adrenaline alone that kept him upright and running after the others.

Janin stopped and turned to him. "Do you have a cloak?"

He opened his pack and was relieved to find his cloak still inside. He nodded.

"Put it on." She pointed. "We're going to be walking through that stone passageway ahead in sight of the night guards who will be on top of the wall above us. Whatever you do, do not run. Walk steady. Our uniforms will be visible so we shouldn't arouse any suspicion."

Rogan nodded and quickly donned his cloak.

"Don't put up the hood, it will look out of place. Follow closely."

Reluctantly, Rogan forced himself away from the safety of the shadows of the castle wall. Similar to the city of Deeport, the royal grounds were made up of a complex network of stone. As they neared the passageway, Dillon turned and waved up to the guards. Rogan didn't dare look up to see if Dillon's greeting was acknowledged. At least, he thought thankfully, he didn't hear any alarm.

It took every bit of willpower he possessed not to sprint for the streets and courtyard gate beyond. Imprisonment was not a fate he ever wished to revisit. He would burn this place to the ground—if only stone would burn—before he would allow the Dwarves to put him back into that cell.

They rounded a corner and Janin guided them briskly to a door that led back into the castle.

Rogan grabbed her arm. "Why are we going back in?" he hissed, unable to keep the fear from his voice.

She stopped and looked at him and then at his hand on her arm. "Unless you are prepared to use magic, get your hand off me or I will slice it off."

Reluctantly, he released her.

"In answer to your question, it is the safest and quickest route. There are tunnels in the castle that will take us underground and outside of the city wall."

He hesitated a moment, sweat beading his brow. "Fine, lead on."

They pushed back into the castle and into complete darkness.

"Dillon, where is the torch?" Janin asked, and Rogan could hear her fumbling around.

Dillon sounded panicked. "I left one right here and it's gone!"

With his eyes now adjusting to the gloom, Rogan could see the outline of the two Dwarves feeling around in the dark for the torch. He called forth a flame of light. "Does this help?"

They both looked up at him with a gasp, a mixture of both surprise and anger on their faces. "Don't do that!" snarled Janin.

"We need light, do we not? This is light."

"It's light created from magic which, in case you haven't heard, is outlawed on this island," Dillon retorted.

"Yes, well, the world has changed, Dillon. The Magical Kingdom of Pyraan has been destroyed, we are under threat of slavery at best and annihilation at worse by a rogue Mage, and we are running for our lives from a King who wants to murder me. Against that, you are worried about a flame to light our way?"

"Good point," murmured Dillon with a shrug.

Rogan turned away from them in frustration. "I just don't understand this fear of magic. Please tell me so I understand!"

"Have you forgotten that you were exiled in Pyraan for a reason, shifter?" Janin asked. "Did they not teach you anything about the legacy of magic use?"

"As a matter of fact, yes, and the legacy of magic before three evil Mages decided to destroy the world was inspiring. Magic was used to heal the dying, to create cures for the sick, to defend the weak. Does having magic automatically make you an evil person? If a Dwarf kills another, does it make all Dwarves murderers? If a dog bites a child, does it mean all dogs bite people?" He shook his head in annoyance. "You simply can't confine the legacy of magic to the Mage War."

Janin took a deep breath. "No, and I will admit that there are valuable uses to magic. But, there is also the ability to cause great harm on a very large scale. If one Dwarf kills another, it is one person. If a dog bites a child, it is one child. If an evil Mage decides to use magic for sinister purpose, he can destroy the world. That, my friend, is why we are afraid."

Rogan shook his head. "The blood oath prevents shifters from ever using magic to harm others and if we are fortunate enough to defeat Ravener, he will be the last of the Mages. So," he continued impatiently, "should I plunge us back into darkness so you can continue to stumble around looking for a torch and flint or should we be on our way?"

Dillon grinned and Janin snorted.

"Your help is appreciated and welcome," Dillon said magnanimously and gestured for Rogan to lead.

Rogan nodded curtly and sprinted ahead in the stone tunnel, the flame in his hand held out before him. As soon as they came to an intersection, he asked Dillon to point the way to his old home.

"I thought you might want to go there first. We better hurry, though, because the King will be thinking the same thing."

As Dillon started to move in front, Rogan grabbed his arm. "Thank you," he said sincerely. "Thank you and Janin both for getting me out of that cell. I honestly don't know how much longer I could have lasted."

Dillon held out his hand, and Rogan took it. "I know you don't remember me, but I have thought of you often over the years. For what it's worth, I think it's foolish to banish magic users." Dillon didn't let go of Rogan's arm, but held it tighter and looked him in the eye. "I am your friend, on that you can depend. I am in this with you to the end."

Rogan swallowed past a sudden burn in his throat. "Glad to have you on my side then, friend." He looked over at Janin who was anxiously looking down both sides of the tunnel. "You as well, Janin."

She smiled for the first time. "As much as I would like to stand around and chatter, a little more running would suit me just fine. We have demons to fight."

"Demons?" questioned Rogan sharply.

Dillon shrugged. "Did I forget to mention that?"

Just then, the alarm Rogan feared finally sounded.

CHAPTER 30

SISTERLY LOVE

Earthshine was less than a week away, but that fact no longer concerned Kiernan. Her relentless training left little room for any cognitive awareness of current or past events. She accepted the fact that she would always have a void in her heart and mind by her separation from Beck and Bajan, but it was slowly filling in with new purpose and activity.

Humming softly, she casually made her way to Gemini's chambers with the intention of discussing this evening's ceremony. Tonight the Gems were hosting a formal affair in her honor, proclaiming her a Friend of the Coven, the first of a three-step process to becoming a sorceress. The second step would be yearlong academic instruction in the use of all gems and their magical properties, and the third, practical training in the gem of choice. This last step usually took two years and at the end, Kiernan would be a sorceress.

She almost laughed out loud at the thought. Kiernan Grace Everard, mindshifter and Princess of Iserlohn, would be a witch.

She deliberately left out the most recent title bestowed on her. She was no longer that person. No longer on that path.

As she rounded the fountain in the center of the foyer, she came upon two of the Sect Leaders. Ruby directed the study of runes and deciphering the obfuscated language of ancient times, and Amethyst led the study of alchemy and the development of magical potions for both healing and spell casting. The two women often worked together in their crafts as many of the early instructions for potions were written in languages and symbols that only the sorceresses of Ruby's sect could interpret.

Ruby smiled at Kiernan and grasped her hands. "Kiernan, I'm so excited for the ceremony this evening. We're both very happy that you're on your way to becoming one of us."

Kiernan smiled, flattered. "Thank you, Ruby. I'm glad to be here, too, I truly am. You have all made me feel very welcome." She nodded politely and moved to step around the women to continue on her way, but they stepped in front of her.

"Why don't you join us for lunch?" Amethyst asked, taking Kiernan's arm and turning her around.

Kiernan shrugged away as politely as she could. "Thank you for the offer, Amethyst, but I really must be on my way. I have to speak to Gemini."

Amethyst barked out a laugh. "Gemini is extremely busy, Kiernan, and she doesn't have time to spare for every silly girl who feels the need to interrupt." She turned to Ruby. "Can you imagine? The woman would never get any work done!"

Kiernan felt her face heat. "I...I didn't realize."

"Yes, well, now you know. Gemini is enmeshed in the multitude of details required to administrate this coven and must not be disturbed. If you can't join us for lunch, then run along," she said, shooing Kiernan away from the stairs with two hands.

Kiernan noticed a calculating look pass between the two Sect Leaders. Her intuition told her something was amiss, but she allowed herself to be ushered away. "Thank you. I will just return to my room then to rest before the ceremony."

Ruby nodded victoriously. "Very good."

Kiernan started back toward her room and watched as the two women continued on their way to the dining hall. As soon as she felt it was safe, she picked up the sides of her dress and sprinted up the staircase to Gemini's office. Halfway down the corridor, she paused with her back to the wall. *Are the Sect Leaders really trying to keep me from Gemini?*

Determined to find out, she pushed off the wall and walked the rest of the way to Gemini's chambers. Light spilled into the hallway from the door left ajar. She didn't dare look in, but as it turned out, she didn't have to. She could hear clearly the voices inside.

"It's none of our affair." *Gemini.*

A hand slapped down on a desk. "It most certainly is, Gemini!" *Diamond.* "You've always had faith in my craft before. Why do you wish to discount it now? There is great destruction in store for Massa, destruction on the scale of the Mage War! I have foreseen that Kiernan is one of the *Savitars!* She must fight!"

Another voice. "Gemini, I trust in Diamond's visions and agree with her that we must get involved. As Kiernan is training to be a member of my sect, I will personally accompany her into battle as will all of my Gems. Harm will not get a peek at the Princess, I promise you that."

"No, Citrine." The reply came so softly that Kiernan almost didn't hear it.

But she did hear the frustrated sighs of Diamond and Citrine. "Why Gemini? Why are you doing this?"

A chair scraped back. Gemini must have risen. "She was my best friend, Diamond. I promised Grace I would protect her daughter—with my life if necessary."

Diamond snorted. "Her life will be forfeit anyway if she doesn't fight."

"Not so. There are three other *Savitars.* Nowhere in your visions or in prophecy does it say that all four have to be there at the battle. Let the three other *Savitars* fight! Kiernan will stay here where she will be safe. It is what her mother wanted and what I swore to do."

Diamond launched into another argument, but Kiernan had heard enough. She walked down the passageway and back toward the stairs, tears welling in her eyes.

It amazed her at the lengths her mother had gone through to protect her. First by concealing her shifting abilities from her father, and then by attempting to shelter her from exile within the Gem coven, and finally by extracting a vow of protection from her sorceress friend. Unlike her father, who banished her from his life and lied about finding Bajan, her mother had done everything in her power to care for her and keep her safe.

I will honor my mother's wishes. It is the least I can do for all of her sacrifice. If she wished for me to live in Elloree, then I will make it so. I will stay here with the Gems and become one of them. Become a witch.

Maximus Everard, Adrian Ravener and Beck Atlan be damned.

***

Kiernan shivered as she waited alone outside of the ceremonial hall. Whether due to her jittery nerves or the fact that she was totally naked under her black robe, she was unsure. Probably a little of both. Tonight was a new beginning for her.

She paused at a sudden errant thought. *Will this really be any different from exile?* The Gems were as cloistered as the shifters had been. How long before she railed against the invisible walls of this new confinement? *No!* There was no turning back now. The Gems had accepted her and she must accept them in return.

The doors to the hall opened and Citrine walked out. She was dressed in a black robe identical to Kiernan's with a black veil covering her face. Kiernan only knew it was Citrine by the distinctive red braid peeking through.

"We're ready for you."

Kiernan took a deep breath and nodded.

"Don't be nervous, Kiernan. This is the shortest and most straightforward of all our rites. It will be over quickly."

Kiernan lowered her eyes. "I'm not nervous, it's just that everything has happened so fast."

Citrine smiled through the veil. "Do you not wish to be one of us?"

"I do! It...has been difficult, that's all."

"I know, but we're going to be sisters soon. I'm here for you any time you wish to talk. Do you hear me?"

Kiernan nodded. "I'm ready."

"Good." Citrine reached for her hand and led the way into the hall. Hundreds of candles were arranged in a semi circle in the center of the room. Soft chanting from many feminine voices drifted to her from above, but she couldn't make out the words or see faces in the concealment of shadows where the candlelight didn't reach. The strong smell of incense filled her nose and she breathed in the piquant scent.

Citrine led her through the breach in the circle of candles to the lone veiled figure standing in the middle and knelt, pulling Kiernan down with her.

"High Priestess," Citrine intoned, "we ask for your blessing in naming this woman, Kiernan Grace Everard, a Friend of the Coven."

"Who asks?"

"We all do!" was the reply from Citrine and all of the Gems in attendance in the dark behind her.

"Please rise."

Kiernan rose to her feet shakily and felt a moment of panic when Citrine left her side and departed back through the glowing tapers. She stood alone now in front of the figure she knew to be Gemini, but kept her eyes lowered.

"In the presence of the Highworld spirits and the entire coven, do you come to us of your own free will? Unencumbered of material possessions?"

"I do," she replied, as instructed earlier by Citrine.

Gemini's hands reached out and gently opened Kiernan's robe and pushed it along the top of her shoulders until it fell to the ground. She trembled as the cool air accosted her body.

"Do you swear to keep secret the arts of our practice? Keep secret the rituals and ceremonies for which you will now have knowledge?"

"I do."

"Do you swear to protect and defend your coven of sisters from all harm?"

"I do."

Gemini lifted her veil back over her head.

Kiernan swayed as she watched her, suddenly feeling light-headed from the strong incense. She closed her eyes and her head rolled back. *This feels wonderful.*

The chanting stopped.

Very softly, almost in a whisper, Gemini said, "As High Priestess, I find you worthy of this coven." She reached out her hand and lightly cupped Kiernan's chin and kissed her on the lips.

"I accept you mind..." she said and kissed Kiernan on the side of her temple.

"Body..." she whispered and leaned down to kiss Kiernan's stomach, right above her navel.

"And, soul..." she said, placing a kiss on Kiernan's left breast over her heart.

Kiernan kept her eyes closed during the intimate ritual and flinched when she felt Gemini walk around her and drape her robe back over her shoulders.

"Let us now close the circle of sisterhood and let it never be broken."

One by one the Gems approached and filled the gap in the circle with one of the candles in the outer ring.

It's over. I am committed now to the sorceresses of Elloree, just as Mother wished.

When at last it was Kiernan and Gemini alone in the ring of candlelight, her emotions ruptured and she began to sob.

"Now, now," Gemini consoled. "Why the tears? You are a Friend of the Coven for now and evermore."

"Forgive me, Gemini. I...I have just felt so alone. I've missed my mother for so long."

Gemini folded her into her arms. "I miss her, too. She was a remarkable woman, and you know what? You're pretty remarkable, too. She would be very proud of you."

"Thank you, Gemini, your words mean more than you will ever know."

"You have us now, Kiernan. You have all of your Gem sisters and you have me. I already think of you as a daughter."

And, that made Kiernan cry even harder.

CHAPTER 31

ELLOREE

Forced to wait for a ferry at the pier in Iserport, Beck paced impatiently. Instead of traveling east as originally planned, he and Bajan would now be traveling west on the Illian River directly to Elloree. *In the opposite direction I need to be.*

No one could tell him exactly where the sorceresses lived, but cautioned him to be wary. Although, the people of Iserport had known about the Gems for some time, unless a shifter daughter was born, they generally stayed as far away as possible.

He wondered why the Gems, a coven of witches by all accounts, would kidnap Kiernan. He asked Bajan to try and reach her, but the Draca just shook his head. Beck wasn't sure if that meant they were too far away for communication or he had already tried and she hadn't answered.

"Beck Atlan?"

Beck turned to a thin man with a tanned, weather-beaten face walking toward him with his hand extended.

Beck shook the man's hand. "I take it you will be our captain to Elloree."

The man laughed good-naturedly. "Well, I'll be navigating the ferry if you can call that a captain, lad. The name is Rafe Wilden, but just Rafe is fine."

Beck smiled. "Rafe it is. When do we leave?"

"Now." He pointed to an open-sided, flat-bottomed boat with sloping square bow and stern. "There she is, the *Blue Lady*. Make yourselves comfortable."

Beck and Bajan boarded and were apparently the only passengers on the *Blue Lady* that afternoon. A cool breeze ruffled his hair as he grasped one of the vertical beams that supported the canvas roof of the ferry and gazed out over the Illian River. The sun sat brilliantly in a red-orange ball right above the western horizon.

The ferry lurched when Rafe jumped aboard with his crew of two young oarsmen. The three men worked as a well-practiced team to push away from the dock and steer in a westerly direction out of Lake Traverse and onto the Illian.

As they set out, Beck's thoughts were a jumbled array of hopes for his fellow *Savitars*. He hoped Rogan had been able to retrieve his pendant and discover word of his birth family. He hoped Airron survived his ordeal in Havenport and was awaiting them in Sarphia. And, he hoped more than anything else in this world that very soon he would be able to hold Kiernan in his arms again.

That final, particularly incredible wish was his last conscious thought as he slid down the rail at his back and fell fast asleep.

He awoke reluctantly sometime later to what felt like a large file being dragged along his cheek. He waved the affectionate Draca Cat away and opened his eyes. "I'm up, I'm up," he said groggily and realized it was afternoon—of the following day!

"Good afternoon to you, lad," Rafe greeted cheerfully.

The short oars of yesterday were replaced by long poles as the three oarsmen navigated shallower waters.

Beck stood, sore from sleeping up against the boat's rails the entire night. "Good afternoon. How much longer to Elloree?"

Rafe pointed with a jerk of his chin. "Right around the next bend. Rope!"

One of the men put down his long pole to retrieve a mooring line with a noose on one end. When the *Blue Lady* steered around the next curve in the river, a lone dock with two wooden pilings came into view.

"Welcome to Elloree, lad!"

Elloree? There was nothing within sight except the dock, a small, pebbled beach and a dirt trail that led into a heavily-wooded forest.

The man with the rope tossed it over the side and looped it expertly over one of the pilings pulling the ferry up tight to the dock.

Bajan jumped from the boat in an impressively long leap that caused Rafe to whistle in appreciation.

Beck followed hesitantly.

"The witches live somewhere along that trail," Rafe said. "Never been there myself, so not sure how far. Good luck to you, lad." Rafe gestured for Beck to unhook the rope and throw it back to him.

"Wait! When will you be back? I'll need to travel back to Iserport as soon as I locate my friend."

Rafe shook his head. "Not going to be back."

Beck stood at the end of the dock with the rope in his hand. "You must have heard the stories," he growled in panic. "I'll need to get back to Iserport!"

Rafe's features were unapologetic. "Of course I've heard the stories! And, that's why *I* have to get back!" he shouted. "I have a sick wife and children to see after."

The pebbled beach under the dock began to stir with Beck's anger. "You would doom the island to destruction, then?"

The ferryman glanced with unease at the beach. "I'm no hero, lad, out to save the world. I only wish to protect my family."

Beck glared at Rafe and then reluctantly threw the rope back onto the ferry. The oarsmen hastily swung the *Blue Lady* around to head back east. Rafe looked back once more, and this time Beck detected remorse from him.

I need more than remorse, Rafe Wilden!

Turning away in disgust, he gestured to Bajan and they walked along the beach toward the forest, the name of which escaped him. He should have known it with all of the time he spent studying Gage's maps, but he didn't.

Doubt plagued him. Even if he found Kiernan this very minute, how were they to travel to Sarphia in the five days left before Earthshine? Short of sprouting wings, it was entirely impossible.

Yet, I have no choice but to keep moving.

The thought sent his heart and legs pumping. "Let's go, Bajan!" He ran toward the opening in the forest and onto the faded trail, the thick boughs overhead immediately blotting out the sunlight, and the long line of trees along the path reminding him of shadowed sentinels rigidly keeping watch and ready to engage in battle at the slightest provocation.

They ran for a full hour before Beck stopped.

"Bajan, do you think you can try and reach out to Kiernan before we go any further?"

The Draca Cat nodded, sat back and closed his eyes.

***

Princess? Princess, I am in Elloree! Can you hear me?

Nothing.

Enough of this silence, Princess Kiernan Everard! I know you can hear me. As your friend and protector, I demand that you answer me!

Nothing. Then...

Go away, Bajan.

His body convulsed in relief. *Thank the Highworld you are unharmed! Where are you?*

Bajan, you must go. I am happy here with the Gems.

Gems? What are the Gems?

The witches of Elloree. I have learned much since I have been here, my friend. About my mother, her last wishes and the ancient bond between our ancestors.

I understand how you must feel as you have longed for your mother ever since I have known you. But, Princess, have you forgotten your duty? We must go to Callyn-Rhe. All of our lives depend on it!

Pause.

I no longer believe that Bajan. It was the half-mad mutterings of a dying man. That's all.

That is not true, Princess! I have been fighting Ravener's demons for weeks. They are very real and we are teetering on the brink of war!

Silence.

Beck is with me.

Silence.

We are coming, Princess. We are coming to get you.

Silence.

Princess! We are coming!

The connection was severed.

***

Beck darted impatiently around the Draca like a hummingbird. He could tell by Bajan's posture and black eyes that he had finally made contact.

Bajan closed his eyes and when he opened them once again, the icy green orbs were furious.

"Well? What did she say?" The Draca turned his back on him. "Is she still here in Elloree?"

Bajan nodded his head in the affirmative.

"Ah, Bajan! This is the best news we have had in a long time! Come!" Beck strode forward onto the path, anxious now to keep going.

The two alternately walked and ran until nightfall before emerging from the forest into an inviting moonlit valley dotted with wildflowers. Unsure how much farther they would have to travel before reaching Elloree, he decided to stop for a rest. After waving Bajan back into the forest to hunt, he sat on an old log and pulled dried beef and cheese from his pack.

As he ate, Beck reached out to the landscape with his magic and found what he was looking for. He waved his hand over the earth between his feet and beckoned the seed of a pink dendrobium orchid to life. The reed-like stem pushed through the soil, the short leaves and dormant buds blossoming with life.

He picked the rare flower with great care as a gift he intended to present to Kiernan when he saw her again. As he was wrapping the orchid to put into his pack, he heard Bajan whine.

"What is it, Bajan?" he asked and walked over to find the Draca digging at the ground.

His eyes widened in surprise at sight of a black grate built into a small hillock. *That's odd. Why would there be a grate here in the middle of nowhere?* He peered through the bars, but could see nothing beyond the inky darkness inside. Grabbing the iron in his hands, he gave it a sturdy pull and the door swung open.

He looked at Bajan. They simply didn't have time for idle explorations, but he was curious to see where it led.

The Draca Cat nodded his silent consent, and the pair stepped into the black hole.

Beck immediately felt around with his hands and his magic, but it wasn't fast enough. He had only taken two steps when the ground disappeared from under his feet, and he plummeted downward into oblivion.

CHAPTER 32

A FAMILY FOR ROGAN

Avalon Ravener stopped her horse at the edge of a sharp precipice and peered out across the Valley of Flame. The deep vale had been named for the profusion of red and yellow birds of paradise that carpeted the valley floor and gave the appearance that the terrain was afire, but now all that carpeted the floor was a profusion of soldiers.

The formidable Starfell Keep sat perched on the eastern hill looking exactly as it had the last time she had seen it despite the passing of centuries.

If only I can make it there, she thought, fighting an exhaustion that threatened to tumble her from her saddle. It had been weeks since she killed the Elven *Savitar,* and it had taken all of her skill as a bodyshifter and sorceress to evade the Elves and animals that pursed her relentlessly ever since. Added to that misery was a string of bad luck with horses and getting lost a time or two in the Puu Rainforest. Oh, yes, her mood was foul indeed.

Her body still pained her where that blasted eagle ripped a chunk of flesh from her back and scored her face. If she had been an amethyst user, she could have made the potion necessary to heal her wounds, but her calling had always been to the sapphire and spell casting.

It may be too late, but she would ask Adrian to reopen the wounds and restore them properly when she reached the safety of Starfell Keep. Her hand lifted to her face to gingerly touch the three raised welts. *If I'm left with these scars permanently, I'll rouse that insufferable Elf from the Highworld and kill him again!*

At least now, her brother had nothing to worry about. The prophecy was dead. Without the Elf and his pendant, the other *Savitars* had no way of finding their way to Callyn-Rhe.

Her mount snorted impatiently in the cool dawn air, anxious now to go down into the valley after catching scent of other horses below. Avalon lashed out and struck the horse cruelly on the side of her head. The mare neighed in displeasure, but didn't bolt. Avalon had too tight of a rein on the animal. "Stupid beast," she muttered, and kicked the mare's ribs to get her moving down the hill.

As she descended, she wondered what her brother had been up to while she had been gone. She heard many disturbing stories during her travels of demons in the night attacking the citizens of Massa. *My brother's doing?* She wasn't aware that he was capable of summoning spirits from beyond, but learned more years ago than she cared to remember not to underestimate him.

The first Cyman sentries that spotted her sprang to attention as she drew near.

"Stop there!" one of them shouted and more men ran forward, creating a wall of defenders.

She continued to approach, and when she was within ten paces of the soldiers, she lowered the hood of her cloak. The sentries recognized her immediately and shrank back, eyeing her distrustfully. Booted feet pounded away to the east and she guessed that a runner was off to tell Adrian of her return. None of the soldiers made any further move to stop or address her, so she directed the mare forward into the heart of the camp.

She passed thousands of soldiers asleep on the bare ground, and those that were not sleeping were engaged in various camp activities. Most watched her pass with thinly veiled hatred. She knew they didn't like her, but it mattered very little to her. As long as they were frightened of her, she was content.

Women's cries could be heard from inside one of the tents. *So, my brother has managed to get his hands on some of the female Elves in Haventhal. Good for him.*

The mare whinnied again as she neared an improvised corral containing half a dozen horses. Spoils for Adrian, certainly. She knew the Cymans wouldn't ride them.

It took her hours to pick her way through the camped army, but she eventually made her way to the road cut into the eastern side of the valley that led upward to Starfell Keep.

For the first time, she noticed shadows in the darkened woods off to her right. At first she thought it just the pre-dawn light playing tricks on her eyes, but quickly realized it was something more. The shadows moved and slithered between the trees with purpose, and the sight sent shivers down her spine.

Arriving at the top of the hill, she found Adrian waiting for her in the courtyard of the Keep. He stood there in all black with his hands clasped behind his back. Seeing him again caused unexpected emotion to well inside of her. *Despite his shortcomings, he is my brother. Love may be too strong a word for what I feel for him, but there is something indefinable there.*

"Sister! How nice of you to return." He frowned as she dismounted. "What happened to your face?"

"A minor sufferance for our cause. I will ask you to heal them later."

"I am a Mage, Avalon, not a bloody miracle worker," he said with a scowl. "Come. We have much to catch up on."

She handed over the reins of her horse to a Cyman soldier and followed Adrian up the stairs to the Keep. At the enormous double doors, Adrian threw them open with a flourish and waved his arm around the marble foyer. "Welcome home."

Her eyes eagerly absorbed every detail as she scanned the bespelled interior. It was exactly as she remembered with the magnificent staircase and elegant cornices with running leaf pattern that ran the length of the room. Stunning, stained glassed doors led to a sitting room on the left, the furniture still covered in dust cloths. And, the nonpareil—a sculpture of Galen Starr standing erect in the center of the foyer holding a staff in one hand and a book in the other.

You are right, Adrian. I am home. And, a Netherworld curse to the next person who tries to take it from me.

Adrian pointed to the sitting room. "Let us go and sit down. I want to hear all about your travels."

She followed him into the room, and he hastily ripped the cloths from the sofa and one of the chairs. He took the chair and leaned forward on his elbows. "Tell me. Do you have confirmation that the *Savitars* are dead? Did they perish in the flooding of Pyraan?"

"No, they didn't."

"What?"

"They are alive, Adrian, but they are children. Just children. Powerful, yes, but young and inexperienced." She proceeded to tell him all she knew about the four young *Savitars* and the pendants that Galen Starr instructed them to locate. "Once fitted together, the pendants contain a map to the power that can destroy our plans."

"How do we stop them?"

"It's done. I killed one."

He sat upright. "You killed one of the *Savitars*?"

She nodded. "Thus, the scars. He was an Elf and a bodyshifter, and I now have his pendant with me."

Adrian's face sagged in relief. "I could kiss you, sister! Well done. But, really, what are the chances that I would have the *Savitars* directly in my sight and let them escape? I actually ordered them to go! Regardless, this is very good news. Without the *Savitars* to interfere, the next phase of our plan is guaranteed to succeed."

"Which is?"

"That the Kings swear fealty to me by Earthshine in five days time."

Avalon stood from the sofa. "I'm not so sure, Adrian. At least not with the King of Iserlohn, anyway. He plans to fight."

"Is he bloody mad?"

"The defeat of Teag and his soldiers outside the walls of Nysa bolstered the King's confidence. Even if it was with the help of the *Savitars*."

Adrian shook his head. "I thought as much when Teag didn't return. He got what he deserved. How many dead Massans did he leave in his wake?"

"None."

"Not one?"

"No, I told you the *Savitars* are very powerful. But, there are only three of them left and they are unsophisticated. They will be but pesky gnats against the full might of the Cymans. And, us, of course."

The front door slammed open interrupting their conversation. Adrian's captain, Lucin, stormed into the sitting room. He glared directly at her. "I 'eard you were back. What news do you 'ave of my son?"

"Nice to see you, too, Lucin," she drawled.

He waited, arms crossed.

She sighed and sat back down. "When I last saw Titus, he was alive. In fact, he seemed to be quite at home with his captors."

"Why didn't you bring 'im back with you?"

"I tried, but I couldn't do so. Not with the *Savitars* and all of the soldiers crawling around King Maximus's palace. If you want your son back, Lucin, you had better be prepared to fight for him."

He narrowed his eye at Adrian. "You think it will come to that, Master?"

"It looks that way. Avalon tells me the Massans plan to contest my rule."

Lucin nodded. "I will ready the men."

Adrian held up a finger. "Before you go, please order one of the soldiers to bring me a woman from the tents."

Lucin glared at Adrian boldly, allowing the disgust to show on his face.

Avalon stood. "Did you hear my brother, Captain? That was an order! Now move."

Adrian snickered as Lucin turned to go. "It's been a while, Captain, since you've seen your wife," he taunted. "If you or one of your officers would like to—"

"Never!" the captain roared, spinning back. "I 'ave never in my life, nor ever will, commit rape against a woman! As long as I breathe, neither will any of the soldiers in my command. I can't stop you from doing what you will, but the spirits know I wish I could."

Avalon laughed at the livid captain and his ridiculous notions.

One of the guards from outside the Keep rushed into the sitting room, eye blinking wildly.

"Captain! They're 'ere! An army approaches the Valley of Flame from the west!"

***

The small brick house sat apart from the others on the street. Neglected and rundown, it was obvious that no one had entered the home in quite a long time. Weeds popped up through the cracks in the stone walk and the windows were boarded with slats of wood.

Dillon and Janin shifted uneasily as they searched the area, but Rogan stood frozen in place, unable to tear his eyes or tumultuous thoughts from the house in front of him. In a chilling torrent, memories he did not know he possessed flowed through him, and he began to recall the events that led to his exile.

The scene unfolded behind his mind's eye as though it were happening at that very moment.

A six-year-old Rogan played in the front yard, and his father ran up behind him and tossed him into the air. Laughing, Rogan turned in his father's arms to wave good-bye to his friend, Dillon.

His mother stood in the doorway with an apron tied around her waist, chestnut hair pulled back at the nape of her neck, calling them both to dinner with a smile on her face.

Somewhere nearby, a dog began to bark frantically.

Then, the ominous sound of horses thundering down the small lane.

His father's head whipped around toward the horsemen. With a panicked cry, he raced toward the house and shoved Rogan into his mother's arms.

She clutched him protectively to her breast. "Gordin! What do we do?"

"Run!"

She sprinted out the back door and lifted him into the back of a wagon hitched to their plow horse. She hushed him gently and told him to stay down and hang on tight as she climbed in beside him.

His father charged out of the house and mounted the horse, slapping his hand harshly against the animal's rump. The horse, evidently not used to such rough treatment, took off with a lurch.

Both versions of Rogan were crying now. The boy because he was frightened, and the man because he knew how it would all end. How could his father hope to outrun the King's men—for that was surely who they were—with a plow horse?

Rogan tried to yell out to him, to warn him, but no sound issued from his mouth.

His father's face looked crazed and wide-eyed as he raced along the narrow and uneven road that ran through the sparse forest behind their house. He tried to maneuver a sharp corner and the King's men gained on them. Predictably, one of the back wheels caught in a rut, and the wagon bed swung around the horse and smashed into a tree, sending all three occupants sailing through the air to the ground.

It was over in an instant, both parents dead from the impact.

They died in an impulsive attempt to save his life. The only reason Rogan survived at all was by landing on his mother's soft body before slamming to the ground.

It's all my fault.

"Rogan!" He was jolted out of his memory-filled trance by Dillon. "Can you hear me?"

Rogan held up his hand to stay Dillon, walked a few feet away into the trees, fell to his knees and vomited. He remained that way for several long moments, grateful that neither Janin nor Dillon tried to approach. It surprised him that he had known all along what really happened to his parents but suppressed the memory because it had been so painful. All it had taken was one glimpse of his childhood home to trigger the recollection of what had transpired that fateful day.

There was consolation in the remembrance as well. He could now vividly recall the faces of his mother and father, heretofore always indefinable, shadowed visages. He could now clearly feel the profound love they had for him. He had never been abandoned. He had been loved and protected until the very end. The knowledge of these truths proved to be the antidote for something inside of him that he wasn't aware was in need of healing.

When he finally felt like he had control of his emotions and nausea, he walked shakily back to his companions. He braced himself for a taunt from Janin, but she only looked at him with concern in her eyes. "Are you all right? Do you want to keep going?"

"I have no other choice." He held out his hand to Dillon. The Dwarf looked at him sideways but took his hand. "I remember you. I remember everything. It's good to see you again, old friend."

Dillon pumped his hand firmly and slapped him on the back. "About time!"

"Your memories came back to you?" asked a shocked Janin.

"Yes, and they were not all pleasant. But, I can't talk about it now. I really must hurry and retrieve the pendant so I can reunite with my friends." He watched Dillon and Janin glance at each other. "Is there a problem?"

"No problem," Janin said. "As long as you realize we're coming with you to Sarphia."

Rogan shook his head. "No, it's too dangerous—"

Janin laughed aloud. "And we have been on a picnic this whole time?"

"You don't understand what we face. *I* don't even know what we face, but it will be formidable magic to be sure."

Janin picked up her pack from the ground at her feet. "Discussion over. We're coming."

Dillon nodded his agreement.

Rogan swallowed in relief, secretly pleased. It would be nice to have his two Dwarven friends with him. "I'll be glad to have you. Have you seen anything?"

"No one," replied Dillon.

"Well, be prepared. The King's men are near, I'm sure of it." Rogan watched them both nod in a form of grim excitement that only a soldier can appreciate and then turned and led the way through the trees. He recalled a back door from his memory and decided it would be safer to go in through there.

Circling around the house at the line of trees, the trio stopped for a moment at the edge of the clearing in back before cautiously approaching at a running crouch.

Rogan went straight to the door and opened it, a flame of fire held out in front of him.

He heard Janin whisper very softly, close to his ear. "Forget what I said earlier. I love when you do that."

The tips of his ears burned with embarrassment as he pushed inside into what turned out to be the kitchen. There wasn't much to see, so he passed through into a living room with two interior doors branching from it, one on each side of the house.

He went into the one on the right. A small bed had been pushed up against one wall and a wooden chest sat atop the mattress. He walked over and lifted the lid to examine the contents. Clothes, shoes and a few pieces of jewelry, but no pendant. Pocketing the jewelry, he left to search the other room. Dillon and Janin were already inside, but there was nothing to see—it was completely empty.

"It has to be here!" Rogan growled in frustration. He went back into the living room and then the kitchen, but his search turned up nothing.

Sudden movement outside the boarded window near the door caught his eye.

"Get down!" he shouted just as the front door opened and someone hurled a lit torch into the living room. The oil from the pitch dripped onto the threadbare carpet and immediately went up in a blaze.

Rogan thrust out his hands, gathered the flames together into a cohesive ball and snuffed out the energy of the fire with little effort.

"Come on out, shifter!" shouted a voice from outside. "Do it peacefully and no one will get hurt!"

Rogan crawled over to the window and peered out through the wooden slats. "Six Iron Fists," he whispered to Dillon and Janin. "Those are your fellow soldiers out there. Go out the back now, and they'll never know you were involved."

Dillon reached out to put a hand on his shoulder. "I am here, Rogan, because it's the right thing to do. I could never live with myself if I left you to face this on your own. She's here," he said, jerking his thumb at Janin, "because she likes a good fight."

Rogan turned to see that Janin still had the same excited glint in her eyes he had seen earlier. He shook his head. "I have to find a way to do this peacefully. I can't kill innocent men."

"We can still thump them pretty good," Janin pointed out.

"Either way, I won't go back to that cell. Too many lives depend on it. Ready?"

After receiving a nod from his companions, Rogan got to his feet, sprinted toward the door, and shouldered into it sending splinters flying as he sailed out into the evening air and dove to the side.

That's when all hell broke loose.

CHAPTER 33

AQUATAINE

Beck tried with all of his considerable might to control his downward drop, but couldn't gain purchase in the steep tunnel smooth and slippery with water and moss. He could hear Bajan scrabbling just as furiously behind him, roaring and spitting all the way. After what seemed like a lifetime of falling, he heard water rushing below him seconds before he plunged into its warm depths. Using his arms and legs to propel to the surface, his head broke through just as the Draca Cat crashed into the pool beside him.

He wiped the water from his eyes.

What is this?

To either side of him, miniature waterfalls that originated from some unseen source splashed down into the lagoon where he now treaded water. Just ahead, a crescent-shaped, white sandy beach led to another lagoon and cave opening. In between, crystallized stalagmites jutted up from the sand reaching for their stalactite kin hanging from a tiered ceiling. Higher still was what appeared to be a sky studded with millions of emeralds, and their glow blanketed the atmosphere in a soft green hue.

"Greetings, stranger! Over here!"

Beck gasped in shock as a group of people pulled themselves from the second pool and hurried across the beach toward him.

There are people here? Beck paused. *Dear Highworld, are they nude?*

"Do not be afraid," one shouted to him. "Come out of the water and join us."

Cautiously, Beck swam to shore with Bajan beside him. A closer look determined that, no, they weren't nude...but, not quite clothed either. People...but, not quite human. Their flesh-toned bodies androgynous in nature with all of the shapes and angles that normally distinguished male from female smoothed out. Yet the face of the man beckoning to him had a definite masculine cast and the woman next to him was decidedly female.

"I'm Beck Atlan," he said, nodding his head in greeting. "And, this is Bajan."

The people made little murmuring sounds of delight at the introduction of the Draca Cat. The same man spoke again, a very tall and lean fellow. "Welcome to Aquataine, Master Atlan. My name is Digby."

Beck puzzled over the sound of his voice. The only way he could describe it was wet, as though spoken around a mouthful of water. Beck narrowed his eyes. *Are those gills on his neck? Impossible*, he thought, shaking his head.

"Digby, what is this place?"

"This is our home, Aquataine," came the slurpy reply.

A sudden shout and splash from the cavern preceded the arrival of a young boy on the back of...a porpoise. The two frolicked in the second pool, the porpoise leaping into the air in a high arc only to dive back down into the water and disappear from view. They would re-emerge a few seconds later, the boy clinging tightly to the leathery, slick hide with his knees and roaring in unrestrained laughter. Beck shook his head in wonder as the playful pair turned and vanished back into the cave.

"Look, Diggy—"

"Digby,"

"Sorry, Digby. Forgive us for intruding. It was quite by accident that the grate we found led us to...Aquataine. We would appreciate your help in returning to the outside as quickly as possible."

Digby motioned for Beck to follow. "First, you must meet with the Elders at the Temple of Grotte."

Beck opened his mouth to protest, but Digby stopped him. "You have no choice, Master Atlan. It is the law in Aquataine. Any outsider who discovers our world must meet with the Elders before they can leave again."

Beck bit back a retort and nodded, figuring it would be faster to just meet with the Elders so he and Bajan could be on their way.

He followed Digby through the stalagmites. Curious, he asked, "Digby, why is it so light here? Not only is it evening, but this place is so far underground, it should be dark all the time."

Digby pointed up toward the cave's ceiling. "Glow worms."

Beck squinted up at the luminescent pinpricks of green light on the ceiling of the cavern. "Glow worms?"

"Yes, the worms are our only source of light and because they are nocturnal creatures, they glow at night and sleep during the day. So, in Aquataine, day is night and night is day," he said proudly, as if the Aquatainians had discovered some form of logic as of yet beyond those that dwelled on the land above.

"I've never seen a glow worm before."

Digby shrugged. "Oh, they are all over the island if you look close enough."

When they reached the end of the beach before the opening to the cavern, Digby led them to a small raft tethered to one of the stalagmites. They boarded and remained standing as Digby took hold of a long pole and guided them into the waterway. The rest of the Aquatainians simply dove into the water and glided through the lagoon with the same ease as the porpoise.

"Digby, does anyone in Massa know about Aquataine?"

"Not many. We use the grates whenever we have to go to the Surface World for supplies, but since you must have the use of magic to open them, visitors are rare."

"Magic?"

"Of course," he said, laughing, and it sounded like a gurgle. "Haven't you figured it out yet, Master Atlan? Everyone in Aquataine is a watershifter."

Beck was stunned. "Watershifter! I...I thought there were only the four metamagics of power?"

"Four? Highworld, no! There are many metamagics known to us and many more that are not. What kind of shifter are you?"

"Earth."

"Well, then, we shift the water the same way you do the ground. As you may have noticed, we have also started to take on the physical characteristics of water beings and can now move rapidly through the water without even shifting." Digby pointed to his bare webbed feet and webbed hands. It wasn't something particularly discernible unless you knew what to look for.

"How many ports to the...Surface World do you have?"

"Four now. We had one in the northern part of the island, but it flooded."

I just have to ask. "Are those gills on your neck?"

Digby nodded with a grin, proud of his magic and the manifestation of that magic on his appearance.

The watershifter steered through the cave entrance and announced ceremoniously, "May I present the city of Ebba!"

A city of waterways instead of roadways, Ebba bustled with activity. The canals were crowded with people swimming or riding porpoises or steering rafts similar to the one he and Bajan were riding. The people came in all shapes and sizes, but it was easier than he first thought to distinguish the men from the women due to their facial features, mannerisms and hairstyles. Most of the buildings perched on stilts, but some sat directly on the sandy shore. Much like any other city in Massa, merchants sold their wares in front of taverns and inns. Along the beaches, couples strolled happily arm in arm, laughing and somersaulting into the water. Children waved and shouted at Bajan as they glided by.

An unbelievable, utopian waterworld. I wish Kiernan could see this magical place.

Digby guided them ashore in front of a modest temple constructed of limestone and clay, the front portico supported by three pink granite pillars. "Word was sent ahead, so the Elders will be expecting you," Digby informed him. "As soon as your meeting is finished, I will show you the way out."

"I will need to go fast."

Digby chuckled with a sly grin. "You have never seen a watershifter in action, have you?"

Beck smiled back. It was hard not to like the young, congenial watershifter. He reminded him of Airron.

Alighting from the raft, Beck and Bajan approached the temple and walked through an archway that led to the dim, cool interior of a vestibule. A young girl appeared and motioned him inside. Her eyes widened in shock when she saw the Draca Cat, but she quickly lowered her head and held out a towel.

Beck looked at it uncertainly and then realized the towel was for him. He took it from the girl and patted the wetness from his hair and clothes, hoping that was what was expected.

The girl glanced up and nodded her approval. When he had finished, he handed the towel back to her and started to walk further into the room.

"Mister!" she admonished in a whisper, her face pale in shock. "Your shoes!"

"Huh? Oh, right." He quickly bent down and removed his boots.

When the girl was at last satisfied, she led them to the back of the temple to a dome-shaped chamber where three men sat cross-legged on the floor, all with varying lengths of white hair.

Beck approached with Bajan.

The man seated in the middle, and who appeared to be the oldest of the three, spoke. "Welcome, shifter," he burbled out in the same watery voice as Digby. "It has been a long time since an outsider has entered our world."

Beck remained silent. Whatever the Elders had to say to him, he wanted them to say it fast.

"We understand that turmoil brews on the island, but we cannot become involved. It is a decision not based on cowardice, but on necessity. My people require water to live and breathe. We can only visit the Surface World for a few hours at a time now."

"I understand. I'm not here seeking aid. I found one of your grates by accident."

The watershifter bowed his head. "Very well. We must ask that you take an oath of silence before you leave. You will always be welcome in Aquataine, as are all shifters, but you must never bring a non-magical entity into our world. Our way of life must be preserved at all costs."

Beck looked into the eyes of each Elder and was surprised by what he found there. Terror. These men were terrified that he would not agree to take the oath. Terrified that, as the protectors and wisemen of the watershifters, they would be unable to ensure the safety of their people.

"With all due respect, Elders, it's not necessary. If keeping your world a secret will protect the people of Aquataine, then I shall keep that secret. The blood oath that courses through my veins is more powerful than any verbal oath I could give to you."

The Elders gave each other uneasy looks.

Beck sighed. "If it makes you feel more confident, I will do as you say." He went to one knee. "Until released, I, Beck Jaimes Atlan, earthshifter and *Savitar*, do solemnly vow to undertake an oath of silence regarding the world of Aquataine to all non-magical entities on the island of Massa."

When Beck looked up again, he could see the relief in the faces of the Elders. "Will that do?"

"Yes, that will do. Thank you, shifter."

Beck nodded. "Great. Now, how do I get out of here?"

***

Adrian drummed his fingers on his desk as he listened to Lucin's report. The Iserlohn Army, now camped on the western lip of the Valley of Flame, had made no further move toward Starfell. Whether they were there to surrender or fight was still uncertain.

Of the twelve demons sent out weeks ago to harass the citizens of Massa, none had returned. Either they were still engaging the enemy or were defeated, the latter being a highly unlikely possibility. The people of Massa were no match for a demon.

There had been no word of the *Savitars*. He had expected to hear from them by now with Earthshine only days away. And, still no sightings of the armies of the Dwarves and Elves. The scouts he sent on foot had not returned. It was taking far too long to obtain the answers he needed. He had no choice but to create more demons.

As usual, Lucin chose to be difficult, refusing to allow more of his soldiers to be sacrificed. The Cyman was very quickly becoming a dangerous liability and would have to be dealt with soon.

He gave his captain a threatening look. "I need them, Lucin."

Lucin shook his head. "My soldiers will fight for you just as well as men instead of the abominations you wish to create."

"And, what are you, Lucin, if not an abomination of my creation?"

The big man's nose flared in anger. "We are not mindless, evil monsters."

"Yes, something went horribly wrong there," Adrian murmured in agreement.

"Give the Cymans a chance, Master."

"I don't have time to take chances, Lucin. We are at war! I need information, and I need it now!" Enraged, he stood up from his desk. "Especially, since you refuse to give me the third prophecy. Don't think for one single moment that I can't retrieve that information from you by force if I so choose. I could peel the skin off your body one strip at a time to get that bloody prophecy! But, you and your army are serving a purpose, so you may keep your hide for a while longer. Now, run along and give me thirty soldiers for this evening's rite or you will no longer serve that purpose. Can I make it any simpler than that for your thick skull? It is either thirty men or the entire Cyman Army!"

The doors to his chambers opened and his sister stalked in, black robe trailing behind her. "Well, well, some things never change. At it again, you two?" she asked, walking directly to the mahogany sideboard to help herself to wine. "Lucin, if this is about Adrian's Demon Army, I can tell you that I was as shocked as you about his ability to spiritshift. Unfortunately, Captain, we do need them."

"For what purpose?"

"Prophecy, Captain. 'For the dark to conquer the land of old, the spirits will need to sing.' Adrian will need the aid of the demon spirits to be successful."

Lucin's shoulders dropped in defeat. "I just want this to be over," he said softly. "I just want to win this war and get my people back to Nordik." He turned and started toward the door. "You will 'ave your thirty men, Master. I will send them at nightfall." And, he was gone.

Adrian joined his sister at the sideboard. "What an idiot. Tell me, sister, is his son really still alive?"

"Of course not. He was too much of a threat to leave behind alive."

"I'm starting to feel the same way about Lucin," he scoffed.

"Have you had any word about the Dwarven and Elven armies?"

He shook his head. "No, none."

"Trust me, Adrian, I think they will fight. From what I've learned, these lands will not submit easily."

"Then they will submit the hard way. It makes no difference to me either way."

"The problem," she reasoned, "is that the Demon Army can only travel at night. They can't walk the land in the light."

Adrian walked away to study the camped army outside of Starfell. "I have been thinking about that as well. If my army can't tolerate light, then I shall give them dark."

CHAPTER 34

HEARTBREAK

Rogan rolled out of the dive off the porch of his ancestral home and crouched, igniting a sword of fire in his hand with a flick of his wrist. The magic in his blood pumped furiously, but it wasn't in response to the King's men—it was the two black wraiths with glowing red eyes hovering in the air behind them.

Unaware of the threat, the six Iron Fists unsheathed their swords at the sight of Rogan's fiery weapon. "Extinguish your magic now, shifter!"

"Get down!" Rogan shouted.

The wraiths swooped over the heads of the Fists and settled on the ground in front of Rogan, materializing into horned demon monsters thick with muscle and shadowy swords of evil clenched in their claws. "By your magic, I name you *Savitar*," one hissed, forked tongue darting in and out. "My Master has been looking for you."

Rogan signaled with his free hand for the Iron Fists, Janin and Dillon to stay out of the way. "Well, here I am, demon," he said, twirling his sword of fire in readiness.

The demon snapped his head around at the movement of the soldiers. In one swift motion, the demon rushed over and grabbed one of the Dwarves by an ankle, lifting him upside down in the air. The dangling Fist lashed out with his sword but dropped it and screamed in pain when the demon ripped open his abdomen with a swipe of its clawed hand. The fiend howled in gratification and let the soldier fall to the ground writhing in mortal agony.

Rogan clenched his teeth together and stalked toward the demon, his blood oath demanding retribution.

It would not be denied.

Sword in his right hand, he summoned a ball of fire with his left and hurled it forward.

The creature sidestepped the fire with an evil smirk.

Rogan continued to advance, lifting his arm to unleash a fiery bolt of lightning. It sliced with deadly precision this time, stunning the demon. With a howl of effort, Rogan leapt into the air at an inhuman height and swung his fire sword, carving the monster's head from his shoulders. Fire licked over the collapsing corpse and it disintegrated into a shower of ash before hitting the ground.

Rogan whirled with a snarl to the second demon.

Janin and Dillon were engaging the creature as another Iron Fist lay dead between them.

The maimed soldier still shrieked in anguish. Rogan grimaced. It would be a slow, painful way to die. The Dwarf's fellow Fists must have thought so as well, and Rogan watched as one of them walked over, whispered a word in the soldier's ear and then stood over him and buried his sword in the Dwarf's chest.

Rogan rushed back into the fight, but wasn't fast enough. He watched in horror as the remaining demon raised his spectral sword high into the air and brought it down on Dillon, severing his friend's arm at the shoulder. Dillon cried out as blood spurted out of the wound, drenching the soldiers closest to him in scarlet strings of matter. Dillon crumpled to the ground.

"No!"

With little regard for her own life, Janin dropped down next to Dillon, pulled a knife from her belt, and cut off a piece of her uniform to try to stem the bleeding.

"Demon! Over here!" Rogan screamed. "It's me that you want!"

The demon moved unbelievably fast and before Rogan could react, he was lifted off his feet by the neck. "Yes, it is you, *Savitar*."

Rogan shrank back from the depravity before him. *This thing loves to kill. It derives great pleasure in destroying the living. I can see it in his eyes. Smell it on his breath.*

The demon tightened his grip. Rogan kicked his legs and tried to pry the clawed fingers free of this throat.

The red eyes narrowed. "If only I had time to play with you before the end, shifter. I would enjoy taking you to the brink of death many times over many days before the final release. Do you know what it feels like to have your face separated from your skull? Your bones pulverized? Alas, prepare to die—"

The demon dropped Rogan as a sword erupted from the middle of his chest. The creature spun around to face a defiant, tear-stained and bloodied Janin.

Rogan did not waver. He bellowed in rage and beheaded the monster in a single mighty swipe. The headless corpse fell first to its knees and then sideways to the ground, crumbling to fiery dust.

Rogan sprinted to Dillon and crashed to his knees at his friend's side. What he found rocked him back onto his heels and he thought he might be sick. Dillon was gone. He lost too much blood and his lips had already turned blue in a ghostly pale face. Rogan pressed his cheek to Dillon's forehead. "Until we meet again," he whispered huskily.

Gentle hands, he never knew who they belonged to—probably Janin—guided him away and they prepared Dillon's body for burial. The sun was just beginning to rise in the east when the last stones were laid on the graves of Dillon and the two Iron Fists who perished in the fight with the demons.

"You'll tell his family that he died honorably and in the defense of his fellow soldiers?" Rogan asked of one of the Fists.

"On my word, shifter."

Rogan thanked the Dwarf and rubbed his neck. He hadn't slept since his last night in the cell of the King's palace, and even then not well, but he needed to keep moving. Earthshine was quickly approaching. Down to days now.

The sound of a large number of horses approaching broke the quiet of the early morning. *Bloody hell.* He sensed Janin step up silently to his side and he looked at her, grateful she had not been hurt.

The King of Dwarves, Rik Rojin, rode into the yard in front of his house, surrounded by Iron Fists. Reining in his white stallion with a flourish, his eyes scoured the freshly dug graves and the blood. Finally, his eyes landed on Rogan and he pointed. "Take this Dwarf into custody," he said to the four soldiers on the ground.

One of the Fists stepped forward and bowed. "Your Grace, if you will permit me to explain—"

"No! I will not permit anything except that you bind that Dwarf's wrists and take him into custody! He is an escaped prisoner and I want him returned before he has a hand in the death of any more Dwarves of Deepstone."

The soldier hesitated, and it was a fraction too long for the King's taste. He raised his sword and from his saddle, swept it out toward the Fist. Rogan rushed forward and knocked the soldier to the ground causing the King's sword to miss all but a lock of the Fist's hair.

Rik's face turned scarlet. "How dare you!" Before the King could articulate another order, a young voice interrupted him.

"What is going on, Father?"

A boy dressed in all white and atop a stallion similar to his father's approached from behind. He looked to be of thirteen years or so and wore a golden circlet upon his brow.

"The Prince," the Iron Fist under him whispered.

The King turned toward his son. "Erik, you must not interfere with this matter. This Dwarf," he said, thrusting a hand out toward Rogan, "must be punished."

The young Prince stared into Rogan's eyes. "What is his crime?"

The King faltered slightly and then said, "He's a shifter, for one."

The boy considered his father's words. "We all know that Pyraan has been destroyed, Father." Erik looked around at the scene and then back to Rogan. "Did you use magic, cousin?"

He winced right along with King Rik at the Prince's use of the familial address.

"Yes I did."

"Explain."

"I used magic to destroy two demons that killed three of your soldiers...cousin."

The Prince smiled slightly and addressed one of the Fists. "Can you verify the truth of this?"

The soldier nodded. "I can. Not only that, our swords were ineffective against the demons. If not for the fireshifter, we would all be dead."

Satisfied, Erik turned to the King. "Father, this Dwarf is to be commended, not punished. He acted in defense of his life and the lives of his fellow Dwarves."

"He has committed other crimes," the King gritted out through clenched teeth, not at all pleased with the way things were going.

"Such as?" enquired the Prince.

The King didn't blink. "He killed my brother, your uncle."

"I did no such thing," Rogan protested. "I was only a small child when my parents were killed!"

"Maybe not by your hand, but by your very existence," he spat contemptuously. "The day you snapped your fingers to ignite fire was the day you killed your parents."

"My parents died trying to flee from *your* soldiers, uncle, not by magic!"

"Do not call me that!"

An uncomfortable silence developed causing the soldiers to shift on their horses. The Prince broke it. "If my father frees you, where would you go?"

Smart boy, thought Rogan. He was giving the King a way to do the right thing and save face in front of his soldiers. "I need to travel to Sarphia to rejoin the other *Savitars*." He looked around at all of the Dwarves. "An oath of the blood resides in the marrow of my bones, but I will swear again to all of you now, with the Highworld as witness, that I am a friend to the Dwarven people and all of Massa. I go forth now to battle the Mage, Adrian Ravener, from enslaving the people of this island, and I will not stop until he is destroyed. If you wish, I will return here to Kondor after the threat is over to stand trial for any crime I may have committed."

"There is still much to resolve," King Rik pointed out, "and I will have you back here as soon as the war has been won."

"You have my word, Your Grace."

"The Dwarves have done their part as well. Two cohorts of the Deepstone Army were dispatched to Starfell yesterday."

Just yesterday? The Dwarves will never arrive in time to help Iserlohn. However, now was not the time to quibble.

"Now, get out of my land," Rik demanded and wheeled his horse around aggressively. As the King thundered away, the mounted Fists scrambled to catch up.

Janin placed a hand on his arm. "I still want to go with you. Now more than ever."

He stared into her eyes and noticed for the first time that they were a lovely shade of gray. "Where I'm going, only the *Savitars* may travel," he said. "But, I very much appreciate the offer."

She looked crestfallen. "You need me."

He realized then that she didn't want to part from him just yet, because he felt the same way. "Would you be interested in traveling to Sarphia with me? I would like to have the company. After I rejoin my friends, you can meet up with the Deepstone Army."

She smiled. "I would like that."

He gestured to the house behind him. "Unfortunately, I need to get a few hours of sleep before we go. I don't think I can take another step otherwise."

"Go ahead," she said. "I'll take watch."

"Cousin!" Prince Erik, dismounted now, hurried over to them. "Cousin, I just want to thank you and apologize for my father. It is well known that he can be a little hot-tempered at times."

Rogan tilted his head with a raised eyebrow.

"All right, *very* hot-tempered," laughed the boy. "But, he does see reason after he thinks things through."

"No thanks necessary," Rogan assured him. "If you'll excuse me, I need to get some rest and be on my way."

"Wait! I came to give you something." The Prince held out his hand and a silver pendant dangled from his grip.

"Where did you get this?" Rogan breathed in shock.

"My father has had a box of keepsakes from your family home for many years. I searched through it once and found this pendant. One look at how the flaming torch flickered confirmed to me that it was infused with magic. I vowed that if I ever had the chance to meet you, I would return it." He suddenly sounded like the young boy he was. "I love magic."

"Thank you, Erik," he said as he put the pendant around his neck. "Your actions today may have saved thousands of lives."

The boy grinned and bowed. "I leave you now to your sleep. I look forward to your return when this is over."

Erik held out his hand.

And it was at that very moment—as Rogan was shaking the hand of the Prince of Dwarves in the early-morning hour with the sun making its climb toward the west—that the world was plunged into darkness.

CHAPTER 35

QUEEN GRACE

Kiernan looked in the mirror and almost didn't recognize herself. Her long wavy blonde hair, pulled back into the severe braid preferred by the Gems, added years to her youthful features. Her cheeks had a hollow look from the constant combat training and her lack of appetite.

Beck is coming.

Bajan is coming.

She had known for almost two days now and still hadn't found the words she would use to tell them that she wasn't leaving Elloree. This was her home now. But, how was she to explain that to Beck? It was hard enough for her to comprehend the emotional journey she had been on let alone adequately describe it to him.

She wasn't even concerned any longer about the women she saw him with on that evening so long ago. This wasn't about him. It was about her.

Bajan had been trying to reach her all morning, so she knew they were close.

A knock on her door startled her and she jumped to her feet. "Come in."

It was Diamond, and the beautiful sorceress wore a grim look. "A young man approaches. Yours?"

She nodded.

"Stay here. Sapphire and Citrine will deal with him."

"No, Diamond, I have to talk to him. I need to make him understand that I'm staying here with all of my sisters of my own free will."

Diamond's eyes were as hard as her name. "Sapphire will make him understand."

"I don't want him harmed, Diamond!"

The witch raised a pale eyebrow. "I guess that depends on how well he takes no for an answer."

***

Beck didn't attempt to disguise his approach to the sorceresses' castle, suspecting that a direct tactic was best. That, and the fact that he didn't have time for anything else. He needed to find Kiernan and get out as quickly as possible.

As he drew closer with Bajan at his side, he observed several women standing on a wide staircase that led to the front entrance of a graceful and feminine castle with spires covered in a pink-hued tile and colorful pennants flapping in the breeze. A narrow road made of colored gemstones cut through the middle of lush, well-shorn grounds.

He didn't see any guards or soldiers, just the women. And most of those, he noticed with more than a little concern, carried weapons. Surprisingly, all were formally attired with their hair in braids.

A raven-haired woman stepped off the stairs and approached. "May I help you?" she asked, cold blue eyes glaring at him suspiciously.

"I'm looking for Kiernan Everard. She is—"

"Not available," the woman finished for him.

Beck drew in a breath. "I came for Kiernan, and I'm not leaving without her."

"Oh, but you are. The only question that remains is whether you would like to leave on your own two feet or be carried."

Beck stared at the woman for a moment and then made a decision. He put one leg out as if to depart, and then forcefully spun away from her and leapt into the air, somersaulting over her head to land on the bottom step of the stairs in front of the other women. The black-haired sorceress screamed out in fury behind him, and Bajan answered her with a mighty roar. The ferocity of his bellow caused all of the witches to hesitate in alarm, and that was all he needed to get past them and into the castle.

"Kiernan! Kiernan, where are you?" he shouted, running into the foyer and sliding along a white marble floor and past a highly wrought fountain.

Blue eyes blazing, the dark witch stalked in after him, her lips moving fast.

"Kiernan! Kier— Ah!" His arms flailed helplessly as his feet were swept out from under him and he crashed to the floor. Before he could recover, an invisible force lifted him into the air upside down.

He saw the fist coming toward his face while suspended in midair but was powerless to avoid it after the sorceress cast another spell that pinned his arms to his sides. She struck him in the mouth, and he spat blood onto the marble floor as the room filled with more and more women. One with fiery red hair approached and began to strike him in a series of what Beck was certain were magically-assisted punches in both sides of his body. His breath left his lungs and he grunted when one of his ribs broke.

The black-haired sorceress grabbed his hair. "Let us try this again, shall we? Your own two feet or carried?"

He looked up at her defiantly. "I will not...leave...without Kiernan."

The women attacked then, and he had never known such pain in his life.

                                  ***

Princess! Are you going to stand by and let them kill Beck? I am shut outside of the castle, but I can hear them beating him. Princess Kiernan Everard! What has happened to you? Help Beck!

"Kiernan, are you all right?" Diamond asked, and spun her around by her shoulder. The sorceress recoiled from her in fright. "Highworld! What is wrong with your eyes?"

Kiernan broke her connection with Bajan and blinked. "I have to go. They're killing him!" She ran to the door, yanked it open and stumbled through, righting herself to sprint down the hall to the front foyer.

"Kiernan!"

She ignored Diamond and kept running, leg muscles straining with the effort. She arrived just as six of the witches opened the front doors and threw Beck bodily down the stairs to land facedown in the dirt outside.

"Stop! What are you doing?" she screamed, pushing the women out of her way to run to Beck. He let out a soft moan as she knelt beside him. She looked up at her new sisters sternly. "Leave us! I need to speak to him alone."

"Kiernan, are you sure...?" began Citrine.

"Yes! Now, please leave. I'll only be a few moments."

The sorceresses reluctantly withdrew, respecting her wish for privacy.

"Beck, are you hurt badly?" she whispered urgently, slowly turning his body onto his back. His face was covered in dirt and bloodied from a split lip, but it was Beck. Her Beck. And, her body trembled at the need to throw her arms around him.

He groaned again. "I will be fine...I think. What was...that all about?"

"Beck, I'm sorry. I didn't know they would react like that. I think they're just trying to protect me."

He sat up, holding an arm around his ribs. "That redhead really packs a punch."

"She is a sorceress of magical combat."

Beck looked at her for the first time in over a month. He took in her dress and braided hair. "You look different."

She lowered her eyes. "I am different, and I don't know if I can help you understand," she said, withdrawing from him.

"Try me."

"The last thing I would ever want to do is hurt you, Beck. You know that, don't you?"

He nodded.

"But, this is my home now. I belong here with all of my sisters."

"Kiernan, you can't mean that! We have to go! Right now! Adrian Ravener is killing people all over the island. Demons walk the earth! We have to stop him." He paused. "It's our sworn duty to stop him."

"No." She stood up and removed the pendant from around her neck and held it out to him. "Take this. It's the pendant you need in the upcoming battle, not me."

Beck took the pendant and got to his feet with a wince. "To hell with the battle! I need you, Kiernan! I love you!"

She turned her back to him. "It's for the best, Beck. You must go."

He spun her around, a tear dropping from his eye. "You promised me, Kiernan! In your mother's dressing room in Nysa, you promised me that we would be together always."

The reminder elicited her own tears and they streamed unchecked down her face. "Stop, Beck! Don't make this any harder than it has to be!"

"Just answer me one question, Kiernan," he croaked. "Do you still love me? At all?"

She turned away again and fell to her knees. She couldn't look at him when she answered. "No. The answer is no, I don't love you anymore."

The ground rumbled underneath her and Beck let out an agonized scream. She turned and watched as he threw his hands out and uprooted a massive oak tree on the grounds in front of the castle and sent it sailing through the air. Face etched in pain, he went down to one knee and wrapped an arm around his ribs.

"Beck..."

Lurching back upright, he didn't look at her as he staggered away down the road.

Kiernan put a fist to her mouth to keep from crying out. Out of nowhere, Bajan appeared in front of her. He didn't say anything, but he didn't have to. His blazing green eyes said it all.

Bajan, I am so sorry.

Why Princess?

I have my reasons, Bajan. Stay with me.

I cannot.

Please, Bajan. You are my bondmate! Stay with me!

While you have strayed from your path, Princess, mine remains clear. I must help the Savitars. Good-bye.

The Draca Cat turned and began walking after the faltering Beck.

Bajan! Don't leave me!

He did not respond.

She stayed outside on her knees until both Beck and Bajan disappeared from sight. When she didn't have any tears left to shed, she stood to go back into the castle and as though in response to her mood, the whole world went dark.

She had no will to question why and numbly retraced her steps back to her chambers. None of her sisters tried to intercept her for which she was grateful.

She lay down on her bed in the dark, not bothering to light the tapers in the heavy bronze holder on her nightstand. Emotions warred in a heated battle inside her mind and body. She tossed and turned for hours praying for sleep to take her away from the unbearable pain of her waking life.

It finally worked. Her eyelids grew heavy, her senses sluggish. That's why it scared her so much when a bright light burst into existence in the center of her room. She sat up in bed and pulled the covers tight to her neck, sure that Adrian Ravener was there to kill her.

"Do not be frightened, my love," said a voice from the light, warm and loving.

She breathed a sigh of relief. She recognized the voice, and it was just a dream.

"It is me, Keke."

Queen Grace Kenley Everard walked out of the light toward the bed, her body silhouetted in an otherworldly glow.

"Maman!" It was a child's name for a mother, but all she knew.

"Yes, darling, it is me."

"I love when you come to me in my dreams."

"I am always with you, my darling, every moment of every day. But, this is not a dream."

"I miss you so much."

"I miss you too, Keke." Her mother was the only one who ever called her by that name and it made her heart soar to hear it again. "I have come to remind you that you cannot give up the fight. You are *Savitar*."

"You know of that?" Kiernan asked in surprise

"Yes." The radiant wraith moved closer, her face pained.

Kiernan tilted her head in question. "But, Gemini said you wanted me to stay here."

Her mother nodded and wisps of vapor trailed around her head sinuously. "That was the foolish wish of a frightened mother for her daughter. I now know that you must be there with the *Savitars* if there is to be any hope for Massa."

"But, Maman—"

Grace Everard swelled in size and Kiernan cringed back. "I will not have my daughter, the Princess of Men, hide her head while innocent people die!"

The words caused the blood oath to flare to life, making Kiernan faint from the magic now swirling inside her body.

"You must fight, Kiernan!"

"Is that what you want?" she cried.

"It is what must be! You are a Princess! A protector!"

"Then, I will do as you say, Maman," she declared, all of the uncertainty shedding from her mind at last. "I will fight! Highworld help me I will fight!"

Her mother's image receded and returned to its former size. "I'm so very proud of you, Kiernan," she said, softly now, teary wisps flowing down her misty face. "Remember that always."

Kiernan swallowed. "I will."

"Do you love him?" her mother asked suddenly, and Kiernan didn't have to ask who she meant.

"With every fiber of my being."

"You hurt him very badly."

Kiernan buried her head in her hands. "I know, Maman, I know."

"Fight for him, too, Kiernan."

She shook her head. "It's too late. He's gone."

"No, he is camped south of the Illian. The darkness and his injuries have slowed his progress."

Hope coursed through her body and burning tears stung the back of her eyes. "This is not a dream, is it, Maman?"

"No."

"But, why have you appeared to me now at this time?"

"Ask Bajan."

"Bajan?"

"I must go. I love you very much. Never forget that." The glowing figure slowly faded away. "Tell Gemini that the cats are singing! She will know what it means."

Kiernan jumped off the bed to reach for her. "I will! I love you, too, Maman!"

And, the light was gone.

Kiernan scrubbed her tears away and fumbled in the abrupt return to darkness for the tinderbox to light her candles. With trembling hands, she managed to get them lit and packed her belongings as quickly as she could. She stripped off the dress the Gems had given her and put on her blue gossamer dress with the arm veils and gold cuffs and her sandals.

As she raced from the room, she ripped the braid out of her hair, tumbling it free.

After passing the fountain, she took the stairs two at a time and came to a frantic halt in front of Gemini's chambers. She pounded on the door. "Gemini! Are you awake? It's me, Kiernan!"

She heard shuffling from behind the door and waited impatiently.

Gemini opened the door dressed in a night cloak, her gray hair hanging loose for sleep. She held a candle out in front of her. "What is it, dear? It's the middle of the night!"

"I'm leaving," she said without preamble.

Gemini's eyebrows knitted together. "Does this have anything to do with that boy?"

She smiled. "It has everything to do with that boy. It also has to do with my mother. She came to me in my room, Gemini. I don't have time to explain. Diamond will figure it out before long."

"I can't allow you to leave, Kiernan. You don't understand."

"I'm not asking your permission, Gemini, but I do understand." She tempered her resolute words by pulling Gemini into a hug. "Thank you for everything. I know you were doing what you thought my mother wanted, but circumstances have changed." She pressed her mouth close to Gemini's ear and whispered, "She told me to tell you that the cats are singing."

Gemini squealed and pulled back. "How...how do you know that phrase?"

"I have to go, Gemini. Can I take a horse from the stables?"

The High Priestess looked dazed. "Yes, yes, of course."

Kiernan turned to leave, but then stopped in her tracks. "Gemini! My sword!"

The sorceress retreated into her room and returned with the Sword of Iserlohn, thrusting it into Kiernan's hands. "May the Highworld be with you, Kiernan."

"It already is!" she shouted over her shoulder as she ran.

***

Kiernan knew it was dangerous to be running her horse at such reckless speed in the dark, but she had little choice. She had to find Beck and that meant putting her faith in the moonlight and the horse's instinct to get her there.

She hadn't realized it before, but Earthshine was only a few days away now. And, with her and Beck on the opposite side of the island! If only she had stayed true and not become so...lost. Wait... That was one of the predictions that Mage Starr warned them about. One of them would be lost.

Well, I'm lost no more.

Drumming the horse with her heels, she sped ahead into the night, the rushing air cleansing the murky tangle of her thoughts. Only when the brackish smell of the Illian River drifted to her nose did she slow the horse to a trot and frantically scan both sides of the road for Beck's campsite.

"Beck!"

Bajan!

She continued to advance more cautiously now and stiffened when she glimpsed a soft glow from a gap in the trees. Heart racing, she dismounted and tore through the coppice only to find the remnants of a discarded fire pit.

I'm too late! They're gone.

Her legs threatened to collapse beneath her. *What now? Should I travel back to Iserport and then continue to the Valley of Flame from there?* She chewed on her lower lip in indecision. *Yes, that's what I'll do. There's really no other choice.*

Decision made, she ran back to the horse. The only marker she had in the darkness was the Illian, and she figured she could follow it easily enough to Iserport as long as the terrain permitted.

She tried one more time. *Bajan!*

Calm down, Princess, we are here. We have stopped at a small stream just through the wood ahead of you.

"Ahh!!" she screamed and jumped off the horse. She hastily tied the reins to the bough of a tree and started running.

Prickly bushes and branches slapped at her face and arms as she dashed through the trees. She tripped over a log and her knee came down squarely on a rock, causing her to yelp in pain. She rose again, limping and bleeding, and finally crashed through the woods into a clearing.

Naked from the waist up with a wide bandage around his torso, Beck was leaning over the stream with cupped hands preparing to take a drink. His head whipped around when he heard her.

"Beck!" She started toward him, fell again and began to crawl, too emotionally and physically spent to continue.

He stood up slowly and stared at her in disbelief, but did not move.

"Beck! I am sorry," she whimpered. "Please, Beck!"

He started toward her at an uncertain walk, and then began to jog, and then ran. She held her arms out to him and it felt to Kiernan like an eternity had passed, but then he was there, lifting her off her feet. She wrapped her legs around him and sobbed into his shoulder. Beck dropped to his knees and they fell to the ground in a tangled heap. She clutched him close, hands digging into his shoulders, terrified that if she let go he would disappear and she would never get him back again.

CHAPTER 36

TAKING THE PLUNGE

Kiernan untied her horse and slapped the animal's rump to set him running free, hoping as she did that he would find his way safely back to the castle in Elloree. With the moonlight to guide her, she returned to the clearing.

Beck asked if she was hungry and offered her a pear.

"Famished," she admitted, and bit into the fleshy fruit with relish, pleased that her appetite had returned after so long.

He reached out and fingered a handful of her hair. "I like it much better this way."

"Thank you, Beck," she said softly. She wasn't talking about the compliment and he knew that. "You took me back," she said incredulously.

"Yes," he said quietly.

"Why?"

He gave her a crooked smile. "Wait here." He went to his pack and pulled something out. When he returned, he unwrapped a crumpled pink flower and handed it to her. "Because on the list of things I can't live without in this world, you happen to be at the top."

Tears pooled in her eyes, blurring her vision. She accepted the flower. "It's beautiful. Thank you." She shook her head. "I don't deserve you."

He laughed quietly. "Probably not, but you're stuck with me nevertheless, Your Grace."

She playfully punched him in the side and he winced.

"Oh, I am so sorry!"

He laughed again. "It's fine. At least one rib is broken, but they don't hurt as much now that they've been wrapped." He removed her pendant from around his neck and placed it over her head.

"Will you finally tell me why you had me send away our fastest means of transportation to Iserport?"

He grabbed her hand. "I'll show you instead. And, we're not going to Iserport. We're going to Kondor."

"Kondor? Why in the Highworld do you—"

"Trust me," he interrupted.

She looked into his blue eyes and the love she found there staggered her. "I do trust you. I go where you go."

He smiled, most likely remembering the first time she had said those words to him.

"Go on ahead," she told him. "I want to have a word with Bajan."

Nodding in understanding, he kissed her and walked away, and she fell back to wait for Bajan. He had been out hunting and his muzzle was stained red. It wouldn't last long. Not on the meticulously fussy Draca Cat.

Welcome back, Princess.

Thank you, Bajan. She paused. *Do you forgive me as Beck has?*

The question is, do you forgive me?

She snorted in her head. *What could you possibly need forgiveness for?*

I have failed you.

What? No! How can you say that?

My Sovereign, Moombai, told me that you were in danger and I needed to be vigilant, that I needed to protect you. I just did not realize that I needed to protect you from yourself.

No one could have, she insisted. *I must tell you that I had the most glorious visit from my mother.*

Did you?

Yes, and she said to ask you about her.

The Draca hesitated and Kiernan had to wait for several long moments for him to respond.

Since the day that Galen Starr died and I was rendered unconscious, I have been having strange visions. I am not sure what they mean, and I am anxious to arrive at Callyn-Rhe so I can ask Moombai. He will know.

I'm here if you need me, Bajan. I won't leave your side again. She threw her arms around his neck and hugged him close, and Bajan purred with contentment.

"Over here!" Beck shouted, waving his arm in the darkness.

"What is this?" she asked, noticing a strange, open grate behind him.

He briefly told her about his discovery of Aquataine and something about glow worms and playful porpoises and a stunned moment later, she found herself hurtling along a slide in the darkness. She would have been frightened to death if she had been alone, but Beck's laughter was infectious, and she found herself laughing with him as they plummeted downward. A muted green light appeared beneath her right before she splashed into a warm turquoise pool of water.

As soon as she surfaced, Beck guided her to the shore where Bajan stood shaking the water from his fur. She looked around in awe. Beck's descriptions of an underground paradise had not been exaggerated.

He pointed upward to draw her attention to the glow worms on the ceiling and told her about the reversal of day and night in Aquataine.

"I'm just glad that Adrian's spell hasn't touched this place," she remarked.

"Oh, it couldn't have because Adrian doesn't know it exists. If you don't know something exists, your spell can't affect it."

She raised an eyebrow at him in question. "How would you know that?"

Beck pulled a small black book from his backpack. "Galen's Protetor."

"He gave that to you?"

"Yes, he wants me to study to become a Mage."

She looked at it skeptically. "And?"

"Let's just say I've read a few pages in the book out of curiosity and that's all. I'm content being a shifter."

"How come it's not soaking wet?"

"A protective spell. It's far too valuable not to be protected from simple things like water damage."

They both turned at the shouted greeting of a man on a raft. "Hello again, Master Atlan!"

Beck grabbed her hand and they ran over the beach to another pool of water.

"Digby! Please tell me you have a port in Kondor."

"We do."

"How fast can you get us there?"

The watershifter thought about it. "A day or so."

"What?" Kiernan exclaimed. "How is that possible?"

Digby looked offended. "You are gazing upon a master watershifter, Mistress."

"Can you take us there now?" Beck interrupted.

"Always in a hurry, Master Atlan! Goodness, you really ought to slow down once in a while." He paused. "Your lady friend is also a shifter, I presume?"

"My lady friend is most definitely a shifter and also the Princess of Iserlohn. May I introduce you to Princess Kiernan Everard."

Digby's eyes rounded to saucers, and Kiernan was surprised when he fell to a knee on the raft.

"You know who I am?"

"Of course, Your Grace! It's only been the past ten years or so that Aquatainians have been unable to tolerate the Surface World for long. Before then, we traveled among Massans regularly."

She shook her head in amazement. *It's now confirmed. I know absolutely nothing about the world I live in.* "Please rise, Digby. It is nice to meet you."

"Thank you, Your Grace," he said, pushing his long, lanky body back to his feet. "Wait until the Elders meet you!"

Kiernan looked back at Beck. "Elders?"

"Come on," he said, waving her onto the raft. "You have to meet with the Elders at the Temple of Grotte. I will explain on the way, but for Highworld's sake, just don't forget to take off your shoes!"

She had no idea what he could be talking about, but he filled her in on the way and after delivering her oath to the Elders, she jumped off the portico of the temple with sandals in hand and raced back across the sand to the raft. Sadly, after departing Ebba, she didn't have much of an opportunity to admire Aquataine due to the speed of their travel. Digby tirelessly propelled them through the channeled waterways for hours, stopping only once at a small village for a quick rest and meal of fruit, cheese and bread.

"Digby, can we pay you for the food and transportation?" she asked during their meal.

"No, your coin is no good here, Your Grace," the watershifter told her with a wink. With that, he jumped into the water again and they were off.

The hours sped by, most of them spent sleeping. But, she did ask Beck at one point, "Why Kondor?"

"I don't want to get all the way to Sarphia only to find out Rogan never made it," he explained. "It's not far out of the way, so better to stop first and be sure."

She agreed, and the next thing she knew, Beck was nudging her awake. Despite all the sleep, she felt woozy when she stood and Beck had to help her on shore. Bajan leapt off the boat with no apparent side effects.

"I'll be waiting here for you," Digby yelled at their backs.

Beck sprinted ahead toward a limestone stairway built into the side of the earth, and they raced upward and came out on top at a grate concealed in an outcropping of rock just outside of King Rik's castle in Kondor.

Darkness still covered the land, but all they had to do to find their way was follow the screams.

Kiernan rounded the boulders and stormed into a clearing where two horned demons menaced a group of women and children trapped tight against the outer wall of the castle. A dozen soldiers in the maroon and blue of Deepstone were attempting to distract the demons away from the innocents.

Several more soldiers lay dead on the ground.

There was no conversation as Beck and Kiernan stalked forward— Beck with hands thrown out to his sides and Kiernan with sword drawn.

Beck struck first by rippling the earth beneath the two demons and sending them crashing to the ground.

Kiernan rushed forward, sword held high overhead with two hands and slashed powerfully at one of the creatures. The demon rolled out of the way just in time and her swing took off one of his clawed hands instead of his head.

The women and children continued to scream in terror.

The soldiers, bolstered by the unexpected aid, started an advance on the other demon. Another soldier died as a result.

"Fire! I need fire!" Beck screamed at the Dwarves. "It's the only way to destroy them!" He lifted his hands and sent an enormous boulder rolling over the ground to crash into one of the demons, pinning it underneath.

The clawless demon howled, put his head down and rushed Kiernan, intending to impale her on his horns. She sprang into the air over his head, but he managed to catch her ankle with the intact claw and slam her to the ground.

Grunting in pain, her sword fell from her grasp. The demon was on her immediately, forked tongue protruding through tiny serrated teeth. The fiend grabbed her hair, stood her upright and hissed in her face. "Your interference has cost you your life, *Savitar*. I will show you pain like you have never known!"

Lightning fast, a muscled ball of white fury hammered into the demon and brought him down. The two combatants rolled over the ground in a vicious clash of snapping teeth and ferocious growls.

"Bajan, move!"

The Draca Cat leapt free as Beck jabbed a fiery brand directly into the creature's mouth. Fire licked out through the orifices in the demon's face in a ghastly show, and he wailed in torment before dying in an explosion of black smoke.

Kiernan grabbed another torch and strode to the demon pinned beneath the boulder and set him afire. In seconds, his body, too, turned to blackened ash and disappeared.

"Is everyone all right?" she asked, spinning back, half expecting another demon to appear.

"Those of us still alive anyway," one of the soldiers murmured with a grimace. "Not that I'm ungrateful for the help, but may I ask why you're here?"

"We're looking for Rogan Radek," Kiernan told the soldier. "By any chance, do you know who he is?"

"I do. He left for Sarphia days ago. He should be close to there by now."

Kiernan nodded, relieved.

"Where is King Rik?" Beck asked.

"Left the same day as the shifter, just behind two cohorts of the Deepstone Army."

"But, it will take weeks for the Dwarven Army to arrive at the Valley of Flame! We need them there already!"

The soldier looked embarrassed. "That's all I know." He ran a critical gaze over them. "Are you *Savitar?*"

"So we've have been told."

"Best of luck to you then and do us all a favor by kicking some demon arse!"

"That is the plan!" Kiernan shouted over her shoulder as they ran back to the grate.

Evening was fast approaching Aquataine by the time they reached the raft, and they found Digby fast asleep in the sand. He looked so peaceful that Kiernan hated to wake him. The watershifter had gone well above the call of duty.

Bajan, not so concerned, emitted a small bellow that had Digby scrambling to his feet and into the water.

Once they were moving again, the soft sway of the raft lulled the fight-fueled adrenaline from Kiernan's body, and she laid her head in Beck's lap. Content for the first time in weeks, she felt reluctant to bring up the subject but, in the end, knew she had to clear the air between them or it would fester like an open wound.

She cleared her throat. "Beck?"

"Hmm?"

"About those women in Iserport..."

"What women?"

Obviously, he doesn't want to discuss the matter. She shook her head. "Never mind."

He looked down and stroked her cheek. "Kiernan, there will never be any other woman for me. There's just you."

"But, I saw you," she pointed out softly and sat up.

"Whatever you saw, it wasn't real. Magic was involved somehow, and I had the headache the next day to prove it. You have to believe me, Kiernan."

She felt incredibly foolish as she realized he was speaking the truth. "Avalon Ravener," she suddenly growled.

"Most likely."

She sighed. "Oh, Beck, how is this all going to turn out?"

He squeezed her shoulder. "We're going to make it, Kiernan. I promise."

CHAPTER 37

REUNITED

"We're never going to make it!" Kiernan exclaimed in a panic as they climbed out of the grate near Sarphia. "We only have two days left!"

"We'll make it," Beck assured her, his voice still full of the confidence she had yet to feel.

"Really? Let's see. We have to find Rogan, find Airron, summon a magical map, find an invisible mystic land, uncover a weapon, and travel to Starfell!" She was babbling now. "We can't do it!"

Bajan growled an instant before a voice drifted to them from the trees and said, "Well, one down and five to go."

Rogan stepped out of the trees with a Dwarven soldier at his side.

"Rogan!" she cried in relief and almost knocked him down as she threw herself into his arms.

The Dwarf turned red and glanced sideways at his traveling companion. "Good to see you, too," he said, hugging her back. He let go and reached out to shake Beck's hand, but Beck was having none of that. He gathered Rogan in an embrace as well.

Rogan finally disentangled himself to introduce Janin. Kiernan hadn't realized the soldier was a female until she spoke in greeting.

"Nice to meet you, Janin," Kiernan said, eyeing the two of them suspiciously.

"We better get going," Rogan said brusquely, putting a halt to any questions that may have been forthcoming. He called a flame to life in his hand and started away on the path that led to Sarphia.

Kiernan smiled knowingly as she followed behind.

"Your pendant?"Beck asked him.

Rogan nodded. "It's a long story, but I have it."

Beck exhaled a breath of relief.

"Any news of Airron?" Kiernan asked as they walked.

"Nothing," Rogan replied. "And, that has me worried. I just hope he's doing well."

"Apparently, you're doing well," Kiernan whispered under her breath. Unfortunately, it wasn't low enough judging by the dark look Rogan sent her and the sly grin on Janin's face.

Beck related to them then all he knew of Airron's misfortune. The news quickened their steps, the group anxious now to see Airron for themselves, and it wasn't long before they emerged from the Puu Rainforest into the Elven capital of Sarphia.

If Aquataine could be described as an underground paradise, Sarphia had to be considered an aboveground fairyland. From the twinkling lights in every tree to combat the unnatural darkness to the magnificent tiered gardens to the raw beauty of the Elven race of people. Every Elf, male and female, possessed an ethereal grace in the way they flitted from place to place that was purely magical to watch.

Kiernan's delighted perusal was interrupted by the arrival of a dozen Elven soldiers that approached them with a gait as light as air.

"We have been expecting you, *Savitars*. This way," one said to them.

Taking positions on both sides of their group, the Elves set a hurried pace that forced the *Savitars* and Janin to trot between them. As they ran, the Elven people in the city stopped to watch the progression and most of their interest was centered on Bajan. If the white marble statue of a Draca Cat in the town square was any indication, Draca Cats were highly revered in the Elven world.

The soldiers halted in front of a wooden building with a thatched roof and long porch. Two Elves dressed in white carried a stretcher inside. Kiernan thought it must be an infirmary of some sort.

"You will find Master Falewir inside," said one of the Elven soldiers, and then the regiment turned on their heels and departed, never breaking formation.

Kiernan and the others went inside to what was indeed an infirmary—one heavily in use. Apparently, the demons had left their mark in Haventhal as well as in Iserlohn and Deepstone.

She enquired about Airron.

"Oh, yes," said a pretty Elven girl behind a desk. "Master Falewir is down the hall in the last room."

Kiernan thanked her, and as they neared the door indicated, Kiernan was surprised to find two guards standing in front of it.

"Is this Airron Falewir's room?" Rogan asked.

"It is," said the stoic Elf. "What business do you have with him?"

"Is that Fireball?" shouted a familiar voice from behind the door. "Let him in, guards!"

The guards opened the door and one by one, they filed into the large room. There sat Airron, propped up in an enormous bed, with four Elven girls attending him. Two were rubbing his feet, one was massaging his shoulders, and one was feeding him grapes. Feeding him grapes!

"Good, you're all here," Airron said through his mouthful. "And, it's about bloody time! In case you haven't noticed, we have a job to do."

Rogan took a step further into the room and planted his feet. "Do you want to kill him, Beck, or should I?"

***

After dismissing the Elven nurses, it didn't take long for Airron to pack. He accomplished the task while recounting his severe injuries at the hand of Avalon Ravener. Without the unsurpassed talent of the Elven healers and an antidote for the venom of the spider, he would have died. He told them of Rory, and they realized that it was Avalon who appeared to them after the destruction of Pyraan, and the young fireshifter had either perished with the others or Avalon had killed him outright.

Also unspoken was the fact that all but one of Galen's prophecies had come true. Airron had been gravely wounded, Beck had been betrayed, and Kiernan had been lost. That only left the most devastating prediction of all.

And, it would come.

Of that, she had no doubt.

"The worst part is," Airron said, continuing his story, "when the bloody witch thought I was dead, she tried to bodyshift me!" He shuddered. "Thank the Highworld something scared her off because she would have realized I was still alive if she had put her hands on me. The last thing I remember was her reaching down and ripping the pendant from my neck."

Three horrified gasps reverberated throughout the room.

"His pendant is gone!" Kiernan said and threw up her hands. "Now what?"

"We're done," moaned Rogan in anguish. "It ends here."

Beck didn't say anything, but the floor beneath their feet buckled.

"Take it easy," Airron said smugly, fighting for balance. "Luckily, I suspected that something was up and I hid the pendant in my pack. Avalon stole a harmless piece of silver I purchased from one of the dockworkers in Havenport."

The room grunted in relief.

"I guess now is as good a time as any to put our pendants together and retrieve the map," Kiernan said and cleared a spot on the floor.

Bajan and Janin looked on as the four *Savitars* knelt in a circle. They each held their pendants out in front of them, and Kiernan yelped in surprise as the four pieces flew from their hands and clinked together with some unseen magnetic force.

The *Savitars* leaned back out of the way as the lodged pendants spun in the space between them, chains whipping around in a gray blur.

A sudden gust sprang up from the center of the whirling metal. The air in the room began to swirl forcefully. Kiernan flinched when an oil lamp crashed to the floor. Her hair twirled above her head, her dress flapped violently against her skin. Yet, she couldn't take her eyes from the transformation happening in the middle of the room. One by one, the links in the chains began to shorten and meld into the pendants. The molten silver pieces continued to fuse and reshape until all that was left was a single round disc.

An explosion of light brightened the room, and the wind abruptly stopped as the silver circle fell to the floor with a tinny clink. A narrow orange flame flared to life over the pendant and etched a design of some sort onto the silver.

When the glow disappeared, Kiernan reached out gingerly to pick up the disc expecting it to be hot, but it wasn't. It was cool to the touch.

"It's a compass of some sort," she said, noticing a thin orange flame still wavering on the surface.

She handed it to Beck and he held the compass in the palm of his hand. "It's pointing due east."

"East it is," Airron said, hefting his pack.

Rogan offered a clumsy and hurried good-bye to Janin, who was remaining in Sarphia to await the Deepstone Army, and together they raced out of the infirmary.

Curiously, the people on the streets bowed down to Airron as they passed.

"They treat you like royalty," grunted Rogan.

Airron laughed, purple eyes sparkling. "I *am* royalty, my friend! A fact I have come to learn since being with the Elves."

"Does King Jerund J'El know that?" Rogan asked with doubt in his voice.

"Of course, although, I will admit that he was shocked at first."

"I'll bet," Rogan snorted. "I have my own royal story to tell when we have more time."

"In any event, I couldn't communicate for weeks," Airron continued, "but once I came around, King Jerund believed my story about the invasion with the help of King Maximus's decree. He departed immediately after with the Gladewatchers to join with the Iserlohn Army at Starfell."

"How many Gladewatchers are there?"

"A thousand maybe."

"What about the rest of the Elven Army?"

Airron shook his head. "He only took the Gladewatchers."

"Dear Highworld, that's not enough," Beck protested.

The soldiers who escorted them to the infirmary earlier intercepted them once again. "You must hurry, *Savitars*. We have just learned that it has begun! Iserlohn has engaged the Cyman Army. They didn't wait for the Elves or the Dwarves."

"What is my father thinking?" cried Kiernan. "They'll be slaughtered without reinforcements!"

Beck held up the silver compass in his hand. "Not if we can help it. Come on!"

CHAPTER 38

THE LAST HOPE

In the midst of the ongoing carnage and bloodletting, King Maximus sat despairingly astride his enormous warhorse at the devastation he could see but not quite comprehend. Hundreds of soldiers in the scarlet and black of Iserlohn lay sprawled across the Valley of Flame in frozen twisted death. Thousands more, at his orders, were now throwing themselves at the mass of Cymans and grappling in hand-to-hand combat. Men who had served the Everard family and the land of Iserlohn for years. Even the sons of those men.

They never had a chance, and it was his fault.

He foolishly disregarded the strength of this enemy and all battle strategies that may have made a difference. The Iserlohn Army alone was no match for the Cymans. These creatures from the north that did not fight with weapons were bigger and stronger and outnumbered his army three to one. The archers were useless as their arrows bounced harmlessly off the tough, leathery skin of their opponents, and the Cyman giants wrestled swords and pikes from the foot soldiers as if they were naught but toys and beat the men to the ground in bloodied heaps with their own weapons.

Atop their powerful and war-ready horses, the Nysian Cavalry held its own against the Cymans, but the foot soldiers were being decimated. The mounted troops were doing all they could to protect the soldiers on the ground, but hour after hour, the bodies continued to pile up.

Maximus growled and yanked hard on his horse's reins as a Cyman grabbed at his leg and tried to pull him out of his saddle. The experienced horse reared up onto his hind legs in response and pawed at the enemy with his hooves. The King heard the satisfying crunch of bone, and the grip on his leg slackened. One more well-placed kick with his boot at the bloodied face was all that was needed to disengage and permanently disable the Cyman.

Scanning the battlefield, he watched his vassals, all expert blademasters, cut into the Cyman horde fiercely with the battle cries of their Houses. Lord Etin called out valiantly to his Flying Eagles and Lady Knapp to her Shadow Panthers. It made no difference. Their colors were just as intertwined with the red and scarlet of his dead.

"Your Grace, you must leave!" a man screamed and then there was Colbie Nash, standing alone in front of him like an avenging angel with his feet spread and thrusting his deadly saber at any Cyman who dared approach his King. One reached out to try to unseat him again and lost his arm to Colbie's sword.

Maximus hacked furiously on all sides, his horse dancing in a circle as he tried to defend from multiple attacks. Within seconds that felt like years, the rest of the Scarlet Sabers closed ranks around him.

With horror, Maximus realized they were too late to help the beleaguered captain. The strength of numbers won out and the animals surged over Colbie and brought him down under flailing fists, some of which held rocks. Maximus howled in rage and broke free of the Sabers to use his warhorse to trample the Cymans crouching over Captain Nash.

"To me!" he screamed, and two of the Sabers slashed their way into the enemy to hoist their captain onto the back of Maximus's horse, only to be cut down in the attempt.

This is it. I'm going to die right here, right now in this valley in front of Starfell.

Regret raked through him in these final moments. Guilt that he had not waited for the Elves and Dwarves to arrive as his daughter had asked him to do. If he had, the island may have had a chance still to prevail. His men may have had a chance to live.

Responding to a harsh wrench on his arm, he dazedly swung his sword at a Cyman and sliced open his belly, the creature's entrails spilling out onto the ground.

All at once, painful, ear-splitting shrieks rang out over the valley from the west. Maximus whirled his horse toward the sound and gasped in panic, unable to believe his eyes.

Hundreds, if not thousands, of children teemed down into the valley like locusts! The implausible sight of children on a battlefield caused defenders and invaders alike to stop and stare in confusion. Dressed in loincloths and wielding small spears, closer inspection revealed that these were no children, but armed warriors. The pint-sized fighters circumvented the Iserlohn soldiers and crashed into the Cyman horde with deadly purpose. Maximus had never before witnessed anything like the scene playing out before his eyes, and was only grateful that the new combatants appeared to be on the side of the Massans. At least, he hoped that was the case.

Brandishing their weapons, they caused a great amount of damage darting in and out between the Cyman giants, stabbing at their legs and inflicting debilitating injuries. The invaders floundered helplessly, unable to offer a defense against the speed and stature of the ruthless little people.

Wherever they came from, Maximus refused to squander the opportunity presented by the distraction. With his captain still on his horse, he yelled, "Forward!" and dug his heels into his mount and thundered back into battle. Buoyed with hope, the Scarlet Sabers and Iserlohn Army smashed into the tide alongside him, hurling it back.

"Again! Forward!" he shouted, and a second vicious blow by the Massans pushed the Cymans back even more.

Straining bodies grunted and howled. Formations disappeared in a mindless tangle of fists and swords and knives. Every detail came alive for Maximus, lasting an age. The brutal combat, the sounds of the dying, the smell of the dead.

Yet, he could feel the enemy line weakening, losing heart in the face of such fearlessness.

"Push!" he bellowed one last time, and that was all it took.

Maximus sagged in relief as the Cyman Army retreated—for the moment—their big bodies lumbering away to regroup.

He called to Lord Etin. "Davad! I need to take Captain Nash to the healers!"

The confident lord nodded. "Go! We will drive these bastards back to Starfell Keep!"

Maximus quickly shook his head. He would not throw any more lives away today. "No! Withdraw! The soldiers need to rest before the next assault!"

Lord Etin's mouth tightened in disagreement, but he nodded stiffly. "As you command, Your Grace."

"I do!" Maximus growled. He reached into his saddlebag for a rope, hastily threaded it under the unresponsive captain and then tightened it around his own waist. Kicking his horse into a gallop, he sped forward, sending soldiers scattering out of his way.

At sight of the red and white flag mounted high on the tent of the healers, he hauled on the reins and had one leg over the saddle before the horse came to a complete stop. He untied Colbie, gently carried him to the ground and knelt beside him.

The pale blue eyes were open, but unseeing to anything in this world.

The handsome young captain of the Scarlet Sabers, who Maximus had once hoped would become his son through marriage one day, had made the ultimate sacrifice of his life for his King's life. As the healers looked on, Maximus tenderly cradled the captain's head, his only wish at that moment that he could take the man's place.

He tried to swallow past the pain lodged in this throat, but it refused to budge. Bloody hell, but this one hurt. Colbie was more than the captain of his Royal Guard—he was family. As was his father before him. Each and every man in the Guard pledged to lay down their life for him, but this was the first time in his reign that it had been necessary.

Finally, he cleared his throat and gestured to a soldier standing nearby. "Find Captain Franck. Tell him to retrieve our dead from the field and burn their bodies in a warrior's tribute." He looked down one more time at Colbie Nash and stood. "Prepare the captain's body as well. He will be honored in death as he was in life. Summon me when the preparations are complete."

He didn't wait for a response, but remounted and made his way back to his tent with what was left of the captain-less Scarlet Sabers following silently behind.

When he arrived, he swung down and ordered that a scout be sent to the south to find out whether the Elves or Dwarves were close to their location yet—something he should have done *before* engaging the enemy.

Fatigue and grief gnawed at him as he ducked inside the shelter and sat heavily on his cot.

A request for entry came from outside and he granted it tiredly.

Captain Bo Franck entered, his uniform torn and bloodied. A long wound across his left eye and down the side of this face oozed with blood. *If he lives, he will be disfigured for life.*

Maximus yanked one of his boots off. "Good, you're here, I—"

"You will need to put your boots back on, Your Grace."

The King looked up with raised eyebrows.

"The Elves have arrived."

"Thank the Highworld, Bo!" he said, his weariness fading with renewed hope. "Now, we may have a chance!"

"I'm afraid that's not all, Your Grace."

"What? What is it?"

"Adrian Ravener approaches as well. Only he is accompanied by an army that makes the Cymans look like a child's plaything."

***

Beck led the *Savitars* into the Puu Rainforest at a ground-eating lope, the beauty of the jungle lost on them as they concentrated solely on putting one foot in front of the other. It had been decided not to expend all of Rogan's energy using magical fire until it was necessary, so Beck guided the way with a torch dipped in long-burning pitch.

They struggled forward, maneuvering through a forest thick with vegetation and trees. The constantly altering terrain put strain on their muscles. The humidity sapped their strength. Minutes turned into hours.

Beck called a brief rest at midday for a meal of dried beef and cheese that the Elves had pressed into Airron's hands on their departure.

Then, they ran again.

Beck continued to take periodic readings of the compass and it always showed an easterly heading. It never wavered from that position, and he began to wonder if the bloody thing worked—

especially when an impenetrable wall of verdant rock emerged in the center of their path.

He turned to look at his companions, shocked at their disheveled state. Faces and clothes were covered in splattered mud, hair was plastered to foreheads. Even Bajan, whose white fur was always impeccably clean, looked gray and limp.

Beck knew he must look the same, and the pain in his ribs flared fiercely, but he pushed the ache down and away from him.

"What do we do?" asked Rogan, hands on knees, breathing heavily.

Beck looked up at the rock wall. "I don't know. The compass is pointing east. This," he said, pounding the leafy rock, "is east!"

"Can we scale it?" Kiernan asked, stepping back to get a clearer view of the wall's height.

"Doubtful."

"We're wasting time," Rogan said impatiently. "We have to find a way around it."

Beck reached out with his magic. The wall itself, behind the profuse covering of jungle vines, was immense in both width and length and built several feet into the ground. Behind the wall sat a mountain of earth leagues long. He sought out any weakness in the stone that he could exploit to bring it crashing down, but found nothing. Broadening his search, he felt a void several feet to the north. "Wait!" he shouted. "I think I found something."

He pulled out of his shifting and walked over to the place in the wall where he sensed a hole in the stone. "Over here!"

Airron ran over to help him clear the dense flora and when they were finished, a man-sized tunnel appeared. The Elf bent down to look inside. "Let me have the torch!"

Beck handed it to him.

A moment later, Airron's voice came back as a hollow echo. "It's going to be wet, but it stretches far into the mountain." His silver head reappeared. "I think we should give it a try."

Beck nodded.

Airron clapped Rogan on the shoulder. "Rogan is going to have to light the way. The smoke from the torch will be lethal in such a confined place."

"Rogan?" the Dwarf asked in disbelief, looking around at the others. "Did he just call me Rogan?"

"Slip of the tongue," Airron said, pushing him forward. "Now, get in there, Fireball."

Rogan grunted and walked hesitantly into the tunnel, creating fire as he went. Beck knew he hated tight, enclosed places as much as Kiernan hated snakes.

Beck extinguished the torch and motioned the others in before him, taking up the rear. Water trickled onto his head and down the back of his shirt as soon as he ducked inside, and it continued to drip incessantly as they trotted. For the next hour, they trudged through ankle-deep water and the only break in the monotonous march was when Kiernan screamed out and kicked a rat against the wall. After that, all Beck could hear was the unremitting seepage of water and all he could see was Rogan's flame flickering up ahead.

As more hours passed, Beck began to regret the decision to enter the tunnel. Then, all of a sudden, he felt a sharp pull in the water and Rogan cried out. "The water is rising!"

Not only was it rising, thought Beck, but a rush of rapids had developed and it was getting harder to maintain his footing in the gush now swirling at his knees.

"We need to get out of here," Rogan said, and Beck heard a slight tremor in his voice. Due to his height, the Dwarf would be swimming long before the rest of them.

"Don't panic," he ordered.

"Grab my clothes!" yelled Airron. "I'm going to scout ahead and see how far the tunnel goes."

Rogan stopped and turned his flame around in time for Beck to see Airron's lanky body shrink down into that of a Hawthorne sturgeon. The large fish leapt out of the water and then disappeared.

Beck reached for Airron's clothes and boots in the soft glow of the magical flame and stuffed them into his pack. "Let's keep going," he said. "Kiernan, hang on to Bajan."

They continued their advance, and the water was up to Rogan's chest by the time Airron returned and shifted back.

"There's moonlight up ahead, but we still have quite a ways to go. We'll all be swimming before we get there."

"Bloody hell, I don't think I can make it," Rogan grumbled. "The magic is draining my energy, and I'm not sure how much further I can keep this up."

Beck urged the party to move as fast as they could but, as Airron predicted, it wasn't long before they were treading water. Amazingly, Rogan still held his hand holding the flame up and out of the water. It was a heroic effort, and Beck knew that Rogan was the only fireshifter alive who could have kept up a constant shifting for so long without interruption. The one thing in their favor was that the water flowed very rapidly now and propelled them forward at a very quick pace.

"Are there snakes in here?" Kiernan asked as she clung to Bajan's neck.

Beck was about to tease her when he heard a grunt and the flame went out, plunging them into darkness. "What happened?"

"It's Rogan! He went under," shouted Airron.

Beck swam as fast as he could toward Airron's voice and together they reached down and pulled Rogan out of the water. Rogan coughed up a mouthful of water and moaned, his head hanging between his shoulders.

"Beck, hang on to Rogan. I'm going to shift into an owl for a different viewpoint and so I can see in the dark. It can't be that much farther."

"I have him. Go on."

Beck couldn't see Airron shift, but heard the flap of wings moving through the air. He flipped Rogan onto his back and put his arm under the Dwarf's chin to keep his head above the water, which now rushed powerfully through the tunnel. Up ahead, he heard a faint sound that grew progressively louder and more worrying as they drew closer. Uneasy, he tried to slow his momentum by reaching out to the wall but with one arm around Rogan, he couldn't procure a grasp on the slippery sandstone. He knew they were near the end of the tunnel when he looked over and could see Kiernan's gray outline beside him, arms still wrapped tightly around Bajan's neck.

She looked terrified.

She said something to him, but he couldn't hear her in the now deafening rush of water.

With a *whoosh*, the owl was back, frantically beating its wings and shrieking. Beck couldn't actually hear the shrieking, but could see the beak opening and closing in alarm. It was as close to a dire warning as an owl can give.

Hang on! Beck mouthed to Kiernan, and tightened his grip on Rogan, motioning for her to do the same. Moments later, the four of them spilled from the tunnel at last, and out into the open night air.

Beck's stomach lurched violently as he fell with his semi-conscious burden held tightly in his arms. The drop seemed unending, and he mentally braced himself for the plunge into the churning froth of rapids beneath him. But, nothing could have prepared him for the physical impact as he slammed into the water. Sharp pain lanced through his rib cage, which now felt shattered into a million pieces.

Darkness closed in on him once again as he was sucked down into the turbulent currents. He fought the instinctive fear of drowning, desperate for a breath, and kicked to the surface, still clutching Rogan.

When his head finally broke free of the water, he drew a lungful of air into his body with a deep gasp. He turned back to look at the height of the towering waterfall in the moonlight behind him and decided it was only through the good graces of the Highworld that he had managed to hang on to his friend during their midair flight over the falls.

Rogan's attempts to cough out his intake of water sounded feeble, but at least he was breathing.

Teeth gritted in agony, Beck swam to the water's edge and dragged Rogan out onto the rocky shore. He scanned the darkness for Kiernan and saw her head erupt out of the water further downstream. When Bajan popped up next to her, she reached out and took a hold of his neck, but the Draca was having difficulty staying afloat with the added weight from Kiernan.

Cursing, Beck ignored his pain, sprinted down the shoreline and dove back into the water.

"Beck!" Kiernan managed to cry out before a wave crashed over her head, her grip torn from Bajan's neck. Beck sliced under the water and caught her by the waist, pushing upward until her head broke free. Clenching his jaw against the throbbing ache in his side, he towed her to shore.

Kiernan stumbled from the water and flopped down to the ground beside Rogan. The sodden Draca Cat crawled out a moment later, and the owl came next, fluttering down from the sky. Airron shifted back into his Elven form and fell back next to the others.

Dear Highworld, we made it.

"Is everyone all right?" Beck asked, an arm held tight against his stomach.

Both Kiernan and Airron groaned affirmatively.

"We're going to need some type of stretcher to carry Rogan. I'll see what I can find. Rest while you can." He consulted the compass. It still pointed east.

"I'll help," Kiernan said, and Beck held out his hand to help her to her feet.

"Are you sure?" he asked. "You're soaked through to the bone."

She gave him a tired smile. "So are you and you can't do everything yourself."

He kissed her on the nose. "Over here, then," he said, leading her. "We need to find strong wood that we can use for the base of the stretcher."

"While you do that, I'll look for some thin vines to lash the frame together," she offered.

It took longer than Beck expected to find just the right size and length of wood he needed in the blackness of day. *Is it still day?* He wasn't sure anymore.

When he returned to the water's edge, Rogan, Bajan and a naked Airron were still lying on the ground, asleep.

He nudged Airron with his toe. "Hey, wake up and help me build this stretcher."

The bodyshifter mumbled something incoherent, but sat up.

"Where's Kiernan?" Beck asked, looking around.

"Dunno," Airron said groggily. "Last time I saw her, she was headed into the forest with you."

Beck cupped his hands to his mouth. "Kiernan!"

He received no answer and his heart skipped a beat. Just like in Iserport when Kiernan went missing, he knew instantly something was wrong. "Stay here with Rogan," he said to Airron and tossed the wood to the ground, striding back into the forest where he had last seen her. "Kiernan!" he shouted again, pushing at the thick hanging creepers with annoyance.

He stopped to listen.

The forest was eerily quiet compared to the rush of noise from the waterfall in the clearing behind him. So quiet that as he stood perfectly still and listened, he was able to hear a small noise that sounded like a muffled cry.

He hacked at the vines in front of him with one hand and shifted with the other commanding the landscape to part and provide him with a path. The leaves and vines untangled before him with a audible groan as he charged through. Not far into the forest, he stopped short in dread.

He had found her.

She hung off the ground tightly entombed in the grasp of a snake.

If you can call what I'm looking at a snake.

A forked tongue darted in and out of a massive head and around fangs the size of his fingers. The only thing he could see of Kiernan was the top portion of her head and her feet. The snake covered every other inch of her entire body.

Beck moved into the open space of the snake's lair, and the serpent watched him come with half-lidded yellow eyes. Kiernan tried to scream out when she saw him, and the snake responded by squeezing tighter. Beck heard the snap of a bone breaking. Seething, he thrust out his hands, fingertips sizzling, and the branch that the snake hung from split in two and crashed to the ground.

As the snake fell, it loosened some of its grip on Kiernan to rush at him. He feigned a move to the left, but then darted to the right just as the snake lashed out to bite him. Spinning around, he slammed his fist powerfully down on the serpent's head, and it released even more of its hold on Kiernan. She pushed at the snake's body and began to crawl away backwards on the palms of her hands. The snake sensed its prey slipping from its grasp and whipped back toward her.

Beck wove his hands again and the forest floor underneath the snake began to roil, sliding up and over the snake to bury it. Kiernan finally managed to disentangle herself completely, her arm hanging uselessly next to her body. She staggered to her feet and started to run, but the snake slithered out from under the dirt and wrapped her up again, this time covering her head. Her feet kicked violently as she struggled to breathe.

Beck growled and cast his hand in a circular pattern. A jungle vine whipped out and encircled the snake's neck pulling it taut. Stalking close, Beck grabbed the enormous jaws in both hands and used every bit of strength he possessed to pull the snake's mouth apart until it cracked open at a hideous angle and the viper fell to the ground, dead.

"Kiernan!"

It took several minutes to unravel the large, sinuous body from around Kiernan, and when he did, her face was blue and she wasn't breathing.

He gathered her up into his arms and ran with her back to the clearing where Bajan's heartrending cry pierced the air.

CHAPTER 39

ACT OF DISGRACE

Adrian Ravener approached the torch-lit battlefield with his sister at his side and hundreds of horned demon soldiers fanned out behind. Across the distance, he watched the Elven King, Jerund J'El, wind his way to the front lines of the Iserlohn Army with his elite Calvary force. Numbering close to a thousand, the hooded Elves made an impressive sight atop their white horses, high-stepping in synchronization and dressed in golden tunics that glistened richly in the soft light. Intelligent violet eyes missed nothing as they scrutinized the scene before them.

Adrian recalled an old battle adage that claimed as soon as an enemy laid eyes on the golden hem of a Gladewatcher's tunic, they were already dead.

Not today, my friends. Today, you will be the first to die.

For some reason, the Dwarves still had not made an appearance. Neither had the *Savitars*. Children, Avalon had called them. Galen should have known better than to send children against him, but what choice did the old fool have really? He was dying and all of the shifters that could have made a difference for Massa were dead.

Adrian tapped his lip in thought. According to his scouts, the Iserlohn Army numbered fifteen thousand strong. Even with the newly-arrived Gladewatchers, it was a puny defense, so Adrian found it difficult to understand why they chose to fight.

His gaze slid over the bannermen rigidly holding the scarlet and black standards of Iserlohn as well as the colors of King Maximus's

Houses and then went to Jerund as the Elf finally arrived at the space made available for him next to Maximus.

The two Kings nodded to each other in greeting, and the Gladewatchers fell into place around the Scarlet Sabers.

The pieces are all in play. Let the games begin.

Two demons next to Adrian suddenly hissed out a warning and he noticed Lucin hastily approaching.

Fool.

"What 'ave you done?" Lucin barked when he neared, his one eye wild with fury.

"What have I done?" Adrian repeated. "I traded up. I realized that thirty wasn't enough for what I needed to accomplish."

"But—"

He leaned over to speak directly into Lucin's face. "Now, step back, Captain, or so help me I will strike you dead this very minute."

Lucin glared at him for half a second longer than was wise before trudging back to his place with the Cyman Army behind the demons.

Adrian nudged his horse forward. "Gentlemen!" he said loudly to cover the distance between the two armies. "By your presence here today, I trust that you have received the directives I issued and are ready to surrender. Although, technically," he added with a twist of his mouth, "you have until tomorrow to do so."

King Maximus tore the black and scarlet standard from the bearer next to him and thrust it into the air. "The Army of Iserlohn will not surrender, Ravener! We will fight with our last breath until you and your monstrosities are defeated! We fight for Iserlohn!" A thunderous battle cheer went up from the throats of thousands of soldiers. "We fight for Captain Colbie Nash!" Louder cries yet rent the air. "We fight for our lives!" The King let the yells continue unabated for several moments while his lords and ladies raced down the line and delivered his words.

When it became quiet once more, Adrian bowed his head in acceptance. "Very well. Let it be known that the King of Men has chosen death for himself and his soldiers."

Even with the distance separating them, Adrian could see the King's shoulders draw back. If there was one thing a righteous old goat like King Maximus feared, it was recklessly costing his men their lives in battle. It was one thing to lose men when fighting on the side of right. It was altogether another to lose men by making terrible decisions.

"King Jerund J'El, what say you?" Adrian asked.

The Elven King's face remained coolly impassive as his calculated gaze fell on Adrian, long silver hair falling over his shoulders from under a burnished golden helmet.

Thousands of men on both sides waited for the Elven King's response.

"We fight alongside our fellow Massans," he declared finally. "You are not welcome here, Mage. You are but a pestilence to be eradicated."

"Odd that you say that, King Jerund, considering that the Elven women have been *very* eager to welcome us here."

Hundreds of purple eyes narrowed in unspoken wrath. Adrian knew he had to enrage the Gladewatchers, goad them into acting emotionally and shedding the imperturbable stoicism for which they were notorious. The only way to do that was through their women.

He gestured and a red-eyed demon pushed through the ranks and shoved a young female Elf forward. The girl's face was bruised and bloodied, her torn tunic hanging from her small body in ragged strips, barely covering her nakedness. The sight of the young girl created an immediate stir of agitation and muttered oaths among the Gladewatchers, their horses dancing beneath them in response to their rider's distress.

King Jerund held up his hand. The old King knew exactly what Adrian planned and sought to settle his soldiers before they acted on the taunt.

It worked for the moment, the King's gesture simmering the situation.

Time to stoke the fire.

At another nod from Adrian, the muscular demon shoved the girl into the center of the open space between the armies and threw her to the ground, where she lay crying.

The Elves turned toward their King, waiting with murder in their eyes for the signal to attack. But, the astute Jerund wouldn't give the signal, and that was something Adrian was counting on. He needed to frustrate the Gladewatchers—to infuriate and shame the Elven males into pursuing reckless action. He needed to provoke his biggest threat to their demise.

The powerfully built demon lifted the young girl by her long, white hair and struck her across the mouth.

The night air rang as hundreds of swords sprang from scabbards. The King's harried hand signals and attempts to communicate with the Gladewatchers were beginning to fail.

Adrian threw up a spell of protection around him and his sister and their horses as the demon stood over the young female. The beast lifted its horned head in a deafening howl and, in a flash of movement, leaned down and ripped off the girl's leggings. The demon shoved her back to the ground, lifted what was left of her tunic, and plunged a clawed hand up inside her body, violating her in a most inconceivable manner.

The girl screamed in pitiful agony, her back arching off the ground. The demon used his other hand to tear away the rest of the material at the girl's chest and ran a forked tongue over her small, exposed breasts.

Inaction was no longer even a remote possibility.

The Elven Gladewatchers roared in a maddened desire to kill and kicked their horses into motion covering the space between the armies in a blaze of white, smashing into the demons that had now stepped out to meet them. The front line of Iserlohn entered the chaotic foray as well, and Maximus's vassals were almost trampled in the violent surge.

The thunderous impact of flesh was staggering. Men and horses screamed. The Kings tried in vain to recall the formations of their units.

"Adrian!"

He turned at his sister's warning shout. One of the Gladewatchers had managed to get past the demons and sprinted at him with a confident smirk. The Elf took a running leap and struck out viciously with his sword, but it bounced harmlessly off the magical shield Adrian had created.

Surprised and off-balance, the Elf hit the ground hard and cried out as he was buried under a swathe of demons.

It had taken less than an hour for the deadly skirmish to accomplish Adrian's goals and it was now nearly finished. A river of red burgeoned under the feet of the combatants. Over the vociferous battle sounds, Adrian heard the aggrieved King Jerund wail in disbelief. The demons had destroyed the Elven Gladewatchers to a man. The revered protectors of Haventhal were no more.

A significant number of Iserlohn soldiers continued the attack, but content that all had gone according to plan, Adrian turned his horse to return to Starfell Keep.

Let them fight it out, he thought. If there was anyone left alive tomorrow, he would accept their surrender then.

***

Beck fastened the last vine around the litter with a grunt. Satisfied it would hold, he walked over to Kiernan, knelt by her side and placed his palm on her forehead. She wasn't feverous, but still breathing very shallowly. Other than the splint he had fastened to her broken arm, there was nothing more he could do for her.

Frustration raged through him. He suspected that the snake's compression had collapsed one of her lungs and if that was the case, she needed proper care from a healer at once or she would die. But, where was he to find one in the middle of a bloody rainforest?

He looked down at her pale face and gently brushed a damp, blonde tress from her cheek, his fingers trembling with worry and fatigue. He pressed his lips to her temple. "Please hold on, Kiernan," he whispered. "I'll find the help you need, I promise. But, you have to hold on. For me." He took another moment in the solace of her scent and then lifted her small frame onto the litter, tucking his cloak securely around both sides of her body.

He stepped in between the roped vines and wound them around his shoulders in a makeshift harness to pull the stretcher.

"Are you ready?" Airron asked, already tethered to the litter that would carry Rogan. Beck looked over at his friend. The tight-lipped grimace and eyes shadowed with exhaustion were a dismal caricature of a face usually creased in a smile. *What happened to him? What happened to all of us? Did Galen Starr really believe we had a chance or were we the only chance he had available to him?*

He nodded to Airron, and they began to trot east down the beach with their burdens, Bajan loping unsteadily behind them. Kiernan's health appeared to be having an analogous effect on the Draca.

He took another reading of the compass as they ran, and frowned as he realized it was leading them back into the Puu. Even with his earthshifting, it would be difficult to maneuver the litters over the dense forest floor. Still, they had no other choice, so they plunged inside the jungle and were forced to stop several times to untangle the wooden slats from the vegetation on the ground. Even more frustrating was the lack of any real indicator of how much longer it would take to get to their destination.

"How much farther can it be?" Airron asked after several hours of grueling travel. "I've smelled the salt of the Arounda in the air for leagues now, yet it remains unseen. We should have run out of forest by now!"

Beck nodded wearily. He knew Airron looked to him for hopeful words, but he simply didn't have any left to give. It was getting harder and harder to run. Every muscle in his body ached and begged for respite. His head throbbed with concern for Kiernan, Rogan and all of the Massan soldiers now undoubtedly in battle. He despaired over ever making it to the Valley of Flame in time to make a difference; despaired over the possibility that they might never find Callyn-Rhe or the weapon they needed. Airron must have been thinking the same, and Beck longed to give his friend the encouragement they both needed to hear, but he couldn't find the energy to do so. "We just have to keep moving," was all he said.

And, they did.

Neither Rogan nor Kiernan awakened during the trek. In fact, the last time he looked, Kiernan's skin had begun to take on a pasty yellow cast.

Running league after league through the darkened trees, the vines cutting painfully into his shoulders, Beck began to see threats in every shadow. Every flutter of a leaf was a snake about to drop down on him. Every rustle of noise, a demon about to rake him with its claws. The threat that eventually did appear before them seemed so harmless at first that he didn't respond fast enough.

Two black shapes appeared overhead swinging innocuously from tree to tree, shadowing them. Yet, the farther they ran into the forest, the more the shapes began to shriek in protest at the invasion of their territory. And, for some reason, their agitation seemed to be directed more at Bajan than the two men towing the litters.

Beck tried to ignore them. *Just a couple of jungle apes frolicking through the trees. They'll lose interest soon.*

"Get lost!" Airron shouted, waving his arms weakly at the apes.

That was all it took for them to attack. One of the monkeys dropped down onto Bajan's back and bit him in the shoulder with large, blunt incisors. The fatigued Draca Cat roared in pain and swept up his spiked tail to dislodge the creature and toss it to the ground.

Beck yelped in shock as he looked down at the aggressor. It was a Moshie! The monkey people of legend with disturbingly human faces and even more disturbingly simian teeth. *They're real?*

Airron stepped out of his harness. "Stand guard over Kiernan and Rogan. I'll handle this."

Even in the dim forest, Beck could see the faint shimmer in the air when Airron shifted into a bear.

Bajan's attacker rushed him once again and the second Moshie jumped down at the bear, who took a mighty swing with an enormous paw. The Moshie darted out of the way, and joined his companion to attack Bajan in a very human, coordinated effort Beck wouldn't have thought possible. They took the Draca Cat to the ground, one grabbing his front paws and the other biting into his hind leg and coming away with a mouthful of flesh and white fur.

Bajan howled and the bear tore toward the Moshies, swiping at one with such tremendous force that the Moshie slammed against a tree and fell to the ground, lifeless. The remaining Moshie screeched and screamed while beating his chest, human eyes glaring with hatred. The maddened humanoid ape dove at the bear with teeth and fists, pummeling it to the ground with unbelievable strength, somehow managing to avoid the lethal claws.

In a final act of dominance, the muscular Moshie jumped down on the bear's leg with all of his weight and then scampered away into the forest, leaving his dead cohort behind.

"Airron!" Beck cried out, stunned by the ferociousness of the attack.

The winded bodyshifter gazed up at him, arms and legs bleeding from bite marks and scratches. "That bloody beast broke my leg!"

"Are you sure?"

"Yes, I felt it crack. Beck, I can't walk. You're going to have to go on without me."

He shook his head. "No, I'm not leaving you alone."

"You have to!"

"Stay where you are," Beck told him, and he hurried over to Bajan lying still on the ground. The Draca lifted a weary head and then let it drop back to the ground with a pained whine.

I can't believe this is happening.

Beck put his head in his hands and took a deep breath.

I can't give up now. We've come too far.

Reaching deep inside, he marshaled the strength remaining to him and called on the aid of the blood oath and his earthshifting. His toes and fingers tingled with the swell of power. The ground trembled beneath his feet. The twin magics clashed inside his body with explosive force, taking him to his knees.

"Beck, are you all right?"

Magic surged through him, energizing his aching body. Adrenaline raced to his heart. Muscles bulged, stretching skin.

With a snarl, he reached down and flung the injured Draca Cat across his shoulders as if he weighed no more than a sack of grain. Ignoring Airron's shouts of protest, he walked to his friend and hoisted him onto his back beneath Bajan. "Hang on!"

"Beck! Leave me!"

"No."

Despite his objection, Airron wrapped his good leg around Beck's waist and left the other to dangle uselessly a few inches off the ground. Beck bent down under his burden to wrap the vines of both stretchers across his body and then he started to walk.

Legs burning painfully, he carried his four friends. Step by step, tears coursing down his face, he walked.

CHAPTER 40

NEW LIGHTS

King Maximus leaned on his sword tiredly, bereft of further stratagems to turn the tide of the conflict and gain an advantage over the Cymans and demons. His newly appointed captain of the Scarlet Sabers, Gage Gregaros, implored him time and again to leave the battlefield, but he refused, even when his horse was mercilessly cut down from under him. He received word moments ago that two of his loyal vassals, Lady Conry and Lord Paxton, had perished in the fight. He knew he was taking desperate chances, but he could do no less. Not after Colbie Nash.

After the Elves' horrific defeat earlier that day, and after a brief retreat, the battle resumed and continued to rage. King Jerund assured Maximus that a messenger had been sent posthaste to Sarphia to summon the main branch of the Elven Army. Although, what form that messenger took was a mystery to Maximus as every last Elf who accompanied the King to the Valley of Flame was dead.

Without thinking, he thrust his sword out to hew at the neck of a Cyman battling one of his Scarlet Sabers.

Where is Kiernan? Where are the Savitars?

As objectionable as he found the thought to be, the Massans needed magic to fight the demons that Ravener introduced to this war. All of the swords in the world couldn't defeat an entity that could disappear into the form of a wraith and sweep away into the night air.

With a heavy heart, he lunged at another enemy soldier and was struck from behind. He hit the ground hard, his breath disappearing from his lungs in a painful grunt. Rolling over, he looked up to find one of the red-eyed demons staring down at him.

He had danced with death for many hours this day and was almost relieved that the moment had finally arrived. His old body had reached its limits. The only guilt he would take with him concerned Kiernan, his beloved daughter. He prayed that she would always remember how much he had loved her. He had made decisions during the course of this life that he now regretted, but that he thought were right at the time. He always assumed Kiernan would be happier living with people like her—people of magic—but realized now how prejudiced that sounded.

Even so, he loved his little girl very much, just as he had loved her mother, the Queen. Grace had magic, too. She tried to keep it hidden, but he knew. He deliberately looked the other way with her because he had no other choice. He couldn't live without her. *Then, why couldn't I do the same with Kiernan?* He supposed it was because magic, any magic, served as a painful reminder of his loss.

He laughed in the shadow of the demon. *She's just like you, Gracie. The girl has mettle, that she does.*

Maximus looked up at the repulsive creature standing over him and rolled away just as the demon's black sword thrust down where his chest had been. *If I'm going to die, it will be while standing on my own two feet and not flat on my back.*

He scrambled upright, two hands on the hilt of his sword.

All at once, the demon roared in surprise as it was lifted into the air and slammed back down to the ground. The creature's limbs snapped tight to its body and it thrashed violently against invisible bonds.

"Hello, Max," said an unquestionably feminine voice from behind him.

He spun around in shock and peered into the face of the woman standing next to him. She looked familiar and he had to rack his brain before coming up with Gemini, one of Grace's friends from down south somewhere.

She had her hand thrust out toward the demon as she smiled at him. "Nice to see you again, Your Grace," she said more formally and bowed her head.

Maximus's jaw dropped. Everywhere he looked beautiful women were fighting alongside the men and tearing into the demons with fervor—and magic.

Gemini flicked her hand and a woman in silk raced to the writhing figure on the ground and set it afire. Within seconds, the demon disappeared in a cloud of black smoke.

"What are you doing here?"

The gray-haired woman shrugged her shoulders. "Keeping a promise."

"Grace?"

She nodded with a wistful smile. "Where is Kiernan?" she asked while throwing out her hands to wrap up a demon stalking behind him.

"I haven't seen her since she left Nysa," he responded and lunged over her shoulder with his sword to stab a Cyman preparing to grab her.

"What are you anyway? A shifter?" he asked

She shook her head and thrust out a hand, causing two Cyman soldiers to slam into each other and fall in a senseless heap to the ground. "I am a sorceress, Max! We all are. And, these witches," she said, waving her arm around with a laugh, "are going to save your royal behind!"

***

Beck stumbled and fell to his knees with a frustrated groan. He readjusted Airron's sleeping weight and pulled himself back upright.

The Elf had stopped protesting long ago which was just as well since Beck refused to talk to him. He focused only on the walking. Hour after hour in the incessant darkness and unrelenting rainfall. Alone. As good as alone, anyway. He had lost all track of time. The tears had dried up and the self-pity was gone. There was only the walking.

The walking and the light.

Less than a league prior, the needle of the compass abruptly spun north and when Beck looked up, he noticed a pinpoint of white light hovering in the air through the trees. He knew instinctively that was where he needed to be. Miraculously, and at long last, the compass had guided him through the elaborate tangle of magic surrounding Callyn-Rhe.

In Beck's solitary existence, the light, much larger now, was the only brightness in a world gone dark. A safe refuge in a world gone mad. There, he knew, he would be able to unfetter his burdens, both physical and emotional. If only he managed to arrive there before his body gave out. The surge of magic-induced energy now consumed, his muscles burned with fatigue and his breathing was labored and painful.

"We're almost there," he announced in a weak, hoarse voice to those beyond hearing.

Suddenly overwhelmed, the tears he thought gone dripped again and mingled with the rain on his cheeks.

This state of weakness was unfamiliar to him. All of his life, his mind and body had been strong. Having strength was what defined him as a person. As an earthshifter. And now, it seemed, when he needed his strength the most, it was failing him.

He fell again and began to crawl on hands and knees through the decomposition of the forest floor, dragging his four friends behind him. Bajan and Airron both stirred, but he ignored their murmurs. He tried to swat at the insects that swarmed over his hands and arms, but it was no use. There were too many, their stinging bites already leaving a trail of welts.

Wait! The light! Where is the light? I lost it!

Crawling more urgently now, he fought down his panic. Reaching for a thick, low-hanging vine, he hauled himself back to his feet.

He briefly considered leaving his friends behind while he searched for the light, but quickly dismissed the idea. Without the ability to defend themselves, it would be too dangerous. And, he wasn't certain he would be able to find them again if he did.

Screaming against the weight draped over his shoulders and back and around his waist, he struggled forward once again.

He reached up to clear his eyes of drizzle and tears and slammed face first into a wall. With a yelp of both surprise and pain, he stumbled back.

Another bloody wall! The light and Callyn-Rhe are behind this wall, I'm sure of it. The end of the journey is here.

Gently lowering Airron and Bajan to the ground and casting aside his harnesses, he reached out to the stone barrier in front of him. There seemed to be no beginning and no end—it just was.

He pounded the wall with both fists and snarled in frustration. After traveling all this way and suffering tremendous loss, it couldn't end this way.

The shifters of Pyraan deserved more.

The legacy of their sacrifice deserved meaning.

Taking several steps back, he bellowed in rage and threw every ounce of strength of will he had into his magic and struck out at the wall. Hands lifted in the air, he pushed and raked and slammed at the mountain of stone before him. The air crackled with the amount of magic he summoned, more than he had ever called before in his life. A strong wind spun into existence above his head and swirled loudly in the tight confines of the forest. The air whipped at his hair and clothes. Branches snapped and fell to the ground. Rain fell in torrents now and lightning streaked through the dark above.

A sudden sinister rumble caused the earth to quake at Beck's feet. The wall shuddered as though alive and the reverberation expanded, spreading over its length.

As the first chips of stone fell loose, Beck cursed and dove out of the way and covered his friends with his body.

The building magic released its energy in a discharge so thunderous the stone barrier exploded in a hail of rock and dirt. The falling debris pounded down all around them in a relentless onslaught. The screeching of tortured stone echoed for an eternity. A cloud of dust billowed overhead.

And, then, there was silence.

Beck lifted his head. Light streamed through a gap in the wall as large as his house back in Parsis, and he had to hold a hand over his sensitive eyes to shade his view. Ignoring the pain, he pitched to his feet, scrambled over the stones from the broken wall and stepped through heedlessly.

Unable to contain his emotions, a strange keening sound burst from his throat as his eyes feasted on blue skies for the first time in more than a week. Endless leagues of grasslands, the likes of which he had not known existed on the island, spread out before him. And it was filled with...

The hair on the back of his neck stood on end. A ferocious roar erupted nearby and from the corner of his eye, he glimpsed an open jaw filled with pointed teeth reaching for his neck.

CHAPTER 41

LAND OF THE DRACA CATS

Sovereign! No! Bajan growled out, watching in dread as the leader of the Draca Cats took Beck to the ground and stood over him, his large white paws pressing into the earthshifter's chest and pinning him down.

The Sovereign swung his amber eyes sharply to Bajan. *Who DARES attack the land of the Draca Cats!*

Bajan wrenched his body to his feet and stretched one of his forelegs out in front of him in a shaky bow. *My apologies for the wall, Sovereign. It is I, Bajan.*

Bajan! I have not scented you in a very long time, but it is you! Moombai moved away from Beck to greet him affectionately by nuzzling his neck. Thankfully, Beck remained where he was on the ground and didn't move.

Yes, he confirmed weakly.

Moombai sniffed at him questioningly. *What is wrong with you?*

He swayed on his feet. *I was injured by a Moshie.*

A Moshie! Those worthless baboons! There is very bad blood between the Moshies and the Draca Cats.

So, I have discovered.

Hold still. Moombai lined up their heads muzzle to muzzle and gently exhaled air into his mouth. A silky, twisting vapor swirled around their connected heads, and Bajan shivered as a cold chill traveled down his body from head to paws. Moombai pulled back and Bajan's eyes widened in surprise. All of his aches and pains and even his tiredness had disappeared and he was left feeling revived and fresh. *Moombai, what...?*

The Sovereign had already turned away and was frowning down at his friends on the ground. *You should not have brought humans here, Bajan.*

It is they who led, Sovereign, but they did not have a choice. They are the Savitars.

The Draca leader made a sharp hissing sound. *Galen Starr?*

Dead.

Has the island been invaded?

Yes. A Mage from the north leads a mutant army and...others. Evil spirits.

So, it is time. I thought as much. The signs have been clear enough that even a blind cat could have seen them. That is why I sent Felice to you.

The Draca Cat began to pace back and forth in thought.

Bajan looked out over the oasis that was Callyn-Rhe for the first time. The sun hung like a fiery red ball in the blue sky and everywhere he looked to the north, east, and south, he saw Draca Cats lounging languorously in the high grasses or atop boulders. Most were lying at ease licking their fur or idly watching the newcomers. Some, Bajan could tell by the red stains on their mouths, were feeding. There were no buildings here in Callyn-Rhe, like the humans built, just the miracle of nature in all of its glory with plains and trees and rivers sparkling in the sunlight.

Moombai walked over to the three humans and scented all carefully, stopping in front of Kiernan. His head snapped up. *Is this my bondmate's daughter?*

This is Princess Kiernan Everard.

What happened to her?

She was suffocated by a forest snake.

Why have you not healed her?

Bajan tilted his head in question. *Healed her?*

Young fool cub! Did you not know that the breath of a Draca heals?

No...I did not know that.

Moombai sniffed. *If you had come back to your pride to learn from us, you would have known.*

Bajan looked the Sovereign in the eyes. *I did not know the way.*

Moombai stopped with raised hackles and emitted a low, distressed growl. He bent to Kiernan and sent air into her lungs. She immediately began to stir.

Bajan sighed in equal parts relief and grief. *I have failed you, Sovereign, and I have failed my bondmate.*

The Sovereign shook his enormous snowy head. *No, Bajan, I have failed you by leaving you alone for too long. I should have come to you. I should have shown you the way home.* He hung his head in remorse and padded to Rogan and Airron. *Tell me, Bajan,* he asked as he worked, *have you had any visions?*

Yes, I have. Of Grace Everard.

The Sovereign's lip lifted slightly in a sad smile before he bent to the humans again.

Bajan watched Beck crawl to Kiernan's side. She sat up hesitantly and looked around in awe at her surroundings. It relieved him to see that she appeared as healthy as ever. Her eyes turned to him. *We made it,* she said incredulously.

Thanks to Beck.

She stood and shook out her arm. Moombai's breath had healed not only the effects of the snake's brutal compression, but her broken arm as well.

How am I healed?

Moombai. The breath of the Draca Cat has curative properties.

Kiernan walked over to Moombai and bowed deeply at the waist. Bajan listened in on their conversation.

Greetings, Sovereign.

Greetings, Princess. Do you know that your mother was my bondmate?

I do know that. Please accept my gratitude for the healing. Moombai. I owe you a great debt as does all of Massa.

Nonsense. This island is my home as well and I will not see it destroyed.

Kiernan nodded.

Now, please ask your large friend if I may heal him, and he pointed with his head toward Beck.

"Beck, the Sovereign wants to heal you. Is that all right with you?"

Beck shook his head. "I'm not hurt. Just exhausted."

Kiernan laughed. "Beck! You have two black eyes, a bloody gash on your forehead, and wounds up and down your arms. And, that's just what I can see! You also have at least one broken rib in case you've forgotten."

Beck put a hand to his face in surprise. "I...I didn't realize."

Moombai snorted a laugh. *Tell him to trust me and bend down.*

Kiernan did and Beck bent his head before the Sovereign. After the cat emitted his magical vapor, Beck looked up and the bruises on his face were already starting to fade. "I thank you, Sovereign."

Rogan and Airron were standing up as well now.

Moombai, you must know why we are here. We have to find a weapon to defeat Adrian Ravener.

It is here. Follow me.

The Sovereign let out an enormous roar and all of the Draca Cats who had made such a casual show of disinterest in the events playing out, rose as one.

Kiernan and the *Savitars* followed Moombai to a large outcropping of red granite rock, the surfaces pitted and furrowed by time and weather. Beneath a natural overhang and among a pile of rock that must have broken from the ledge at one time, stood a stone altar.

Moombai bounded onto the altar and faced the gathering.

Draca Cats! Brothers and sisters! Listen carefully! For over three hundred years, a formidable and ancient power has been locked away in our homeland. You may be surprised to learn that the power I refer to is us. It is the Draca Cats.

Kiernan flinched as the cats began to pace and mew anxiously.

Moombai turned their way. *Savitars! Around the time of the Mage War, Galen Starr cast a Spell of Forbidden Use over an ancient form of shifting called spiritshifting. He knew that war with his brethren was imminent and wished to protect Massa from the evil spirits that could be summoned by a Mage skilled in spiritshifting. Due to Galen Starr's unfortunate demise, the spell he cast hundreds of years ago has been purged, and the ability to spiritshift has been resurrected.*

Kiernan finished her translation, and the *Savitars* looked at each other in disbelief.

Bajan informs me that Galen Starr's fears have been realized, and our island has been invaded by a Mage spiritshifter.

The Sovereign paused.

What this Mage cannot know is that the Draca Cats are also innate spiritshifters.

The Draca Cats' mewing turned to howls, and Kiernan had to suppress the urge to howl right along with them.

Moombai looked down at Bajan. *That is why you have had visions of late. Until you know how to recognize and control the shifting, you inadvertently beckoned spirits to your side.*

The Draca leader lifted his head again to the gathering. *Naturally, we would only call upon the angels of the Highworld while the dark Mage calls upon the demons of the Netherworld. In order for any spirit to gain entry into the mortal world, a portal is required. The demons demand their portal be a human sacrifice whereas the angels only require an object of magic through which to pass. And, the time to call them is now!*

Kiernan had to cover her ears when the Draca Cats, including the Sovereign, lifted their heads and yowled out a battle call with all of the ferociousness for which they were once notorious.

Savitars! Who has the portal?

Kiernan repeated Moombai's question, and her friends were at as much of a loss as she was by the question. "A portal? The only thing we have with magical properties is the compass."

"Wait!" Beck said and pulled the Protetor from his pocket. "Will this work?"

Kiernan held out the black book to Moombai and translated Beck's question

The Sovereign nodded. *It is a device of great magic. It will be sufficient. Please place it on the altar.*

As she did, Moombai said regrettably. *I wish I could give you more time to adjust to the significance of what I have just told you, but we are simply out of time. Dracas!*

The Draca Cats edged in closer to their Sovereign, and Kiernan noticed a female Draca sidle up next to Bajan and purr quietly.

Felice?

Yes.

The Sovereign paced the edge of the altar. *Every young cub in Callyn-Rhe is required to learn the Dracan Chant. Let us sing it now in our hour of need!*

Hundreds of Draca Cats bowed down with a bent foreleg out in front. A voiceless chant droned through Kiernan's mind, softly at first and then with more fervor. The Protetor lying open on the stone altar began to glow and tremble as the air ignited with magic. The intensity of the power emanating from the portal riddled Kiernan's body with goose pimples and her hair stood on end.

A small whimper escaped her throat, and she instinctively stepped back along with the other *Savitars* when long white fingers started to claw their way out through the open spine of the book.

CHAPTER 42

A CALL TO ARMS

The fingers lengthened and a head, arms and then the body of a man stepped from the book. The silvery apparition, at least ten feet tall, whipped a head of white hair purposefully as he scanned the area, a luminous white sword gleaming from his fist.

Kiernan gasped as she recognized Galen Starr. Only, not as he appeared on his deathbed, but more like the man she first met, full of vitality and drive, and something new—menace. The mischievous twinkle was nowhere to be found. This Galen Starr looked ready for battle.

Beck reached over to grab her hand tightly in his. She glanced to the side. Rogan's face was deathly pale, and Airron looked like he was preparing to flee.

"MOOMBAI!" the Mage thundered, the resonance of his voice deep and terrifying.

I am here, Mage.

"Is it you who has summoned me?"

It is.

"The battle has begun." It was a statement.

Yes, Mage.

"The *Savitars*?"

They are here.

The white wraith swooped close to hover in the air before them. "I am pleased to see that I made the right choice. It was with the utmost remorse that I set you on the path to Callyn-Rhe, but you have proven yourselves more than worthy." Galen bowed down to them. "My eternal gratitude, *Savitars*."

Beck spoke up. "Thank you...Grandfather."

For a fleeting second, the sparkle was back in the blue eyes, and then it was gone.

"ANGELS!"

Bajan leaned into her when more ghostly forms emerged from the Protetor one after the other. The glowing wraiths launched high into the air and then settled down onto the ground, their shapes resolving into more solid human forms. Although not quite as large as Galen, they were just as formidable, all with a look of supreme strength and power.

Kiernan cried out as her mother, Grace Everard, stepped toward her. "Maman!" she cried and fell to her knees. "I was right...it wasn't a dream."

"No, darling. Bajan summoned me to your side. He was so worried for you that his spiritshifting responded to your distress. Luckily, your young man had the Protetor in his pack, and I was able to cross over into this world and go to you." Her mother reached out to touch her hair and it felt like the tickle of a light breeze on a summer day.

More shapes stepped up behind the Queen, and the reunions played out simultaneously.

***

Jaimes and Constance Atlan stood tall before Beck, swords of light glowing from the scabbards at their hips.

Constance smiled down at her son from her immense new height, head and shoulders above him. "We are so proud of you, Beck."

"Why?" he demanded guiltily. "I couldn't save you. I tried, but I couldn't break the shield!"

His father reached out to put a hand on his shoulder. "It was meant to be, Beck. Do not weep for us. We walk in the light now. Find peace in that knowledge until we are together again."

***

Two Dwarfs dressed in battle gear approached Rogan. The male said, "You may not remember me, but I am your father."

Rogan trembled. "I do remember you. After all of these years, I finally remembered." He reached a hand out toward the woman. "Mother..."

"I am here, my son."

Rogan soaked in the sight of the parents he now knew gave their very lives for him. "You never left me," he stated in wonder.

"Never!" replied his mother adamantly. "Do not for one moment ever believe that to be so. You were my life, Rogan Radek, and you must never forget!"

***

Airron wore a wide smile at sight of his parents, Jeni and Joshe. "I never thought I would see you again."

Joshe's face donned a grin to match his son's. "*Asha*, my beloved."

"*Asha*." Sudden tears welled in Airron's eyes. "If I had not been sent away during the battle in Pyraan, maybe I could have—"

"Done what, my son?" his mother interrupted. "We are all where we should be for a reason. Yours is to protect this island."

"Because I am *Savitar?*"

"Because you are a shifter."

***

A young Dwarven male stepped out front to greet Rogan.

"Dillon!" exclaimed Rogan. "Why? Just when we were getting to know each other again."

Dillon shook his head. "Do not question fate, my friend. Are you watching over Janin?"

***

Bret Schwan, the Scarlet Saber who accompanied the *Savitars* to Iserport, traded grips with Beck and Airron.

"Avalon?" Beck questioned.

The Saber nodded ruefully. "She got the best of me. Make sure the witch does not do the same to you!"

***

Another tear slipped down Kiernan's cheek when Titus emerged looking around hesitantly. As soon as he saw her, he glided over to hover in front of her. "'Ello agin," he said shyly.

Kiernan reached out her hands to him. "I am so sorry for what happened to you, Titus."

He nodded. "I know. I just wish we 'ad more time to get to know each other."

"Me, too. Oh, Titus!"

"I must go," he said. "Tell my Da that I am in a safe place and love 'im!"

"I will, Titus, I promise!"

***

Several shifters from the Magical Kingdom of Pyraan glided past, including young Katrin Allendale who looked like she could bend an oak tree with little effort.

Kiernan held her fists to her stomach in pain when Colbie Nash appeared before her. She reached out to him. "Oh, no. Colbie," she moaned.

"Princess," he acknowledged and bowed to her.

"My father?"

"Alive, but needs our help."

"What happened to you?" she asked.

"Exactly what was meant to happen, Your Grace," he said smiling.

***

"ANGELS! DRACAS! *SAVITARS!*" roared Galen Starr interrupting the gatherings. "The time is now!" The Mage soared high into the sky, raised his radiant sword above his head and swung it down, pointing it north.

"WE FIGHT!"

With those two words, the angels took to the air and flew after the departing Mage. The Draca Cats let out deafening roars of aggression and plunged into the Puu Rainforest headed toward the Illian River and Starfell.

The *Savitars* nodded to each other grimly and turned to follow.

"Wait!" Beck shouted, humbled in the presence of such unadulterated courage. Despite the fact that one would not survive the night, the determination to rush to the aid of their fellow Massans was immutably etched into each of his friend's faces.

He looked into Kiernan's eyes, so alive and full of passion. A life where she did not exist would be bleak and empty. He turned to Rogan who watched him questioningly while fingering the short beard on his chin. Beck knew he would grow out that beard with pride and adorn it with gems in the Dwarven custom if he lived. And, Airron, with his violet eyes that sparkled in the moonlight. A world without Airron would be a world without laughter.

Bajan nudged him warmly as if to remind Beck not to forget about him.

"There are some words that must be said before we go," he said quietly.

"Beck," Kiernan said sadly. "It's too painful—"

He stopped her and shook his head. "It's more painful to live with words unsaid. I don't want to have any regrets, so I will tell you now what you already know in your hearts. You are my family, my best friends, and I want to thank you for the meaning you've brought to my life. In this world or the next, remember that always."

His friends murmured their agreement.

"Despite this!" he yelled with a paradoxical grin. "Despite knowing the outcome! We will still fight!"

The air around the *Savitars* glowed as the blood oath coursed through them in a burst of magic as bright as that of the angels.

"We fight together! As one!"

Impossibly, the light glowed brighter.

The *Savitars* and Bajan screamed out in unity and sped away north after the angels and Draca Cats as fast as superhumanly possible.

CHAPTER 43

THE VALLEY OF FLAME

It was dawn of the first Earthshine in Massa's history without light. Unrelieved darkness blanketed the skies, land and souls of the defenders like a death shroud. The battle for the Valley of Flame had raged all through the night at a terrible cost in lives.

For a while, Maximus dared to hope that they might have a chance. King Jerund, now without his Elven Gladewatchers, had admitted to an inborn talent of all Haventhal Elves of the ability to influence animal behavior, and he was able to call forth the most aggressive beasts of the Du-Chu Forest and Puu Rainforest to aid them in the battle. King Rik Rojin finally arrived with General Klay Arsten and his preeminent Iron Fists, the remainder of the Deepstone Army marching at full speed toward their location. Gemini Starr and her sorceresses proved to be particularly cunning against the enemy. It was somewhat of a challenge initially for the men to get used to fighting alongside women dressed in silks, but their opinions were soon assuaged by the witches' unique talent for destruction. And, there was Vinni Vee and his Halfie tribe who caused more damage to the enemy than all combined.

Even so, there were simply too many of the Cyman soldiers. And, with the demons now in the fray, his hopes had crumbled to ash.

"We're beating a dead horse," he told those gathered around him. "We've lost too many men." The leaders were all there, crowded outside of his tent. Bo Franck, Gage Gregaros, and Lords Etin, Winslow and Hamilton and Lady Knapp. King Rik and King Jerund and their captains and vassals. Gemini Starr and Vinni Vee. He couldn't see the Scarlet Sabers, but knew they were nearby, surveying his every move. "We're simply outmatched and outnumbered."

"Are you suggesting surrender, Max?" King Rik asked gruffly. "Because if you are, the Kings will not live out the day. Ravener could never afford to let us remain alive."

Maximus shrugged with an indifference he had to struggle to maintain. "Better me than more Iserlohn lives. We can't throw back another advance of the enemy. When they come again, it will be the last time. We will break." He looked carefully at the faces around him. Their eyes told him they knew it as well. He went on relentlessly. "As Kings of this island, we have failed our people. If we had not become so isolated and suspicious of one another, we may have had a chance. We should have been working together to create a strong united army, not closing our borders to one another!"

"You're right, Maximus," King Jerund replied, "and if we have an island left standing after this, we'll discuss all of our inadequacies at that time. Until then, we have to find a way. I haven't given up the fight yet. We can—"

The Elven King didn't get a chance to finish his thought as a strident bugle alarm went up.

One long and two short bursts.

Enemy advancing.

The assembled group sprinted to their horses and mounted.

"Gemini!" Maximus reached down and grabbed the sorceress by the forearm and swept her up behind him on the saddle. He spurred his horse roughly forward and dodged men and campfires with careless disregard. Gage Gregaros and the Scarlet Sabers pressed in dangerously close behind him.

Their headlong flight came to an abrupt end when they reached the rear infantry, and Maximus was forced to slow. He pressed his mount aggressively through to the front line. He had not seen Adrian or Avalon Ravener since yesterday morning, but they were there now at the head of their armies.

Gemini hissed in his ear.

"Good morning, High Priestess," Avalon called out from the space between them. Her mouth moved soundlessly and Maximus's horse unexpectedly reared. While he managed to stay seated, Gemini was tossed to the ground.

Avalon laughed. "No, no, don't get up for me," she said mockingly. "You're fine right where you are."

Gemini glared at Avalon as she got to her feet. "Still playing childish games, I see, Avalon."

Maximus wondered how Gemini knew Avalon, but had no opportunity to ask as the other sorceresses smoothly moved in behind their leader.

Adrian, sitting atop his horse, raised a hand in the air. "Enough! I have no quarrel with the witches." His eyes narrowed with malicious intent. "I have come for the Kings. This is the dawn of a new day, a new world, and there is no room in it for ignorant and cowardly leaders. When the three of you are dead, the fighting will cease." He laughed. "The people of Massa will probably thank me as soon as the deed is done."

"You are despicable, Adrian."

"Good to see you, too, Gemini. What has it been? A few centuries?"

The sorceress spat toward him.

"Why do you call me despicable, Gemini? Because I wish to return to my homeland?"

Gemini stalked forward. "Because of the innocent lives you are taking along the way, Adrian!"

"A means to an end, Gemini, that is all." Ravener suddenly screamed out in pain. One of the Halfies stood below the Mage pressing a knife into his calf. Ravener kicked out and sent the Halfie flying through the air. Vinni Vee let out a howl of rage, but Maximus jumped down from his horse and restrained the Tribe Leader.

Gemini sucked in a breath. "Citrine! No!"

Maximus whipped his head up. A sorceress with a braid of red hair had also managed to infiltrate the enemy line. She leapt into the air behind Avalon, grabbed her around the neck and threw her to the ground. The witch pummeled Avalon with lightning speed, each fist falling like a heavy mallet.

Avalon groaned in pain, but managed to murmur a spell that flung Citrine to the ground.

Avalon got to her feet and strode to the prone woman. Without an ounce of hesitation, she lifted Citrine's head and gave it a vicious twist, killing her instantly.

Gemini and her sorceresses screeched in fury.

"Stand back!" Adrian shouted, lifting his hand. "Gemini! We don't wish to fight you! Listen to me! We need magic in this world. Unlike these feeble Kings, I will make sure that you and all of the witches have a place in the new world! It's really quite ironic if you think about it. King Maximus hates magic so much, he exiled his own daughter and all the while he had a coven of witches living in his backyard! King Jerund is so blind, he doesn't even realize that *all* Elves have magic in the way they can summon animals! It's not some innate Elven ability. It's magic! And, King Rik! He killed his own brother because of magic! I promise each and every one of you. Massa will be better served with me leading than these three bloody fools!"

"Avalon must die," Gemini growled as if she didn't hear a word he said.

"Step out of the way, witch," Adrian threatened.

"Over my dead body."

"Very well..."

"ADRIAN RAVENER!" The fearsome voice boomed from the Puu Rainforest to the south, and every man, woman and animal in the Valley of Flame shrank back in fright.

Maximus looked up in shock as Galen Starr and an army of white wraiths drifted over the valley in the sky above.

"Demons! Formation!" Adrian bellowed.

The Demon Army responded at once and launched from the ground to meet the threat. Hundreds of white and black wraiths took positions facing each other midair and all was momentarily quiet on the battlefield as the mortals watched from below.

There were a few hushed gasps as several of the soldiers recognized departed comrades now in their spirit forms. One of the wraiths gracefully peeled away from the assemblage to swoop down in front of Maximus.

He fell to his knees. "Gracie."

"Yes, Max, it's me." She reached out and ran the back of her fingers down his cheek. "I am with you, Max, always. Remember that and take care of our daughter."

He nodded mutely, too overcome with emotion to speak.

Standing behind her as though still on royal guard, was Captain Colbie Nash. Maximus let out a half-mad laugh when his fallen captain winked at him.

His beautiful Gracie bestowed one last heartrending look at him, and then the duo swept back into the sky to take their places among the angels poised for battle.

Galen Starr, at the front of the line, lifted a sword that glowed brilliantly with light. "You will not have this island, Adrian Ravener!"

The angel Mage dropped his sword in a grand flourish, and the demons and angels rushed to close. The concussion of the clash lifted the hair on every person on the battlefield not weighted down by helm. The power of the colossal struggle between the Highworld and Netherworld, the angels and demons, echoed through the air, the ground and the flesh of every being present.

Maximus felt insignificant and small and could only look on impotently.

Bestial roars swung his gaze south to witness hundreds of Draca Cats pour out of the rainforest and over the Illian River to crash into the Cyman's southern flank.

Then, came the *Savitars.*

Stalking toward the battlefield with a deadly grace, the air around them crackled powerfully as their eyes swept over the chaos. One by one, they unleashed their magic into the enemy. The earth rumbled and heaved, throwing soldiers several feet into the air. The sky and the battlefield lit up with sorcerous fire. Confusion rang out as mindshifted Cymans turned on one another. Unbelievably, an enormous mantath sprouted up out of the body of Airron Falewir and with terrible noise brushed men out of its path and squashed them into the earth.

At the sight of his daughter, Maximus immediately seized the reins of his horse and mounted. He dug his heels into the animal's ribs and plunged ahead. "Forward!" he screamed to his front line.

Ravener saw him advancing and turned his horse to flee. Avalon clutched at his legs and Maximus could hear the panic in her voice. "Adrian! Take me with you!"

The dark Mage looked down. "You'll only slow me! You're on your own, sister!" Ravener kicked his horse and the surprised animal lunged forward, crashing through the Cyman Army toward Starfell Keep.

The galvanized Iserlohn Army collided with the Cymans in a barrage of violence. Maximus tried to drive through the horde to give chase after Ravener, but one of the Cymans yanked him from the saddle. As one, three lethal sabers lashed out of the dark to deal with the threat.

"Father!"

Maximus barely heard the call over the clamor of battle both on the ground and in the sky. He spun around to see Kiernan running through the throng to reach him. "Kiernan! I'm here!"

She looked so tired and frail as she pushed through the fighting men. He just wanted to wrap her in his arms and carry her away to safety.

Suddenly, she stopped and turned her head to the side.

Maximus stretched to look. Someone was calling to her.

Kiernan produced a weary smile for the woman who approached her.

Maximus's eyes widened in fright at sight of the redheaded witch Gemini called Citrine. How could that be? Avalon had killed her. He had seen it with his own two eyes!

His blood froze in his veins. "Kiernan, run!"

Kiernan heard his warning and crouched, unsure where the danger was coming from.

The dead witch continued to stalk Kiernan, a knife in the palm of her hand.

He ran as fast as he could, shoving soldiers out of his way and screaming to his daughter. "Look out!" He would never get there in time, he realized. "Oh, Kiernan!"

Galen Starr's prophecy blazed through his mind. One of those that went forth on the journey to Callyn-Rhe would not survive. He fell to his knees and hung his head in anguish. "I am so sorry, Gracie."

Daring to look up one last time, Kiernan disappeared from view when a streak of white flashed past her and tackled the witch to the ground. The sorceress landed flat on her back, and the large Draca Cat stood over her commandingly. The witch surreptitiously slipped her hand out from under her body and pulled her knife free.

No.

Her face twisted in a sneer, she jerked the knife upward with both hands and plunged the weapon deep into the chest of the unsuspecting cat.

Red blood stained the Draca's fur, and he looked down in surprise. Very slowly, as though movement had become too difficult for him, the snowy head lifted and he turned to find Kiernan. Twin green eyes locked for a long, poignant moment, and then the enormous body crumpled down to the ground. The witch scrambled out from under him and disappeared into the embattled mass of men.

"Nooo!" The heart-wrenching scream from his daughter propelled him into action. He pressed forward forcefully, and when he arrived at her side, she was cradling the Draca in her arms.

It was Bajan.

Tears poured down her face and she moaned and rocked in mortal agony as her lifelong companion took a final ragged breath and was still.

***

"Get out of my way!" Adrian screamed, slashing at the neck and shoulders of any Cyman soldier who found himself within striking range of his sword.

I'm almost there!

The road that cut into the eastern side of the valley would conceal his passage until he arrived at Starfell. There, Galen Starr would be powerless against him. Not even the Mage for whom the fortress had been named could penetrate the potent wards surrounding the Keep in his current spirit form.

Adrian struck out at another Cyman standing in his path. The soldier reacted instinctively and swung around, backhanding Adrian so viciously he was swept from the saddle.

"Idiot!" Adrian landed on his feet and cast out his hand. The Cyman scratched at his throat as he began to choke, his face turning first red and then purple as he fell thrashing to the ground.

An angel swooped down close to where Adrian stood. With a wordless snarl, he dove behind an overturned wagon.

They were hunting him. He could end this now and kill everyone on the battlefield, but that would cost him his own life as well, for surely Galen would know where he was if he tried to conjure magic of that magnitude. His only chance was to make it to the Keep unseen.

Suddenly, two big hands reached out and dragged him from his concealment.

"What are you doing? Stop this!" he commanded, but sighed in relief when he saw that it was Lucin.

"It's all over, Mage."

Adrian shook his head. "Not yet, Lucin. Get me to the Keep! There we will live to fight another day!"

Lucin's eye narrowed. "I am not taking you anywhere."

The skin around Adrian's eyes tightened. "I should have killed you a long time ago, Lucin. The only reason I kept you alive was to keep these mutants controlled while I slowly changed them into demons! And *you*," he bellowed, pointing, "would have been my last!"

Lucin smiled at him. "I made a promise to myself the night you killed twelve of my soldiers and the innocent Elven girl, Siole, that I be the one to personally see to your death. I do this for Maree and Miah and Titus and all of the Cyman people you 'ave tortured and abused."

"A little early to declare victory, is it not, Captain? You see, I have powerful wards set at the Keep. No one will be able to touch me there! And, let me *promise* you something, Lucin. As soon as Galen has gone back to the Highworld where he belongs, I will travel back to Nordik and hunt down your wife and daughter. I *promise* you, Lucin, that their deaths will not come quick or easy."

The Cyman captain just stared at him. "Would you like to finally 'ear the third prophecy, Mage?"

"This is your last chance, Lucin! Get me back to the Keep now, and I will let your family live!"

With battle raging all around them, Lucin recited the words. "*At the final battle, there is hope for the land, all Men, Elves and Dwarves, it is out of your hand; The angels will battle for liberation, the demons will battle for domination; It all ends as it once began, between the raven and the star; who will prevail at the end of the day, is yet to be decided from afar.*"

"GALEN STARR!" Lucin roared into the night.

"Lucin! Quiet!"

Lucin continued to scream over the mayhem. "GALEN STARR! GALEN STARR!"

The forbidding white angel with flowing hair and a sword of light heard the call.

A binding spell rooted Adrian in place, and he could only look on in contemptuous acceptance as his mentor and nemesis rushed toward him.

He didn't utter a sound as Galen's white sword cut him in half. With a powerful jolt, the world turned light.

Epilogue

A New World

The island of Massa won the battle, but would be forever changed by it. Adrian Ravener was right—it truly was a new world, and the aftermath brought many surprising events as proof of that fact.

After learning from Galen that the passive Cymans only fought for the Raveners under extreme duress and the threat of death for themselves and their loved ones, the Kings agreed to allow them to return to Nordik and reunite with their wives and children. The huge Cyman captain, Lucin, was so overwhelmed with emotion that he cried. He wept even harder when Kiernan Everard told him of his son's final words.

The three Kings of Massa agreed to institute a new council for the unification of the island. They would meet once a month to discuss all matters necessary to strengthen and revive the island and its people.

King Rik Rojin reminded Rogan Radek of his promise to return to Deepstone. There was much they needed to discuss the King told him with a pat on the shoulder, and Prince Erik was anxiously awaiting his cousin's return.

King Jerund J'El pledged to Airron Falewir that he would teach him what all Elves but he knew how to do—summon animals. He also agreed to teach him the Elven Morning Song to Elán.

King Maximus Everard declared to his daughter and all on the battlefield that day that there would be no more exile for magic users.

Gemini and the sorceresses of Elloree gave farewells to their sister, Kiernan, with heartfelt assurances to stay in touch. They did not seem surprised when Kiernan told them that she would not be advancing to the next level within the coven.

The Tribe Leader of the Halfies was most pleased with the outcome of what was being referred to as the Demon War. Not a single Halfie had been killed in battle. Vinni Vee and his Halfies vowed to try to be good citizens of Massa as they searched for a new home. Then, Vinni reflexively kicked Beck Atlan in the knee.

Of Avalon Ravener, there was no sign. The witches of Elloree declared that they would hunt her down, but it was generally agreed that without her brother, she would most likely remain in hiding. If she did reappear, the people were confident in the sorceresses' ability to deal with her.

The angels, having defeated the demons, returned to the Highworld through the Protetor. Unless dire circumstances arose, it would be the last time they would see each other, they said, but that was the way it was meant to be.

They said that often, thought Rogan Radek.

The biggest shock came from one of the Draca Cats. After they laid Bajan to rest in a touching ceremony that Kiernan translated for the Massans, Felice approached to tell her she was going to have Bajan's cub. She promised Kiernan that the baby Draca would be Kiernan's first child's bondmate. This touched Kiernan profoundly, and it took some time before she was able to stop crying. Prophecy took one of their own, but left another in his place.

Finally, it was just the shifters left. Plus one. Unbeknownst to King Rik, the resourceful Deepstone soldier, Janin, infiltrated his entourage of Fists and traveled unobserved with them to the Valley of Flame.

***

Janin snuck up behind Rogan and wrapped her arms around his waist. Startled, the Dwarf turned to look at her and his face and ears turned bright red. But, he didn't move away. He put his arm out and Janin ducked under, still clutching his middle.

"Don't worry, Janin," Kiernan told her, "it took Beck a long time to figure it out, too."

"I figured it out!" countered Rogan. "A long time ago, I might add. But in case you haven't noticed, Kiernan, I have been a little *busy* lately."

They all laughed as they started south after the Draca Cats. The four friends didn't know what the future held for them—knew only that they were not yet ready to go their separate ways. The Dracas invited them back to Callyn-Rhe for rest and time to heal from the effects of battle.

They were at peace.

The fighting was over and there was profound comfort in knowing that their family and friends were safe in the Highworld. They had much to look forward to in their new magical life ahead of them.

"Besides," Rogan said, "what kind of decent young lady would want to be with a magic shifter like me?"

"Decent? You never said you were looking for decent!" Janin teased with a smile.

Airron barked out a laugh, and when Airron Falewir laughed, they all found it hard not to join in.

The End

RULING NOBILITY OF MASSA

ISERLOHN
King Maximus Everard
House Colors - Black & Scarlet, Sigil - Golden Lions
Princess Kiernan Everard

MEN AT ARMS
Colbie Nash - Captain, Royal Guard, Personal Guard to King Maximus
Bo Franck - Captain, Iserlohn Army
Greg Gregaros - Scarlet Saber
Bret Schwan - Scarlet Saber
Kirby Nash - Lieutenant, Iserlohn Army

COURT MEMBERS
Lord Davad Etin
House Colors - Red & Blue; Sigil - Flying Eagles
Lord Abram Winslow
House Colors - White & Gray; Sigil - Crouching Wolves
Lady Isabella Conry
House Colors - Brown & Black; Sigil - Savage Badgers
Lady Lillian Knapp
House Colors - Gray & Purple; Sigil - Shadow Panthers
Lord Paxton
House Colors - Black & Green; Sigil - Thundering Bulls
Lord Johan Hamilton
House Colors - Red & Yellow; Sigil - Red Dragons

DEEPSTONE
King Rik Rojin
House Colors - Blue & Maroon; No Sigil
Prince Erik Rojin

MEN AT ARMS
Klay Arsten - General, Iron Fists, Personal Guard to King Erik

RULING NOBILITY OF MASSA

HAVENTHAL
King Jerund J'El
   House Colors - Brown & Green; Sigil - Ficus Tree
Prince Thorn J'El

MEN AT ARMS
Raine Aubry - Gardien, Gladewatchers
Leif Oliver - Gardien, Gladewatchers

AFTERWORD

Thank you very much for reading Book One in the Island Shifters series. I hope you enjoyed it! Please reach out with comments at my website at www.valeriezambito.com. The next book in the series, Island Shifters – An Oath of the Mage, is now available at most online retailers.

Thank you!

It is nearly unthinkable. A child has disappeared. But, Beck and Kiernan Atlan know exactly who has their daughter, and she is the waking nightmare that has haunted their dreams for years.

The kidnapper will stop at nothing to exact revenge against the shifters of Massa but will soon discover a powerful truth. The fierce love of a parent burns eternally, but when stoked, it threatens to explode.

ABOUT THE AUTHOR

Valerie Zambito lives in New York with her family.   A great love of world building, character creation, and all things magic led to the publication of her first adult epic fantasy series, ISLAND SHIFTERS, in October, 2011. Since then, she has added five additional novels to her repertoire.   Visit www.valeriezambito.com for the latest information.

Other Books Published by Valerie Zambito:

Book One: Island Shifters - An Oath of the Blood
Book Two: Island Shifters - An Oath of the Mage
Book Three: Island Shifters - An Oath of the Children
Book Four: Island Shifters - An Oath of the Kings
Angels of the Knights - Fallon
Angels of the Knights - Blane
Angels of the Knights – Nikki
Eden's Creatures

www.ingramcontent.com/pod-product-compliance
Lightning Source LLC
Chambersburg PA
CBHW070800180626
46818CB00001B/40